runaway bride's guide to love

Guide to Love
Book One

chelle sloan

Cover Design: Chelsea Kemp Art

Paperback Formatting: Y'all That Graphic, Kate Farlow

Editing: Kiezha Smith Ferrell, Librum Artis Editorial Services

Proofreading: Michele Ficht, Kelly Latham, Amanda Marcello

To all the women who know, and survived, the smallest man who ever lived, this book is for you.
Just remember: He ain't shit.
And your tits look great.

guide to love rule #1

Red is a good color for lipstick, not flags.

1
stella

"To Duncan and Stella!"

Our families and the wedding party all raise their glasses. "To Duncan and Stella!"

Cheers fade in and out as people take sips of their drinks and resume their conversations. I lower my champagne flute before turning to my soon-to-be-husband, my whole body filled with love and excitement. I'd love to steal a kiss after the beautiful toast my brother Simon just gave at our rehearsal dinner.

But there's no return look from my fiancé, let alone a loving glance. There's no kiss. If I wasn't holding his hand I doubt he'd even know I'm standing next to him. Hell, he still might not.

No, the only thing Duncan is looking at with hearts in his eyes is the bottom of his glass of scotch.

Get you a man who looks at you like Duncan Hughes looks at a glass of Macallan 18.

I shouldn't think things like that, especially the night before our wedding. I'm just being dramatic. I have a tendency to do that—or so I've been told. Tonight is a happy night, and tomorrow is a day I'm going to remember forever.

Tomorrow I'm becoming Mrs. Duncan Hughes.

So I'm not going to hyperfocus on the fact that Duncan is half a bottle of scotch in. He's celebrating. The man loves scotch. So much so he has an entire room dedicated to it at our condo. He calls it his office, but that requires a desk. I don't say anything about his hobby, though. I know if I say one word about the booze room then he's going to object to the number of shoes I own and the two closets I need to store them.

And no one—and I mean no one—touches my babies and lives to tell the tale.

But that's marriage, right? Compromise. Learning to blend your lives together. He has Jameson, and I have Louboutins. He has his poker nights, and I have my Thursday night dates with my best friend, Andi. Instead of buying a house in the suburbs, he wanted us to continue living in the condo I moved into with him last year. I didn't want that. Then again, he didn't want the big wedding I had dreamed about since I was a little girl, and even more so since the day we met.

So he's getting married in front of four hundred people and I'm staying in a space that doesn't have enough closets.

See? Compromise.

We're already killing this marriage thing.

"Stella?"

I feel a tap on my shoulder and turn to see our wedding planner, Whitley, standing next to me with a worried look on her face. It's the opposite of what you want to see from the woman who has been taking care of every facet of your wedding weekend since you realized four months ago it was too big to handle yourself.

"Everything okay?"

She doesn't say anything, instead just tilting her head as she signals me to follow her. I nod and give Duncan's hand a squeeze. "I'll be right back."

He barely acknowledges me as I follow Whitley through the private dining room at the Italian steakhouse we rented for the rehearsal dinner and into a hallway. It's not private, but it's about as out of the way as you can make it. My stomach drops with every step we take. If this were good news, we wouldn't be back away from everyone. And considering we're about to go through the fire exit, this has to be bad.

"Okay, you're scaring me," I admit.

"I'm sorry," she begins, though I don't know if she's apologizing to me for what she's about to say or what's about to happen. Maybe both. "Something is up that you need to know about."

Those are the last words a bride wants to hear the night before the wedding. "Just tell me Whitley. Rip the Band-Aid off."

Whitley bites her bottom lip, clearly nervous to say what she's about to say.

"The florist called me because she said she hadn't received final payment."

I feel the color drain from my face. "What? That can't be right. Duncan was supposed to call in the payment this week. Did he not?"

Whitley shakes her head. "Doesn't sound like it. The problem is, she's not the only vendor who's called to tell me this."

I feel my head starting to spin. "Excuse me?"

"The DJ called me right after the florist. He said the card you had on file is declining. Which means he doesn't have final payment either."

"Declined?" That can't be right. There's plenty of money in that account. It's the wedding fund that Duncan and I have both been contributing to. "Did you try the credit card you have on file for backup? That's not tied to the bank account?"

"I did. Also declined."

This can't be happening. That card, which is in both of our names, has a high, *high* five-figure credit line. "Something has to be up. Maybe our identity was stolen and our account was drained? And they hacked our credit card too."

"Maybe?" Whitley might say the word, but it doesn't sound like she believes it. Honestly, neither do I. "I know this is the worst time to tell you all of this, but if they don't get paid now, there won't be flowers or a DJ at your wedding."

I shake my head. "No. Thank you for telling me. I'll go get Duncan. Maybe he knows what's going on."

She nods. "Okay. Let me know if I can help you in any way. I'll call in the final payments once you get it sorted out."

"Thank you," I say, my mind now racing about how in the world not just one, but two, errors like this could have occurred.

It has to be a fraud thing. That's the only thing that makes sense. There should be thousands of dollars in that account. And plenty on the credit card. Not only should it have been plenty to cover the flowers and the DJ, but we're also using the leftover money and credit card for our honeymoon next week.

I can't believe this is happening. Especially since these were the only two big expenses Duncan and I were taking care of for the wedding. When we told my parents we were engaged, they gave us plenty to cover everything we could want. Duncan's eyes looked like a cartoon character when he saw the figure, but something didn't feel right with me about not contributing at all. Plus, Duncan and I have money. I do well for myself as the head office administrator for the law firm Carter, Banks and Fairchild. It's also the law firm where Duncan is an associate. So, I politely told my parents that we were going to pay for a few things. Those things were the DJ and the flowers, bridal party gifts, and all the other odds and ends that keep seeming to pop up when you're planning a wedding of this size.

Here I was, trying to be an adult—and responsible and not a spoiled little rich girl—and this is what happens.

Being an adult sucks.

I walk back into the dining room, quickly adjusting my tight, white, strapless dress to make myself feel a bit more put together on the outside. I give my hair a shake and push back my shoulders, giving every impression that nothing is the matter.

Fake it till you make it, right?

I say hi to a few guests as I try not to look like I'm hurrying back to my table. I quickly take my phone out of my purse and log into the bank app.

Except I can't.

I try again, completely convinced I have the password correct because it's the same for everything I use, but nothing.

What the hell?

I swallow a groan as I go through the pain in the ass process of changing my password. Reluctantly, I use the password they suggest because I just need this to go quickly. Alarm bells are sounding off in my head as I finally am able to log in to the account to see my worst nightmare.

There, on the homescreen, is nothing but zeros.

Well, not all zeros. The savings account has a *negative* balance. A negative balance of more than six thousand dollars.

What the hell? How did I not get an alert on this? This doesn't make sense.

I quickly toggle to the transactions in the checking account and one large wire transaction that took the checking to zero. Over on the savings, it's three large amounts, and one that took it to heavily overdrawn.

What the hell? I need answers.

I stand up and search around the room for Duncan, who is leaning against the bar with his best man and a few of the groomsmen. He's laughing and having the time of his life.

At least one of us is.

"Duncan? Can I talk to you for a minute?"

"Not now, babe," he says, barely making eye contact with me before turning fully to the bar where a round of shots was just placed in front of him and his groomsmen.

If this were any other night, and any other problem, I'd probably move on. I don't like to stir the pot with Duncan. I know sometimes I can be a bit crazy and don't think things through, so most of the time I ask myself if it's a problem I'm willing to die for. Most of the time that answer is no.

Tonight the answer is a resounding yes.

Duncan and his boys hoot and holler after they slam their glasses back down, giving each other a round of high-fives like they just won a game. I don't say anything, instead continuing to shoot a death glare at my soon-to-be husband, hands on my hips and foot tapping.

I'll wait here all night if need be. I'm as stubborn as I am Southern.

And I am *very* Southern. I have the monogrammed towels, bag, and water bottle to prove it.

Duncan finally turns to face me, letting out an audible sigh as I signal with my eyes that I need to talk to him. After a few more seconds of a silent stare-down, he starts walking back to where Whitley and I just came from.

"Fine. Here I am. What is so important that you had to drag me away and cause a scene?"

I swallow the laugh that bubbled to the surface at the thought that my request was a scene. Since we've gotten together, I've calmed my dramatic ways. I'm an adult, after all, in an adult relationship, with an adult job, and adult money. I'm too old to be causing scenes.

Now college and early twenties Stella? She's a whole other story…

"I just talked to Whitley," I begin. And it's at this moment I decided to play a little dumb. I don't know why my brain is telling me that's the move, but I'm going with my gut. "She informed me that none of the vendors that we were responsible for have been paid, which means they aren't showing up tomorrow."

I might not be a lawyer, but I work with enough to know that a face can give anything away. The slightest movement. A tick in their jaw. Irregular breathing. Removing eye contact.

But Duncan's face doesn't move. Not even a millimeter. He

does hesitate to answer, but that's not uncommon for him. The man is always careful with his words. He is a lawyer, after all.

"Stella…babe…Whitley has her facts mixed up. I paid this week, like you asked me to. Clearly she's trying to pull one over on us. Maybe she thinks she'll get paid more if she saves the day?"

And there's lie number one.

"Really, Duncan? *That's* your theory?"

"I don't know, Stella. Why is this my problem?"

Maybe because you're lying to me? Maybe because it's our fucking wedding?

"Duncan, you have one chance and one chance right now to tell me what's going on. And the truth. None of your lawyer bullshit. Because if you thought that was a scene, you have no idea what's in store for you."

My parents always called me tiny but mighty. Which made sense. I was always short—even now with my stilettos I might hit five-foot-five—but the mighty part was their polite way of saying to not fuck with me. Or those I care about. I've never cared if I was a foot shorter than someone; I wasn't going to be bullied. Someone messing with you? Excuse me while I take off my earrings so I can properly swing. I might love my shoes, but I'll throw one like a ninja star if the situation calls for it.

Though I don't know if Duncan has ever seen that side of me. I've tried to tame the crazy since we got together three-and-a-half years ago. I learned that you can still defend those you love without having to make a spectacle.

Though I have a feeling a spectacle is exactly what's about to happen if he doesn't fess up.

Duncan looks around before taking my hand and pulling me even farther into the hallway. He tilts his head back, pinching the bridge of his nose. When he looks back down at me, an overwhelming look of sadness is written across his face. "I fucked up."

I do my best to stay calm. At least he's telling the truth now. "What happened?"

He lets out a defeated sigh as he reaches for both of my hands, giving them a simultaneous squeeze. "I got caught up in a few deals."

"What kind of deals?" My voice is shaky. How could it not be? I feel like the world is falling out from under me.

"That's not important. I just…I thought…they seemed like sure things."

They never are—that's one thing my dad taught me years ago—but I know my commentary isn't what's needed right now. "I'm guessing they weren't?"

His face is remorseful, maybe the most sorry he's ever looked in our time together, and that's including the time he forgot to pick me up from the airport. "I'm so sorry Stella. I know I should've told you, and I know this is all my fault. And I'm sorry, but I turned off your alert notifications because I didn't want to stress you out about this. I wanted to fix this. I owed money, and I needed it quickly, so I had no choice but to take it from our account."

He changed my settings? Did he change my password too? I'm adding that the list of questions for later.

"And the credit cards?"

His face flashes signs of guilt. I hadn't brought up the credit card on purpose. And I bet if I hadn't, he would've just played off the fact that he maxed out a card. Or just emptied the bank account.

And as for saying cards, as in plural? That was on purpose. Let's see what he has to say about that.

"I'm so sorry. I should've told you." I give him credit—his face and body are all showing signs of guilt and being in the wrong. "Things just got away from me. Before I knew it, I had all my credit cards maxed, so I took ours and used that too. I'm going to get out of this, I promise."

He trails off, either not knowing what else to apologize for, or what else to say.

"You're right. You should have told me. And you shouldn't have used our money. Our *wedding* money. Or our joint credit card."

He nods. "I know. But I thought I could get it back before you found out."

How's that going for ya?

That's what I want to say. It's on the tip of my tongue. But I don't. A smartass comment isn't going to fix the situation. It's just going to cause a bigger fight.

Ugh! Why does adult Stella need to be mature? I want to scream and slap him and throw a drink in his face and call him every name in the book for fucking up like this. I mean, what else did he do? Invest in an MLM and now we have to invite his downline to the wedding? Send money to a Nigerian prince?

That's what I want to say, and in my mind when I'm saying all of this to him, it's poetic and perfect and I don't stumble over a word. He gets the tongue lashing he deserves, and I feel better in the process.

Still broke. But a little better.

But I don't. Because I'm not that girl anymore. I'm not the one who starts shit at bars. Or speaks before she thinks. Plus, Duncan hates when I let the sarcasm slip out. And by the look on his face, he's beating himself up enough right now.

So I do what I'm sure I'm going to have to do many times over the next how-ever-many years of marriage: I lie to save a fight.

Welcome to wedded bliss...

"It's okay."

His face turns from regretful to shocked and hopeful. "It is?"

No. It's not. But in this moment, I don't have a choice for it to be anything else but okay. I have guests that are probably wondering where we're at. We have four hundred people coming to a wedding tomorrow that I've been planning for a year. Is this the best way to start a marriage? Absolutely not. But it's just money. We can figure it out.

After the honeymoon. That is if there's even any money for it…

"It has to be," I say, doing my best to sound comforting and reassuring. "I have my emergency credit card, so I can finish the payments with the vendors. And I'm sure we'll get plenty of gift money so we can at least enjoy our honeymoon."

"Oh, babe," Duncan says in relief as he kisses my cheek. "I knew everything would be okay. What would I do without you?"

Oh, the comments smartass Stella could make…

"We'll be okay." I try to be hopeful, though I don't know if that's coming through. "Though I really didn't think we'd be putting into effect the wedding vows of 'being there for each other through tough times and bad' so early."

"For richer, for poorer."

I narrow my eyes. "Too soon."

He smiles and dammit, my worries somehow melt a little.

He's been able to do this since we got together. His smile has always been my kryptonite. It's how he went from just the guy I worked with to the guy I saw a future with. It's the smile I hope our kids have.

It's the smile I want to see for the rest of my life.

Right?

Yes.

Maybe.

Huh?

I'm so damn confused.

Because that smile that's trying to comfort me is also coming from the man who just stole money from me. And wouldn't have told me about it had the vendors been paid earlier. Or if Whitley hadn't told me. Or that I chose to unsuspiciously call him out on the hunch about multiple credit cards.

How is this happening right now?

The rest of the night goes by in a haze. People come up to us and shake our hands and wish us well for tomorrow. We smile and take pictures and everything on the outside is business as usual.

On the inside, though? I'm having feelings I never thought I'd have twelve hours before I'm supposed to get married.

Do I really want to get married to Duncan Hughes?

guide to love rule #19

Go with your gut. It's usually never wrong.

2
stella

Since I got engaged last year, I've been waiting for *the* moment.

The moment when I felt like a bride.

I'm now an hour away from hearing the wedding march played, and I'm still waiting. At this point, I've given up that it's going to happen. Because it didn't happen when he proposed. Or when we had our engagement photos taken. Or at the engagement party. Even last night when we were practicing for today, I didn't get a single butterfly that this is real.

Maybe I missed out because I didn't go wedding dress shopping. Yes. That has to be it. I didn't get my *Say Yes to the Dress* moment and that's when I was going to feel like a bride.

Why didn't I go wedding dress shopping? Great story, would love to tell you.

I'm what you call a people pleaser. Not as much as my sister Ainsley, but I generally want to be liked. Whether it's being the go-to girl at the office for anything and everything, or being the friend you call on for the range of grabbing drinks to burying a body, I want to be that person.

And when it comes to being liked by my future mother-in-law? I was willing to do almost anything. Including wearing her wedding dress.

From the moment we started dating, I had a feeling Sheila Hughes didn't like me. And that wasn't going to do. No matter what I did, I couldn't get her to budge. I hosted dinners. Asked for recipes. I found a first edition book she loves to give her for Christmas. I even watched her little yappy dog that bit me.

Still, nothing but cold shoulders.

Then one night we were at her house for dinner, and I was telling her that I was going dress shopping that weekend with my mom and sisters. Next thing I knew she was in tears. And I'm not talking about "a little choked up" tears. I'm talking full-on, need a pill, meltdown. She was going on about how she always wished she'd had a daughter so she could wear her wedding dress. She kept going on and on about how fashion forward it was for the late eighties and that it made her heart hurt that it was sitting in her attic collecting dust. In a moment of panic and desperation, I said that I'd wear it. That I'd be honored to.

Now today, as my own mother puts on the veil that went with the dress—which looks like it's sprouting baby's breath from sixteen directions—I'm regretting that decision.

I think I'm regretting this whole thing…

No. I'm not. Probably. I'm just thinking those thoughts because I'm staring at myself wearing a dress with more tulle and taffeta than should be legal in a garment—not the strapless, fitted mermaid-style dress with a sweetheart neckline that I had on my wedding vision board.

At least I'm wearing my white satin Louboutins. There's still a little Stella in this look. Even if you can't see it under the thirty-seven pounds and ten feet of fabric.

"There we go," my mom says as she steps away to look at me through the full-length mirror. "My baby is officially a bride."

I stare at my reflection, willing myself to have the feeling.

But nothing. Nada. Zilch. The only thing I'm feeling are tears welling in my eyes, because this is not how I expected to feel on my wedding day.

I didn't expect to not feel like a bride.

Or have the knowledge that my husband squandered our money.

And then tried to lie about it.

I don't know how a bride could feel worse hours before she says "I do."

I turn around from the mirror to look at the room full of the women I love the most. My three sisters; my mom; Charlie, essentially my sister-in-law; and my best friend Andi. I had invited Sheila to come back with us, but she declined, saying she wants to see me in the dress for the first time when I walk down the aisle.

Which is probably good. I don't know if I can hold my face back much longer.

My sister Quinn tries to say something, but can't find the words. And she never struggles with what to say.

"It's…"

"It's a dress." That comes from my oldest sister, Maeve, whose eyes are now twice the normal size. I hope she doesn't play poker with that face.

"That it is!"

Gee, thanks, Mom.

I push back the threatening tears as I turn to Ainsley. The girl can always find the silver lining. She doesn't have a mean or negative bone in her body. She'll make me feel better about this.

"Ainsley? What do you think?"

She doesn't say anything. But she doesn't have to. The combined look of horror, panic, and shock says everything she isn't vocalizing.

I'm the most hideous bride to ever walk down an aisle.

This is *not* the moment I was hoping for.

"Stella?"

I hear the words from my mom's mouth, but I don't move.

It's like I'm frozen as I watch everyone in the room start to circle around me. My breath is picking up speed. My heart is racing.

Then…out of somewhere deep inside my gut…I let it out.

And I just fucking scream.

"Ahhhh! I can't do this! I can't get married!"

Somehow I push back the tears, because like hell I'm going to cry off this makeup. I paid good money for it—with my *own* money since my dumbass fiancé lost all of ours—and like hell am I going to be in an ugly-ass dress *and* splotchy makeup.

Before anyone can say anything, I hear a pounding on the door. My eyes go wide in a panic, not wanting anyone to see or hear me in this state.

Or in this dress.

"I got it," Andi says, staying calm as she opens the door. But not all the way. Just enough to see who it is.

"Is everything okay?"

The voice is coming from Sheila. When Andi looks back to me, I furiously shake my head. She's the last person I want in here.

"Everything is fine, and actually, you're just the person I was looking for! I need your opinion on how we set up…" Andi's voice drifts off as she exits the room and presumably guides Sheila away. I don't know what lie she's pulling out of her ass, but I'm really glad I'm friends with a woman who works with lawyers.

Because she knows how to lie like one.

Maeve claps her hands so all attention turns to her. "Quinn: Tissues. Ainsley: Drink. Charlie—

"I'm going to watch the door," Charlie says. "You know, just in case Monster-in-Law breaks away from Andi."

I want to laugh, but I can't as Maeve sits me down between her and my mom on the oversized couch in the bridal suite of the hotel. Ainsley hurriedly hands me my comfort drink—Diet Dr Pepper, in a can, with a straw, so I don't mess up my lipstick.

She's the best.

"Okay, it's just us," Mom says, her voice gentle and soothing. "I thought you might have pre-wedding jitters, but something tells me there's more to this than cold feet and a hideous dress."

I don't know why, but my mom calling this dress hideous makes me laugh. Demetria Banks is as properly southern as they come, so a direct insult means you know it's bad.

"It's..." My words trail off because I don't know what I want to say. Do I want to tell my family about Duncan's stupidity? I mean, I will and I should, but now doesn't feel like the time.

What I want to admit is how I've been feeling since Duncan and I got engaged. A feeling I've pushed down for months but is now bubbling at the surface. How I've never been truly excited. How sometimes I've wanted the wedding more than the marriage. That I think I'm only getting married because he's the first one to ask.

I want to ask them about every doubt that seems to be rapid firing in my brain. But I don't say or ask any of that. Instead, I say the only question I can properly articulate.

"Mom? How did you know?"

The question is vague, but from the look on my mom's face, she knows exactly what I'm asking.

"I wish I had these great words of wisdom, but I don't," she says. "I just knew. Though that was probably because since the day we met, your daddy was telling me he was going to marry me, so after a while I didn't have a choice."

We all laugh, knowing that my dad might talk a big game, but when it comes to my mom, the man does whatever she wants.

"I know that doesn't help much," she says, motioning me to stand up with her. "But I want you to do something for me."

My mom positions me back in front of the mirror. Unfortunately the dress hasn't gotten better in the last ten minutes. My hair and makeup still look flawless, though.

"I want you to look in the mirror. Just at your face. Not at the dress." This makes everyone in the room chuckle. "Now I want you to think about walking down the aisle to Duncan. Think about holding his hands as you say your vows. Think about kissing him for the first time as his wife. Think about all the good moments you've had before and all the memories you're going to make in the future. Can you see them? Because if you do, then you're going to be just fine. If you can't, then maybe this isn't just cold feet."

I nod and do as she says, closing my eyes and thinking.

But I don't think about the wedding or anything that hasn't happened. No, I think about the day when he became more than just a lawyer who worked at my firm.

As the office administrator at Carter, Banks, and Fairchild, it's my job to know every employee. And not just their names. What makes me the best at my job is that I remember everything—law specialties, coffee order, marital status. And those are just to name a few. You want to know it? I can find out for you in three to five business days. Background checks have nothing on Stella Banks.

Duncan Hughes was an associate who was on a fast track to making partner. His specialty was in contract law, and he was making a lot of money for the firm. He was single, no wife or kids, and never had a girlfriend. At least, he never brought a woman to the office parties, and his social media was woman free beyond the pictures with his mom. His go-to lunch order was a turkey club, he drank exactly two cups of coffee a day, but when the days were a grind, he'd slam a Red Bull in the afternoon.

Basically, he's your standard late twenties/early-thirties lawyer in Nashville. Which is probably why I never really paid attention to him. He just blended in with the rest of the associates. In fact, and I'll never tell him this, sometimes he looked so young a few of us thought he was an intern. I mean, he's five-foot-seven on a good day, in his good shoes, and has a face that takes two weeks to sprout stubble. On the outside, he wasn't my type: he wasn't at least five-foot-ten with perfectly styled blond or brown hair who could rock a suit during the week and had his country club look down for the weekends. In college I went after the frat guys who smelled like daddy's money. As an adult, they became finance bros. The more expensive the cologne, the more attracted I was. And if he was a few years older? Your girl was down bad.

Duncan had a few of those qualities—he's three years older than me, has sandy brown hair, and is from a well-to-do family —but that's where the list ended.

That was until the day I realized that a list is nothing more than an arbitrary piece of paper.

It was the company Christmas party on December 23, nearly four years ago. Everyone at the firm was laughing, drinking, and dancing. Everyone except me. I was sulking at the bar.

Why? Because yet another of my sorority sisters had gotten an engagement ring for Christmas.

That was six so far during the holiday season, with ten days to go before the new year. Then there were the three weddings I'd been in that summer and the four others I went to as a guest —a dateless guest, nonetheless.

And there I was. So single I didn't even try to get a date to the party. Hadn't even been on a date in months. Serious relationship? Never heard of it. While my friends were leaving the University of Tennessee with their M.R.S. degrees, I was leaving with a degree in marketing and memories of good times but not long times.

But that was the story of my college experience. In a sorority, but not on the board. Good grades, but not graduating with cords. Good internship, but didn't feel real because my dad set it up with one of his clients.

So when it came to my personal life, I felt on the outside looking in—again. Granted, I thought I was good with being single. I loved my life. At the time, I was twenty-three, living in Nashville, working a job I loved. I had friends, went to concerts, and saw my family frequently. I had the occasional date, and the occasional overnight guest, but no one I was bringing home to Sunday dinner. But deep down I had wondered when it was going to be my turn.

Normally, I was good about keeping those feelings of loneliness and "why not me" at bay. That Christmas, I couldn't do it anymore. When was it going to be my turn? Why hadn't I met someone? Was something wrong with me? Was I too short? Too blonde? Not pretty enough? Too pretty? Did I go too hard on the halcyon ho days of college and my early twenties? Was I not smart enough? Did I have a piece of toilet paper permanently stuck to my heel?

Seeing yet another engagement social media post was a wakeup call. A slap in the face that it was time for me to get serious about dating. I wanted the happily ever after, I wanted what my friends had, so that meant I had to be done with my wild days. It was going to become my New Year's resolution to start seriously looking for a relationship and moving into the next part of my life. Becoming a real adult.

And like he could hear my thoughts, there came Duncan sliding up next to me at the bar. His shy smile hit me right in the heart, and all I could think was that Santa had brought me an early Christmas present.

He made me smile. He made me laugh. And he made me grow up, which was a good thing. I couldn't be crazy party girl Stella forever. And I was good for him. If for no other reason than I started making him style his hair and expand his tie collection.

We took trips. We went to wineries and drove to Knoxville to tailgate for UT games. He was a good guy with whom I'd share a good and comfortable life. Stable. Sure, there weren't a ton of sparks or fireworks, but who needs that when you're planning for the rest of your life? He was the man I wanted to spend the rest of my life with.

But now I'm not so sure.

Because I can't see me kissing him at the end of the aisle. I can't see us celebrating tonight at the reception. I see portions of good times, but as soon as I see those they are replaced by last night, when he told me that he lost all our money. And that he's never sent me flowers. Or given me an orgasm without the help of my own hand.

I'm confused. I don't know which way is up. Which is the only reason I decide that there's one way to put an end to this mind fuck.

"I need to see Duncan."

"What?" Ainsley exclaims as the rest of my sisters let out audible gasps. "It's bad luck for you two to see each other!"

"I'm wearing this dress, can my luck get any worse?" I leave out the part where we're also broke, so clearly luck has already taken a backseat. "I'm not scared of a superstition."

"Stella," my mom begins as I go to my bag and grab my cell phone and the keycard for the honeymoon suite. It's where Duncan and I are staying tonight, but today it's where him and his groomsmen are getting ready. "Are you sure?"

I nod, suddenly feeling more confident about this decision than any I've had to make for months. "I am. This is probably just cold feet and wedding nerves. Once I see him and talk to him, everything will be much better. I just know it."

"If you say so," Maeve says, though her tone doesn't sound very confident. "If we don't hear from you in thirty minutes, we're going to assume you ran away."

I laugh as I unlock the door. "Don't you worry, big sister. Even if I wanted to, these red bottoms were not made for a sprint. They were made for getting married."

guide to love rule #26

Communicate your kinks with your partner.
How else are you supposed to know he likes
to be spanked?

3
stella

I might have grown up a lot since being with Duncan, but one thing I don't know I'll ever grow out of is acting—or speaking—without thinking.

Sometimes I'm able to catch myself. Others not so much.

Like right now. Now is other times.

All I knew in the moment was I needed to see Duncan. I didn't think about how I raced out of the room in my hideous wedding dress. I didn't think that guests of the hotel, along with guests of the wedding, were going to see me get in the elevator. Heck, I barely remembered to grab my cell phone and shove it into the pockets I had sewn in.

If I'm going to wear an ugly dress, let's at least make it practical.

"Getting married?"

I'm startled by the voice that's apparently inside the elevator with me. I turn to see a woman, probably in her fifties, looking at me up and down. And is she serious? Why else does she think I'd be wearing a dress that literally takes up half the occupancy of this space?

"Yes," I say with a very fake smile. "About an hour from now."

"How nice," she says. "Your dress is beautiful. Looks just like the one I wore when I married my first husband."

My smile goes from fake to mortified, and I've never been so happy to have the elevator stop on a floor. Hers, thank God, because I need her to exit so I can internally scream, which is probably going to become an external scream the second the door closes.

"Ahhhh!!!" Yup. External. "What am I doing?"

I'm pacing back and forth in the elevator—which is three steps each way—as that question rolls through my head. I don't even know what I'm specifically asking about. The dress? The wedding? Duncan? It feels like that question covers all of those topics at the same time.

I hate this feeling of indecisiveness. That's not me. I'd like to say that one of my strong qualities is I know what I want and I go for it. I might not always get it, but I'm not afraid to shoot my shot. I want a pair of shoes? I buy them. I want to settle down and find a husband? I did it.

Just don't ask me what I want for dinner. I'll never know the answer to that question.

You'd think on the day of my wedding I shouldn't be playing a should I-shouldn't I game in my head. Yet, here we are, exiting the elevator on the twenty-fifth floor of the Omni Hotel with the wrong kind of butterflies in my stomach and more questions than I should have, hours before my wedding.

"Duncan?" I knock on the door, and at first don't hear anything. Weird. I mean, I didn't expect to hear a party, but I figured he and his groomsmen would be laughing or chatting, since they were all getting ready in here.

I tap the keycard to the reader and let myself in to a sound I wasn't expecting.

A crack.

And moans.

And a woman's voice.

What the hell?

I don't bother shutting the door quietly. I don't bother announcing myself. I barely remember to hike up my dress so I can march the few steps down the hallway to be able to see into the room. I don't realize that I pick up speed when I hear another crack, followed by what can only be described as a yelp, and words that I think I'm going to remember for the rest of my life.

"Does my good boy like that?"

It's at that moment I turn the corner and see my fiancé on all fours on the king-sized bed, completely naked, ass in the air for all to see.

Well, except for the tie that was a part of his tuxedo hanging from his neck. And black socks.

And standing behind him is a redhead, wearing expertly placed leather and holding a flogger.

"What the fuck!" My outburst gets the attention of Duncan and Leather Lady. Their eyes are wide. Duncan's face turns quickly to panic. Hers to confusion. "Since when do you like being spanked?"

That's my first question? Really, Stella? I mean, it probably shouldn't be the first, but it was definitely something at some point I'd want to know. Duncan is as vanilla in bed as they come. One time he said I sucked his dick too hard and told me I was hurting him.

I know that wasn't true. I give phenomenal head. I have references.

He just has a pencil dick. And I'm not being petty, because in this moment my fiancé is getting his ass literally beat by a dominatrix. Dude is tiny. And I was willing to overlook a life full of unfulfilling sex and minimal orgasms for the happily ever after of marital bliss.

But now I want to rip that tiny fucking dick off with my bare hands and stuff it down his throat.

Then again, he might like that, considering the position he's in.

"Stella!" Duncan jumps from the bed—and now it's

confirmed that the only thing he's wearing is the tie around his neck and black socks. It's quite the look. "It's not what it looks like!"

I watch as Duncan crawls on the floor, looking for his boxers. "Really Duncan? That's what you're going with? Please then, explain to me what this actually is?"

"I mean…it's…" He can't even get out a damn sentence as he hurriedly steps into his boxers, only to almost fall back on the ground. If this was a sitcom I'd be laughing hysterically. Alas, it's my actual life, and I am not amused. "It is. But it's not. It's…"

"How about I take a stab at what this is," I say as I take another step into the room. His eyes grow wide as I approach the bed that he has just found his way back to. Probably because I look like I'm about to rip him a new one. Which he'd be correct about. "This is you getting spanked by a woman, who is not me, an hour before our wedding. Or is it flogged? I'm unfamiliar with the proper terminology."

"What? An hour before your wedding? Dude…that's fucking low."

I nearly forgot that Leather Lady was still in the room—and apparently not in dominatrix mode anymore. I must say, now that I'm looking at her, she's quite stunning. And apparently on my side.

Hoes over bros, especially when their pants are literally down.

"Yes. An hour before our wedding. Can you believe that?"

"I cannot."

"Thank you! Oh! I'm so sorry, I didn't introduce myself. Stella Banks."

"Nadia," she says, extending her hand that's sporting blood red nails filed into near daggers. "So sorry you walked into see this. I promise you he didn't tell me that he was getting married. I'll do some stuff for a payday, but had I known, I would've said no. Or hit him harder."

"Not your fault," I say as we shake hands in the oddest

exchange I think I've ever had in my life. "I must say, you are gorgeous. Your hair is beautiful."

"Thanks, and your dress is…"

"Hideous. But it has pockets."

"Nice. And I wasn't going to say hid—"

"Will you two stop!"

Oh, shit. Pencil Dick is still here. *And he's talking back.*

"I'm sorry. Was I interrupting your spanking time? How dare I do such a thing."

"Stella, don't take that tone."

"Oh, Duncan…" Nadia groans, shaking her head. "Just shut the fuck up."

"Thank you, Nadia! Because you know what? I'm going to take whatever fucking tone I want to! I came up here to get reassurance. That last night was just unfortunate timing and a complete one-off. That you're the man I want to marry. That I'm the woman you want to spend the rest of your life with."

"You are."

"Really? I am? Is that why you cleaned out our accounts? Lied to me about it? Is that why you're here with Nadia getting your fucking ass beat before we walk down the aisle? No offense, Nadia."

"None taken."

"And speaking of Nadia! How do you have money to hire her? I hope to God you're paying her, because every woman deserves to make her money however they so please. But we didn't have money to pay for our flowers or DJ. Which means I assume *you're* also broke if you resorted to stealing from our joint account. So please tell me Duncan, who's paying for her?"

"Oh, he didn't pay me yet," Nadia chimes in. "Asked if he could pay me after. I'm starting to wonder if he wasn't going to conveniently not have any money…"

"Stella…Nadia…let me explain. This is all a big misunderstanding."

I look down to Duncan, who has never looked more pathetic in his worthless life as he cowers on the bed.

"Is it a misunderstanding that you're a broke piece of shit? Or a liar? Because if it's not any of those I don't want to fucking hear it"

"Stella…we don't need to use that language."

Oh no he didn't…

"The fuck I don't!" I scream, ripping the engagement ring off my finger and throwing it at him. It bounces off his head and falls to the carpet. "I'll use whatever the fuck language I want. Because I'm not yours anymore. You don't get to tell me how to talk. Or how to act. Or remind me to keep the crazy away. It's not your problem anymore because I'm fucking done."

"Done?"

Is he serious? Why does he look like that's the most shocking thing I could have said? For a smart man he really is an idiot.

"Yes, we're done! Do you have selective hearing? We. Are. Done. Over. Broken up. Engagement off. You can go down and tell everyone that the wedding is off. Make up whatever excuse you want because I doubt you'll tell the truth. But I couldn't care less what you say. I'm out of here."

I turn on my heel, somehow remembering to maneuver the hideous dress so I don't trip over myself during my dramatic exit.

The dress…

I happen to stop in front of a mirror on the closet of the suite. My face is red. I'm breathing heavy. And I'm wearing a fucking ugly dress because I was trying to make him happy.

I did everything to make him happy…

"I gave you everything," I say, though I don't turn around to direct my words to him. He doesn't get to see me cry. "I changed for you. Because I wanted the fairy tale. I thought you were going to give it to me. I became the woman you wanted me to be. I was ready to do that for you. Because I loved you."

"Babe…" I hear his footsteps coming closer but I hold up a hand behind me.

"Don't." I turn around, quickly willing the stray tears to go back in. "Don't 'babe' me. This isn't something you can smile and talk your way out of. I mean it, Duncan. We're done."

He doesn't try to stop me. He doesn't say another word as I turn and exit the hotel room.

I feel like a zombie as I walk toward the elevator. I don't remember pushing the button. I don't remember people coming on and off as I bypass the fifth floor and keep heading down.

All I remember is stepping out of the cart and walking through the lobby and outside, right into downtown Nashville.

And then I just run.

4

emmett

You never know who—or what—you're going to see at a downtown Nashville bar. Doesn't matter the day or time, the people watching is always top notch.

Granted, I don't come down here often. Too loud. Too many people. I'd much rather be at my quiet house with my dog and a ballgame on in the background. Reading a book. But some days a man just needs a drink and a burger after a long week.

And to say I had the week from hell is an understatement. My business partner and former college roommate, Simon Banks, is on the longest paternity leave in history. And even if he was working, his sister is getting married today, and he insisted he needed to be available for any impending wedding duties. Five of the properties I manage for our business all of a sudden had major repairs that I needed to coordinate to fix. A site we're building on suddenly had permit issues I had to deal with. And a storm just hit our Florida rentals, which means I have to head down there next week to check the damage.

So yes, a Jim Beam and Coke and a burger was what the doctor ordered.

Luckily it's still the afternoon, so it's not crazy yet, but the usual suspects of the Nashville summer bar scene are here. Bachelorettes and their crews whooping it up. Corporate suit guys playing credit card roulette after eighteen holes of golf. Tourists who don't think they look like tourists but are given away by watching the aspiring country music artist playing on stage and thinking it's the best thing they've ever heard.

And a woman sitting across the bar from me in a wedding gown.

Okay, that one isn't something you normally see.

"Here's your burger. Can I get you anything else?"

I don't even look at the BBQ bacon cheeseburger I ordered or the bartender who's delivering it. I can't take my eyes off the woman, who looks slightly familiar but I can't put my finger on it. "Is she okay?"

"I'm not sure," he says, looking over to her then back to me. "She got here about an hour before you. Asked for a lemon drop martini then quickly changed to straight shots of tequila. I've been trying to pace her out and give her water, but since I have a feeling she's not wearing that dress because she lost a bet, I'm fighting a losing battle."

The bartender walks away, but my gaze doesn't move.

Yes, she's beautiful. That's partly why I can't take my eyes off her. She's been looking down most of the time, but from the glimpses I've gotten, she's a stunner. Beautiful features. Blonde hair that is pulled up under a rather large veil. I'm not hip to wedding styles—or any fashion styles really—but even I know what she's wearing on her head is a bit much. Her makeup is a mess from crying, which breaks my heart.

Why is she here? Is she okay? Who did this to her? Who, or what, happened to drive her to a downtown Nashville bar on a Saturday afternoon still wearing her dress? I know it's none of my business. I don't know this woman from Eve. But something makes me want to be sure she's okay.

If my sister Maddie were here, she'd joke that this is my Prince Charming complex coming to the surface. You save one kitten from a tree when you're thirteen to make your baby sister stop crying and you're tagged with the "my hero" persona for life.

I'm no Prince Charming. Far from it. I'm just a country boy from East Tennessee who was raised to hold doors open. To say please and thank you. To help those who need it. I can't stand by and see people hurt. Or cry.

Or get hit on by douchebags.

Just as I'm about to pick up my burger, I watch as one of the corporate douches walks over to her. What makes *any* man think it's appropriate to hit on a woman wearing a wedding dress at a bar is beyond me. Especially one who's clearly distressed.

She looks over at him, and I can't make out what he's saying, but I know a forced smile when I see one. She's shaking her head and trying to look away. To look at anything but him.

Which in any universe means "no" and "leave me alone."

But apparently this motherfucker isn't from our solar system because he inches closer to her. Her body stiffens. He leans in. She leans back in retreat.

My blood pressure spikes.

That's it. I can't watch this anymore. I see her say the word "no" and shake her head even more as I push away from the bar. I feel like I'm running, though it probably looks like a march into battle, as I make my way around to where he's hovering over her. When I make my way to her side of the bar, I push down the urge to just grab and punch the shit out of him. Instead, I stop and catch her eye, making sure she knows I'm a friendly face. See if she gives me any clues of how to proceed.

Crystal blue eyes meet mine. They're sad. A little scared. Pleading.

And so fucking gorgeous.

I force myself not to get lost in her eyes and make a slight motion to the asshole before looking back to her, hoping she can read my mind. I'm going to defend her in whatever way she wants, but I'm not going to insert myself into a fight if she doesn't want me to. I don't mind throwing hands first. Won't be the first time. Probably won't be the last. But I won't do it unless she wants me to.

When she nods with a worried look, I don't hesitate. Especially when I hear the next words out of his mouth.

"I mean, if you're not taking that dress off for your husband tonight, why don't you take it off for me?"

"The fuck she will!" I pull him away by his back collar and throw him behind me. He stumbles as he tries to catch his balance, which gives me just enough time to put myself between him and her. "You're going to leave. Right the fuck now."

He finally regains his balance and does his best to puff out his chest. "What the hell, man?"

"She said no. No means no. Didn't anyone teach you that?"

I'm staring down at this man—literally because I have at least five inches on him—but I'll say one thing, he's not backing down. Then again, that's probably the liquid courage and sheer stupidity taking over.

"How the hell do you know? Were you here? I don't think so. Me and the lovely bride here were just getting to know each other. So you can just go ahead and fuck off."

"Listen here and listen good." My voice is deep as I take a step closer to him. "You're going to walk away. You're going to go grab your friends and not come near her. Actually, let's make sure of it and just leave this bar all together. I think it'll be best for everyone involved."

"And why would I do that?"

I take another step closer, the height difference becoming more apparent as I look down at him. Am I trying to intimidate him? Yes. Is it working? Judging by his eyes bugging out of his head, yes.

"Because if you don't, the only article of someone else's clothing you'll be removing tonight is my boot from your ass. Now. Get the hell out of here before I throw you out myself. Got it?"

He rolls his eyes, but not before I see him take another huge gulp of air. "Whatever. She's not even worth it. Dude probably dodged a bullet not marrying her."

I don't bother replying, wanting this interaction to be over with. That's why I'm startled when I hear the most feral scream I've ever heard in my life.

"You fucking asshole!"

Everything in front of me happens all of a sudden, and somehow also in slow motion. First I see a giant white cloud run past me, sounding like a banshee that just freed herself from barbed wire that's still digging into her as she chases down her next victim. I turn back to the idiot, who looks more terrified of her than he ever did of me.

I can't say I blame him. I'm not the one she's going after, and I'm petrified.

She's two steps away from cold-cocking this guy before I snap back to reality and pick her up around her waist. Shit… she's fucking strong! Her arms and legs are flailing, and it's taking a good amount of strength to hold her back. I wish I could see his face, but I really can't see much past the dress that keeps floating up with every swing she makes.

"I would've been a great wife! I was going to be a great wife! He's the one who was getting spanked before our wedding! SPANKED! WITH A FLOGGER! You don't know what you're talking about, you little-dicked fuck boy!"

I peek around this five-foot-nothing firecracker only to see the asshole and his friends making a beeline for the exit. Probably for the best. I don't know how much longer I can keep hold of her.

And I have a feeling her screams could hit a few more octaves if she really wanted to.

"You good, Tiger?"

She nods as I lower her back to the ground. The second her feet land, she does her best to smooth down her wedding dress. I have to stifle a laugh because she's not exactly having the best luck. Though I don't think it's her fault. I don't know much about mechanics of wedding dresses, but it looks like it has a mind of its own. I mean, it's big enough to host a small colony of animals, so I'm guessing it also has smart technology built in.

"What are you laughing at?"

Oh, shit. Now the banshee has her sights set on me.

"Nothing."

She narrows her eyes. "Are you laughing at my dress?"

"No, ma'am."

Her face is back to feral. "Don't ma'am me."

"Yes, ma'am."

I internally cringe for saying it again, because I think she's about to bite my head off. Literally. But I also don't think this is the time to tell her I call every woman whose name I don't know "ma'am."

"I'm not a ma'am!"

She starts pacing in circles, which makes her dress do this weird funnel thing. I'm just going to stand here because I'm a little scared to say anything, or move. Yet at the same time I feel like I need to be here to catch her when she eventually trips on the approximate fifty pounds of fabric. "I'm…I'm a…" She stops for a second. Is she thinking? Going to scream again? "I'm a mess!"

Tiger melts to the floor, her wedding dress pooling around her as she starts crying in the middle of the bar. I look around, and the few people who are here are definitely staring at her. I see the bartender coming around to make sure she's okay, but I wave him off.

I got her.

I don't know why that's the only thought going through my head right now, but it is.

"Hey," I say as I kneel down so I'm eye level with her. "What do you need?"

She looks at me like this is the most off-the-wall question I could've asked. "Excuse me?"

"What do you need?" I repeat.

"I don't know if there's a list long enough to answer that question now."

"Fair," I say. I don't know how she's making jokes right now, but it's earning her points in my book. "Let's start with the easy stuff. Water? A Lyft? To follow that guy out of the bar so you can get a clean shot?"

This earns me a small smile. "How about we start with helping me up?"

"Of course." I pop up and hold out my hands for her, gently pulling her to her feet. "There we go."

She tries again to smooth her dress, which gives me a chance to really look at her.

She's much younger than I realized. If I had to guess, I'd say she's around my sister's age, so in her mid-twenties, meaning a solid ten years younger than me at thirty-seven. I also didn't realize how short she was. I'd have to guess at least a foot shorter than me, and I believe I saw high heels under that dress. I don't know why that makes me smile, but it does.

My smile only gets bigger when she looks up at me. Her cheeks are red from the combination of fighting and crying at the bar. Her eyes are pooled with new tears that haven't leaked out. But that only enhances the blue in them. Then there are her lips. They're pouty and perfect, heart shaped. I'm guessing at one point today she was wearing red lipstick. Lips that, under any other circumstance, I'd be figuring out a way to kiss.

She's a mess. The most beautiful mess I've ever seen.

No. Stop it right the fuck now, Collins.

What the hell is wrong with me? I'm no better than the douchebag who hit on her. This girl has clearly gone through it today, and all I can think about is kissing her? Not only am I a fucking asshole but also a creepy old man.

I need to snap out of this. I need to leave. I need to make sure she's okay and get the hell home to my silence and my dog.

"Can I ask you a favor?" Tiger says.

"Of course."

"Can you sit with me?" She signals back to the bar. "I…I don't have anywhere else to go and, well, after all that, I'd rather not be alone. I also don't know if they take ApplePay because I don't have my purse so I might need some assistance with that."

Fuck…I don't think I could say no even if I wanted to…

"Sure," I say with a sigh. "I guess I should introduce myself. My name's…"

"No," she says, shaking her head. "No names today. If I tell you my name and you tell me yours then this whole day gets a lot more real, and I can't handle any more of that. I need to escape as long as I can, and if that means no one calling me by my name, or what my name was supposed to be, that—that just sounds fantastic."

Somehow that makes sense. "Okay. But on one condition."

Her face gets a worried look. "What's that?"

I smile to try and reassure her. "I get to pick your name, *Tiger*."

The smallest smile graces her face, and it's in this moment I decided that my goal tonight is to see her real smile. Because I bet it's fucking gorgeous.

"Okay, I'm Tiger and you're…" She trails off. "I'm not sure."

"It's okay," I extend my hand to guide her back to the bar. "I'm sure you'll think of something."

When we sit back down, the bartender places my burger and drink in front of me, and two shots of what looks to be whiskey.

"Should we toast?"

She nods as we pick up our glasses. "To not getting married."

I clink her glass. "I'll drink to that."

5

emmett

"You're kidding me? He stole from your wedding account *and* maxed out your joint credit card? And you found this out last night?"

"Yup! He did and I did!" Tiger slams her hands on the bar. "Credit card declined. No money in account. Vendors weren't going to show up. And you want to know the worst part?"

"That wasn't the worst part?"

"Nope. The worst part was that I was going to go through with it. He tried to lie to me. Only reason he told me any part of the truth was because I caught him in a trap. He had every excuse. Every reason. Hell, he might not even be telling the truth now. And I was still going to marry him. Forgive him. For richer or poorer and all that bullshit. That's the worst."

"You were in love." I mean, I assume she was. That's why you'd get married, right? I wouldn't know. I've never seriously dated anyone, let alone have thoughts of marriage. But I assume love has something to do with it.

"I was stupid." She finishes off her beer in record time. Good lord this girl can drink. "Jim…why was I stupid? Was I in love or stupid?"

"Jim?"

She nods down to the drink in front of me. "Your drink. You're drinking Jim Beam and Coke. I thought we could test run Jim as your nickname."

"Not the worst I've had," I say, taking a sip. "But I think you can do better."

She thinks about it for a second before nodding. "You're right. I can. I can do better with nicknames. With men. With…" She stops for a second before picking up her beer. "With drinking!"

I laugh. "I think you're doing just fine with that."

"I think that's the only thing." She hangs her head, which causes her veil to cover her face. It would be comical if this wasn't so heartbreaking. "I'm an idiot, Jim. Can you believe that I almost married a man who spent our entire savings on a Ponzi scheme and hookers? Though the hooker I met was very nice. I don't know if there were others."

Did I hear her right? "You met his hooker? You mean you were *actually* there for the whipping and spanking thing you were screaming about earlier?"

"It was flogging. And yes."

Tiger throws back her who-knows-what-count shot of whiskey. The fact that she isn't flinching when the burn hits her is quite impressive.

Then again, we are both very, very drunk. Me not as much as her, but holy shit, this little thing is giving me a run for my money.

"I did. Well, I feel like hooker has a negative connotation. Sex work is work, you know? And she was more of a dominatrix. Her name is Nadia. She looked like a Nadia. She told me I was pretty. That was so sweet of her."

How is she saying all of this like it's everyday conversation?

"I didn't know he liked to be flogged. I smacked his ass once, and he told me I was too rough. Oh, and did I mention this all happened an hour before our wedding? In our honeymoon suite?"

I nearly drop my drink. "You found out about the money thing and the hooker thing in twenty-four hours?"

"You bet your sweet ass I did." She only pauses to take a sip of the refilled beer that magically appeared in front of her. What kind of alcohol hasn't she drank tonight? "Which is how I ended up at the bar. I got in the elevator and just ran. Didn't go get my purse. Didn't tell my family or friends. Luckily had my phone in the handy dandy pockets I had put into this fugly wedding dress."

"Fugly?"

"Yes. Fugly. A combination of fucking and ugly."

"Oh. My bad. Continue."

She shrugs, toying with the pint of beer. "That's about it. I caught him. I ran. I texted my mom and siblings that the wedding was off before turning off my phone. Then I walked into the bar. You know the rest."

Damn. I knew shit had to have been bad for a woman to end up alone at a bar in the middle of the afternoon in a wedding dress. But that…no one should have one of those things happen to you, let alone both in less than a day.

"I'm sorry," I say. "That's…a lot."

She nods and lets a silence come down between us. This isn't the first time since we've sat down that this happened, and I'm guessing it won't be the last. But like hell am I going to try and insert random conversation or questions I have no business asking. This is her rodeo. I'm just along for the ride.

"Woo! I'm getting married!"

The announcement of an incoming bachelorette party grabs everyone's attention.

"Ignore them," I whisper to Tiger, who is currently shooting death glares at the bachelorette and her crew of twenty that are skipping up to the bar.

Tiger nods as she turns to look at them. Because of her rather large veil, I can't see the look she's giving to the soon-to-be-bride, but I'd guess it's not a friendly one.

"Oh my God! Bride bestie!" The bachelorette skips—literally skips—over to us. Between her high-pitched tone and her barely-there dress, I doubt Tiger and this girl would be besties.

And I immediately hate myself for even thinking that word in my head.

"Don't do it," I hear Tiger say. Which makes Bachelorette Barbie go from bubbly to confused.

"Excuse me?"

"You heard me. Don't do it. Marriage is a fucking sham. Men are liars. Get out while you can."

Barbie tsks. "My man doesn't lie. He loves me."

Tiger laughs. And not just a little laugh. A loud, straight from the gut laugh that gets everyone's attention. It's almost the laugh of a mad villain in a Bond movie. "That's what they all say. Ask him about his sex worker. I wonder if he has the same one mine did. If it's Nadia, she's at least good people."

Now, I realize I don't know Tiger well. But it's going on three hours since we met, and in that time she's been in one fight. And I have a feeling another is about to happen. Especially when I see Barbie give her a onceover.

"Whatever. I keep my man satisfied. He'd never call someone like that. Then again, if I looked like you do right now, I can't say I blame the guy."

Ah fuck…

Tiger doesn't say anything. No, like a true wild animal, she just pounces. Somehow she launches herself from the barstool at Barbie in a haze of white fabric and guttural screams, her feet never touching the ground.

Wait…is she pulling her hair?

"I gave him everything!" Tiger yells as she rips off the bachelorette's tiara. "And this is his mother's dress! I was trying to be a good wife! He's the one who stole money from me. He's the one who fucked around! I suck good dick!"

The bartender looks at me and I nod, knowing that we've

now just officially outstayed our welcome. Thankfully I paid the tab after the last round.

"Let's go, Tiger," I say as I pull her off Barbie. "I think it's time to relocate."

Her arms and legs are still flailing as I throw her over my shoulder. Which is the easier way to carry her, but I didn't account for the monstrosity of a wedding dress flying in my face due to her feet kicking wildly. I can barely see where I'm going when I hear the final words from Tiger as we exit the bar.

"Don't do it! Save yourself!"

———

"How the hell? How do you keep making them?"

Tiger does a little victory dance after bouncing the quarter into the shot glass.

Again.

"Drink up, Cap!"

I do, because that's how the game's played. "Cap? Is that the nickname now?"

"Yup! Tiger and Cap. For Captain America, obviously," she says as she takes another sip of her beer in front of a devilish smile. "You came in and saved the day, just like my favorite super hero. Though I'm not sure if you have America's Ass. Maybe Tennessee's Ass. I haven't checked it out yet. Stand up. Let me get a look at ya."

I suddenly feel my cheeks turn red. Am I blushing? I don't blush. Why am I blushing?

"I like Cap," I say, ignoring the ass comment. "Better than Prince Charming."

Tiger's face goes from playful to terrified in a heartbeat. "Wait? Who calls you Prince Charming? Oh my God! A wife? A girlfriend! Oh my God! I'm a runaway bride *and* a home wrecker!"

"No, no," I hurriedly say as she dramatically drops her head to the table. "No wife. No girlfriend. Just a little sister who has annoyed me with a Prince Charming nickname since we were kids."

She peeks out from underneath the veil. "Really?"

"Really."

"Good. That's good." Tiger sits up and takes a reassuring breath. "Not the nickname. I mean it's cute. I like it and it's fitting, but not if you hate it. But it's good that I'm not forcing another woman's man to hang out with her on the most pathetic day of her life. That wouldn't make me much better than…"

Tiger's words trail off, but I know where she was going. This has happened a few times tonight. Seemingly innocent conversation that couldn't be farther from what was supposed to happen turns suddenly into topics too close for comfort.

More specifically, about her ex. Who I hate. I don't know him. I don't even know his name. But I know if he walked into the bar now I wouldn't wait for her permission to lay him the fuck out.

How could she want to marry that guy? I mean, I know it couldn't all be bad. Right? But this woman…this beautiful, drunk, semi-dramatic, slightly crazy spitfire of a woman had to have better options than a man who apparently is a thief and a cheater. Right?

Then again, who am I to question decisions about marriage? I was raised by a woman who thought marriages and relationships were things you collected.

"Here you go," the waitress says, putting down two shots in front of us. "Anything else?"

I look to her, then over to Tiger. "When did you order these?"

She shrugs and puts on a fake innocent face. It's really bad.

And really adorable.

"No clue," she says. "I bet the Booze Fairy brought it for us."

This makes the waitress laugh. "You two enjoy."

I give her a side eye. "Last one."

She salutes me with the wrong hand. "Yes, sir."

"I mean it."

The devilish smile reappears. "What's the matter, Cap? Can't hang?"

"I can hang."

Her eyes glimmer with mischief. "Prove it."

Now, I'm a gentleman. I'm here to make sure she's safe. That she doesn't get so drunk that she ends up in a dangerous situation.

But what I don't do is turn down a dare. Or a challenge. Or anything that can be construed as one. It's why I'm always everyone's first pick for teams. It's why I was always Simon's beer pong partner in college. I don't back away from a challenge.

And I never lose.

So what will one more shot hurt?

"Bring it on, Tiger."

She makes a show of holding up the shot glass before clearing her throat. "To hookers with floggers and strangers at the bar saving the day!"

"It takes a village."

We clink our glasses together, then hit the table before shooting back another shot of whiskey. Usually I pretend to be man enough to not take a chaser, but that went out the window four shots ago.

"Where did you learn to drink?" I ask between sips of the beer.

"University of Tennessee," she says before holding her beer in the air. "Kappa Delta, baby!"

"No shit," I say. "I went to UT too."

She slams her beer down and her eyes double in size. "No way! When?"

"A long time before you did," I joke.

"Oh, it can't be that long," she says. "I graduated in 2020."

"Fuck me…" I don't want to tell her that in 2020 I was wrapping up construction on my house. Or that I found my first gray hair. And if my drunk math is doing things correctly, she's about twenty-six years old. "Let's just say that was a long time after I was there."

"I'm betting you know someone in my family. I'm a third-generation Vol, and all my siblings went to UT. I'm the youngest of five. So I bet at some point you'd know someone in my family. Maybe my brother? He was there around the mid-2000s. Oh! Oh my God! I love this song!"

Any conversation of me knowing her brother, or any of her family out of the estimated 28,000 that go to the University of Tennessee each year, are forgotten as she jumps from the booth, her dress trailing behind her, as she makes her own dance floor in the middle of this Nashville dive bar.

And all I can do is sit back and watch. Not in a creepy way. Hopefully. I don't mean for it to be like that. More in a…proud way? I don't know what it is, but watching Tiger right now is something special.

This girl doesn't give a shit that the entire bar is watching her. She's dancing and singing without a care in the world, wearing a fugly wedding dress that's now been through it and singing at the top of her lungs about keying a man's car and slashing his tires. She's horribly off key and her hair is a mess. She looks more like a zombie bride than one that was supposed to get married earlier today.

And all I can do is sit back, watch, and smile. Admire. I know she's in pain. I know she's hurting, and tomorrow everything is going to come crashing down on her. But for right now? In this moment? She's going to let it all out however she needs to. And I say more power to her.

"Cap! Come over here!"

I shake my head. "I'm good."

"Oh, come on!" She comes back over to the booth and grabs my hand. "Dance with me!"

I reluctantly get up, but not because I want to dance. I *don't* dance. But more because I don't want her making a scene. I've been to this bar a few times, and it takes a lot to get kicked out.

That's why I picked it. But the way Tiger's going tonight, I wouldn't put it past her.

She releases my hand when we get back to the makeshift dance floor and resumes dancing in her own world. I don't move an inch because I have a feeling the combination of alcohol, dancing, and a dress that has its own zip code is about to catch up to her.

"Come on, Cap! This song is so fun!"

The words are barely out of her mouth before I watch her start to stumble to the ground. She tries to catch herself, but she somehow takes out two couples, knocks over a pub table, and runs into a waitress all in one swoop.

I bend over to pick her up from the floor. "Come on, Tiger. Time to go."

"No!" She yells as she kicks her feet, sending her dress up in the air. "I gotta dance!"

"Dancin' time's over. Time to sober up."

"You're no fun."

"So I've been told."

———

"You don't have to carry me."

I reach into the backseat of the Lyft and pick her up fireman style as we walk to my house. "You fell, therefore I do."

"I'm not hurt."

"You could've sprained your ankle."

"I wouldn't know, because I haven't put any pressure on it."

"Let's be safe and not test that." I stop in front of the keypad to my garage. "Can you open it up and type in my code? 1017?"

"Sure," she says, though at the angle I'm holding her, it's not the easiest. And let's be real, she's probably seeing double after what she drank tonight. The fact she hasn't passed out yet is impressive and a little terrifying.

"Ta-da!" she exclaims as the door to my attached garage

begins to open. "Also, you must be a very trusting person if you gave me your garage code before you even know my real name."

I turn the door handle into my laundry room without dropping her. "If your drunk ass can find your way back to this house, and remember the code, I'll let you break in. No questions asked."

"Deal," she says, and I have to chuckle as I hear her mumbling 0217 over and over again. "Here, let's get you down. I need to let my dog out then I'll get you ice for the ankle. And water for your liver."

"Thanks, Cap. You're too kind."

I put her down in the living room as an excited Winnie comes racing through the house. I never leave her home this long alone, so I know she has to be dying to go outside.

"Oh my gosh! Puppy!" she squeals.

"She thinks she is," I say as I guide my golden retriever, Winnie, to the patio door to let her outside. "She's seven but has the excitement of a two-year-old."

I leave Tiger as I hear her going on and on about what kind of dog she would want as I hurry to the kitchen to grab supplies. I'm glad she's talking because that's keeping her awake. The last thing I need is for her to pass out before she drinks at least one glass of water and takes a few aspirin. As I make my way back to the living room, I hear her laughter filling the air.

"Care to share what's so funny?"

"I always wanted to be carried over the threshold on my wedding night. Guess I still got my wish."

Fuck...I never even thought of that.

"I'm sorry," I say as I sit next to her. "I didn't mean—"

"Don't apologize," she says. "You're the last person to apologize for anything. Plus, I need to thank you. I haven't said that tonight, and I should have said it no less than a hundred times."

"You don't need to thank me."

"Yes, I do. You didn't need to come over and help me at the

bar. You could've said no when I asked you to stay with me. So thank you. This day was shit, but you made it a little less shitty."

Warmth runs through my body at her praise. "I couldn't have left you."

"Most men would've."

"I'm not most men."

There's a moment between us...an electricity of some sort, but I quickly shut it down as I grab her ankle and bring it up to my lap so I can apply the ice pack. I begin to take off her shoes when I notice my hunch from earlier was right.

Stilettos. With a red sole.

Fuck me.

I might be a country boy at heart, but a woman in stilettos will be my downfall every single time.

Snap out of it. Right. The fuck. Now. You're drunk. And horny. It's been a while, but that's no excuse to be thinking any sort of thoughts about Tiger. She's drunk and depressed and had a hell of a day and is no less than ten years younger than you.

"You know I used to be that girl."

I don't know what she's talking about, but I'm grateful for the change of subject.

"What girl?"

"The bachelorette." Tiger relaxes into the sofa. "That was me just a few months ago, only my bachelorette party was in Miami. I had the same sash. Same tiara. Hell, I think we were wearing the same dress. It was like I was looking in a mirror."

I resist making the comment that she's ten times more beautiful than Bachelorette Barbie.

"You're not her," I say. There. The truth. Just...disguised a bit.

She looks at me like I'm an idiot. "That's where you're wrong, Cap. I'm that girl down to the perfume and expensive jewelry. But thanks for trying to make me feel better."

I don't know what else I can say—if there is even anything to say—so I choose not to. I usually default to silence, but I have a feeling on most days that's not how Tiger operates. But in this moment, I think it's the remedy she needs.

I don't know how much time passes by when I hear an adorable snore. When I look over to see Tiger, passed out, still in her wedding dress, hair a mess, I can't help but smile. I know this has been the shittiest day of her life, and tomorrow might be shittier, when she goes back to reality, but I hope she wasn't lying when she said I made it a little less horrible.

Because this was one of the best days I've had in quite a while.

I carefully move her and do my best to gently pick her up. She stirs a little, but finds a nook in my shoulder to lay her head as I walk her down the hallway to my bedroom. I'd take her to my guest room, but I'm ninety percent sure there aren't sheets on the bed. Most of the time that room is the place I store things when I don't know where else to put them. Plus, the girl has been through it; the least I can do is let her sleep in a comfortable bed.

She stirs a little when I lay her down on top of my comforter. Her cell phone falls out of the pocket of the dress, so I plug it in and set it on the nightside table. I head to my closet and grab an extra blanket, along with a pair of boxer shorts and a T-shirt. I lay the clothing next to her, figuring when she wakes up tonight she can put them on. I drape the blanket over her, tucking in the edges around the massive gown.

"Goodnight, Tiger. I know it doesn't mean much, but I'm proud of you."

I brush her hair off her forehead before walking to the door, careful to leave it just a sliver open to let some light in. I'm sure when she wakes up she's going to be confused and disoriented.

And honestly, I think I'll be the same way.

Because this might have been the most random, strange, and memorable day I've ever had in my life.

guide to love rule #30

If you're going to do the walk of shame,
at least make it a good story.

6

stella

"I now pronounce you Mr. and Mrs. Duncan Hughes. You may kiss the bride."

I lean in to kiss Duncan, except he's not there. Where'd he go? I turn to where the guests are sitting, only to see them pointing and laughing. I look back to my sisters, who are in a line next to me, but none of them are making eye contact. What's going on? Why are they laughing? Where's Duncan?

Wait. Is that Nadia standing in the back, swatting a whip against the palm of her hand? And next to her is Bachelorette Barbie, who looks smug as hell. Wait! Is her arm linked through Cap's?

What in the actual hell is going on?

I let out a gasp as I jolt awake, breathing heavy as I sit up in bed, desperate to leave that hellish dreamscape behind. I pull the fleece blanket up to my chin, like it's going to protect me from the dream that featured every character from yesterday's hell.

Wait, why do I have a blanket? Where am I? My head is pounding. There's a sliver of light coming through the curtains, which allows me to see that I'm in a light gray room with strategically placed pictures on the wall. There's a couple dressers, but no other furniture. This room screams minimalist bachelor pad.

Wait! Is this…*shit*…is this Cap's room? I bet it is. The last part of the night takes center stage in my mind. The singing and dancing, the falling, Cap carrying me out of the bar, then into his house. I remember Sad Girl Stella coming out for an appearance. But that's the last I remember.

Did I pass out? Did we…no. We couldn't have. I wouldn't have. He wouldn't have. At least I don't think.

Right? I mean, I would have remembered something like that. God, I hope I would've. Because I have a feeling that man would be unforgettable.

But to be safe, I check under the blanket, just to make sure everything is where it should be.

I don't know if it's a good or bad thing that I'm still wearing the hideous wedding dress.

"Fuck me," I groan, flopping onto my back as the weight of yesterday starts to crash down.

I got drunk yesterday to forget. To forget about Duncan. His lies. The wedding I ran from. I didn't want to remember a single thing.

It was a bandage on a problem that needs an amputation.

So now not only do I have to deal with the fall out, I have to do it with a raging hangover.

Super.

Just as I'm wondering if I can ask Cap if I can move in—all in the sake of avoiding my problems—I hear a vibration from the nightstand next to me. By habit I look over to see that it's my phone. And it's plugged into a charger. And it's next to a pair of boxer shorts and a T-shirt.

Did he do that? He had to have. I don't even remember to plug in my phone at night when I'm sober and my battery is at five percent. And the clothes? Are they for me?

Why is that simple gesture hitting me so hard? I'm talking straight in the feels. Maybe because he didn't have to. Maybe because in nearly four years together, I can't remember Duncan doing anything like that. Maybe because I'm overly emotional as I feel everything starting to come back to life.

But no matter how I feel, it's sweet.

He's sweet.

Oh Cap…poor, sweet, didn't-sign-up-for-yesterday, Cap…

I don't know why he's single, but the ladies of Nashville are missing out. If my drunken memory is serving me right, he said he built this house himself. Which is fucking hot. Oh, and he does nice things like plug in cell phones for drunk girls he randomly meets and gets suckered into taking care of.

This man should be scooped up and accounted for. Not by me. No. I'm a hot mess. But by someone.

And she'd be the luckiest girl in Nashville.

Buzz…buzz…buzz….

Shit. My phone is still vibrating. And another one. And another one.

Without even looking, I'm going to guess the family text chain is in full effect.

"Time to pay the piper, Stella," I say as I grab the phone off the charger. "You've avoided life long enough."

> **MOM**
>
> Stella Leigh Banks. Enough is enough. We let you have yesterday, though I was worried SICK. Answer your phone.

> **AINSLEY**
>
> Stella, just send one letter. Or an emoji. Anything to let us know you're alive. I'm really worried.

> **QUINN**
>
> See! You worried Ainsley.

> **MAEVE**
>
> Not that I'm not worried about you, I'd just like to say that you ran, and therefore I won the bet.

SIMON

Stella, I'm going to need you to come over to Mom's house because I've been wanting to kill Duncan for a day now, but I can't kill him without justification, so I'm going to need to know things very soon or I'm going to be going to jail and then you're going to leave my new daughter without a father. Is that what you want? IS THAT WHAT YOU WANT, STELLA?

STELLA

Sheesh. Enough of the dramatics. I'm here. I'm alive.

AINSLEY

Oh, thank goodness. You didn't have your location on so I was trying to keep a positive outlook. But after a while I naturally assumed you were dead.

STELLA

Not dead. Just hungover, so dead would be better.

MOM

Stella! Did you get drunk?

MAEVE

No, Mom, she ran away from her wedding and planted a garden. Of course she got drunk.

SIMON

Where are you? Do you need a ride?

Yeah, that's exactly what I need: My brother driving to a location I'd drop him because I don't know where I am, only for him to be greeted by the man who owns this house whose name I don't actually know.

STELLA

I'm good. I'll call a Lyft.

MOM

Have it come to our house. I'll cook breakfast.
Everyone come over.

MAEVE

Wow, we get a Sunday breakfast out of this?
Thanks, Stella!

STELLA

Glad to help the cause. I'll be there in an hour.

DAD

See you then, sweetheart.

I laugh at my dad's last message—he's always the one to end the conversations, and usually it's the only text he sends—as I swing my legs over and reluctantly get out of bed. I somehow maneuver out of the dress, ripping it in the process, and put on the most comfortable pair of boxer shorts and T-shirt I've ever felt against my skin.

Then again, they aren't made of lace and tulle and taffeta, so it has to be a step up.

I ball the dress under my arm and grab my phone as I quietly leave the room. I happen to see a door open across the hall and peek in to see a passed-out Cap on a bare mattress that is way too tiny for him, rolled up in a blanket, his dog laying at the foot of the bed.

He let me sleep in his bed. How in the world is this man single?

I want to thank him, but I also don't want to wake him up, so I tiptoe down the hall of his ranch-style home and luckily end up in the living room. I snag my high heels before walking to the kitchen island. I order a Lyft, and while I wait, I find a scrap piece of paper and a pen because I need to say thank you, even if I can't do it in person.

Cap — Prince Charming is pretty spot on. Thanks for everything yesterday. I'll never forget you -- Tiger.

And it's true. I won't. Never in a million years.

————

I had a mantra in college: If you're going to do a walk of shame, you better have a good story behind it. And the hookup better have been worth it.

I have the story. It might not be good but it's...something. And even though I didn't have the hookup, meeting Cap was definitely worth it.

Except now I'm doing a walk of shame at my parents' house.

In my defense, this is so many degrees above a walk of shame there isn't a name for it. I highly doubt anyone in the world has had to walk into their childhood home, wearing a strange man's T-shirt and clothes, hair and makeup a mess, and carrying their wedding dress under their arm.

Yup. This is the worst walk of shame to ever shamefully shame.

With one more deep breath, I tuck the dress securely under my arm and enter my parents' house.

And I'm met with silence.

If there's one thing to know about the Banks family, it's that we're never quiet. Loud is an understatement. With five kids, and one of them being my brother Simon, there was never a moment of peace. I don't even know if it was silent when we were all sleeping.

I was nervous before to tell everyone what happened. Now? I'm slightly terrified.

"Hello?"

No one answers as I walk down the front hallway. That's when I start to hear whispers coming from the family room.

"What are we going to say? We need to be gentle, especially since we don't know what state of mind she's in." That comes from Ainsley, which makes sense. She's the most empathetic of my siblings.

"How about 'what the fuck did Duncan do so I can kill him?'"

"That's not how we're going to start this, Simon," Maeve says.

"Can we just come out and ask? I feel like a rip the Band-Aid off approach might work." I giggle under my breath at Quinn's suggestion. She's the most blunt of the siblings. A true middle child if there ever was one.

"Really?" Maeve asks. "Just dive right in?"

"No, not exactly," Quinn says. "Maybe like, 'Hey Stella. You okay? Want some leftover wedding cake?'"

"Quinn, that is the absolute worst idea I've ever heard," Maeve says. "And Simon is here, which should really say something."

"Well, we have a lot of cake!"

I can already feel the tears, and a little laughter, starting to come as I turn the corner. "Cake might help. Booze didn't. Might as well try desserts."

Six sets of eyes snap to me, all wearing different versions of sadness, pity, and worry. The worry is obviously my parents. And looking back, what I did yesterday was pretty stupid, so I really need to apologize for that.

The combination of sadness and pity is from my three sisters. I mean, I'm the baby. I expected them to have these looks.

Then there's my brother Simon. The only way to describe his gaze is relieved with a splash of anger that I'm pretty sure is reserved for Duncan.

But as he walks toward me and brings me in for a hug, and his eyes don't soften, I wonder if I'm reading him wrong. Is he mad at me?

"One, are you okay? Two, where did you go last night, and does it have any correlation with whose clothes you're wearing?"

Of course Simon has to point out my walk of shame outfit. "Yes, I'm okay. And I'm safe. That's all that matters."

He grunts something under his breath, though I can't hear him because my mom is tearing Simon away to wrap me in a hug of her own.

No, not a hug. This is a vise squeeze.

"I was so worried," she says, somehow making her hold tighter. "Are you okay?"

My first instinct is to say that I am, though I think everyone in this room would know that's a lie. So I say the only thing I know to be truthful right now. "I don't know."

———

"Shut the fuck up…"

"I'm going to fucking kill him."

"No fucking way…"

"Language! We aren't damn heathens!"

"A hooker! As in a prostitute?"

"I need to call the firm…"

Two hours later I've showered, put on clothes that I had in my suitcase from yesterday because I'm an over packer by nature, and have a full stomach of breakfast food. I've also given the full post mortem on how Stella Banks became a runaway bride.

I told them about the money.

I told them about the maxed-out credit card.

And I told them about Nadia.

That's the one that shocked them the most. I mean, I can't blame them. I don't think anyone had "catch Duncan getting flogged by a dominatrix in the honeymoon suite" on their bingo cards.

After I wrapped up all the details—and I spared none—Simon and my dad exited the room, likely to come up with a plan to have Duncan conveniently disappear. Which means it's just the girls now, which I'm grateful for. I love my dad and brother, but sometimes you just need your sisters and your mom to tell you everything's going to be okay.

Quinn breaks the silence, though she doesn't have much to say. "I…I just…"

"Yup." It's all I can say. I try to think of something more as I take a long sip of the hot cup of coffee. Normally I'm an iced vanilla latte girl, but today, strong, hot, black coffee is exactly what the doctor ordered. "I do need to say that I'm sorry. I reacted in the worst way possible. I shouldn't have just run off. I should have sent more than a text. I feel horrible for that."

"Don't apologize for the reaction," Maeve says. "No one could ever know how they're going to react to a situation that is so out-of-left-field it almost doesn't seem real."

"I know it wasn't something I could have practiced a reaction for, but just sending y'all a text message saying that 'Duncan cheated. And lied. Wedding's off. Don't look for me.'? That was shitty of me. So yes, I do need to apologize."

Mom leans over and puts her hand on my leg. "You said enough. Plus, I saw your face before you left. You already had one foot out the door. You just didn't realize it."

I nod, knowing she's right. She's always right.

I think back to those minutes in the bridal suite before my world went upside down. The worry I felt. The uncertainty. Staring at myself in the mirror and not knowing who I was anymore.

She's right. I did have one foot out the door.

But that still doesn't give him an excuse to hurt me like he did.

Because he hurt me. He hurt me so fucking bad.

"How could he do this? We were supposed to get married. Why did he do this?"

My last words come out in a scream as the avalanche pours on top of my head.

The money.

The cheating.

The years of manipulation I never saw.

The time I wasted on him.

The parts of myself I let go to make him happy.

The need to have what everyone else had so compelling that I lost sight of who I was.

I knew today everything would come crashing down on me. Once the first tear comes out, I know there's no stopping them.

And frankly, I don't want them to.

guide to love rule #4

There are five stages of grieving a breakup.
There are also the sub-stages, which include eating, drinking,
crying, and swearing.

7

stella

Even when I was shit-faced drunk on Saturday night, delusional enough to pretend like I didn't have a care in the world, I knew the real tears were going to come.

I didn't realize they weren't going to stop.

Don't you run out at some point? I mean, how much can one person cry in a twenty-four-hour span?

The answer is apparently all day, all night, through eating and sleeping and everything in between. Though after breakfast yesterday, I haven't eaten anything. And calling what I did sleep is laughable. Every time I think I'm done with the tears and I can move on to the next stage of grief, which is anger, they start again. Which sucks, because I *really* want to be in the anger stage. I'd pay any amount of money to be in the anger stage. Breaking shit right now sounds fan-fucking-tastic.

Like Duncan's nose. Or his precious bottles of rare vintage Jameson. That would hurt him more than anything else.

But no…I'm sitting here in the crying/denial stage, where I can't believe that instead of leaving for my honeymoon today, I'm wondering what my next step should be. When do I have to go back into the world? What will people say? What *are* people saying? How do I show my face at work? Will Duncan still have a job or will my dad call in a few favors and get him fired? Can that even happen?

And if he does get let go, would it be worth it? Sure, I wouldn't have to see Duncan every day, but the not-so-subtle comments about me getting everything because of my dad will fire back up with a vengeance. That's all I heard when I got hired. I was the nepo baby of Carter, Banks, and Fairchild. It took me a full year to prove myself. If Dad pulls strings to get Duncan fired, I have a feeling the talk will be worse than before. Not only would it remind everyone that I'm a partner's daughter, but that I'm also a real-life runaway bride. One I can handle. Two might break me. A woman can only tolerate so much when trying to put on the brave face.

"Stella?" The whisper and light knock comes from Ainsley. "Can we come in?"

Ugh...she said we. That means all of them.

It's time for a meeting of the Banks Sisterhood.

Ainsley I could handle. She's gentle. And even when she disagrees with you, she does it in the nicest way possible. But the other two? Them I'm not sure about.

Don't get me wrong, I love my sisters with my entire being. I'd give them kidneys. I'll fight for and with them any day of the week. Hurt one of us? You hurt us all. But I don't know right now if I can take Maeve's need to be the second mother or Quinn's directness.

Then again, I eventually need to get out of this bed, and if anyone can help me do that, it's my sisters.

"Come in," I say as I push myself to a sitting position. I know my hair is a mess, and I'm sure my face is an absolute train wreck, but bless their hearts— they don't say anything. Instead they circle me on the bed, each giving me some sort of comforting gesture.

"I'd ask how you're doing, but I know the answer is 'shitty' so I'll skip the formality."

Yup. Direct Quinn is here. "I appreciate it."

"Even though we know the answer, that doesn't mean we're not worried about you," Maeve says as she wraps an arm around my shoulder. "Stella Banks doesn't cry like this, which means I'm guessing there's more to the story."

Leave it to all my sisters to see right through me. Which isn't surprising. There are no other people on this planet who know me better than the three women sitting on my bed. There might be roughly eight years between me and Maeve, with Quinn and Ainsley falling in the middle, but the differences in age have never stopped us from being in tune with each other.

And many times doing it sitting in one of our beds, just like this.

I remember the first council meeting of the Banks sisters happening when I was around eight. Maeve was going into her senior year of high school and Ainsley and I heard a sound we'd never heard before—Maeve was crying.

Maeve didn't—and doesn't—cry.

So, being the curious little sisters we were, we walked into her room to see her with her head in Quinn's lap, crying like we'd never seen her before. Ainsley and I laid next to Maeve, holding her hands as Quinn brushed her hair off her face. It was over a boy—because they sucked then just like they suck now. I don't remember what was exactly said during that first bed talk, or even who the guy was that made the big bad Maeve Banks cry, but I do remember the feeling of knowing that we had a bond that was rare.

We were friends. Best friends.

And God help the man that fucks with one of the Banks sisters.

"Yes, I'm mad at Duncan. The money and the lying and the cheating were obviously the reasons I ran. But I'm more mad at myself."

"How on Earth are you mad at yourself?" Maeve asks. "You did nothing wrong."

I shake my head. "That's where you're wrong."

"I'm going to need you to elaborate," Quinn says. "Because unless you hired the woman to spank him, then I don't see how this falls back on you."

I grab a tissue to blow my nose as I gather how I want to tell this to my sisters. "It's not the lying and the cheating that are my fault. I know that. But, part of me wonders because I let go of who I was during this relationship that maybe if I hadn't, I would've seen clues to his lying and cheating. Does that make sense?"

"Yes," Maeve says. "I think. Before I weigh in, I want you to elaborate. I don't want to assume your headspace right now."

I do appreciate Maeve wanting clarification. She usually just weighs in whenever she wants. "I don't know if there are specific examples. I just know who I was when Duncan and I met and who I was days before the wedding. I found out he had stolen thousands of dollars from me, and us, and I was going to stay with him. I told him we'd figure it out. All because I needed to get married so badly that I was willing to ignore a glaring red flag."

"That's not a red flag," Quinn says. "That's a full-on flashing neon sign that was saying 'get the fuck out of this.'"

"Exactly. It was inches from my face, and I completely ignored it."

"The Stella I know wouldn't have done that," Ainsley says. "You once chased a frat boy down the street because he walked out on a tab and you felt bad for the waitress. You jumped on his back and started beating him until he agreed to come back and pay."

"She didn't deserve that," I say hotly.

"And neither did you," Maeve says. "But I want to ask you about something you said. You said you needed to get married. Why?"

I wasn't expecting that question. "What do you mean, why?"

I know the answer, I just really don't want to say it in front of my sisters because I know how it's going to sound.

Pathetic. Weak. Sad.

And those aren't the words we use to describe the Banks sisters.

"No. You're not going to get off that easy," Maeve says. "Why did you need to get married? Who was pressuring you?"

I shake my head. "Me. Only me."

"Why?"

How do I say this that doesn't make me sound completely pathetic? "Because everyone else was."

"Oh, Stella…" Ainsley's sympathy makes me feel slightly better.

"Who's everyone?" Quinn asks. "It sure as hell wasn't us. And Maeve was already divorced by the time you and Duncan got together."

"Thanks for the reminder," Maeve says dryly.

Quinn brushes her off. "Oh, like you miss being married."

"You're right. I don't. Good riddance to bad orgasms."

"I don't think that's how the saying goes," Ainsley deadpans, which of course makes us all laugh.

"It should," Quinn says. "But back to Stella. Who was getting married that you needed to marry the first guy you dated seriously?"

I look down and suddenly become very focused on the pillow next to me.

"Stella?"

"Everyone," I say. "Everyone was. Every sorority sister. Every person I went to high school with. You know how many weddings I went to the year before I met Duncan? Seven. I'd seen six of my friends get engaged just in that holiday season. And there I was, no boyfriend. Barely dating. Thinking that I had all this time to have fun, when clearly I didn't. And then along came Duncan…"

"Oh, Stella," Ainsley says. "I hate that you felt that way."

"Me too," I say. "Because that feeling has led me here."

"Don't beat yourself up," Quinn says. "This is who you are. You've always thought you wanted what others had."

Now I know Quinn is the blunt one of the four of us, but that dagger she just threw hurt more than others. "Excuse me?"

"What our sister meant to say with more tact..." Maeve gives Quinn a glare before turning her sights back to me. "You're the little sister. You grew up wanting what we had. You wanted to dance because Ainsley did. You wanted to ride horses because Quinn took lessons. When I said one time at dinner that I was becoming a vegetarian, you quit eating meat too."

I laugh at the memory. "That only lasted a week. I missed chicken tenders."

"Exactly. That's the point. They weren't your ideas. They were ours. Some of them you stuck with. The dance choice was great. Meat and the horses? Not so much."

Ainsley reaches over and takes my hand. "We love you. And you're one of the most amazing people I know. But you've always had a tendency to follow. To just want what others have wanted. What does Stella want? Without thinking of anyone else, what does Stella Banks want right now?"

Holy shit, when they put it like that, everything makes so much more sense. I have always been a follower. I've always wanted what my big sisters had. Or thought was cool. But it didn't stop there. I pledged a sorority because it was the one my sisters were in.

But even in college, the need to not be left behind, or not have what others had, didn't go away. I was smart, but never the smartest. I never had the popular boyfriend. Or any serious boyfriend at all. I was always scrounging up dates for formals because I refused not to go while my friends were taking their significant others.

I've always felt a step behind. That I needed to have what others had to measure up.

And I was willing to get married to fill that hole in my life.

"Fucking hell," I say, falling back to the bed. "What the fuck is wrong with me?"

"Absolutely nothing," Quinn says. "You are who you are, and we love you. And now that we know the problem, the next step is how we fix it."

"Yes. How does Stella get her groove back?"

I sit up, wondering why Quinn is snickering at Maeve's comment. "What?"

"You're too young," Quinn says. "But just know it was a wonderful, well-timed joke."

"I'll believe you," I say. "But Maeve's right. How do I get my groove back? Because now that all of this is out there, I feel even more lost than I was an hour ago."

Silence falls over the room before Quinn throws her finger in the air, like an actual lightbulb just clicked on in her head. "You go on your honeymoon."

"What? I'm not doing that."

"Yes, you are."

"No. I'm not," I say with authority. "I already feel like shit and pathetic. Now you want me to go on my honeymoon alone?"

"One, it's not pathetic, it's empowering," Ainsley says.

"Two," Maeve continues. "It's not like you were going on some super inclusive, romantic honeymoon where you have to be reminded of what didn't happen. You're staying at a vacation house owned by your brother because your fiancé wanted to drive to fucking Florida."

"So don't think of it as a honeymoon," Quinn says. "Just think of it as a solo vacation. Which is badass. You took the time off work, and it would be better if you didn't jump right back into that swamp. Get away from here for a few weeks. Lay on a beach, read a filthy book featuring blue alien dicks with a horn in just the right place, get a tan. Hell, maybe get laid."

"Quinn!"

"What? I'm just saying rebound sex isn't a bad idea." She

gives me a wink. "The best way to get over someone is to get under someone else. Am I right?"

"Ignore that last part," Maeve scolds. "But she's right. Pack your bags. Book a flight. Get out of here and clear your head. I think it'll do you some good."

I think about it for a minute. "I've never traveled by myself before."

"Even better," Ainsley says. "This will give you the time to find yourself. Not Stella who thought she was going to be the future Mrs. Duncan Hughes. Or Stella who thinks she needs to follow the pack. But find out who Stella *really* is. And more importantly, what Stella really wants."

I look at my sisters, who are giving me nods and looks of encouragement.

They're right. I do need this. I need to get out of here. I need to find myself. I need to figure out what's next. And I can't do that here.

I need to get my groove back.

"All right, then, that settles it," I say, rolling out of bed for the first time in hours. "Destin, here I come!"

8

emmett

There are some phrases I never thought I'd say in my life. To this day these are ones that are holding strong:

Roll Tide. (Over my dead Tennessee Volunteer body.)

I like my bacon floppy. (Crispy or I don't want it.)

I'll hire someone to fix that. (It'll be a cold day in hell before I let a stranger fix anything that belongs to me.)

Until today, "I can't wait to go to Florida" was on there.

Not anymore.

Because I can't wait to get the hell out of this town. Even if it's just for a few days.

When Simon asked me last week to head to Destin to check on our rental properties, I admittedly pushed back. We have locals who we keep on retainer to check on things. Simon insisted I needed to be the one to check out any storm damage.

Now I'm glad he did.

It's been roughly three days since my night with Tiger that somehow fucked me up more than I care to admit. So, yeah, maybe a change of scenery will do me some good. Even if it's at the beach.

I hate the beach. Too much sand. Too many people. And frankly, I don't fuck with sharks.

I've been on the road for roughly two hours on my way to Florida, and this is only the third time I've thought about her. I think that's an improvement. I don't know what spell she put on me, but I can't get her out of my head.

When I woke up Sunday morning, I knew she left. I just had a feeling. I mean, if it were me, I would've gotten the hell out of Dodge too. On the rare occasions I spend the night with a woman, I usually leave before the sun rises. And those nights weren't fueled by the worst day of my life. So I don't blame her one bit.

However, when I went to the kitchen and saw the note she left, I felt a pain I wasn't expecting. I can't describe it, but I know it wasn't pleasant.

I shook that off and was fine for most of the day. That was until I sat down at night with my beer and my dog and turned on the television to an Avengers movie.

Fucking Captain America…

That was my sign that I needed to get the hell out of Nashville. I needed to get my mind right. On that same note, I hope Tiger's taking some time as well. If it was me in her situation, I'd have been out of town the minute I ran from the wedding. A lying and cheating fiancé that you found out about right before the wedding? No one deserves that. Especially her.

Luckily, I can't get too much more in my head about Tiger as I see my sister's name on the dashboard signaling an incoming call.

"Winnie secured?"

I hear my dog barking in the background. So I guess the answer is yes. "Yes, she is. I always forget how much she loves car rides."

"They're one of her favorite things. And if you go get her a pup cup, she'll never come home to me."

"Wouldn't you know it? I was thinking I needed to make a coffee run. This seals the deal."

I laugh as I change lanes. "Thanks again. I hated the thought of boarding her."

"It's no problem," Maddie says. "You know I love her. Jack was over the moon that we get to watch her for more than a night. We're already headed to the dog park."

I smile when she brings up my nephew. Jack is three years old and the best damn kid in the world. Granted, I'm a biased uncle, but my sister hit the jackpot with him. And he's all hers, since the sperm donor bolted the second she told him she was pregnant.

"Well, thanks again," I say. "Now, to change to a less pleasant subject. Have you talked to Mom?"

Maddie lets out a long sigh, which is the normal reaction when bringing up our mother. "I did. She's on a trip with Larry…or is it Gary? Something with an 'ary.'

"I thought it was Barry?"

"Maybe? Who knows. Honestly I quit learning their names until they get married."

"I mean, she's been seeing him for a month, so it'll probably happen soon."

"And they did go to Vegas, so it's completely possible."

"Fucking great…"

Our mother is…how do I put this? Incapable of being alone. Single isn't in her vocabulary. Never has been and never will. It's just something Maddie and I have come to terms with when it comes to Rhonda Collins-Marrs-O'Leary-Moscowitz-Giordano-Zaharopoulos-Smith.

Yes. That's seven marriages. Eight, if Larry Gary Barry sticks around. I'm the product of marriage number one. Maddie came from number three. At her ripe age of twenty-five years old, that's a twelve-year age difference between us—so do the math of the average amount of time for each husband. I liked Maddie's dad and was sad to see him go, though I do talk to him every once in a while since he still lives in Nashville and has a great relationship with Maddie. My father, on the other hand, didn't even lie and say he was going for milk and cigarettes before leaving. I had just turned four.

I was the ring bearer in wedding number two before I started kindergarten.

Thus began the revolving door of boyfriends who turned into husbands, who turned into ex-husbands.

And that is the reason why I'm in no rush—and really have no desire—to ever get married.

I've seen marriage. Many times.

Fuck that.

"So when Mom inevitably comes back married from Vegas, I'm sure there will be a reception. Will my brother be bringing anyone?"

I huff out a laugh. "Not subtle, Sis."

"What? I was simply asking if there's a woman in my brother's life?"

Don't think about Tiger…Don't think about Tiger.

"And, just like the last time you asked, the answer is no."

And the time before. And the time before that.

"Unacceptable. I command you to go to Florida and meet someone. Have a fling. A vacation romance. Something."

"I don't fling."

"You should."

"Why do you say that?"

"Because…" She pauses before continuing. "You don't date. At least, that I know of. I'm sure there are…women…you meet when…things need done."

I cringe. "Please don't talk about my sex life."

"Do you have one? I'm not being sarcastic. I truly don't know. And if you do, that's great. Because you don't date. I've never seen you with a woman. Aren't you lonely, Emmett? I know Rhonda didn't give us the best example of a healthy relationship, but you do know that being with someone doesn't make you her, right?"

I know this. The rational part of my brain knows that just because she birthed me, doesn't mean I'm like her.

My true worry is that I'm like him. The parent I don't know.

So I made the decision a long time ago not to experiment with "which parent am I" and have opted to stay single.

Honestly, it's worked out well so far. I get what I need when I need it. The Nashville bar scene usually leaves plenty to choose from when I need to scratch the itch. And even better, I can usually sneak out before the sun comes up.

No long term. No leaving. Nice, clean, and easy. Just how I like it.

"I know," I say. "Please don't worry about me."

"I am and I will," she says. "It's not healthy to be that alone."

"I'm not alone," I protest. "I have Winnie."

"Your dog doesn't count."

"Quiet!" I scold mockingly. "She'll hear you."

"She's too distracted by Jack. And I'm getting her a pup cup. She's on my side now."

"Even getting my own dog to turn against me," I groan as I pass the signs that say I'm entering Florida. "Are you done with the brother bashing?"

"For now," she says. "But please, I know you're there for work, but try and have a little fun. You're in Florida. Maybe see a beach. A night club."

"I'm too old for night clubs. And I hate beaches."

"Not in Florida you aren't," she says. "And who hates beaches?"

"I'm hanging up now."

"Love you, big brother!"

I sigh. "Love you too."

As I head to a rest stop to fill up on gas and grab something to drink, I try to picture myself at a nightclub. It's laughable. I didn't even like going to dance clubs in college, when I was admittedly more fun than I am now. My idea of a night out starts at a reasonable time—no later than seven—and it's at a bar with a reasonable volume for music, a few beers, and a game to watch on the television.

Night club? Thumping music? Sweaty bodies and shoulder-to-shoulder crowds? No fucking thank you.

As I put the car in park, my phone vibrates with a text message from my best friend and boss. Good. Work things. That I can get behind.

SIMON

When you get down there check on 2254 first.
That's where Stella's staying this week.

Ah yes. Stella. The sister who got married. I forgot she and her husband were using that unit for their honeymoon.

EMMETT

Will do, boss.

SIMON

Thanks, man. And check on her, won't ya? I'd
appreciate it. Oh. And have some fun.

Check on her? On her honeymoon? That's fucking strange. Then again, I've met her now husband. He's…a piece of work is one way to describe him.

Jackass would be the other.

So without thinking I type back "no problem" before tossing my phone to the side and filling up the truck. Fifteen minutes later I'm back in the driver's seat, ready to make the final haul for a week of work and…beaches.

Nope. Won't be doing that either.

Destin, here I come.

guide to love rule #67

If you give a man a fake name, make sure
you're never going to see him again.

9
stella

MUCH LIKE THE DREAM WEDDING I WASN'T GOING TO GET, I ALSO wasn't getting my perfect honeymoon.

I wanted to go to Greece. Duncan, who preferred not to fly because his lips got chapped, wanted to go somewhere drivable. When he heard that Simon bought rental properties in Destin, he somehow talked my brother into giving us access to one for two weeks. For free. I thought he was being frugal. Now I wonder if it it's because he knew we'd be broke.

I mean, who needs to see the Parthenon when you have the Destin Fishing and History Museum? The sad thing is I didn't even fight for Greece. Didn't leave subtle hints like having baklava around the house or watching *Mamma Mia* every time Duncan came home.

Nope, like so many other things I didn't fight for while we were together, I just agreed. Now don't get me wrong, I love Destin. My family vacationed here every year when I was a kid. But for a vacation. Not for a trip that's supposed to be romantic and once-in-a-lifetime.

God, I was an idiot. So blinded by what I thought I wanted that I was agreeing to two weeks in Florida. I don't know in the stages of grieving a relationship if you're supposed to beat yourself up for your past blunders in judgment, but that's where I'm at. I'm calling it Stage 1.5: Stupidity.

The Uber driver pulls up to my beach house and helps me unload my bags. I wonder if I tip him extra he'll help me bring my bags inside. Because now that I look at the suitcases I brought, I'm wondering what the heck I packed for, while also wondering if I remembered to pack bras.

Two full-size suitcases with clothes and shoes. A smaller one for makeup, face products, and hair tools. A carryon for electronics. And of course my Louis Vuitton oversized purse that is bigger than most suitcases.

It looks like I'm moving in. Which, if I'm being honest, isn't out of the question. Here has a beach, peacefulness, and no one who knows what happened to me in the past week. There has Duncan, regret, and everyone who knows what happened to me.

I wonder which one I'll choose…

"Here you go, ma'am," the driver says as the bags are safely out of his trunk. I give him a cash tip—we're not about to make this nice young man claim that on his taxes—but he takes off before I can ask for extra help.

Smart man.

It takes me longer than I care to admit to wheel and carry my bags down the driveway, through the garage, and into the house. When I get inside I throw down my purse and wipe the sweat off my forehead. I feel gross and disgusting, which is only amplified by the one-million-percent humidity outside. Without looking in a mirror I know my hair and makeup are a mess. My clothes are sticking to me. Yet, I somehow don't care. Normally I would. But right now, all I want is to lay down and let this glorious air conditioner cool me off before taking a shower so cold my teeth chatter.

I abandon my bags in the entryway—that's future Stella's problem—as I walk the few steps I need into the living room and fall face first into the oversized sectional. I kick off my tennis shoes and just lie in air-conditioned bliss. I know I should be looking at the beach because I'm at the beach, but I need AC more.

This might be heaven. Then again, my bar is extremely low for what qualifies as heaven right now. I'm exhausted. I haven't had a peaceful night's sleep since…I don't know when. Not the night before the wedding. Not since. Actually, the only time I slept like a baby was when I was at Cap's…

Oh, Cap…

I feel myself smiling as I let my mind drift off to that night, which was the only shining moment in the shit show that has been my life. But just as I feel my eyes starting to grow heavy, and memories of Cap's smile flashing in my mind, I hear a door slam. I think it's coming from the back of the house. My eyes shoot open, but I don't move from my position on the couch. I don't breathe. I don't move. I just do my best to hear where the noise is coming from and formulate a plan, because I refuse to be the dumb blonde who gets killed first in the horror movie.

How does my brother not have a security system? Nothing went off when I walked in, though I was too tired to realize it at the time. I didn't think going on your honeymoon alone could get worse. Nope. It can. Because you can be the victim of an ax murderer.

I hear footsteps growing louder. They are heavy. Like he's wearing boots. Which is also odd for Florida in August. But not odd if he plans on dumping my body in a nearby forest.

I really need to stop watching true crime shows before bed…

I slowly roll off the couch, trying my best not to make a sound. When I get to the floor I reach around and find one of my shoes. It's not the best weapon, but at least they have a little platform on them. I'm sure it could do some damage if I put some weight behind it.

Oh, who am I kidding…I'm a one-hundred-twenty pound, five-foot-three female who is surviving off caffeine and stubbornness at this point.

But as my parents say, I'm tiny but mighty. And the ax murderer is about to learn that firsthand.

The footsteps stop, but they got pretty close. Maybe he's at the edge of the living room? I take that as my cue to slowly creep up from a crouching position, priming myself to pounce on the intruder.

There he is. His back's to me so I can't tell what he's doing. But it gives me a few more seconds to size up my adversary.

Fuck, he's hot…

Well, at least from the back. Strong thighs wrapped in denim. An ass that looks damn good in said jeans. He's wearing a white T-shirt that's clinging to his back muscles, and his light brown hair is curled out underneath a ball cap. It's giving sexy modern cowboy, and I'm here for it.

Which is odd since that's not usually my type.

And odd because he's about to kill me.

Stella! Focus! There's a stranger in the house and you need to go all Home Alone on his ass.

With an internal pep talk, and fueled by the pending anger stage and a lack of sleep, I launch myself in the stranger's direction.

"Ahhh! Danger! Danger! Get out of my house!"

I wield my shoe above my head as I run toward him. My plan is to jump on his back and just start beating him with it. I think. I mean, that's the plan. Except it doesn't matter because right before I jump onto him, the man turns around. His reflexes are definitely catlike as he catches me mid-air. Somehow my legs wrap around his hips.

But these aren't just any hips.

They're *Cap's* hips.

Cap is catching me.

Cap is the ax murderer.

Cap is here.

In Florida.

In Simon's house.

"Tiger?"

I wiggle and push myself out of his hold, which he doesn't protest. My breathing is heavy, bordering on hyperventilation, as I take a few steps back.

Because what the actual fuck?

I have to be dreaming, right? That's it, I fell asleep on the couch and I'm having the realest dream of my life. Yes. That's it. Because Cap isn't here, and that wasn't his ass I was staring at, and those weren't his arms holding me like I was nothing.

"What are you doing here?" I ask, my breath still heavy.

"I should be asking you the same thing."

"I asked first."

"Really, Tiger? That's how this is going to go?"

"It is," I say sternly, my shock now being replaced with determination. "You're going to tell me why you're breaking into my brother's house."

He looks confused and gives his head a quick shake. "For one, I didn't break in. I have a key. And I don't know what you're thinking, but this isn't your brother's house. This is one of the rental properties that my boss owns that I'm checking out, along with numerous others over the course of this week."

"Are you calling me a liar?"

He shakes his head and puts his hands up in surrender. "I didn't say that. I'm just saying that maybe you got the wrong house. Because I work for the man who owns this house, who isn't your brother."

"This is the right house, and my brother does own this property."

"No, he doesn't."

"Yes, he does."

He groans. "Are we really having a kindergarten argument over this? Just admit you're in the wrong house."

Okay, now I'm mad. I've just spent the better part of the last four years with a man who would gaslight me into submission. Or argue with me until I gave up. I'm not about to spend one of my first days of freedom being treated the same way.

No matter how sexy Cap looks in those jeans and that hat.

"I'm not in the wrong house. This is the house I'm staying at, owned by my brother, Simon Banks. I'm staying here for two weeks. So now I'm going to ask you again, what are you doing here?"

Cap's jaw drops a little. No. Not a little. A lot. Think cartoon character with the jaw that hits the floor and the eyes that bug out.

"Are you…Stella?"

Did he…how does he…

"How do you know my name?"

He shakes his head and starts pacing in circles. He takes off his hat and runs a hand through his hair. He looks panicked. I'm just confused.

"No…no, no no," he mutters. "This is supposed to be occupied by his sister, named Stella, who just got married. It's supposed to be for her honeymoon."

"It *was* for my honeymoon. And as you know, that didn't happen."

"Fuck," he groans. "Now it makes sense that he asked me to check on you. He just forgot to tell me that one small detail."

I notice Cap's hat as he puts it back on, which says Magnolia Properties.

The name of my brother's company.

And then it hits me.

I've heard about my brother's one and only employee, his property manager, Emmett. One of his best friends from college whom he reconnected with over the past year.

We've never met. At least I thought we hadn't.

Emmett is Cap. Cap is Emmett.

The one who saved me on the worst day of my life.

The one who took care of me when he didn't need to. When I

was a stranger in a bar wearing a fugly wedding dress and crying into my martini.

He's the man whose ass I was having the most wicked thoughts about just a few minutes ago.

"Cap?" I pause, swallowing the lump in my throat. I know the answer to the question, but I need to hear it from his lips. "What's your real name?"

He stops his pacing, and my heart immediately hurts when I notice just the slightest bit of sadness in his eyes. "Emmett Collins. Nice to officially meet you, Stella Banks."

10

emmett

SHE'S HERE. THE WOMAN I HAVEN'T BEEN ABLE TO STOP THINKING about is here. She tried to beat me with a shoe.

And she's the little sister of my best friend.

Fucking great…

I remember thinking the night we met that I needed to get my mind out of the gutter because of her vulnerable state. Now I need to quit because Simon will kill me.

Well, he'd pay someone to do it, because God forbid the pretty boy get his hands dirty. Either way I'd end up dead.

But at least my final view would be one of absolute beauty.

After the shoe incident, each of us declared we needed to get our bearings. I went back to the house I'm staying in, which is right next door, to splash some cold water on my face. I told myself no less than twenty times that I needed to make sure all of my thoughts about her stayed friendly and platonic.

Maybe I needed to say it twenty-one times, because as I walk into her house, where she's currently standing over a pot of pasta she insisted on making, my thoughts are definitely not platonic. Her blonde hair is piled on top of her head. She's wearing a matching tank top and short set that is so tight it might as well be painted on. I wondered what her body looked like under all that fabric the night we met, but even my wildest thoughts didn't do her justice.

As I take a step closer, I realize just how short she is. Is she even five-foot-three? She was short when she had her heels on, but the closer I get to her, the shorter I realize she is. Where would she come up to on me? How would it look if she looked up at me with her gorgeous blue eyes?

Shit. Maybe I needed a twenty-second time. Clearly I didn't get the message. Stella Banks is off limits.

For so many reasons.

"Emmett?"

Hearing my actual name from her lips startles me. "Yeah?"

"Did you hear me?"

Shit. How out of it was I? "Sorry. What'd you say?"

"Just wondered if you wanted tomato sauce or Alfredo?"

"Oh." Yup. I didn't hear any of that. "How about both?"

She scrunches her nose in the most adorable way. "Both?"

"Have you never had the two together?"

She shakes her head. "No, because that's not allowed."

"Says who?"

"Normal people."

I chuckle. "Oh, Tiger, not only is it allowed, but it's going to change your life."

I head to the pantry and take out the bottles of sauce I picked up earlier today. Actually, I was putting away the groceries when Stella arrived. Simon had sent me a detailed list this morning and asked if I could pick them up. Which again, I thought was odd. And that was on top of his message for me to check on her.

It all makes sense now. Then again, it could've made a lot more sense if he just would've fucking told me she didn't get married. Would I have pieced it together that his sister was Tiger? Who knows. But still, you'd think since Simon tells me everything from his newborn's diaper changing schedule to what he thinks about the Roman Empire, he would've told me his sister didn't get married and was traveling to her honeymoon alone. Instead I got the news from Stella jumping on my back, ready to beat me to death with a tennis shoe.

I laugh at the memory, which gets her attention when I put down the jars of sauce next to the stove.

"What's so funny?"

"Oh, nothing. Just thinking back to when you thought you were going to take down a home invader with a Nike."

A blush creeps over her cheeks. It's also adorable. I really need her to stop being so damn cute. "In my defense, I wasn't left with a lot of options. And it had a platform to it. Gave a little extra weight."

"Whatever you say, Tiger."

"You don't have to call me Tiger anymore. We can go by our real names."

"What if I want to?"

Stella turns to me with a small smile. "So I can still call you Cap?"

"I kind of like having a nickname only you use."

Her blush heightens as she grabs the sauces and puts them in pans to warm. "I'm sorry," she says. "About the shoe. And the jumping on your back thing."

"Don't apologize. You didn't know I was here, and you were scared. I don't blame you one bit."

"I'm going to kill my brother," she says. "He could've told me that someone might be here."

I walk to the freezer to get the garlic bread I bought. "Can we do it together? Because it would've been good to know that it was just you and you weren't on your honeymoon."

"Yes!" she yells, slamming down the plastic spoon she's been using to stir the pasta. "How does he not tell either of us this? The man has no filter or sense of when to stop talking any other time!"

"Maybe we should fuck with him when we're home," I say.

"Oh! Maybe you kicked me out and I had nowhere to stay."

"I like the way you think," I say as I preheat the oven. "But that might not work since you'll be here for two weeks. Maybe we could just tell him we burned the house down."

"That's good," she says, tapping a manicured finger to her lips. "Or maybe we go with that you walked in on me in the shower. Then one thing led to another and now we're dating. Thank him for playing matchmaker."

Her eyes go wide as the last words come out of her mouth, like she didn't mean to say it out loud.

"Maybe we should go with the house fire," I quickly say.

"Yup. House fire. Good call."

Stella doesn't say anything else, instead becoming very focused on the pasta. I do notice the blush creeping from her cheeks down to her neck. God, I love that I can tell when she's bothered. It also makes me feel better that I'm not the only one affected by the thought me seeing her in the shower. Just the thought of it makes my cock ache.

I busy myself with getting the table set and drinks poured. Anything I can do to take my mind away from the image of a dripping wet Stella.

Fuck, I need out of here. I came here to give myself some space from thoughts of my mysterious Tiger. Now she's not a mystery. And she's going to be next door for the week I'm here. All because I'm the asshole who was trying to be economical and stay at one of the houses instead of getting a hotel.

Great move, Emmett. How's that working out for you?

We each make a plate of pasta in silence before going to the dining table. When we're seated, I look over to see just the red sauce on top of her angel hair pasta.

"Didn't want to try the mix?" I say, taking a sip of my beer.

"Alfredo gives me bad breath, so I don't eat it anymore."

"Anymore?"

She shrugs like she's embarrassed. The fact that she's staring at her pasta confirms that suspicion. "Duncan didn't like when I ate it, so I stopped. He said my breath was horrible after and he didn't want to kiss garlic breath. Actually, I grabbed this garlic bread without thinking. If you want it you can have it."

Another tally to the reasons I want to kill the man Stella was going to marry.

Garlic breath? Really? Does he not know there are things called mouthwash and it's not permanent? Also garlic is lovely and flavorful and an ingredient you should use while measuring with your heart.

I bet Duncan thinks salt and pepper is spicy.

Fuckwad.

I stand up and walk around the table, pulling an empty chair right next to Stella. I don't sit though. Instead I go back to the kitchen and make another plate of pasta, making sure to put an ample amount of Alfredo on the angel hair.

"What are you doing?"

"Giving you options," I say as I sit next to her. "Now, if you truly don't like Alfredo, or don't like the lingering taste it gives you, then by all means, don't eat it. It's your world, Tiger, and I'm just visiting. But, if you want to eat the sauce, then eat the fucking sauce. Pour it on your pasta. Dip your garlic bread into it and go double garlic and make vampires scared of you."

That makes her laugh. It's a sound I've never heard from her, but one I want to hear all the time.

"I know you're still processing everything that's happened. I can't imagine what you're going through. But he's not here anymore. He's not here to control you, or tell you what to do, or what you can eat. You're Stella fucking Banks. You attack home invaders with shoes. You hold your head high when everyone else would be crumbling. And you eat the fucking Alfredo sauce."

She looks at me, a smile slowly forming on her face. "I'm Stella fucking Banks."

Now it's my turn to smile. "Damn right you are."

With a nod she takes a piece of the garlic bread and rips a

portion off, gently dipping it in the creamy sauce on top of the pasta.

"Oh, come on, Tiger. Get in there."

With a giggle she does, coating it fully before dropping it into her mouth.

"Ermygod," she says. "That's sooooo good."

"Glad to hear it," I say with a smile, pride swelling in my chest as I watch Stella dip the rest of the bread.

Pride? Over someone eating food? What the hell is wrong with me?

Just as I'm about to shake away that feeling, I watch as Stella tilts her head back and drops the bread into her mouth before letting out the most sensual moan I've ever heard in my life.

Fuck…

Does she know what she's doing? She's not making eye contact with me or making any other movements to indicate that she's doing this on purpose. She's just genuinely enjoying her meal.

And I hate to admit that I'm enjoying the show.

"Want some?" she asks, dunking another piece in the sauce and holding it out to me.

I shake my head. "I'm good. That's all yours, Tiger."

She shrugs. "Suit yourself."

She takes a bigger bite, which leaves a small trail of the white sauce at the corner of her mouth.

Head out of the fucking gutter. You aren't a fourteen-year-old boy.

Apparently my dick doesn't get that message, because it's starting to stir again as I watch her slowly swipe it away before sucking it off her finger.

Fuck my life.

What is this woman doing to me? She's eating bread, for fuck's sake. Nothing about this is supposed to be sexy. Or any sort of emotion-stirring. Between this feeling and the thoughts earlier of Stella in the shower, it's abundantly clear that I need to get the hell out here.

I've now spent in total two days with her. The wedding day and today. And in those two occasions, she's sparked feelings I'm not at all comfortable with.

Desire. Pride. Want. Contentment. Happiness.

And I might not know much, but when you put those together that seems like feelings you'd have toward someone you're in a relationship with.

And I don't do those.

Especially with Simon Banks's sister.

———

"I don't think I could eat another bite," Stella groans.

"You do know there's ice cream, right?"

She pops her head up from the couch where she was laying, a hopefulness in her eyes. "Birthday cake?"

I'd never heard of that flavor until it was on the list Simon sent me. I'm now very glad he put it on there. "Along with vanilla, chocolate, and my personal favorite, cookies and cream."

"Okay, maybe just a little bit. Since you went to the trouble of buying it."

I crack a smile as Stella falls back onto the couch in the living room. I finish loading the dishwasher and scoop us each some ice cream, adding some toppings to both.

I mean, what's ice cream without some syrup, whipped cream, and a cherry on top?

Boring. That's what.

I take our two bowls over to the couch where Stella's lying, scrolling through one of the streaming services on the television.

"One birthday cake sundae."

She sits up on the couch, but doesn't take the bowl from me right away. She's staring at it like she's unsure what to do next. I swear to fucking God if she says that her fucking ex didn't let her eat ice cream, I'm going to drive to Nashville tonight for the sole purpose of killing him.

"Please tell me you also didn't give up ice cream for that asshole?"

She shakes her head. "You made me a sundae."

Her reaction is one of surprise. It's throwing me. "Yeah? I hope that was okay."

She nods, and I think I see a tear forming in her eye. "You put away dishes *and* made me a sundae."

Am I missing something here? "Well, you cooked. So that means I clean. And as for the sundaes, I was making myself one, and thought that your birthday cake needed some fixins. It wasn't a big deal."

"I know it shouldn't be a big deal, but it is." She pauses for a second then turns her eyes from the ice cream to me. It breaks my heart when I see the sadness behind them. "We're…friends. Are we friends? Acquaintances? Random people who keep running into each other?"

"Friends," I quickly say. "We're absolutely friends."

I see the hint of a smile forming at the corner of her mouth.

"Okay, friends. Friends who have seen each other twice. In that time, you've done more for me than Duncan did for me in the entirety of our relationship."

"Really?" Surely not. I mean, I know what she's told me. And I'm remembering back to the one time I met him at Simon's baby stag party. Duncan felt slimy. He was asking about strippers and details of other people's sex lives. I didn't like him then and I sure as shit don't like him now.

"Really," she says. "Maybe not at the beginning. You know, during the stage where everything is great and you want to be around each other all the time. The sunshine and rainbows stage."

"Sure." I don't mean to have a sarcastic tone, but I hear it slip it out. If she notices, she doesn't say anything.

"Duncan and I had that stage for about three months. Three blissful months of no fights, cuddling on the couch, and doing the small things for each other. Surprise flowers. Lunches. Those kinds of things."

Stella trails off for a second, but I don't fill in the silence. Like I told her earlier, this is her show. I'm just along for the ride.

"That leaves roughly three years and nine months of slowly losing myself in our relationship. Gradually giving up some of the foods I liked. Making sure I always woke up in the morning before he did to wash my face and brush my teeth because of one comment he made about how I looked in the morning. This? What we did tonight? We used to do that. Cook dinner, have a drink, laugh about stories from our day. Clean up and curl on the couch together to watch television. By the end it was me being his cook and maid before he retreated to his booze room as soon as dinner was done."

My heart aches listening to her talk about him. I swear every story she tells me about their relationship just makes it worse. "Can I ask you a question?"

She nods as she takes a big bite of the sundae.

"Why did you stay? Why did you want to marry this guy?"

I'm probably out of line for asking. I might have said we're friends—and we are—but I've also known this woman for less than forty-eight hours in totality. She doesn't have to tell me shit.

Yet, I want to know. I want to know why this woman—this beautiful, brave, strong, woman—would want to be tied down to what sounds like the most insufferable and dickless man on the planet.

"Just jumped right to the million-dollar question?"

"I like to aim high."

My response doesn't brighten her mood. If anything, I watch her slip deeper into the couch, her eyes drifting down.

"I thought I loved him," she begins. "And I did. At least at one time. But love made me blind. Or stupid. I haven't decided which one. All I know is that I wanted to be married so bad that not only did I lose myself, but I made excuses for his shitty behavior."

She trails off, and I give her ankle a squeeze. It's all I can think to do to show her that she can take her time. I'm here as long as she needs me.

"I wanted the fairytale," she continues. "Devoted husband. House with the wrap-around porch. Maybe a porch swing? Two-point-five kids and a husband who would dance with me in the kitchen. I think as time went on that's what I was in love with—the *idea* of that life. I had felt like all my friends had it, and I wanted it too. I loved Duncan because he was the man I *thought* was going to give me that life. And I wanted the life. Some part of me still does. But when you catch your fiancé getting flogged with his dick out, wearing nothing but a tie and black dress socks, that's one red flag you can't ignore."

I don't mean to laugh, but I can't help it. "I'm sorry, Tiger, I know that situation isn't funny."

"Don't feel bad. The flogger thing is funny."

"You're right, the flogger thing *is* funny. But the rest? Don't feel like you have to put on a brave face. Grieve the loss of the relationship. Take the time you need. And for the first time in a while, be completely selfish. You've earned it."

She nods. "Thanks. I've been trying to. My sisters helped me see that before I left."

"That's good."

"And I'm getting a little better each day, at least with coming to terms of how we got here. Though now I'm getting angry. Which is great."

"Great?"

"Oh yes," she says, a wicked smile coming across her face. "I want to break shit."

"Breaking stuff is fun. I'm always down to do that."

"Really?" The excitement in her tone is a one-eighty from where it was a minute ago. "Because I want to find one of those smash rooms."

"Smash room?" I echo, suddenly feeling like I've walked into something I might regret.

"Really? You've never heard of a smash room?"

I shake my head. "Can't say I have."

"Oh, we're going to one." Stella puts down her bowl of ice cream and grabs her phone from the coffee table, her fingers flying as she brings up a picture for me to see. "They give you a sledgehammer and baseball bats and goggles and a padded room where we can just break shit."

"We?"

"Yes, we. Aren't you in town for the week?"

"Yeah." I swallow the admission that I was going to move up my exit date. "That was the original plan."

"Original? Are your plans changing?"

Yes…no…I don't fucking know anymore.

"Undecided."

She sits up a little straighter and slaps her hands to her lap. "Well then let me decide for you. You're staying. And we're going to a smash room. Along with the beach and to dinner. Oh! I bet they have mini golf here. Duncan would never mini golf with me because he said it was for kids but I *love* mini golf. He was just pissed I always beat him."

"Stella…" My voice trails, because I hate to be the one to take the excitement away. As I try to figure out how to tell her gently, and only lying slightly, of why I need to go back to Nashville earlier than expected, she reads my face and fills in the blanks for me.

"Oh." I feel the proverbial knife go through my heart as I watch her shoulders slump. "I understand. You have work to do. This wasn't a vacation for you. It was stupid of me to ask you to stay and do all that stuff with me. Forget I brought it up."

I reach over for her hand, needing her to believe what I'm about to say. "Hey. Don't talk about my friend that way. I don't think she's stupid at all."

The shy smile she gives me when my words register makes my chest swell in a way it never has.

And make me say the words I didn't intend to.

"I can stay."

She raises an eyebrow. "What?"

"I'll stay," I say with a sigh. "I was only going back because I'm, what my sister calls, 'not fun.' I'm not much of a beach guy. Or a vacation guy. So I was going to head back early. But I don't have to."

Was that a lie? Partially. My sister does call me a stick-in-the-mud. "Plus, Simon told me to stay and take some vacation time. The fucker owes me after taking the world's longest paternity leave. So let's go smash some shit and let me beat you at mini golf. I'll even sit on the beach with you, but I won't be happy about it."

Her smile lights up the room. "Really?"

"Really." I give her hand a squeeze before I release it. "And I'm being serious. I'm not letting you win. I play for keeps."

"Noted," she says. "And thank you. Truly. Though, I was ready to play the single-girl-alone-after-I-just-ran-out-of-my-wedding card."

"Really, Tiger? Sweet and innocent? Woe is me? That was your ace in the hole?"

She faux-innocently shrugs. "Would it have worked?"

Of course it would've. Because I'm quickly learning that when it comes to Stella Banks, I can't say no.

And that's a very, very, big problem.

guide to love rule #55

Drinks with umbrellas are a key part
of curing heartbreaks.
A hot man in swim trunks also helps.

11
stella

I know I wasn't sold on coming to Destin when it was my honeymoon.

But being here for my non honeymoon? Well, this isn't too shabby.

I have the hot sun on me and a frozen drink with an umbrella in my hand as the salt water hits my legs. Every time the tide hits me, it washes away another piece of anger that has been building inside me all day.

At least I hope it is.

Because I'm mad. So damn mad. And I don't know why today it's all bubbling to the surface, but it is. As I lay here and try to bask in the sun, all I can think about is everything I want to be mad about.

I'm mad that I wasted time and money on a day only I cared about.

I'm furious that he drained our bank accounts. Maybe more so now than when I found out about it. I'm so mad that I shot a text off to my dad asking if I could sue Duncan. He said we'd talk about it when I got back. Which is his way of saying, "let's think this through when you're not emotional and drunk."

Which is fair. These frozen drinks are going down way too smoothly.

My dad also knows I wouldn't *actually* sue. Duncan might be a lying, stealing, cheating scumbag, but he's a good attorney. The battle between him and my dad would go on for years. No one has time for that. Plus, years of working at a law firm has made me hate tiny, revenge-filled, lawsuits. Though I would contend this wouldn't be a petty lawsuit. No, I feel that I'm entitled to compensation for money that was stolen, my money that I paid for the wedding. Oh, and the emotional suffering I endured from wearing his mother's wedding dress. Hell, I should sue just for that.

But I can't, because I did that. I did a lot of this. Which brings me to who I'm mad at the most—myself. I want to slap myself for ignoring every red flag that is now so glaringly obvious. I'm furious that I made excuses for his behavior. And how I let myself change for him. I'm mad for having such a narrow focus and the need to have what others had to the point I didn't see what was happening right in front of me.

I know I'll move on. I know I'll get over the hurt in my chest for the life I thought I was going to be living. But I don't know when, or if, I'll forgive myself for letting all of that happen.

"Room for another chair?"

I crack an eye open to see Emmett standing over me, completely blocking the sun. I didn't know one person's shadow could completely engulf a person.

And why is that so hot?

"Sure," I say, signaling next to me. "Though, I don't know if I'm good company today."

"That's fine." He unfolds the chair he brought down from the house and starts to take his shirt off. "I'm more of a silent beach-goer anyway."

Sweet baby Jesus…

I don't mean to stare at Emmett's chest, but…I am. He's not even doing it in a sexual way. He's just a man taking off his shirt at the beach. And I don't blink for a single second as I watch in awe.

In my defense, I've never seen an eight-pack of abs before. I've also been with the human version of a Q-tip for the past four-ish years.

Emmett is…manly. Bronzed skin. Defined muscles without it looking like he lives at the gym. A slight trail of hair that leads down to, then disappears, inside his trunks. Trunks that I bet cling to his muscular thighs if he were to step into the water. I find myself biting my lip at the thought of a wet Emmett, his hair slicked back and the drops of water running down his face and the sweat pooling on his chest.

"You okay, Tiger?"

Emmett's words, in conjunction with the water smacking me on the legs, snap me out of my fantasy.

And what a fantasy it was…

"Yeah," I say, fumbling for an excuse as to why I was gawking at the man. Because judging by how he's looking at me I've been clearly caught. "I've been drifting off a lot lately."

Yes. That's a good one. I hurry to talk again just in case he doesn't buy it. "I thought you said you didn't like the beach."

He shrugs, turning his backward hat around to block the sun in his eyes as he takes a seat. "I don't. But I'm here for the week, so, when in Rome, right? Plus, I thought you could use some company."

"Thanks. But you don't have to spend pity time with me. You said you don't like the beach, and I'm already making you do things that you weren't planning on."

Emmett sits up a little in his chair. "Who said anything about pity?"

"Isn't that what it is?"

"On the contrary." He turns to me and the sincerity on his face hits me right in the heart. "This is me being done with work for today. This is me wanting to spend the day with my friend, relaxing on the beach. And who knows, maybe she can tell me what's so great about beaches. And why getting sand up my shorts is relaxing."

This makes me laugh. "Well, for starters, at this beach, you get frozen drinks."

Emmett looks around. "Is there a bar?"

I shake my head and grab the cooler that is next to me and pull out a pitcher of strawberry daiquiris. "There is. Bar Stella."

"Very nice," he says. "I'll take one, please."

"Coming right up."

I pull the plastic cocktail glass from the cooler and pour Emmett a drink. Because yes, I maybe, might have, on purpose, packed an extra glass for him.

I mean, a girl can hope, right?

It's not that I was looking to see if he was coming down every five minutes. I knew he had work to do today. And he said he wasn't a fan of the beach.

So I only looked every ten minutes.

In my defense, I don't do well being alone. I grew up in a house with four siblings. I shared a room with Ainsley until I was thirteen, and even after that she was in the room right next to me. When I went to college, I lived in a quad before moving to the sorority house. After I graduated, Ainsley and I got an apartment together in Nashville, where I lived until I moved in with Duncan.

I've never been completely on my own. And I don't think I thought of that when my sisters gave me the grand idea to do a solo vacation. At first it sounded freeing. Then on the plane ride I realized it was terrifying. It's probably why I all but forced Emmett to become my vacation buddy.

Yes. We're going to go with that. I was lonely, and that's why I asked him to stay. Not because he's male perfection and he made me a sundae.

"Cheers," I say, needing to get my mind back on track. Except when I go to extend my glass, he doesn't meet mine. "What? Did I do cheers wrong?"

He shakes his head. "Not wrong per se. I've just always been of the belief that if you're going to cheers, you have to make it count for something. Otherwise it's just two people clinkin' glasses to say they did."

"Never thought of it that way. That actually makes a lot of sense."

He sends me a wink, and I choose to ignore the fact that it sends a jolt of something through my body. "So, Tiger, if you want to cheers, tell me what we're doing it to. Small or big. Just make it count."

I think for a second. I know he said it didn't have to be this huge thing, yet I feel this enormous pressure to make this meaningful.

That's when it hits me.

"To making it count."

This earns me a smile that I swear the sun radiates off. "I like that. To making it count."

We tap our plastic glasses and take a sip before setting them down on my makeshift table—a.k.a. the top of my cooler.

We each lay back in our chairs as a comfortable silence falls between me and Emmett. The warmth of the rays combined with the slight breeze off the Gulf is the perfect balance. The beach is loud—it's August in Destin, and people are getting in their last trips before the school year starts—but somehow I'm able to block all that out. It's weird. This is the first time in days my brain has almost shut itself off. Not completely. But for right now, I'll take it.

"So this is how you beach?"

I giggle. "Did you just make a Ken reference?"

"What's a Ken reference?"

I shoot up from my chair so fast I nearly knock my designer sunglasses off my face. "Emmett Collins, do you not know about Ken and Barbie?"

"The dolls?" His confusion is adorable.

"Well, yes, they are dolls, but the movie. The *Barbie* Movie?"

He shakes his head. "Can't say I do."

"Well, that's just a shame," I say. "It's an American classic. A true cinematic masterpiece of the patriarchy and women in society."

Emmett turns his face to me. "Then what does the beach have to do with it?"

This makes me laugh, which only leads to a more confused Emmett face. "You'll just have to watch and find out."

He shakes his head and turns back to his lounging position. "No thanks, Tiger. There's no way I, as a thirty-seven-year-old man, am going to watch a movie about dolls."

Thirty-seven. Huh. I guess he is. I knew he was Simon's age, but I never really thought of it until now. When he was in high school, I was still playing with Barbies. I remember because I took one to Simon's high school graduation. I always felt the age difference between me and Simon was huge. Though that was probably aided by the fact that he's the oldest of the siblings and I'm the youngest.

But when I'm with Emmett, I don't feel that gap. He's Cap. I'm Tiger. An unlikely, yet amazing, duo. He doesn't look at me like I'm young. He doesn't treat me like it either. Which is refreshing. For years, especially at the office, I've battled lawyers thinking I'm a young girl who only got the job because of her dad. And I know Emmett and I haven't had a lot of deep conversations, but I somehow know he doesn't think that about me. When I'm with him, I'm with a guy who's easy to talk to and doesn't look at me like I'm a dumb blonde who's only goal in life is to get married and have kids.

The Barbie of it all…

"You know," I continue, "Simon watched it."

"Good for him."

"Don't you want to be on an equal playing field? Make a reference that now he can't monopolize?"

He turns back to me. "You're going to keep going until I agree to watch it, aren't you?"

I shrug. "I never did get to play the runaway bride card."

He groans, but it doesn't sound like he's really mad, which makes my smile as big as I've had it since he said he'd hang with me for the week.

"Fine. But we're getting all the movie candy I like. And ordering dinner of my choosing. I'm talking burgers and fries and not a vegetable to be found."

Is he really tempting me with a meal that I've not had in years because Duncan couldn't eat greasy foods because he'd get a stomach ache? Hell yes.

"Can we get mozzarella sticks? And onion rings? Oh! And maybe some fried pickles? With ranch, obviously."

Emmett gives me a wink that warms my body more than the sun ever could. "You got it, Tiger."

———

I can't believe what I think I'm seeing.

Emmett is crying.

Over the *Barbie* movie.

"Hey," I say gently, putting down my ice cream bowl so I can hand him a tissue. "You okay?"

He rips it out of my hand and dabs his eye. "That song should be illegal."

I laugh as I push pause on the movie. "Yes, it should."

He quickly sniffs back the stray tears and tosses the tissue on the coffee table. "You are *not* going to tell your brother about this."

I cross my heart with my finger. "You have my word."

"Thanks." He reaches for his beer and takes a long pull. I don't mean to stare, but his jawline makes it virtually impossible. It's perfectly defined without being too rigid and is covered by a beard that is, in my opinion, the perfect length. Not that I would know what the perfect beard length is. I've never dated a guy with one. Duncan tried to do No Shave November and he barely had stubble by the end. But I have a feeling Emmett's beard is perfect. Just long enough to feel the scratch against your skin.

Focus Stella. No staring. No fantasizing. He's your vacation buddy. And Simon's friend. And business partner. There can't be anything more. Even if that beard is making you think things.

"Can I ask you a question?"

"Of course," I say, hoping his question isn't about his beard.

"I've known Simon for more than fifteen years. How have we never met?"

"Actually, I've wondered this too," I say. "But, I was still in elementary school when you guys went to college together."

"I'm aware."

Why did he say it all growly like that? "So yeah, the few times I went to campus was for football games, and Simon would tear himself away from his tailgate to hang with us. And by the time I was in college, he was off living his life. He'd try to be the cool older brother occasionally when he was in town for games, but that's it."

"That makes sense," Emmett says. "But in the past year since we reconnected, I feel like we should've run into each other."

"Were you at the New Year's Eve gender reveal?"

He shakes his head. "No. I was invited but was told by my boss not to attend."

"Really?" Then it hits me about the timing of the party. "Did Simon keep you away because of his idiotic lie that he was telling Charlie about the restaurant?"

Emmett nods. "Exactly."

I still to this day don't know how Charlie puts up with him. "What about after the baby was born? That big party they had where Simon Simba'd my niece?"

He shakes his head. "I'm still mad I missed that one. That one, though, was random. I just happened to be out of town and couldn't make it."

"Wow," I say. "The fact that we had multiple chances to meet, yet it took a random day at a random bar after the most unpredictable thing of my life."

"Funny how life works."

"It really is."

We share small smiles before falling into a comfortable silence as I turn the movie back on. We're not even in another five minutes when I get a calendar alert on my phone.

"Shit," I mutter, clearing away the notification.

"Everything okay?"

"Depends on your definition of okay," I say with a sigh. "Part of Simon's honeymoon present was dinners he made reservations for at my favorite restaurants. I'm assuming they're also paid for, knowing my brother. I told him not to cancel, feeling confident at the time that I'd be able to solo honeymoon much better than I am. The first is tomorrow night."

"So don't go," Emmett says, like it's just that easy. "You can do whatever your heart desires."

I bite my bottom lip, for some reason nervous to say this out loud. "That's where the conflict comes in. I want to go. It's my favorite restaurant in Destin. When I was young and our family would come here, we always went. It was our big night out. We'd get dressed up, my dad would order sparkling grape juice for the kids as he and my mom shared a bottle of wine. It has this amazing seafood—I swear they've got the best clams I've ever had in my life—and the ambiance is so romantic. I remember seeing couples around us and they were always so in love. In my little girl fantasies, I imagined one day going there with my boyfriend or husband. Which I know is silly. And it's also why I can't go. I can't let that little girl down, you know?"

I look away from Emmett, because the last thing I want him seeing are the tears pooling in my eyes. Which is why I don't see him place his hand on my leg.

But I feel it. I feel it in every cell of my body.

"Hey," he says gently. When I turn to him I see a smile that is quickly becoming a source of comfort for me. "You want to go to that dinner?"

I nod.

"Then we're going."

I have to blink a few times. "Excuse me?"

He shrugs like it isn't a big deal, when it's in fact the biggest of deals. Bigger than what he did for me the day of the wedding. Bigger than anything else he can do for me while he stays in Destin.

"I said we're going to dinner tomorrow. Unless you'd rather go by yours—"

"No! Oh my gosh, thank you!" I launch myself at him, hugging him as tight as my not-very-muscular arms can manage. My cheek connects with his, letting me feel every itch and scratch of his beard. Except I'm too excited to process that the itch feels way better than I thought. "Thank you, thank you, thank you!"

When I pull away, I can't help but notice that Emmett clears his throat like he has a frog in it.

Could he—? No. That's absurd. Me hugging Emmett didn't make him need to compose himself. Even though I needed more than a few seconds.

Because the more I spend time with him, the more I realize I'm a fan of the beard. And his tanned body. And his smile.

I'm a fan of him. A big, *big* fan.

"I have to work tomorrow, so I won't see you during the day," he says, breaking the semi-awkward silence. "What time is the reservation?"

"Seven-thirty. Come by around seven?"

"It's a date."

Date.

I know it's just a phrase. I know it doesn't mean anything, and he didn't mean it that way. And I know that because Emmett has already turned the movie back on and is paying no mind to me.

Which is good. Because I'm officially freaking the hell out.

12
emmett

I roll my eyes at the text from my sister, but quickly reply with a full-length picture of me in tonight's outfit.

I can't be mad at Maddie's interest in what I'm wearing. This is the consequence of my actions. I'm the one who texted her earlier today, asking what someone would wear to a five-star seafood restaurant. She wanted to know why I needed to know. I said it was none of her business. After a slew of messages going back and forth, she declared that I had a date and she wasn't going to be convinced of anything else.

I didn't correct her.

In my defense, I was desperate. So desperate I not only recruited Maddie for fashion advice, I actually went to a men's store, where I bought three button-down shirts, four pairs of dress pants, two ties, a suit jacket, shoes, and a vest. Maybe more. I was scared to check the bags.

I don't know how it happened. One second I was asking my salesman, Javier, to help me find a simple white shirt and black pants for my dinner tonight with Stella. I think Javier put something in the cucumber water he gave me, because the next thing I know, I'm staring at a total I've never seen at a clothing store in my life.

I don't wear dress clothes. I'm a jeans and T-shirts guy to my core. In the fall and winter it's flannels. My "nice" clothes that I brought for this trip are a white short-sleeve button-down and a pair of khaki shorts. And even if I were at home, the options I'd have for date clothes would be skimp. I don't date, therefore I don't have date clothes.

Except apparently tonight I do date. Or at least, that's what it feels like.

And that *is* what I said.

Though I didn't mean it. Not like that, anyway. It just slipped out.

This isn't a date. This is a friend wanting to help another friend. A guy wanting to give a girl a nice night out. A man not wanting a woman to feel self-conscious eating alone at a restaurant.

That's what I'm playing on repeat in my head. Because if that loop stops for even a second then I'm going to think this is a date.

And it's not. It can't be.

This is Simon Banks's sister. The little sister of my boss and best friend. Then there's that whole fact that she's at least a decade younger than me. I'm sure there are more reasons why this can't be a date, but those three are strong enough for me to take hold of.

MADDIE

Looking good, big brother. Have fun on your date!

EMMETT

Not a date.

MADDIE

Then what is it?

EMMETT

Dinner.

MADDIE

With a woman?

EMMETT

None of your business.

MADDIE

That's all the answer I need ☺ Have fun!

"Pain in the ass," I groan as I pocket my phone. I grab my wallet, put on my watch, and give myself a spray of cologne. I'm usually not a big cologne guy but Javier gave it to me today and said it was a gift with purchase.

I think he just felt bad for drugging me.

A few minutes later I take the short walk from the beach house I'm staying at and knock on Stella's door. I fidget for a second, pushing my hands in my pockets, before taking them out and playing with the new watch. I'm about to start messing with the buttons on my cuffs when I hear the door open.

I think I stop breathing. I don't mean to stare, but how can I not? Stella is standing in front of me looking like a god damn goddess.

She's wearing a sparkly gold dress that should be illegal. The deep, low vee in the front is breaking the laws of physics. How is it covering what it needs to while tempting me in the most infuriating way? The sleeves are long but fitted to her toned arms. And the skirt? It's so short I have to swallow a moan and will my cock to behave. As my eyes continue to travel down her tanned legs I see that she paired the outfit with a pair of stiletto heels that make my knees nearly give out.

There's something about a woman in heels that has always done it for me. And Stella can fucking wear a pair of heels. How well? So well that I'm starting to say fuck the age gap and conveniently forget that she's my best friend's sister.

"Hi," I remember to say.

Her smile is bright, and it's just now I'm noticing the red lipstick she's wearing.

Fuck me…

"Hi, yourself. I just need a few minutes. Come in."

I do as she says, forcing myself to not stare as she turns her back to me to grab her purse. Fuck…is there a piece of her body that dress doesn't hug perfectly?

I try to shake away every inappropriate thought that is running through my mind right now. Which includes, but is not limited to, Stella wearing nothing but those heels as her legs wrap around me. Or waking up in the morning and seeing that glittery dress in a pool at the foot of my bed.

"You clean up nice," I hear Stella say.

"Thanks. You too."

Thanks? You too? Fucking idiot…

"Ready?"

I nod and cough at the same time, needing to get my bearings back. "Ready."

Ready to go to hell, that's for sure.

———

"Congratulations!"

Applause erupts around us as a man slips an engagement ring on his brand-new fiancée's finger.

Now I'm really glad I came here with Stella tonight. After what she told me about this restaurant, I can't imagine how she's feeling watching a couple get engaged two tables over from us.

"You okay?"

She nods, but considering her eyes are glued to her bowl of seafood linguini, I highly doubt she is.

"That's how Duncan proposed."

Fuck, I wasn't expecting that.

"I mean, not here, but at a restaurant." She pauses again

before going on. I notice she does this a lot. Like she's picking her words strategically. I don't know if it's because it's hard to talk about her life before she became a runaway bride or because she wants to make sure she says the right thing. But no matter what, I'm not about to fill in the silence when the floor is hers. "We were in Nashville. A steakhouse that he loved. It was where we had our first date."

"I mean, I guess that's romantic?"

Stella shakes her head and adds in an eye roll for good measure. "You'd think. But he knew I didn't want it in public. We'd talked about it. One night we went to a hockey game and a guy proposed on the Jumbotron. Luckily, she said yes. I'd told Duncan that I didn't want it like that. Too much pressure and I didn't want to ugly cry in front of strangers."

"So then he turned around and proposed to you in front of strangers? What a fucking putz."

This makes her laugh. "Yes. Putz. That's actually the perfect word to describe him. But it was okay in the end—the proposal that is."

"Okay? Proposal's shouldn't just be 'okay.' Plus, he did it in a space you said you didn't want. Did he even get you a decent engagement ring? I'd like to also go on record that if I ever see him again, I'm punching him square across the face. I'm not asking permission, and I'm sure as shit not going to ask for forgiveness."

I don't know why this is making me so angry, but out of all the things that I've heard about Duncan, this one is making my blood boil more than anything else he's done to her.

Apparently my declaration of violent intent is the right thing to say as Stella's hand reaches across the table and rests on top of mine. And the smile she gives me? I'll tell her every day how I want to hurt him if she smiles at me like that.

"While I appreciate the hypothetical act of violence, it's really okay. I didn't ugly cry. I was ready."

"Ready? Did you know he was proposing?"

"I did. I saw him put the ring in his pocket when we left for dinner. And even if I wouldn't have seen that, he was being weird all day. Fidgety. I knew it was coming, so I could stave off the tears."

I start to respond before Stella slams her hands on the table.

"No. No more Duncan talk. Not tonight. He's not going to ruin this restaurant for me. And you know what? Enough about me. You. Let's talk about you."

I agree about the Duncan talk, but there has to be other subjects. "Do we have to?"

"Yes, we do. I feel like all we do is talk about me and talking about me always goes back to Duncan, and I'm not going to let him ruin this night. So, Emmett Collins, tell me something about yourself."

"Um…" I'm suddenly unable to remember anything of interest about myself. "I work for your brother?"

Stella gives me a look that Maddie has given me many times. I don't know what it means in their age demographic, but in mine it translates to "no shit, Sherlock."

"I know that," Stella says. "I know this isn't a date, but what would you talk about or tell your date if this was one?"

I shrug. "I wouldn't know."

"How would you not know?"

"Because I don't date."

She stares at me like I have horns growing out of my head. "What do you mean 'don't date?' I thought you were single?"

"I am."

"But you don't date?"

"That's right."

"How does that work?"

"Is that a trick question?"

"It's not."

"Okay. Then the answer is I just don't."

"At all?"

How do I tell her that my version of dating is picking up a

woman's bar tab and heading back to her place? "Not at all. I just…I have a very abbreviated version of dating."

It takes her a second before I see the recognition in her eyes. "Oh…gotcha."

Stella doesn't follow it up with anything else, but I can tell in her eyes that she wants to push. To ask more.

And for some reason, I want to tell her.

"Aren't you curious as to why?"

She shakes her head, pauses, then tips it side to side. "No. Yes. No. It's none of my business. If you want to tell me, great. I'd love to hear more. If not, I get it too."

Stella isn't the first woman to want to know about this part of me. Pretty much all of the women I've told this to have been curious for an explanation. For them, I usually give a variation of "it's just not for me." But with Stella? She gets the whole story. It only feels right.

"I didn't exactly grow up with a good example of a loving relationship."

"Are your parents divorced?"

I nod my head while taking a sip of my whiskey. "Yes. And if that was it I'd probably be okay. Except when my dad took off I never saw him again, and my mom decided to try and set the world record for marriages."

"There's a world record for that?"

"There is. Twenty-three."

"How do you know that?"

"I'm a curious person," I say, trying to laugh it off. "Plus, I made the joke once to Mom and she got very excited so I had to bring her down to Earth. She's only at seven, though she is in Vegas right now, so eight could be happening as we speak."

Stella's jaw drops a little more with every word that comes out of my mouth. "Seven marriages?"

"Yup."

"Wow," Stella shakes her head a bit and takes a sip of her

wine. I follow suit with another drink of my whiskey. "That's something. Seven weddings and she never ran out of one?"

How I don't spit my drink out at Stella's comment I'll never know.

"Did you really just say that?"

She gives a coy look with a small shrug. "If you can't make fun of yourself, who will?"

I hold my glass up. "To dark humor."

She returns the gesture. "The best kind."

———

"Thank you."

I turn to Stella as we sit on a bench with a view of the beach, ice cream cones in hand. Or as Stella calls it, "sweet treats."

"For what?"

"This. Tonight. Everything."

"You don't need to thank me."

She shakes her head. "No. I do. You didn't have to do any of this. But you did. Hanging out with me. Dinner. This wasn't on your itinerary for the week. Hell, you didn't even want to stay. You don't know how much this means to me, and I need to tell you thank you."

I feel choked up when I finally get the words out. "You're welcome. But truly, it's been my pleasure."

And it has. I know she assumes I had this grand itinerary for the week, which I didn't. I brought golf clubs that I didn't intend to use. I brought swim trunks that until Stella talked me into the beach I didn't plan on wearing. My days would've consisted of working, inspecting the properties, and handling anything I'd need to before dinner at some sports bar or a spot off the beaten path.

Instead I'm enjoying fine dining with a beautiful woman and days ahead I'm actually looking forward to that don't revolve around work. I really should be thanking her.

Because I don't hate this. I don't hate it one bit.

"I know you said you don't date," Stella says, her mouth half-full of her strawberry cheesecake ice cream. "But you should know, that if you did, you'd be really good at it."

This makes me laugh. "Please don't tell my sister that."

"How old is she?"

"About your age. The product of husband number three. If she found out that I'm apparently good at dating, she'll have a field day with it."

"There's no apparently. You are."

Not that I'm looking for compliments, but I'm genuinely curious how I am. Because as I quickly retrace the events of the night, nothing sticks out that should put me in the "good at dating" category.

"Can I ask how?"

"Just little things," Stella begins, her eye line turning back toward the Gulf. "You opened my car door for me. Pulled out my seat at dinner. Let me order my own food. Bought ice cream."

I have to blink a few times because she can't be serious. Is the bar that low? I know Maddie has complained about the dating pool, but I didn't realize it was this fucking bad.

"Stella." I don't know what else to say. I'm literally stunned. Did this asshole not put in any fucking effort?

"I know what you're probably thinking."

"What's that?"

"That I'm a dumbass for staying with him."

"Not in the slightest."

She lets out a humorless laugh as she polishes off her sugar cone. "You should. I do."

"Hey." My quick word gets her attention. "I need you to stop beating yourself up. You were in love. You thought you were getting the life you wanted. You were going to get married. He hurt you and treated you badly. That's on him. He's an asshole. Don't let his actions make you feel bad about yourself."

Her chin falls, but I need her to hear one more thing. I take my fingers and tip it up, locking in with her beautiful blue eyes that I could easily stare at for hours and never get tired of.

"I need you to do something for me."

"What's that?"

"I know you still need to process what he's done. And you can do that. Be mad at him and be mad at the world. Grieve how you need to. But I need you to quit looking at this like it's something you lost and instead start seeing all the things you've gained."

I see the moment my words hit her right where I wanted them to. Something shifts in her eyes. Maybe it's hope? A glimmer of positivity? Whatever it is, it makes my heart swell that I did that for her.

"I like that," she says. "If we had a drink, I'd toast to the glass being half full."

"We'll save it for the next one."

I slowly drop my fingers away, but miss the touch of her skin the second I do. I might not be touching her, but I'm still locked in her orbit. The moonlight is hitting her in the perfect way. There are a million stars in the sky, yet somehow Stella is shining the brightest.

I want to kiss her. Fuck, I want to kiss her more than I want my next breath. And by the look on her face, she wants it too. I know we're both feeling the pull between us. I thought I felt it before, but chalked it up to circumstances. The only problem is you can only have so many circumstances before you realize it's more than that.

It's something. Something big.

Something that scares the hell out of me.

guide to love rule #13

Sometimes you just need to scream at the top of your lungs to Taylor Swift to fully heal.

13
stella

The smash room was exactly what I needed.

I felt powerful. Strong. A little violent, but in a good way. When I first took the mallet and swung it down on an old printer, I don't think I've ever felt more fierce in my life. When it cracked into a hundred pieces, a noise escaped me that sounded like a beast in the wild.

There's just one problem: It's hours later, and I'm still mad. There's still energy inside me that I don't know what to do with. It doesn't help that there's a thunderstorm brewing, which somehow feels metaphoric.

Well, that and Duncan contacted me today.

So to say I'm ragey would be an understatement.

I knew who it was despite the call coming from an unknown 615 area code number. Something in my gut said it was him. But like a dumbass, I answered.

And then proceeded to roll my eyes for a solid ten minutes.

He asked where I was. I wouldn't tell him.

He asked if we could talk. I said I didn't have anything to say.

He asked if I'd consider forgiving him. I laughed at that one.

He said he was sorry. I didn't believe him.

He asked if he could get any money back from the deposits. I promptly hung up.

And then I went and smashed shit. And the whole time I pictured me taking the bat to his balls.

Best therapy ever.

Then there was Emmett. Dear, sweet, man I don't deserve, Emmett. I don't know if he truly knew what to expect at the smash room, and at first, he just sat back and let me have at it. But pretty soon he got in on the fun.

And staring at him while he was swinging a mallet? It was not the worst sight to have. I might have thought a few times what it would look like with him wearing one of his tight white shirts, swinging an ax. I bet it would be manly. Rugged. Sweat dripping off his handsome bearded face.

Then, realizing that I was ogling at the man, I snapped myself out of it by throwing empty beer bottles against the wall. That seemed to do the trick.

I think Emmett knew something was off, but he didn't push me and I didn't say anything. Which is the best part of Emmett. He listens. He doesn't talk to hear his own voice. In fact, if he could say nothing at all, he'd prefer to.

He's truly one of a kind. And I can't imagine being here without him.

Which is insane. Two weeks ago I didn't know who he was. I mean, I guess I did, because I knew my brother had a business partner named Emmett. But I didn't know he'd be the person who would be getting me through the hardest time of my life to date.

But he has, and I'll never be able to repay him for that.

Cap…my own personal superhero.

I hear a low rumble of thunder as I start getting myself ready for bed. I'm grabbing a T-shirt and the boxers I might have not returned to Emmett as I hear a call coming through. My entire body goes solid for a moment before melting when I see Maeve's name on the caller ID.

"Hey there," I say as I head downstairs. Might as well make my nightly sweet treat while we catch up.

"How you doing?"

What a loaded question. "I'm hanging in there."

"You don't have to do that."

"Do what?"

"Lie."

"I'm not."

"Stella Leigh. You know I can tell."

And she can. It's one of her super powers. As the oldest daughter of the Banks clan, Maeve has always had a way about spotting the bullshit from a mile away. When we were kids, she always knew who was throwing who under the bus for whatever crime was committed. When I was in high school, she knew I was lying about a cheerleader sleepover when in fact I was sneaking out with my boyfriend. She wasn't even living at home at that time. And in the bridal suite that fateful morning, I could tell she also thought something wasn't right.

Maeve knows all, and I don't know why I ever think I can get anything past her.

"I'm having good days and bad," I say. "Two days ago was great. Yesterday was all right. Today was…both."

And that's as honest as I can be. Two days ago was my night out with Emmett. That night was as close to perfect as one can have. Yesterday was just okay. It rained for most of the day, so I stayed in the house. Emmett had to work but came over after, and we ordered pizza and watched a documentary about the JFK assassination. It was Emmett's choice, and I found it fascinating that he chose that over an action movie. Based on Duncan and guys I dated in college, I thought that was the standard. Come to find out Emmett is somewhat of a self-admitted history nerd.

Buff and brains. The man really does have it all.

Then there was today, and no amount of time in the smash

room can make up for the amount of rage and grief that occurred when I heard Duncan's voice.

"That's to be expected," Maeve says. "I mean, it hasn't been that long."

One week, but who's counting?

"It feels like it happened yesterday and also six years ago."

"Also to be expected. But are you getting out? Or are you staying cooped up in that house?"

My mind runs through everything I've done since I've been here. I feel myself smile as I think back. Probably because Emmett is attached to every single moment.

"I've been getting out," I say as I take my ice cream and go sit on the couch. "I've gone to the beach. Went shopping. Bought a new pair of shoes."

"Of course you did," Maeve says with a sigh. "What about meals? Please tell me you're doing more than ordering Uber Eats every night."

"Some nights yes," I admit. "Some nights no."

"Oh!"

I didn't think she'd sound *that* surprised. Then again, I don't even like going to the bathroom by myself in public.

"Look at you, trying new things. Solo dining is a big one."

"Yeah." The guilt is laced in my voice. I can hear it, which means I know Maeve can too.

"Stella…what aren't you saying?"

I have two options here. Lie my face off, only for my big sister to call me out on it. Or I could just skip that part and tell the truth.

Ugh, I hate being a grown-up and doing the mature thing.

"I've…met someone."

My admission stuns her silent. Or so I guess. She's not replying, and I can't even hear her breathe.

"Maeve? Are you there?"

"Did you say you met someone? As in a man?"

"Why do you assume it's a man?"

"Because if it was a girl or a gay you met at the shoe store, you wouldn't have stopped talking. You wouldn't have paused in the middle. You would have went on for five minutes and given me the full Stella FBI background check on them."

Ugh. Damn Maeve and her damn know-it-allness.

"Fine, it's a man." I start to tell her about Emmett, but I stop myself.

Should I tell her it's Emmett? I assumed we'd tell Simon we met when I got back to Nashville, but something right now is stopping me from admitting who he is to Maeve. Not because I'm ashamed, but because somehow telling Maeve about him—which is the same thing as telling the rest of my siblings, because she will report it immediately—will ruin what we have.

And selfishly, I want Emmett all to myself. At least while we're in Destin.

"He's staying nearby. Traveling for work. We saw each other on the beach and struck up a conversation. We've been to dinner a few times. That's it."

There. Perfect. Not any lies. Just not the whole truth.

"Stella…"

"Maeve, you don't need to worry. I'm fine. Plus, it's not like that."

I mean, it's not. Technically. So what if my eyes roam a little? Or I melted when his fingers held my chin delicately in his hand? Or that every time he calls me Tiger I have to stop myself from thinking that it's anything more than friendly. Because it is. He's said it many times. We're friends. That's it. I'm Simon's little sister, whom he's become friends with. That's it.

"I'm not going to tell you how to live your life."

"I appreciate that."

"I'm just going to give you a warning."

"I figured you were."

I hear Maeve tsk through the phone. "You've been with Duncan for a long time. And before that, you never had a serious boyfriend. This is likely a rebound, and you need to know how to handle that."

"This isn't a rebound," I defend. "Emme—we're just friends."

I flinch when I almost say Emmett's name. Luckily Maeve didn't catch it. "You say you're just friends. But it only takes one night for a rebound. And you love hard, Stella. You fall fast, and that's not how rebounds work."

"I know how rebounds work."

"I love you, Stella, but you don't. You've never had one. They aren't meant to catch feelings. They're meant to be quick and fun and to help you bounce back. I'm just saying if you do, please keep that in mind."

"I will," I say. "Plus, even if this was something like that, which it's not, I'm not in any place for a relationship. I'm going to need months to get over this, and probably a lot of therapy. The last thing on the to-do list is to catch feelings."

"I'm glad to hear that." Maeve stops, and I have a feeling she wants to say something, but I'm not sure what else.

"Maeve?"

She lets out a big breath. "There's another reason I called. It wasn't just to catch up."

"Oh." I feel my stomach drop to my feet. "What is it?"

I put down the bowl of ice cream on the table. I have a feeling this is a smart, preemptive move.

"Duncan came to the house today."

"He did what?"

"Yup. We were all over for Sunday brunch, which was rudely interrupted by your ex-fiancé banging on the front door."

"The nerve," I say. "He must have had 'talk to the Banks family' on his to-do list today because he decided to call me as well."

"Really? What time?"

"I don't know, maybe around noon?"

"Interesting. Because he arrived around one, demanding to speak with you. Dad answered the door and said you weren't here. I know this because I watched everything from the hallway. I wasn't about to miss that show."

"Of course not. Tell me everything."

"Well, after Simon stepped in and said you weren't here, Duncan demanded to come in and check. I thought Dad was going to punch him."

Now I'm laughing for real. The thought of William Banks, the calmest man on the planet, punching anyone is laughable. Though Dad still hits the gym. He could take him.

"When Dad blocked his entrance, Duncan started throwing a hissy fit. His last words were that the only reason he was coming by was to deliver papers to Dad on his intention of suing you."

Did I hear her right? Suing me?

"For what?" I yell.

"Right? According to the filing, it's for the emotional damage you caused with running out. And to recoup funds that he paid for the wedding he's unable to get back."

"Emotional damage? He was the one getting flogged! I'm scarred for life with that image on my head. And does he not remember the fact that he *stole* from me? From us!"

My breathing is heavy because I'm about to blow. Who does he think he is? I know I joked that I'd sue. But now…well, *now* I'll sue for everything. Dad might be retired, but I know he misses practicing. And I'm a woman scorned. It's a recipe for lawsuit heaven.

"It's silly, and it won't go anywhere," Maeve tries to reassure me. "Dad's on it and has informed the partners at the law firm. I have a feeling they will be talking to Duncan very soon."

Good. I hope he loses his job and has to move back in with his mother. She can wash his fucking underwear.

"I'm sure he's going to call you again," Maeve says. "Don't answer. Don't interact. If you do, for some ungodly reason, say you can't speak without your attorney present. Be on the safe side. Dad thinks he's bluffing, but I had an eye on him and I don't think so. He looked angry. Determined. I have a feeling this is going to get worse before it gets better."

I rub my temple as I slide into the couch. "Thanks."

Maeve and I say our goodbyes and as soon as I hang up the phone, I feel my head starting to pound. But not with a normal headache. No, this is my anger. I'm boiling from the inside out. I know I was worked up earlier, but this is a whole new feeling.

This is rage.

Fucking Duncan. I knew he'd pull some shit. But a lawsuit? The nerve. The audacity. The little dick syndrome of it all.

"Ahh!" I yell just as a clap of thunder hits outside. I watch a flash of lightning through the glass doors that leads to the patio area that faces the beach.

I need to yell. I need to scream. I need to let all of this anger out or it's going to detonate inside me.

So I do what any midtwenties woman would do in my situation. I find the playlist aptly called "Female Rage," blast it to full volume, and let myself out of the door and into the storm.

I don't care about the rain. Or the lightning. In fact, I embrace them as I hold my arms out wide and start screaming about the smallest man who ever lived.

14

emmett

I'VE NEVER BEEN A SCIENCE GUY—HISTORY AND MATH WERE MORE my speed—but I've always been fascinated by thunderstorms.

Something about the brewing clouds and the air changing. The distant rumbles of thunder that grow closer and closer. When that perfect strike of lightning hits. I'm watching it all from a lounge chair on the patio that thankfully has an adjustable canopy, allowing me to take this in while staying dry. It's the perfect way to get lost in my thoughts.

And all of them circle around Stella Banks.

Something was off at the smash room today. I expected her to get in my car and be busting at the seams to go to the one place that's been on her to-do list since we got here. But she wasn't. She was quiet. Sullen. I could tell something was going on. She was fidgeting, which I've never seen her do. Biting her nails. Barely said two words on the drive over. I don't gamble a lot, but I would've gone all-in that it had something to do with Duncan.

Then something snapped when we stepped inside the room. I had to step back to make sure she wasn't going to hurt herself. She was absolutely feral. I thought at one point she was going to throw her shoulder out. I had a feeling she'd be a bit on the unhinged side ever since she told me about this idea, but the look in her eyes today was downright terrifying.

Stella was on a mission—to break every item in that room.

I even got in on the fun. Though I was smashing away my sexual frustration because Stella is getting too tempting for my sanity.

Our missions were very different.

I don't know if hers was accomplished, but mine wasn't. If anything, I'm even more frustrated now than I was before.

Is part of that physical? Of course. Stella is by far the most beautiful woman I've ever laid eyes on. Her blue eyes and perfect smile keep me up at night. Her body, no matter what she wears, is downright sinful. And the feel of her skin the few times I've made contact? I had to force myself to pull away.

If it were just physical, I could push my feelings aside. But it's becoming more and more clear that this is more than that. These are feelings I'm not comfortable with. Ones I've never had before. And they were confirmed in the smash room today.

When I was watching her, I wanted to take away every ounce of pain I could see in her eyes. I wanted to keep putting bottles in front of her to break just so she could get rid of all the anger and resentment she had inside. I wanted to hold her and let her cry, because I could tell she was a ticking time bomb of emotion. I want to take away every ounce of hurt and pain because I don't want her to feel like that ever again.

I have no prior experience in this area, but I'm pretty sure friends don't have these feelings about each other. Some? Maybe. But all together and combined with the overwhelming feeling of rage and jealousy on my part every time I think of her with Duncan? Or the lust I feel when I see her wearing her bikini on the beach? Or how I have to bite the inside of my cheek when she throws her head back and laughs, because all I want to do is plant my lips on her neck?

Yeah…those aren't friendly feelings.

Those are feelings that clearly say I'm fucked.

I'm just about to go inside because thinking about Stella means I need my third shower of the day, until I hear music blasting from next door.

And then a voice that's screaming…singing? No. Definitely screaming.

"Were sent by someone! Who wanted me dead!"

What the hell?

The music and the "singing" is coming from Stella's house. When I turn to see what the hell is going on, I see her standing outside, past her patio, with her arms out wide. It's like she's begging the storm to take her.

What the hell is she doing?

I don't recognize the song she's singing, and from this distance I'm only hearing every other word. It sounds like something about someone trying to maybe kill someone? Or having them gunned down? Whatever it is, it sounds angry, though I don't know if that's a strong enough word. I might be a house away, but I can feel the rage and hurt rolling off her with every lyric she yells.

I'm watching Stella exorcise a demon.

I doubt she can hear me, but I don't move an inch, not wanting to interrupt her. Because what I'm witnessing right now is hauntingly beautiful. Seeing this woman, who I know has been trying to put on a brave face while going through every emotion there is on a daily basis, has to be hard. I also know she's only telling me parts of it. Today's a great example. She said she was fine, but her eyes gave her away. I know she's trying to limit talking about every feeling she's having in front of me. For one, I've not been shy on my feelings about Duncan, and he's tied to every one of her emotions right now. Two, I have a suspicion she thinks she has to put on a brave face for me. That she doesn't want to come off as this whiny woman who can't get over it.

That's where she's wrong. There's nothing she could do, or say, that would change my opinion of her. She's the strongest woman I've ever met. And she's showing it right now without a goddamn care in the world.

The song changes, but her voice doesn't stop. If anything, like the storm outside, it only gains speed. It's like she's channeling the sea to go into battle with her. This goes on for at least a minute when her singing suddenly stops. The music doesn't. I can still hear it in the distance, but she's not singing.

I train my eyes on her when I see her collapse to the ground. It's like in slow motion. She just slowly drops to her knees, which is followed by a cry so loud it's like she's right next to me.

I don't think. I don't hesitate. I don't bother with an umbrella as I race across the beach and maneuver past the rocks that serve as a divide between the houses. I almost slip a few times as the water pools in the sand, but I keep my stride until I reach her.

Her cries are loud and painful as I bend down to pick her up. She doesn't fight me, instead wrapping her arms around my neck like a boa constrictor. I blink away the rain drops pelting my face as I carry her back inside the house.

I feel her hot tears despite my wet T-shirt as we sit on the couch. Fuck…I want to do more than just hold her. I want to take away every ounce of this hurt. I'd do anything to be able to do that for her.

"Why'd he do it?" Stella asks between sobs.

I brush back her hair and continue to gently rock her. "I don't know, Tiger. I wish I did."

"He said he loved me. He said he wanted to marry me. Why would he lie and cheat and steal? Why would he live almost another life?"

I'll admit I've wondered this too. "I don't know Duncan well. I only met him once, but my guess would be because he's one of those pompous fucks who thought he could have his cake and eat it too. He wanted to live this risk-filled lifestyle with bad business deals and cheating. But he also wanted the life everyone told him he was supposed to have with his stable career and beautiful wife."

"What about the life I wanted? Did that not mean anything?"

Stella finally looks up at me, and my heart breaks instantly. It takes every ounce of strength in me not to cry for her. She looks beaten down. Still beautiful. But just…drained.

"Of course it does," I say. "Maybe not to him. But it does."

"I thought we wanted the same things," she says. "I was a fool."

"No. Not a fool." I tip her chin up, forcing her to look me in the eye when I ask her this question. "What do you want? What does Stella Banks want in life? Truly. Not what she thinks she wants because others have it. What do *you* want?"

She doesn't say anything for a second, but doesn't move off her seat on my lap either. The tears have pushed back a little, but I can tell they could burst again at any moment.

"I want a job I love that doesn't feel like work. I want friends I adore and my sisters and family to have everything they want." She takes a deep breath before she continues. "And I want a man who loves me so much it hurts. And I want to love him with everything I have. I want date nights out and lazy nights in where we're wrapped around each other. I want him to pull me into his arms and dance barefoot in the kitchen just because the moment strikes. I want to learn about things he does and him to not bitch when I want to go shoe shopping. Or think it's stupid when I say that I want to volunteer at the animal shelter. Or that will write down my overly complicated coffee order in his phone so he knows what my order is when he wants to get me a drink just because. I want to try new foods and not feel self-conscious about them. I want to walk down the aisle and our eyes be glued to each other and let the rest of the guests fall away. I want to start a family that will be loving and supportive emd crazy, just like how I grew up. I want it all. I don't want to settle. But most importantly, I want someone who wants that too."

I don't say anything. I don't think she expects me to, which is good. How can I when I'm pushing down the burning sensation of jealousy, knowing the man she wants—the man she deserves

—can never be me? I'm not that guy. She wants the fairytale. And no matter how many times I've been told otherwise, I'm no Prince Charming.

"Do you know what I want right now?" Stella asks.

"What's that?"

"I want you to kiss me."

My entire body goes still. I don't say anything. Hell, I think I forget to breathe.

She turns toward me slightly. "I want to feel something more than sadness or hurt or anger. That's all I've known since I ran. And I just…please Emmett…help me feel."

Her blue eyes are begging. Her voice is pleading.

And my willpower is crumbling.

"Stella…"

She tries to turn her head away from me, assuming I'm about to say no. I quickly catch her chin in my fingers, making sure she hears what I'm about to say.

"Please," she begs. "Don't say anything. Don't make this even more embarrassing than it already is."

I shake my head. "Nothing to be embarrassed about."

"Says the man who isn't going to kiss the girl who just made a fool of herself."

"Who said I'm not going to kiss you?"

Her eyes go wide at my words, and I think for the first time since I've met her, I've rendered Stella Banks speechless.

"I'm going to kiss you, but I need you to know one thing," I begin. "I want to kiss you more than anything. I want to be the man who relieves a little bit of this pain. But you have to know: the man you described earlier? The forever guy? That's not me. So if that's what you're looking for…"

She shakes her head. "I don't want that. Not now. And I know you aren't that forever man. But that's not what I need. I just need you, Emmett."

The groan that passes through my throat is low and primal. My name on her tongue rips my last thread of self-control.

"Fuck it," I growl, and I close the last remaining gap between us.

My mouth is on hers before she can say anything else, taking what I've dreamed of since I got here. Oh, who the hell am I kidding? Since the day I met her. Then I could convince myself to push down my desire. But now? With Stella in my lap? Asking me to take her out of this dark place? To help her feel again? It's all I want in this world.

Even if it's just for now.

guide to love rule #75

Get over your ex by getting under
your brother's best friend.

15
stella

When you've been kissed for a certain way for years, you forget there are other ways to be kissed. And when you've been kissing Duncan Hughes, you forget that kisses ever contained things like sparks and butterflies.

I forgot. Holy cow, did I forget.

Or did I ever know? I couldn't have. This is a feeling I don't think I'd forget. And at the same time, I couldn't describe it for all the money and shoes in the world.

Emmett's lips are soft yet claiming. His hands are gently holding my face, but the strength is there. And his tongue? It's taking what it wants, yet somehow I feel like I'm still in control. The combination is setting my body on fire.

I know I asked Emmett to just kiss me, but I'm already contemplating asking for a lot more.

"Emmett…" His name spills off my tongue as he starts kissing across my cheek. His hands move from my face to my hair, where he gives it the slightest tug, making me tilt my neck back so he has the perfect opening to leave a trail of kisses across my pulse.

"Oh!" I let out as Emmett hits a spot that I didn't realize was sensitive in a very good way. He's kissing and sucking and…

Holy shit…

Can you have an orgasm through kissing? No. That's not possible. Is it? I mean, I don't remember the last time I had one the normal way, and when I did it was because I helped my own cause, so maybe there's just a whole new other world I'm missing out on. I mean, this isn't how I thought kissing went, so who knows what I've been missing out on? I thought kissing was just a boring means to an unsatisfying end.

I was wrong. So damn wrong.

Emmett breaks for just a second to lie me back on the couch. He lays next to me, half of his body covering mine as he goes right back to work. I let my fingers play at the nape of his neck like it's the most natural thing in the world. Our lips find a rhythm that feels like we've been doing this for years.

And even better? I don't feel angry or mad or sad. I don't feel like I want to scream. I'm just feeling. I focus on Emmett's lips on mine and on his hands tracing my body. I bask in the feel of his beard against my cheek. Our bodies are touching and his erection is growing. I'm covered in a warmth I'm feeling in my entire body.

And I know one thing—I haven't felt like this in a very long time.

If ever.

Is it because this is new? Is it because I've been so down lately that anything was going to make me feel up? Maybe. But I have a strong feeling this is all because of the man whose kiss is bringing me back to life.

I know my sisters joked that I should have a rebound while here. But if this was a stranger I picked up at a bar, would it feel the same? Sure, I'd probably have some fun. Maybe a little regret. Probably a good story. And even if the sex was bad, it would be a few hours of a distraction.

But I doubt I'd feel like this. And not just what he's physically doing. I don't think I'd feel free and sexy and beautiful and wanted, while also becoming empowered and in control.

No, that's all because of Emmett. The man who has saved me more than once. The man I just met who I can't imagine my life without.

The man I want to fuck me, right here, right now.

I watch him as he traces my body, his fingers finding a sliver of skin as the T-shirt has gotten pushed up ever so slightly. He looks up to me and I nod, giving him the silent permission to keep going.

He doesn't hesitate as he lifts me back up, settling me over his lap so I'm straddling him. His hands immediately go to the bottom of the shirt where he lifts it over my head and tosses it to the side. I watch as his eyes heat as he takes in my topless frame.

My first instinct is to be shy. My body is nothing special. My barely B cups aren't anything to get excited about, and I'm just curvy enough to not be a stick. Duncan used to joke—but I now don't think it was a joke—about me getting a boob job.

No! Quit thinking about Duncan. He has no place here. Enjoy this moment. Enjoy the fire in Emmett's eyes as he looks at you.

Because that's the only way I can describe Emmett's gaze right now. His brown eyes are nearly black. The grip on my hips is becoming tighter but not in a hurtful way. Like he's trying to hold himself back.

Well, he doesn't need to do that. Not at all.

"Take me, Emmett."

The groan that passes through his lips sends a shot straight to my pussy.

Oh damn, that's definitely new.

"Stella." His forehead falls so it's resting against my chest as his fingers dig into my hips. "I need you to be one-hundred-percent sure. Because if I do, this isn't going to be gentle. It's not going to be romantic. There are no hearts and flowers. I've been holding myself back because you needed a friend, not an asshole trying to get in your pants. But if we cross this line? There's no going back."

I tip his chin up, making him look at me like he's done to me so many times. "Fuck me until I forget."

My words hang in the air, and just as I'm about to wish for a black hole to suck me down, he stands up and somehow effortlessly tosses me over his shoulder.

Oh! This is new too…

I can't keep the excitement out of my voice as Emmett stands up and starts walking toward the back of the house. "Where are we going?"

Emmett takes the stairs two at a time. Why does that make me so giddy? "The first time I fuck you is not going to be on a couch. I'm going to lay you out exactly how I want so I can look, and lick, and taste every inch of you. Then I'm going to fuck you until you beg for more. You'll forget him. But I'll make sure you never forget me."

Licked? Begging? What kind of sex am I about to have? I bet it's going to have more than two positions.

And did he say the first time? Is he already predicting there will be more?

Before I can voice any of those questions, Emmett tosses me on the bed. I didn't know what to expect, but him standing over me, staring at me without movement, wasn't it.

"Is everything okay?"

He nods, and a predatory glint flashes in his eyes. "Last chance, Tiger."

The warning, with its touch of playfulness, sets my body on fire even more than it already is. "Show me what you got, Cap."

In one motion he puts his arm behind his back, lifting his T-shirt over his head in one pull. The movement is mesmerizing—so much so that I don't realize that in another lightning-fast move, he's pulling my shorts down and taking my panties with them.

"Oh, Stella," he says as he kneels before me. "You have no idea…"

Emmett slowly spreads my knees apart and…yup! That's his tongue. Licking my pussy.

Because he wants to.

I know I need to quit comparing the two, and I'm not trying to. I don't want Duncan anywhere near my thoughts. But it's hard not to when he once told me that he wouldn't go down on me because it was gross. Honestly, it was fine. If he ate pussy like he kissed, it wouldn't do much anyway.

But Emmett? Whose tongue has lit every nerve in just a few seconds? The man is acting like I'm his last meal and he's not going leave a single crumb.

And who am I to let a hungry man starve?

I lay back and revel in the feeling of Emmett's mouth on me. My hands pull at his hair, which seems to excite him. Every time I pull tighter, it only makes him dig in more. I couldn't think of anything else if I wanted to. Through the power of his tongue, or his mouth, or the two fingers he's now inserted, he's taken all the thoughts out of my head.

Emmett Collins…how many different ways can this man come to my rescue?

I didn't think anything could pull me out of this zen feeling, but the first rush of an orgasm does just that, making me open my eyes as I start feeling it through my stomach down to my center.

"Emmett," I whimper, gripping his hair tighter.

"That's it, Tiger. Come on my face. I want to taste it all."

It must be his dirty words accompanied by a sinful mouth that does the trick, because in seconds I'm exploding onto him. I think I might pull out a chunk of hair as I hold on for dear life, the orgasm hitting me in every part of my body.

"That's my girl," he says, slowly bringing me back down. "Just breathe. I got you."

How does he make a command like that sound gentle and dirty all at once?

"Holy…" My words fall off as I try and catch my breath. "That was…"

He smiles and stands up, grabbing a condom from his wallet. Our eyes don't leave each other as he somehow undoes his belt with one hand and then snaps it off his waist. And just when I don't think I can stare any harder, he slides down his boxers, freeing the hardest and biggest cock I've ever seen in my life.

My God…how is that…is that legal?

"That's not going to fit."

His eyes get a little twinkle in them as he rolls on the condom and crawls on top of me, planting a hard kiss on my mouth before moving away. "You can take it. I promise."

Emmett's elbow is holding him up as he uses his other to line himself up. We don't break eye contact as I feel his tip enter me, sending my body into a spasm as he slowly pushes himself the rest of the way in.

"I've got you," Emmett whispers, his motions so slow I don't know if he's actually moving. "I've always got you."

And he does. I know he does. Not just here, as he gives me a second to adjust to his size. Since the moment I met him, when he was Cap and I was Tiger and we were two strangers at a bar, he had me then.

He's had me all week.

And now he's not just having me. He's claiming me. His body is caging me in like I might go away. Our hips are meeting in what started as slow but are now hard thrusts.

The roughness is keeping my feelings in check. This isn't anything romantic. This isn't anything more than me needing an escape and Emmett being the one to give it to me.

That's all this is.

And I'm going to escape as long and as many times I can.

Emmett rolls me over on top of him, and I let out a little yelp as I situate myself. I shiver when I feel the hair on his chest. I love the feel of it as I grip down on him, beginning to ride him as I chase the orgasm I'm desperate for.

"That's it," Emmett says. "Take what you want, Tiger."

I look down into his brown eyes that are staring right back at me. There isn't a word out of his mouth he doesn't mean. This is for me just as much as it's for him. He wants me to have this. He wants me to take it.

And if that doesn't send a shot of confidence through you, I don't know what would.

I begin to ride him faster, letting my hips bounce as I hold on for dear life. I watch him bite down on his lip as he grabs each of my tits, squeezing them as I use his dick as my own personal joyride. When he pinches one of my nipples, I arch back, my hands gripping onto his thighs, loving the conflicting sensations I'm feeling.

This new angle is stirring something inside me—something I wanted but wasn't sure could happen twice in a night. I heard about it. People said it was true. I had called bull until right now.

Because holy moly…another one is coming.

And it's coming hard.

"Emmett…"

His name is a plea that he understands immediately.

He sits up and holds me to him, as close as two people can be. Our hips are still meeting, only now the pace is frantic. We're both chasing ends that we desperately want, yet don't want at all.

At least that's me. I can only hope Emmett feels the same way.

Emmett's mouth latches on to the spot on my neck that I knew was the ending to a live wire. In a matter of seconds I'm exploding onto him, my entire body quivering from the release. Emmett follows right behind me with a guttural groan, squeezing me to him as we both finish.

Neither of us say anything for a few moments. The only sound in my bedroom is our breathing and the rain hitting the window.

Emmett slowly lifts me off him, lying me back on my bed

before he goes to take off the condom. My eyes are growing heavy when I feel a warm towel at my center.

Oh! Another new thing.

"Sweet dreams, Tiger," Emmett says, kissing my forehead.

I want to ask him to stay. I want to ask him to lie down with me. I know he says he doesn't, but maybe he will?

Except I don't. I can't. Because Emmett Collins fucked me into an orgasm coma.

And I'm not mad about it at all.

16
emmett

I meant to leave.

Because I don't stay. I don't wake up with a person. I sure as hell don't cuddle.

But I couldn't make myself go.

As I watched Stella sleep, I kept telling myself just a few more minutes. I had convinced myself that I was just making sure that she was okay. Tonight might have been more of a roller coaster of emotions than the night we met.

Then I laid down. Then I slowly start running my fingers lazily along her arm. Then she rolled into me. Her head found my shoulder, and I was a goner.

I don't remember the last time, if ever, I woke up with someone in my arms. The closest I've come is when Winnie has found her way onto my bed. And that usually just means she wants something.

Here's the problem: It's now the morning. The sun is shining, and a new day is here. And I still don't want to leave. Hell, if I had my way, we'd stay in this bed all day and continue what we started last night. There are many—and I mean many—things I still want to do with Stella Banks, but I have this gnawing feeling that if I leave they're never going to happen. That somehow the bubble will burst. Maybe she'll realize last night was just a one-time thing fueled by emotion. Or I'll come to my senses and remember she's too young and her brother might kill me.

Let's be real. I'm not coming to my senses. The longer I lay here, the more my logical thoughts go out the window. Stella Banks is now in my blood. And I don't know if she's ever going to leave.

I take in a deep breath when I hear the ping of my cell phone somewhere in the room. The sound is coming in rapid fire so I get up, careful not to wake Stella as I slip my boxer briefs on and find my phone in the pocket of my jeans.

SIMON

You alive?

SIMON

Or did you get eaten by an alligator?

SIMON

Or is it a crocodile? I never remember which one lives in Florida.

SIMON

But for real, where are you? You haven't texted. You haven't called. For all I know you went to Florida and joined the circus.

All I can do is shake my head at the idiotic texts from my best friend.

EMMETT

I don't even know where to begin with all that.

SIMON

I'm just glad you're alive. Wait. Maybe this isn't you. Maybe it's your kidnapper and they're pretending to be you. How can I be sure this is Emmett?

EMMETT

It's me, jackass.

After all these years, I still can't help but laugh at the utter ridiculousness of Simon Banks. Yes, he's a grown man-child. Yes, his overall demeanor has been described as a golden retriever on crack. Yes, he doesn't think before he acts or speaks, nine times out of ten. But I wouldn't trade him or his friendship for anything in the world.

And to think it all came to be from the luck of the draw. We were randomly paired to live together our freshman year at Tennessee. We both majored in business and had close enough areas of interest—he wanted to get in on the real estate market while I one day wanted to open my own construction firm, which is why I minored in engineering. We were complete opposites. He was from old money and was the fourth member of his family to go to UT. I was from the hills of Chattanooga and was only at college because of scholarships.

Yet, more than fifteen years later, here we are.

SIMON

Oh good. I'm glad you aren't kidnapped.

EMMETT

Glad to know I'd be missed.

SIMON

I wouldn't go that far.

EMMETT

Asshole.

SIMON

How's Florida?

EMMETT

Fine.

SIMON

That's it? Fine? You've been in Destin for five
days. All I get is fine?

I look back at Stella and I'm thanking the Lord above that this
conversation is over text and not FaceTime. Because I don't know if
I'd be able to hide my smile right now. Which would also raise alarm
bells because I rarely smile, which he'd definitely call me out on.

EMMETT

Yes. That's all you get.

SIMON

Oh my God! Did you meet someone? Vacation
fling? Emmett Collins, you dog you. I'm so
proud.

EMMETT

I'm not discussing this with you.

SIMON

Yet. You're not discussing it with me yet. I'll
accept that and get the full rundown when you
get home.

EMMETT

I won't.

SIMON

Whatever. You will. Change of subject. Have
you seen Stella? How's she holding up?

I sit a little straighter on the bed. Coincidentally, I feel the bed
move as Stella rolls over.

Does he know? Is that why he's asking?

No. He can't know. It's coincidence. I'm being paranoid.
Which is another reason why I need to come to my senses and
make last night a one-time thing.

I won't. But I should.

EMMETT

I have. Could've told me she didn't get married.
Would've been helpful information.

SIMON

I told you.

EMMETT

I assure that you did no such thing.

SIMON

Oh. Shit. My bad.

Oh. Shit. My bad. That's his answer? Can I use that as my response if Simon ever finds out that I slept with his sister?

EMMETT

She's fine. We've actually gone to dinner and
hung out a few times. She even got me to the
beach.

SIMON

No shit! You? On the beach? I thought you said
the beach was a sandbox cesspool?

EMMETT

Eh. It's not so bad.

With Stella. It's not so bad with Stella.
Which is giving me an idea…

SIMON

Well I'm glad you're enjoying yourself.

EMMETT

I am. And actually, do you mind if I take a few
more days? You were right, this was what I
needed.

You know I'm pulling out all the stops when I tell Simon he's right.

SIMON

I'm right? Did you just say I'm right? I'm going
to print this text out and frame it. Put it on my
desk.

SIMON

And hell yes you can stay a few more days.
You've earned it.

For some reason, that compliment sends a pang of guilt
straight to my gut. Simon suggested I get away because I hadn't
taken a vacation since I started working for him. It was actually
years, but he didn't need to know that. He wanted me to clear
my head, decompress, and blow off some steam. In none of those
instructions was "blow off steam with my baby sister."

EMMETT

Thanks. I'm going to get going. I'll call you
when I'm back in town.

SIMON

Sounds good. Give Stella my love.

EMMETT

Will do.

I drop my head and lean my elbows on my knees, regret
washing through me.

How could I do this? I slept with my best friend's sister.
There has to be some sort of bro-code rule that I broke. I made
her scream my name and fucked her until she passed out. I
remember the taste of her on my tongue and can still feel how
she tugged at my hair.

I look over my shoulder as she starts to wake up, her blonde
hair a mess, naked underneath the white sheets.

Maybe the guilt isn't that we did it, it's the guilt that I want to
do it again. It's that I can come up with a dozen reasons why
what we're doing isn't so bad. Or maybe it's that I know in my

heart of hearts I'm never, ever going to tell Simon about this. Or that I'm selfish because I want all of her while we're here, but I know this is temporary.

God, I'm fucked in so many ways. Because I know this is wrong for an abundance of reasons. Yet, I still don't care.

I want her. For as long as I can have her.

"You stayed…"

Her words come out like a purr as she opens her eyes, squinting a bit as she adjusts to the light coming past the curtains.

"I did." I crawl across the bed and drop down next to her. "Sleep well?"

She nods and lets out the most adorable yawn.

Since when are yawns adorable? Get it together, Collins.

"I did. Who knew a day and night full of smashing, screaming, crying, and fucking would tire you out?"

I can't help but laugh at her sarcasm. "You're pretty funny, you know that?"

She shrugs, her eyes averting down.

Nope. Not happening. Not anymore.

I take my free hand and tip up her chin. "No hiding. Say what you want to get off your chest."

"I hate that I keep talking about him," she says. "I don't want to talk about him. I don't want him anywhere near my thoughts. Yet, there are things that come up every day that makes me realize how much I let slide. Or how much I let him walk all over me. And put me down, even if it wasn't with words. And I hate it."

"I know you don't want to think about him," I say. "But think of it this way. Every time you realize anything about that relationship, just think of it as one more thing you're reclaiming. One more piece of you that you're taking back."

"Wow. I never thought of it like that."

"Well let me help." I inch a bit closer to her, taking my fingers and tracing down the side of her face. "I think you're funny as hell. Witty. Impeccable timing. A little dry and dark, but that's my kind of funny."

I thought I felt good this morning. Nope. That's nothing compared to how I'm feeling now as Stella's smile grows with every word I say.

"I'm going to take it he didn't think you're funny," I continue. "Which to that I say, fuck him. You're Stella Banks—let that sarcastic wit fly. Claim it."

She nods. "He told me it wasn't ladylike. And that the other wives I'd be around don't crack jokes."

I shake my head and roll on top of her, my erection starting to grow as our bodies make contact. "Then I think you were hanging out with the wrong kind of people."

"I agree."

I lean down to kiss her, and I can't help but notice the familiar feeling that washes over me. Like this is something we've been doing every morning for years.

What is this woman doing to me…

I need to rein this in, but I don't want to stop it. Far from that. But on the other hand, feelings like this seem like a dangerous thing.

Boundaries. That's what we need. Rules. Regulations. If I know what the rules of the game are, then I know what I can and can't feel.

Yes. Brilliant idea, Emmett. Ten out of ten. Actually five bonus points for coming up with that before coffee.

I slowly pull away, which leaves Stella a bit confused, considering my dick is hard as a rock right now and begging to be set free.

"Everything okay?"

"Yes," I try to say with some sort of authority so she doesn't get worried. "It's just…before we…"

Why am I having trouble spitting out these words? I've had a version of this conversation plenty of times with other women, and I've had no problem laying out the expectations. Yet with

Stella, I don't know what exactly to say. "I think we should put some ground rules on the table if we want to…"

"Have sex again?"

I laugh at her bluntness. "See? It's all about the timing to land the joke."

She sits up and brings the sheets with her, covering her chest. I can still see her peaked nipples through the white cotton, which does not help my focus for this conversation.

"You're right," she says. "Last night was a bit spontaneous. And a bit emotionally charged. But I meant what I said. I'm not looking for anything serious. I'm not in a place to handle anything like that."

I feel my shoulders relax. "And I meant what I said—I'm not a long-term relationship kind of guy."

"Well, then, it looks like we're perfect for each other," she says with a devilish smile.

She's right. In the past, I've always wondered if women were pacifying me when they said they were okay with no commitment. With Stella I have no worries that's the case.

"So, we just continue what we're doing," I say. "And then when we leave Florida, we're back to normal? You go your way, I go mine."

"And when we see each other at functions involving my brother, we'll share a secret smile, knowing we've seen each other naked."

"Emphasis on secret," I say. "You're okay with your brother not knowing? Because this is something I'd rather not tell him."

"Agree. Simon knows too much about me anyway. The last thing I need him knowing is that you gave me my first real orgasm in four years."

I think my eyes just fell out of my head. *Four years?*

"Oh, Tiger." I pounce back on her as her giggles fill the room. My dick has come roaring back to life with that information. "You really shouldn't have told me that."

Her fingers immediately start playing with my hair, her nails scratching my neck with just enough pain to make it perfect. "And why is that?"

I lean down, pressing kisses along her cheek until I get to her ear. "Now that I know you've been neglected, I feel that it's my job to catch you up."

"And how do you intend to do that?"

"Easy." I nibble on her ear lobe as my hand reaches down and cups her already wet pussy. "Until we leave Florida, this pussy is mine. Do you understand?"

Her nails are now scratching down my back, pulling me into her.

"Yours."

And that's all I need hear before I get my wish—we don't leave this room for the rest of the day.

guide to love rule #82

Sometimes it's the simple things that
mean the most.

17
stella

I DON'T KNOW IF I WOULD CALL THIS THE BEST DAY OF MY LIFE, BUT it's definitely the best day I've had in years. And I'm purposely not trying to count back to the last good day because that makes me think about people I'd rather not.

Because right now, I just want to think about Emmett.

I didn't think anything could beat yesterday—he went shopping with me and even carried my bags. And he didn't complain once, or make a snarky comment, about a pair of shoes I bought. In fact, he even said I should get the taupe ones instead of the black. That earned him a blow job last night.

But today? Today wipes the floor with yesterday.

It started with breakfast in bed, which was much needed after the most intense morning sex of my life. I thought morning sex was supposed to be slow and lazy. Nope. I was seeing stars. Literally. At some point I ended up with my head hanging off the bed as Emmett drove into me.

How I had the energy to go parasailing this afternoon I'll never know, but any amount of tired I was feeling was quickly washed away the second I felt the wind blow through my hair. Sailing over the Gulf, the crystal blue water beneath me, and the white beaches around us, was something I'll always remember. And doing it with Emmett, who had the most genuine smile and laugh during the excursion, was the perfect cherry on top.

We got lunch at a spot on the water before being beach bums the rest of the day. I worked on my tan while Emmett sat and read his book. It was also during this time I realized I'm very turned on by men who read.

Or maybe it's just because of Emmett. Because I'm pretty sure he could be mopping a floor and I'd find it sexy.

Oh, what am I talking about? A man cleaning? *Emmett* cleaning? That's hot as hell.

After our hours in the sun—followed by a shower I'll never forget—we're now sitting at dinner at the best place in the world that I haven't eaten at in years because of the Douche Who Will Not Be Named.

Chili's.

Don't laugh. It slaps.

"You never cease to amaze me, Stella Banks."

I raise an eyebrow but don't say anything. Mostly because I'm savoring a mouthful of southwestern egg roll.

"You bought shoes yesterday that I'm pretty sure are a mortgage payment. I don't know much about purses, but I'd venture to say the one you're carrying also cost a pretty penny. But when I ask you the one place you want to go to dinner, you say Chili's."

I dab the corners of my mouth with a napkin. "I'm an enigma, Cap. Get used to it."

We share a smile as I see his cell phone light up on the table. I can't help but look at it, because I'm a nosy human. I also can't stop myself from grabbing it, because I see the background and fall in love.

"Oh my God, I forgot you have a dog!" The golden retriever is so adorable I ignore that a girl named Maddie is texting him. Well, I don't completely ignore. I just swallow the twinge of jealousy, because I'm not allowed to be jealous because this is just Florida fun times and by no means anything serious. "What's its name?"

His face lights up as he takes the phone back. "That's my girl Winnie. She's the most golden retriever to ever exist."

"I always wanted a dog growing up," I say. "But we had Simon."

I'm smiling from ear to ear as I watch Emmett do his best not to spit out the sip of beer he just took.

"Now that was a good joke." His laugh continues as he types something in his phone before turning it around to me. "This is the photo my sister just sent me of Winnie and my nephew, Jack."

I feel my shoulders immediately relax.

Maddie is his sister.

"Jack loves Winnie," he continues. "He was so excited to keep her for the week. I'm about to make his day when I tell him I'm staying longer."

He's staying? I had wondered why he was still here, but I didn't want to make a big deal out of it. No, I'll do that by myself later.

"That's adorable," I say, picking up my glass and taking a healthy sip of my margarita, being cool and totally nonchalant.

"Relieved?"

I look to him with wide eyes and fake confusion. "What? No. Why would I need to be relieved?"

He gives me a knowing look with an adorably cocky smile. "You don't hide your crazy well."

I let out a dramatic gasp. "I don't know what you mean! I've hid my crazy for years! I've perfected my crazy hiding."

When Emmett Collins laughs, there's something about it that hits me in the heart. Maybe because it sounds genuine. It's not boisterous or loud. It's subtle, but it's true.

Actually, that describes Emmett perfectly. The man is calm

and collected. Everything he does is low key. Which makes the bigger things he does that much more meaningful. There's something pretty great in that.

He reaches over and takes my hand, and I try not to relish in how good it feels. "Stella, you are many things. But what you aren't is a good actress. Or calm. Your crazy is a part of you. Embrace it."

"I disagree." Though the smile I can feel on my face is proving his point. "I'm tame, completely sane, and an amazing actress."

"You keep telling yourself that."

We share a smile as our main courses are dropped off—cajun pasta for me and a steak and a baked potato for him.

"If I'm being honest, none of my sisters are good actors," I say. "No one could keep an act up for anything."

"I still can't believe after all these years of being friends with Simon, I never met any of the sisters other than Maeve."

"Actually, given the age difference, it makes sense," I say. "Maeve is closest in age to Simon. Quinn, Ainsley, and I weren't old enough to go visit Simon alone. If we did, it was family tailgate outings. Plus, I don't know if that town could have handled all five Banks children in one spot."

"What's that like?" Emmett asks. "When you're all together?"

When I think about my siblings, I can't help but light up from the inside. "Chaotic. Amazing. Borderline anarchy. Loving."

I trail off, because I could go on and on. Between Simon and me, there's an eleven-year age span, and all of us are different in our own ways. But when it comes down to it, I'd dare anyone to find a family tighter than ours.

"I can't fathom growing up in a house with five siblings," Emmett says. "Then again, I can't imagine growing up in a normal house, either."

My heart breaks for Emmett. I know he's mentioned his childhood, which couldn't have been further from mine. I can't imagine growing up not knowing my father. Or in a house with a revolving door of stepfathers.

"Well I don't know about normal. One of those children was Simon." That comment seems to lighten the conversation. "Though I can't be too hard on him. He might be the odd combination of middle-child antics in a firstborn body, but he's the best. Looks out for us even when we don't know it. Wants to fix everything because he can. Wants everyone to have everything they want. He's pretty great like that."

"He's done that since college," Emmett adds. "One time I didn't have a ride home to Chattanooga for Christmas. He had a car. Even though it was an hour out of his way, he drove me back, no questions asked. Refused gas money. He just did it because he could. He did stuff like that all the time. But let's not tell him we're giving him this credit. His head is big enough as it is."

We clink our glasses for that one. "Deal."

We go back to our meals, which I take a second to get lost in. Cajun pasta from Chilis is my favorite, and it was out of my life too long.

Out of all the red flags I should have noticed, Duncan saying that Chili's was trash should've been the biggest one.

"It's funny you say that Simon acts like a middle child," Emmett says, "because for years I thought Maeve was the oldest."

"She should've been," I say. "Maeve is everyone's second mother. She has texted me every day since I've been here and called twice to check in on me."

"I believe it," Emmett says. "The first time we met in college our freshmen year, she was making sure we all drank water and took aspirin before we went to bed so we didn't have a hangover."

"That's Maeve. If you look up 'oldest daughter syndrome' in the dictionary, Maeve's picture is next to it. But don't get me wrong, she had her fun before her marriage, divorce, and kiddo. But now? She's Mother Maeve. Super successful interior designer. Mother of the Year. Family coordinator. And those are just a few of her titles."

"What about the other two? I've never met Quinn or Ainsley either."

I smile, thinking about the two middle sisters of our crew. "Quinn lives and teaches middle school in Arizona. I don't see her as much as I'd like, but we talk all the time. She's what we call…unfiltered. Which we love about her. She's always been like that—she's the friend to tell you if the jeans make you look fat—but it heightened when she moved from teaching elementary school to middle school. I've heard teenagers today are unhinged."

"I can only imagine," he says. "And Ainsley?"

"Ainsley's the sister I'm the closest with. We shared a room growing up. We lived together when I graduated from college. We lived together until…" I trail off, but I feel a squeeze on my hand. When I look at Emmett, and his reassuring smile, I know I don't have to finish that train of thought. "Ainsley's the good girl of the Banks clan. Doesn't drink. Doesn't swear. God forbid she ever smoked or did drugs. We're pretty sure she saw Maeve and Simon during their high school parties and decided to go the other way. Ainsley is what Mary Poppins would call, 'practically perfect in every way.'"

Emmett puts down his fork and knife and leans a little toward me. "And what about Stella? What's Stella's role in the Banks family?"

"I'm the baby." I open my mouth to say more, but I'm not sure what else to add.

"Is that it?"

I shrug. "Pretty much."

"Don't sell yourself short, Tiger," he says. "You have to be more than that. Actually, fuck that. You *are* more than that."

I feel my cheeks heat at Emmett's words. "When you're the

youngest of a big family, especially with three older sisters, you just want to be like them. I wanted to be fearless like Quinn. Or put together like Maeve. Or like Ainsley, the teacher's pet, who everyone loved. I wanted Simon's confidence. But I was just Stella. Just a bit short in everything I did. Smart, but not the smartest. Danced growing up, but was never the best. In a sorority, but never an officer. Don't get me wrong, I had an amazing childhood and life so far. But I've always been just a bit behind. Majored in marketing, but couldn't get a job so I took the job at daddy's law firm. I didn't leave college with a boyfriend or engagement like my friends, so I said yes to the first serious boyfriend I had, because I wanted what I saw others having. Look where that got me."

I hate admitting that all to Emmett. Yes, he's heard snippets, but I never put it all together. Yet, it feels good to get it all out there. Say what you want about Destin, Florida, but it has been quite therapeutic.

"Oh Tiger." Emmett takes both my hands in his. I feel immediately better as I concentrate on the feeling of his thumbs stroking over my knuckles. "Like I said, you might not be a great actress. And you might not be what your sisters are. But you are definitely too good for that asshat, and I, for one, am glad that part of your plan didn't work."

"I am too," I admit for maybe the first time. "Running away from that day was the best thing I ever did."

"I agree. And I know it's always hard to see yourself for what you truly are, but let me tell you what I see." Emmett brings my hands to his lips, placing a gentle kiss on the top of each one before he goes on.

Holy swoon…

"You're beautiful and smart. You're brave and bold, and yes, a little crazy."

That last one makes me chuckle. I don't know if anyone has ever called out my crazy but make it sound like a good thing. But if anyone could, it would be Emmett.

"I know you feel like you haven't figured out where you fit yet. And that's okay. You're young. You have time. There's no timetable for life. When you find where you fit, you'll know, because it'll be as easy as breathing."

I've gotten a lot of advice over the years from friends and family. Mostly family. Mostly Maeve. But I've never felt more put at ease by words than I have right now.

"Thank you," I say. "Sorry this got all serious."

Emmett gives my hands a squeeze. "Don't ever apologize for saying what you need to say. Ever."

The waitress has perfect timing as she comes over with the bill. I try to grab it—I feel like it's the least I can do since I forced him to stay on this vacation with me—but I'm not fast enough.

"You really think you're paying, Tiger?" He shakes his head with a smile as he slides in a credit card. "You don't pay. Ever."

Don't think ever means forever…

He didn't mean it like that. Ever is short. Ever for us has an expiration date. Five more days and counting. In five days I go back to Nashville. In five days this vacation getaway is over. In five days Emmett and I will go back to normal—whatever that means.

Which is what I need. I need to get back to, and figure out, my life. I don't need any extra distractions.

But what I do need right now is my nightly sweet treat.

"Yes," Emmett says without me saying anything.

"What?"

"Yes, we'll go get ice cream."

My smile is huge as the waitress comes back with the receipt and we both stand from the booth. "Say what it's really called."

He rolls his eyes as he pulls me in to him, his hand immediately going to the small of my back. "A sweet treat."

I can't help but smile as the words leave his mouth. "I think you'll like this one."

"Oh really? What flavor tonight?"

I raise up on my toes so I can get closer to his ear, which isn't possible even in my three-inch wedges.

"You."

The low groan that I feel vibrating from him sends a shiver through my body.

We have five days left, and I'm going to make every one of them count.

18
emmett

I've always been a fan of consistency. Monotony is okay in my book. As long as you're enjoying it, why rock the boat?

I just never knew monotony could be this…exciting. Or maybe it's just because every night with Stella is the same, but each night somehow tops the last.

Take tonight, for example. We weren't even inside five seconds before I had her pressed against the wall, kissing her like I'd die if I didn't. Before either of us could catch our breath, we were ripping each other's clothes off and I was fucking her in the entry way.

Most nights are like this—each of us so desperate for the other we barely make it inside before things escalate. I don't know what it is about her. But each night when we come back to our respective houses, it's like I can't wait anymore. The need to touch her is overwhelming. The pull to kiss her is too strong to fight off.

And I don't want to fight it off. I want as much as I can get for however long I can have it. Which in my case is two more days.

And that fucking sucks.

I'm not ready for this to be over. Not even a little bit. And as I stand here in front of the open freezer on the mission to get us ice cream, all I can think about is how I'm on a running clock. It's the countdown I never want to end.

Before Stella, I'd never woken up next to a woman, but now I can't imagine not seeing her first thing in the morning. I've become quite used to the feeling of her head on my chest and her arm slung over my stomach as she sleeps. Sometimes in the middle of the night I'll reach for her, because I can't sleep without holding her.

And it's not even just the physical that I'm going to miss. I've gotten used to our nightly sweet treats. Or lazily watching television together. Or the boring days we spend lounging around the house or at the beach. Hell, I'd even go shopping with her again. While I'd never personally spend that much on a pair of shoes, I'd buy her a hundred pairs to see the pure joy on her face when she put them on. I'm going to miss her laugh. Her witty sense of humor. And her blush when I catch her looking at me.

Fuck….I'm going to miss all of it.

Which is how I know without a shadow of a doubt this needs to stop. Nothing this good lasts forever. That's one thing I know for certain. We're living in a fantasy world right now. When we're back in Nashville with jobs and lives and families and everything else, it won't be like this. So while I might be enjoying my time with Stella, this needs to stop while we're ahead. It's the smart thing to do.

Though sometimes I hate being fucking smart.

"Are we out of ice cream?"

The sound of Stella's voice shakes me a little, but I'm immediately calmed when I feel her arms wrap around my waist.

You're still in the bubble. This is okay. Enjoy every minute while you're here. Don't waste a single one.

"We're not." I grab the ice cream from the freezer before turning around. I place it down on the counter but quickly pick her up to set her on the island. We're eye level, which gives me the chance to gaze into her eyes for a few seconds. Fuck, they're gorgeous. She's gorgeous. But she's more than that.

She's...everything.

"Got in my head for a second. Sorry."

"Nothing to apologize for." She gives me a sympathetic look as she softly runs a hand through my hair. "Want to talk about it?"

I slowly shake my head as I lean into her touch. "Not important. Definitely not as important as tonight's sweet treat."

I take her hand and place a kiss into her palm before taking a step back. Except when I step away, I catch a glance at the bottoms she's wearing.

Boxer shorts. My boxer shorts. And not a pair she grabbed from the clothes I've started keeping over here. But the ones I gave her the night we first met.

"What are those?" I shift my glance from the shorts to her blushing face. She's biting her lip as if she's nervous. I can take a guess as to why she is, but little does she know she should be nervous for a whole other reason.

Because seeing her in my clothes is doing something to me in ways I've never felt. And it's making me think things I've never thought.

Like this woman is mine.

Like the thought of her wearing any other man's clothes makes me murderous.

Like I don't want this to end in two days.

"Your shorts?"

I grab the waistband with both hands and step back to her. Her legs instantly go around my waist so she has no choice but to feel my cock pressing against her through the fabric.

"Have you worn them before?"

I see her swallow before she answers. "Yes."

"Why have I never seen them?"

Her smile goes from nervous to playful. "Because when I'm with you I'm usually naked."

Fair. And a naked Stella is never a bad thing.

"If I would've known this was an option, I might have kept you clothed more."

"Really?" She raises an eyebrow as her hand reaches down and inside the sleep pants I'm wearing, slowing beginning to stroke me. "You don't want me naked?"

The growl I let out echoes through the room. "I never said that."

My mouth finds the base of her neck, which is open for me because of the off-the-shoulder T-shirt she's wearing. Stella starts moving around, but it's not her normal fidgets when I'm hitting the spot that sends her wild. I quickly take a peek to see that she's trying to take off her—my—shorts.

Except that's not going to do.

"Stop."

The worried look on her face quickly disappears when I give her a reassuring kiss. "I know we've done this a few times now, but I do have a rule that I should probably tell you about."

"And what is that?"

I lift the shirt over her head, leaving her topless for me on the island.

"When you're with me, you don't open a car door."

I lean down and give a quick suck to one of her perky nipples. "You don't ever pay."

I switch over to the other, giving it a pop as I release it.

"You always come first. In every way."

I lean in closer to her, my lips next to her ear as I hook my fingers into the shorts. "And you don't ever rob me of the plea-sure of taking off every last piece of your clothing. Understand?"

"Yes..."

With that one word, I strip the shorts off her, leaving her gloriously naked for me.

Sweet treat indeed.

I tilt her back slightly, looping my arms under her knees so I can put her in the perfect position. I lick my lips as I lower my mouth to her beautiful, and waiting, pussy. It's wet and glistening and fucking mine.

"Oh!" Her gasp comes with an accompanying pull to my hair. But she's not trying to pull me away. Oh no, she's holding on for dear life.

Little does she know I've got her. I'll always have her.

That thought should scare me. It should make me run, even though right now my tongue is licking the sweetest thing I've ever tasted. But it doesn't. And I'm not going to think too hard into why. No, I'm going to enjoy this night. I'm going to enjoy her. I'm going to let my mouth suck at her clit. I'm going to let my fingers enter her and find new spots that send her hips bucking into my face. I'm going to flick my tongue until she screams and begs for me to stop.

And then I'm going to fuck her like only I can do. I'm going to make sure I stay with her as long as she's going to stay with me.

"Emmett…"

I feel her pussy starting to pulse around me. She's so close. I insert another finger and hook them just where I know she likes it as I give a few more flicks to her clit. The combination sends her into an orgasm that leaves her literally shaking and screaming.

"Fuck!"

"Soon," I say as I bring her down. I rise up to her, making sure she watches me as I lick my fingers, making sure to get every drop of her pleasure. "So sweet."

It's at that moment I see the tub of ice cream I got out earlier. Stella doesn't see what I'm doing as her eyes are closed, still recouping from the orgasms. I quickly grab a spoon from the drawer next to me and take off the lid, scooping up a bite.

"Open for me, Tiger."

She first opens her eyes to see the waiting spoon with vanilla ice cream on it before slowly opening her mouth. I place the spoon on her tongue and watch as she takes the bite. I take it out, but quickly dive in for a kiss so I can feel the coldness in her mouth with mine.

"Another?"

She nods as I repeat the gesture, only this time our kiss lingers longer. When I reluctantly pull away I watch as she opens her mouth again. Only she doesn't realize that's not where I'm putting the next bite.

I take a scoop of the melting ice cream and carefully let it spill onto her breast. The moment the cold touches her peaked nipple, Stella's eyes go wide and a tiny scream comes out. It's quickly followed by a moan of pleasure as I dive in, licking every drop of it off her perfect tit.

"Holy shit…"

I smile as I do it again, this time on the other side, resulting in the same "yip" followed by the same sob of pleasure.

There are a lot of things I know I'd miss, or feel differently about, when I went back to Nashville. Ice cream was already going to be on that list. But now? I don't know if I can ever eat it again without thinking about Stella, laid out for me, as I lick ice cream off her perfect body.

"Emmett…" Stella's words grab hold of me before I can take another scoop. "I need you. Inside of me. Please."

Her desperate words hit me square in the chest. I quickly lower the flannel pants I came downstairs in, freeing my aching dick that's been begging to be freed since the moment I felt Stella's arms around me.

I start to line myself up at her center when I realize I don't have a condom down here.

"Fuck," I groan as my arms fall to the island and I hang my head. "We need to go upstairs."

I move myself so I can pick her up when her hands grab my forearms. "No. I want you here. Nothing between us."

My eyes grow wide. "Are you sure? I'm clean, but…"

I don't know where my sentence was headed, but I don't need to as Stella shakes her head. "I'm on the pill. And clean.

After…before I came here…I got a blood test. My results came back today that I'm clean. I just…I know this is almost over, and I want to feel you. All of you."

Her words hit me straight in the heart as I crash my lips to hers. My hands reach behind her back as I pick her up and lift her up to bring her closer to the edge of the island. Our mouths stay fused together as I enter her, which is the only reason I don't wake up the entire Florida Panhandle the second I feel Stella's warm heat on my cock.

"Fuck, Tiger," I groan, burying my head into her shoulder as I slowly start working in and out of her. "You feel so fucking good. Too good."

Her hands reach around to my back, pulling me into her as if I can get any closer. "Make me yours, Emmett. Even if just for tonight. Make me yours."

There's no way Stella could've known what I've been thinking about all night, and I don't tell her. Instead I do as she asks.

I make her mine. I pretend she's mine. I fuck her like she's mine.

Mine.

The single word lights a fire in me as I begin driving into Stella. She's clutching onto my biceps, her nails leaving marks in my skin. It's not long before I spill inside of her, her orgasm coming within seconds of mine.

We don't say anything as we come down from our highs. Or anything as I slip out of her. Or when I take a warm towel to her throbbing pussy. We don't say a word as we go back to bed.

Instead we slip under the covers, our bodies connecting like magnets. Her head finds my chest and her body wraps around me like if she doesn't hold onto me I might disappear.

I'm not. At least not for another two days.

Because as long as we're here, Stella Banks is mine.

guide to love rule #54

You can learn a lot about a man by how he treats you when you're a passenger princess.

19
stella

I slowly blink my eyes open, which is hard because at some point my sunglasses fell off my head and the bright mid-afternoon sun is reflecting straight into my eyes off the windshield of Emmett's truck.

"Where are we?" I say groggily.

"At a rest stop. We're just about to cross into Tennessee," he says as he shuts off the truck. "I didn't know if you needed to use the restroom or get any snacks. This will probably be the last stop."

My heart sinks as those words hit me. "Thanks. No to the snacks. I'll head in and splash some water on my face."

Emmett leans in and kisses the top of my forehead before exiting out of the truck. I tilt my head back and forth as I walk into the rest stop, trying to get it to crack since I apparently fell asleep in the worst possible position in Emmett's passenger seat.

I hate that I fell asleep. The whole reason I decided to cancel my flight back to Nashville and ride home with him was to spend our last few hours together. Instead, I passed out somewhere between Birmingham and wherever we are.

Then again, the sleep can't all be blamed on me. There was an outlet mall in Alabama I wanted to stop at real quick. Emmett said no, citing that there was no such thing as a quick trip when it came to me and shopping. I begged and even offered a quickie in the cab of his truck in exchange for just three stores. He countered by fingering me in the passenger seat, which not only put on a show for the semi-truck next to us, but also put me into a slumber so I slept as he drove past said outlets.

I really can't be mad, though. Who needs new shoes when you can have an orgasm on I-65?

As I exit the restroom and find the map for "you are here," I realize that we're not far from Nashville. About two hours.

Then it hits me like a freight train—reality.

Back to work.

Seeing Duncan.

The fallout of the wedding that wasn't.

Figuring out where I'm going to live.

Figuring out if Duncan is really suing me.

Not seeing Emmett.

That last one might hit the hardest.

I've known since the first night that we were on a clock. It seemed so far away then.

It wasn't. In fact, it wasn't nearly long enough.

"Two more hours." I say to myself. As much as it's a countdown until I go back to the real world, it's also one for how much longer I can let myself pretend that Emmett and I are more than what we are.

I know this needs to end. We've both made this very clear that this was a Florida-only thing. It was a win-win. That's what we said.

What we said fucking sucks.

I take my time walking back to the truck and stretch a little while I wait for Emmett. When I see him walking toward me, I don't try and hide my stare. He's carrying two plastic bags and looking so good I might ask him if we can have engine problems that need us to find a hotel for the night while it gets fixed.

I wonder if I can cut a wire? I saw it in a movie once. I bet I could. I'm pretty handy.

"Hello? Earth to Stella?"

I blink my way back to reality and out of the delusion of being stranded at a cheap hotel with Emmett for the night. "Sorry. Still asleep. What's in the bags?"

I can tell from the glint in his eye he knows I'm full of crap, but he doesn't call me on it. "Waters because I'm pretty sure you haven't had actual water yet today. Diet Dr Pepper so you didn't yell at me for only getting you water. Cookie dough bites for you. Skittles for me."

I feel my mouth drop open in shock and awe. "You got me snacks?"

"Of course." He walks around to unlock the truck and open my door. "I saw how much Diet Dr Pepper you went through in the last two weeks, so that was an easy one. And you ordered cookie dough ice cream enough that I figured that was a safe bet."

"But I said I didn't want any snacks."

"You were half-asleep. I knew that wasn't the answer. Plus, it's always smart to get snacks. Get in, Tiger. It's time to go home."

I do as he says, and I'm surprised that I'm not dwelling on the words "time to go home." Instead I'm marveling at the thoughtfulness of this man. And it's not just the snacks. It's everything over the past two weeks.

Saving me on the wedding day.

Going to the beach when I know he hated it.

The smash room.

Holding me while I cried.

Letting me scream when I needed to.

Reminding me of who I am and who I want to be.

Kissing me as if he was bringing me back to life.

Making me feel things I didn't know were real.

Being a friend.

Becoming so much more than that.

"Thank you."

He quickly glances at me before turning his eyes back to the highway.

"For what? The snacks? Stella, you really don't need to—"

"It's not just the snacks," I quickly say. "It's everything."

"Everything?"

I turn to face him, though his eyes stay focused on the road as we enter back onto the highway. "Do you know how thoughtful and considerate you are?"

"It's just good manners."

I shake my head as I turn in my seat to face him—and do my best not to stare at the veins in his forearms that are slightly more prominent than usual as he grips the steering wheel.

"It's more than manners," I continue. "There's polite, then there's thoughtful. And you're both. You're without a doubt the most considerate man I've ever met in my life. Not many men would do what you did for me."

"Are we talking about the orgasms or carrying your suitcases?"

I playfully smack his arm. "You know what I mean. You're a good man, Emmett Collins. Probably the best I've ever met. And you don't give yourself enough credit for it, so I'm going to be the one to do it. Especially if…"

I trail off, not wanting to finish that sentence. I close my eyes, willing myself to not get emotional, but when I feel his hand on my thigh that quickly becomes a losing battle.

"We're going to see each other," he says, somehow reading my mind and finishing the sentence. "You'll just have to be a better actress so no one knows I've fucked you six ways from Sunday."

That makes me laugh. "I'm an amazing actress."

"Whatever you say, Tiger," he says. "But seriously…we'll see each other. It'll be a little awkward at first. But pretty soon it'll just become a memory we look back at fondly. Hell, maybe someday we'll tell Simon."

We exchange a look before cracking up laughing. No way in hell will my brother *ever* find out about this.

Our laughter dies down and we fall back into a silence, the only sound in the cab is the low hum of the country music station Emmett has on his satellite radio, playing a fitting song about wanting to stay a little longer.

The lyrics hit even harder when I see the "Welcome to Tennessee" sign on the highway.

One hour and forty minutes…

"When do you have to go back to work?"

One thing I want to talk about less than Emmett and my time together ending is going back to the office.

"Monday morning," I say. "I have no idea what I'm walking into, or what's been said. I'm sure Duncan has told them a million outlandish lies about what happened, so I'll be putting out a ton of those fires. It won't be the first time I've had to battle office gossip. I just never thought I'd have to do it again."

"When did you have to do that?"

I lean into him so I can wrap my arms around his bicep, my head resting on his shoulder. "When I graduated from college, I had no idea what I wanted to do. I had a degree in marketing, but nothing felt right. I was a bit lost, but I needed a job. If there's one thing my parents instilled in us, it was a work ethic. So, until I figured out what I really wanted, my dad got me a job at the law firm as the office administrator."

"I'm guessing you had to fight off talk that Stella Banks was only there because her dad was on the nameplate?"

"Exactly. It didn't matter that I was really good at it. No—I *am* really good at it. And I love it. I really do love my job. But unfortunately, none of that mattered. To some I was just a nepo baby hire who had her daddy buy her the red bottom shoes she was wearing."

"They really said that?"

"Right? How dare they? I bought those shoes for myself, thank you very much."

My joke earns me a smile from Emmett before giving me leg a reassuring squeeze. "Has it gotten better?"

"It has. I've made friends. My best friend in the world works down the hall from me. I've shown my worth. It's barely a blip on the radar anymore. Though I have a feeling whatever rumors Duncan is spreading are going to be ten times worse than anything I dealt with back then."

"Could you get a new job?"

"I don't want to," I say. And that's the truth. I love my job. I have friends there. I'm proud of the fact that I help run that place. "Can that be future Stella's problem?"

"Sure." I feel Emmett's lips kiss the top of my head. God I'm going to miss that. I don't even know if he realizes he does things like that. Little kisses or touches. Small gestures. Few words. He's the king of the little things. The small gestures that mean more than any grand gesture ever could.

"How about you?"

"What about me?"

"What's life for Cap when he returns to the land of being Emmett Collins?"

"Back to normal I'd assume," he begins. "I'll go pick up Winnie from Maddie's house. Probably spend the day with her and little man before heading home. Grocery shop. Get ready for the week. Back to business."

Out of all the words, thoughts, and feelings I've had today knowing our time was up, "back to business" somehow stings the worse. He's going back to normal. I'm going back to chaos. He has a life he's happy with. He's going back to his days of work and his dog and his sister and nephew and bachelorhood. I'm going back to...fuck if I know.

We fall into a silence for the rest of the drive back. Which I'm glad for. Gives me a chance to get my mind right as we approach the Nashville city limits. Because I need to remind myself of about ten thousand things before I step out of this truck. *Yes, this stings right now. Yes, the bubble is three seconds away from popping. Yes, you are walking back into a shit show. But remember that this vacation, the time with Emmett, was always temporary. It was what you needed at the time. It was time you needed for yourself. Now it's time to turn the page. Face the music. Find the old Stella, and with it, become a new and improved version. Just remember, even though this is going to suck for a few days, the alternative is being Duncan's wife, washing his tighty whities, and having pictures of your wedding day in that fucking dress.*

Before I know it, we're exiting the highway toward Ainsley's apartment—or I guess I should say my apartment. It's where I lived before moving in with Duncan. And before I left for Florida she told me I was more than welcome to come back until I could figure out what was next. Little does she know that I have no clue what's next.

I don't text her to let her know I'm here. If I did, she'd come down and see Emmett, and I don't want our final minutes together spent answering a million questions. For all she knows, I'm taking a Lyft here from the airport.

When he turns off the ignition, the sudden sound of silence is deafening.

This is it. When I step out of this truck, Emmett will go from the man who made me whole again to my brother's best friend. He won't be my Cap anymore. I won't be his Tiger. I'll just be Simon's little sister.

It's for the best. And soon I'll realize it.

But not now.

Now, for just a few more minutes, I can be sad.

I reach to open my door when I feel his hand grip my arm. When I turn to look at him, the smirk he's giving me is the one I want to remember when I think of my two weeks with Emmett Collins.

"I know we're back in Tennessee, and the new rules are about to start, but that doesn't mean you now open your door."

I chuckle through the threatening tears as he walks around the truck to open the door, giving me his hand as I step out. He lets go so he can grab my mountain of bags out of the bed of the truck, and it gives me the chance to take one final look at the man who saved me in more ways than I can count.

When the last bag is out, Emmett looks over to me just as I lose the battle with the tears. He doesn't say anything as he pulls me into him, bringing me against his hard, yet comforting, chest that I already miss.

"Best vacation ever," he whispers as he buries his face into my hair.

"Best vacation ever."

He pulls back, but just enough so now our foreheads are resting against each other. We've shared countless kisses and touches over the past two weeks. Yet none of them have conveyed more emotions and feelings than this one right here.

"See you around, Tiger." Emmett takes a step back, giving my hand one final squeeze before stepping toward his truck.

"Thanks, Cap. For everything."

We share one more knowing look before he gets in his car and drives away into the summer sunset. I feel myself crying, but I don't do anything to push away the tears. I don't even know how long I'm standing here, because eventually I feel two hands on my shoulders, giving me a familiar and comforting hug.

"Hey," Ainsley whispers. "You okay?"

I wipe away the tears and throw on an invisible coat of armor.

Back to reality…

"Yeah…I will be."

guide to love rule #49

Winning a breakup is key to moving on.
Telling people your ex
has a small dick also helps.

20
stella

I watch the elevator light up for each floor as I ride to the twenty-fourth floor. With each number that flashes, I remind myself of everything I need to do as I walk back into Carter, Banks and Fairchild for the first time since the wedding that wasn't.

20…Smile, no matter what.

21…Hold your head high.

22…Tits up.

23…Let's fucking go.

When the door opens, I see the normal buzz of seven-thirty on a Monday morning. A few of the junior associates are already working, wanting to show the partners how dedicated they are to the firm. The assistants are zooming around, getting everything ready for the day and week.

Yet, with every step I take toward to my desk, I feel the eyes starting to drift my way. I hear the whispers growing louder. I wish I could say it's all in my head, but that theory is quickly debunked when I make eye contact with two interns who work closely with Duncan. They can't look away fast enough.

You knew it was going to be like this. The little bit of gossip is worth the peace of mind that your life is now Duncan free.

"Welcome back."

I relax at the sound of Andi's voice. I don't sit down. I don't turn on my computer. Instead I bring her into a hug that is long overdue. "I'm so happy to see you."

"Same." We give each other one more squeeze before letting go. "How are you?"

I shrug, because what else can I do? "Not ready to come back here."

"I was going to call you." Andi trails off as two of her fellow paralegals start walking slowly past my desk. Can they make it any more obvious they are trying to eavesdrop? "Actually, let's go somewhere more private."

The paralegals fail to look innocent as we walk past them toward the break room. It's not exactly private, but at least there's a door and full glass windows, so we can see who's coming in. Or trying to eavesdrop.

"Okay, lay it on me," I say as I lean against the counter. "How bad is it?"

Andi's face immediately squinches up.

"That bad?"

"I didn't say anything!"

"Your face said everything."

She slumps into a chair. "I didn't mean to."

I chuckle as I take a seat across from her. Andi is not a good liar. It could be something as small as she took the last donut, to something complex like parading around a fake boyfriend. No matter the scenario, her poker face is shit. In her defense, she did pull off the fake boyfriend thing. It worked so well he's now her real boyfriend.

However, in this instance, she's not hiding a damn thing.

"Let me guess," I begin. "My former fiancé is saying that I'm an unfeeling bitch who left him at the altar. That he had no clue it was coming, and my sudden, and unexpected, choice to flee has caused him so much pain and anguish that the only remedy he can come up with is filing a lawsuit against me for emotional damages."

"Pretty much," she says. "Wait! How did you know about the lawsuit?"

I stand to make myself a cup of coffee. I have a feeling I'll need one or ten of these to get through today. "Maeve called me while I was in Florida. She didn't want me to be taken by surprise."

"I'm sorry," she says. "I knew and I should've called you."

"You have nothing to apologize for."

"I do. I'm a bad friend. When it came to the suit, at first a bunch of us thought he was bluffing. Or just trying to talk shit. Duncan being Duncan, you know? Then he went parading around, showing the filing like he had the winning lottery numbers."

I roll my eyes at the image in my head. I'm sure he was puffing out his nonexistent chest thinking he was so smart. "Sounds about right."

"I wanted to trip him every time he came back to our department. Especially knowing what I know. Which no one does, and that kills me. I've wanted to defend you, but it's your story, you know? I've quashed what I could, but it's been hard. He's a piece of shit and everyone is taking his side. *Please* let me start dropping hints about the flogger. Or the money. Anything. Hell, it can be a lie or a truth. I don't care. He doesn't deserve the sympathy he's getting."

I had a feeling this was how it was going to be when I returned. Taking that time off was absolutely what I needed for my mental health, but it's putting me at a massive deficit when it comes to damage control in the office. Especially since I don't have my dad here to play defense for me. Not that I'd want him to, but it would be nice to have more than Andi in my corner.

Damn him for retiring.

"I knew it was going to be like this," I say. "I'll take a little office gossip and a few weeks of being looked at funny if it means I'm not married to that lying, cheating asshole."

"That's a very healthy way of looking at it. Though I'm going to warn you, it's more than a little gossip," Andi says. "I'm pretty sure one rumor I heard was that you actually rode away from the hotel on a motorcycle."

I nearly spit out my coffee. "Can you see me on a motorcycle? Please. That helmet would crush my hair."

I don't know why, but at that moment I start smiling as I wonder if Emmett has a motorcycle. I'd battle helmet head to ride on a bike with him.

Oh…motorcycle sex…

"Why are you smiling like that?"

Shit. I didn't mean to actually smile. Just do it internally. "How am I smiling?"

"Like you're thinking about good sex."

"Andi!" I gasp, though I can't think of anything to say in rebuttal, because she's not wrong.

"Stella Banks! Did you hook up on your little vacation? Oh my God! Did you fuck a cabana boy!"

This time I don't even try to keep the smile off my face. I also wish I could see Emmett's reaction if he were to find out that in this version of the story, he was my cabana boy.

"Holy shit! That good?"

"Shhh," I whisper as I sit back down next to her. "It was, and I'll tell you more later, but—"

I can't finish that sentence as the break room door swings open so hard it rebounds off the wall. And that's when I stare straight at the man who is responsible for everything.

"Hello, Duncan."

His snake smile isn't fooling anyone. "Stella. Welcome back."

Andi looks to me, then to Duncan, before back to me. I give her a nod that it's okay to go. Yes, I'd like a witness in case I murder him, but at the same time she needs plausible deniability.

Duncan watches as Andi leaves the room, shutting the door behind her, leaving the two of us staring at each other with nothing but disgust. At least that's my view of him. I don't know what he's thinking, but if I were to guess, it's mock arrogance and a bit of anger.

Because, you know, he's the one who should be angry because none of this was his fault.

Oh wait…

"You look well," he says, unbuttoning his suit jacket before sitting down across from me.

"You look like a lying asshole. Or an uncircumcised penis. Can't decide which."

"Oh Stella," he says with extra slime in his voice. "Do we need to be like that?"

"Why? Is this causing you more emotional damage? You going to up the damages? Because I'll take back the penis dig. But you *are* a liar, and I'll scream that until I'm blue in the face."

"Stella, baby…come on now."

"Don't baby me, Duncan Hughes." My voice is growing louder. Judging by the eyeballs trying not to stare into here, they can hear me. I couldn't give two shits. "What do you want?"

"I wanted to see if you'd have dinner with me tonight."

I think my eyes jump out of my head. "Dinner? With you? For what, Duncan? What possible reason would I have to go to dinner with you?"

Is he serious? He can't be. He's either dumb or delusional if he thinks I'm going anywhere with him.

Oh, who am I kidding? He's both.

"To talk. About us. We need to put all this behind us so we can make up and start fresh."

I let out a laugh so loud even the people who aren't trying to eavesdrop heard us. I know because a group of heads all popped up from their cubicles at the same time.

"There are only a few things to talk about. One is when I'm going to be paid back for your shady business dealings. Second, to schedule when I can come to the condo to get my things. Neither of those are getting back together, and it never will be. Going forward, when we have any conversations that aren't pertaining to business at the office, it will be with my father next to me as my lawyer. And I'll want Simon there simply so I can watch you piss yourself when he just stares at you for hours, thinking about how many people he'll need to call in to hide your body."

He tries to hide the gulp he swallows, but he can't. The man is scared shitless of my brother.

"Stella, come on," he says. Is he asking again? Does he not understand the word no? "You had your time away. I let you take the time you needed. You got to lay on the beach and get everything out of your system. It's now time to get everything figured out."

The fucking audacity of this man. He's *actually* serious. I know because he's leaning forward, his head tilted like he's trying to show that he cares, while holding out his hand for me. I can now see clearly all of the times he did this to manipulate his way out of a fight, or to get his way.

Not anymore.

"You want me—the woman you lied to, stole from, and cheated on, on the day of our wedding, mind you—to just brush it all way because you asked me nicely? Because you think some time on the beach washed away all my issues, so now I can forgive you?"

Holy shit. His eyes say it all—that's exactly what he thinks.

"Well yeah. Don't you forgive me?"

"No the fuck I don't!" I yell as I pop up from my chair. This is no longer a sitting conversation. "And even if I did, which I *never* would, you spent the last two weeks telling everyone here that I'm a bitch and you're suing me. Why would I get back together with you when you have an actual lawsuit out against me?"

Judging by his reaction he didn't realize I knew that. Did he think my family wouldn't tell me? With every conversation I have with him, the more I realize that he's a fucking idiot.

"Who told you about the lawsuit? Andi?"

"Yes, Andi. And my sister. And my father. You know, my lawyer? Who you served papers to. How would you think I wouldn't know?"

"The suit was just something I did out of anger," he says with a mock apologetic tone. "I'll drop it right now if you'll just have dinner with me. Talk this out. Give me another chance."

I almost—almost—start to give in. Not fully, but I feel myself begin to say, "Fine, I'll have dinner." Because that's what old Stella would've done. She would've given in because she didn't want to fight.

That was the old me. The new me isn't putting up with this shit.

No, I'm Stella 2.0. A little crazy, a little bold, and knows what she fucking wants. In the past two weeks since I figured out who Duncan was, I've also figured out who I am.

I'm not that needy woman who just wanted what everyone else had.

I'm not the woman who's going to forgive to avoid conflict.

And I sure as shit am not the woman whose going to be with a man just for the sake of it.

I'm strong. I'm capable. I know my worth. I also know that no one is going to drag my name through court because his feelings are hurt. Nope, I'm going to countersue him for a dollar just to say on the record how much of a piece of shit he is.

And I want Nadia to testify on my behalf.

Actually, I want more than that. I want *everyone* to know what he did. I don't want to sit back and just let the gossip die down. Why does he get to have the last word and use his status at the firm to win the breakup?

Fuck. That.

Before I can think about what I'm doing, I swing open the

door of the break room and head into the bullpen of the office. As I march to the middle so everyone can see me, I'm remembering back to the night of the rehearsal dinner when Duncan told me not to cause a scene.

I didn't then, but I sure as shit am about to cause one now.

"Hey! Everyone!" I yell as everyone turns their eyes on me. I'm surrounded by associates and interns, and even a few of the managing partners are making their way out of their offices.

Good. I thrive on an audience. I'll even stand on a desk so everyone can see and hear me just fine.

"I'm assuming by now you all know that I left Duncan at the altar," I begin as more eyes focus on me. "And I'm also going to assume that he, or someone in his circle of law bros, has told you that I'm a bitch. That I hurt him, and he's the good guy in all this, and no one can fathom why I left."

I hear low murmurs and see head nods. I also see glares from the law bros I just mentioned. I know they're trying to intimidate me. Joke's on them. Their presence is only fueling my fire.

"What I'd like to let you know is that he stole from me. Thousands of dollars. I'd rather not go into more detail than that because I'm sure if my father— you know, the man whose name is on your paychecks—were here he'd tell me to not talk about details of a lawsuit. And not just the bogus suit he's filed against me for emotional distress. Which is horseshit. Because actual emotional—and visual—damage is the thought and memory of Duncan Hughes getting flogged on a bed by a dominatrix an hour before our wedding in nothing but his tie and dress socks while being called a good boy. Now *that* will give you nightmares."

I hear a few gasps as I watch all the eyes turn to Duncan. I take a peek over to him just in time to see the color drain from his face. I want to stare, but I also need to keep going. I'm on a roll.

"So yes, everyone, please know that before you go believing

everything you hear, that there are two sides to a story. One is from a woman who was going to give everything to the man she thought she loved, only to find out she was being lied to and cheated on. The other is coming from a pencil dick who fell for a Ponzi scheme and barely gets hard with his three inches paying a woman to flog him."

It's at that moment I see Stanley Carter, the most senior partner of the firm, walk into the room. I know I have about a minute before he says that he needs to see me, but I'm not quite done. I climb down from the desk because I have one more thing I need to make sure that everyone, but especially Duncan, knows.

"I was the best you were *ever* going to fucking do," I say as I stare at him dead in the eyes. "Goodbye, Duncan. And go fuck yourself."

I walk toward Stanley with my head held high, not looking directly at anyone as he opens the door to his office. I don't sit down even though he walks behind his desk and does so himself.

I know what's coming. So I'm going to do it before he can.

"Stella…"

"I know," I say. "I'm resigning. Effective immediately."

He lets out a sigh and hangs his head for a second. "I didn't want it to be like this. You know how much I think of you. Of your father. You run this office better than anyone we've had in thirty years. I wanted to fire him. I know what he did to you—and not just because you announced it. Your dad told me."

I wince for a second, hating that a man I admire knows about all the shitty things I let happen because I was too…whatever… to see what was right in front of me.

"Stanley…"

He shakes his head for me to stop. "Don't. Whatever you were going to say, don't bother. Personally, I'm on Team Stella. But unfortunately, professionally, I have to be neutral. And since

Duncan didn't do anything that was in direct reflection of the company or to harm his clients…"

"I know," I say as the adrenaline crashes around me. "Can you do me a favor?"

"Name it."

"Don't call my dad right away," I say. "Let me tell him."

He nods in the fatherly way he has about him. "Done. We're going to miss you around here."

I look back to the office, where everyone is seemingly getting back to work. "I will too. Mostly."

I leave his office, my head held high, as I go to my desk and quickly pack up my belongings. Andi helps me, but doesn't say anything as she carries one of the boxes to my car.

"Call me later?"

"Of course."

I'm in a haze as I spend the next hour driving to my parents' house in Rolling Hills as I replay the last hour of my life on repeat.

And each time it finishes, I don't regret a single second.

Except that I don't have a job.

And I only have a place to live because Ainsley's an angel.

Oh, and I'm getting sued.

Still no regrets. All of these are small prices to pay to avoid what would've been the biggest mistake of my life.

When I pull into my parents' driveway, I see my dad sitting on the front porch swing. Does he know? Or is this coincidence?

"Stella?"

Surprise. Good. I can handle that.

"Hey, Dad."

"What's wrong?"

I wince a little before telling him an abridged version of the events.

"I might or might not have just told the entire law firm that Duncan likes to be flogged. And why I ran from the wedding. Oh, and I called him a pencil dick and then I quit."

Dad laughs. "Did you throw in that he's a cheating asshole?"

"Of course."

"Do you need a lawyer?"

"Probably."

He throws his arm around me as he leads me into the house. "That's my girl."

21

emmett

ONE OF THE BEST PARTS OF MY JOB IS THAT EVERY DAY IS A LITTLE different, but has enough continuity to keep me sane. Some days I can stay in Nashville and inspect our properties here. Some days I can work from home and check on permits and do any coordination I need to do.

Every Tuesday I drive to Rolling Hills to check on our work down there, which again, I don't mind. It's only an hour drive, and I'm promised to get the best coffee and breakfast in Tennessee from Mona's, which is Charlie's diner.

Today is Tuesday. Today I was met with a text from Simon on my way into town asking me to meet him for breakfast. Today is the only day I wanted to skip my weekly ritual, because I didn't want to face my boss and best friend.

He's going to ask me about Florida. He's going to ask me about Stella and how she was down there. And I'm going to have to lie. I can't say that I fucked her brains out and it's been three days since I've been back and I can't get her out of my damn head.

"He's alive!"

I chuckle under my breath as Simon waves at me from the

breakfast counter. "Yes, I'm alive. I went on vacation, not on an extended medical leave."

"For you it's the same thing."

"Can you not be dramatic?"

This earns me a haughty laugh from Charlie as she pours me a cup of coffee. "If you didn't want dramatic, you should've never said yes to this partnership."

She's not wrong. I knew what I was getting into when I teamed up with Simon last year and left my cushy job at a high-end firm in Nashville. Usually I'm not one to wonder about what could be or to take the risk for more. I like stability. I had a well-paying job in a field I enjoyed. Sure, the pipe dream I once had about owning my own construction company was still there, but I wasn't chomping at the bit to take the gamble on that when I had a six-figure job with a healthy retirement plan and bonuses.

Then I came into Rolling Hills one day, sat on this very stool, and met Mona, the original owner and namesake of this diner. I came to try to get her to sell to my firm, but something about the interaction felt different. I'd approached numerous people over the years asking if they'd be willing to sell. Hell, I was sent on those missions because I was good at getting people to say yes. But there was something about her, and this town, that made me not want to be the guy that my corporate bosses sent out on buying missions. I wanted more than just being the guy on the other side of the email when people needed something.

And then Simon Banks sat down next to me, and the rest is history. Before I knew it, Simon was buying this diner, I agreed to work for him, and a year later we're growing Magnolia Properties on a daily basis.

And I get the perk of free coffee when I'm in town. I'll take that any day of the week.

"So how was Florida?"

I feel my face instantly flush. I hurry and take a sip of coffee to try to hide any blush creeping in. I knew he'd ask me this. I even practiced what I was going to say. I just thought I'd have a better handle on my outward reactions.

"Good," I say. "A much-needed break."

Well done. The less words the better.

"A break? That's it? That's all you're going to tell me?"

"What do you want to know? It was Destin. I worked. I played some golf. I laid on the beach. I went to a few bars. That's it."

Simon's raised eyebrow means he doesn't buy my half-ass, and half true, story. "Oh come on, you had to do more than that! You were gone for two weeks. I highly doubt it was because you suddenly found a love for the beach."

I mean, I did, but not for the reasons he's thinking.

"My guess is you met a woman," he continues. "But Charlie thinks I'm crazy. And I know meeting a woman and spending time with her is a little out of the box thinking, but that's how well I know you. I know when you go off script and meet a woman and have a sex vacation."

I nearly choke on my coffee when he says the words "sex vacation." Because essentially that's what I had, even though it was much more than that.

"Oh my God, you did!" Simon yells. "Bug! Come here! I was right! Emmett got laid!"

Charlie responds to her nickname and walks over to us. "Emmett Collins! Did you have a vacation fling?"

"Change the subject," I grunt before taking a sip of coffee. The two of them laugh at my expense, and I will myself to fix my face. I need this line of questioning to stop. Right now.

"Sorry," Simon says as his laugher dies down. "Anyway. I'm glad you had fun. Got laid. Blew off some steam. And thanks again for checking in on Stella. I hope she didn't bother you too much."

"No problem," I choke out. "Was happy to help. So what's new with you?"

I say that answer a little too fast, which Simon doesn't pick up on. He also doesn't say anything to the fact that I rarely ask what's new with him. Not that I don't care. I do. Simon just has a tendency to ramble.

As he's going on about what he's been doing the past few weeks, and pulling up videos on his phone of his three-month old daughter, Lainey, I see Charlie giving me a questioning look. I try not to make eye contact to avoid the guilt that I'm sure is written all over my face, but I can tell she knows something's up.

"So, you might be wondering why I asked you to meet me here," Simon says.

"Not really."

"Really? Not even an inkling?"

"Simon, you're technically my boss. For starters, it's Tuesday, and I always come here on Tuesdays. And a boss asking an employee to meet is one of the most basic tenants of a boss-employee relationship."

"Huh, I guess so," he says with a shrug. "Anyway, the reason I brought you down here today is because while I was on paternity leave, I had a chance to think about the future of Magnolia Properties. More specifically, how we can make this bigger than either of us imagined."

This makes me sit up a little straighter. Simon might be a tad on the ridiculous scale. But when it comes to business, he doesn't mess around.

"Okay?"

"When I brought you on, I was at the brim of what I could handle myself. Between my real estate deals, and the properties I'd already acquired, I needed you to help manage the day to day. You were my saving grace and the reason we've been able to double the amount of properties we have in less than a year."

Damn…has it been less than a year? "Thanks, man. It's been everything I'd hoped."

"I'm glad. But that being said, we're about to be in a similar situation. We're at our max. You handled so much for me on paternity leave, and honestly, I don't know how you did it all."

"It was nothing," I say.

"No. It was a lot. I tried to do what you normally do when you were in Florida, and I was in tears."

"It's true," Charlie chimes in as she walks by with an arm full of plates. "He missed you."

"Don't listen to her," he says. "Actually, do listen to her. She's right. I was a wreck without you."

"Aw, Simon…you flatter me."

"Don't go getting a big head. The reason I'm telling you all of this is because I've been debating for a while now about expanding Magnolia Properties. Actually having an office. Hiring someone to help us with more day-to-day so I can focus on buying properties and you can focus on managing. Hell, I'm hoping even one day we can grow even more, put that construction background you have to good use and build developments in and around Rolling Hills. High-end homes. Affordable starter houses. You name it, I want us to create it."

Now that gets my attention. "Simon, wow, I'd love to."

"I thought you'd say that," he says. "Which is why I already started our expansion."

"Explain?"

"The space next door to here?" Simon signals to the left, like I don't know what we've been working on. "We'd already been turning it into offices, so I took the listing down and decided that's where we're setting up shop. Plus, now I get to work next door to the love of my life."

"Yay," Charlie deadpans. "I can't wait for you to be here more than you already are."

"Oh quit," he says, leaning over to give her a kiss, which she accepts with fake reluctance. It's their thing. He's a cocky, mildly ridiculous man, and she keeps him grounded but also can't resist him. They're truly made for each other. "You love me."

"Yeah, yeah…" she says with a smile before turning to me. "This means you'll need to figure out something else to order. Unless you're going to eat a patty melt every day."

"I don't see a problem with that." I'm a man of routine. On Tuesdays at breakfast I get coffee and eggs. Lunch I get a patty melt and an iced tea. Why mess with a good thing?

"Yes! Patty melts for all!" Simon says, clapping his hands. "Now, I know right now you only come to town once a week. Are you good coming in more? Not every day, as I know we have a lot of business in Nashville. But it's a decent commute, and I know you aren't interested in moving."

He's right. I'm not. I built my house myself and have no intention of selling it. Plus, my sister and nephew are in Nashville.

"The commute is fine," I say. "Maybe I'll start listening to some audiobooks."

"You can expense them for all I care, as long as I can see your handsome face a few times a week."

"I'll hold you to that," I say as I tip my cup of coffee to him.

"Great! It's settled. We'll move in next door. We'll both have offices. You have a space to work when you're in town, but also are free to work from home when you need to stay in Nashville. When you're here, you'll clog your arteries with patty melts, and we'll continue to take over Middle Tennessee one house and building at a time!"

"Sounds like a plan," I say.

"Fantastic." Simon stands up. No—he *jumps* up. Because he has more energy than he knows what to do with. I told you: golden retriever on crack. "Want to go next door and see your office?"

"Would love to."

Charlie pours me a to-go cup of coffee and we take the thirty steps we need to go next door.

"Welcome to Magnolia Properties," Simon says as he switches on the light. "Front desk here. Your office is in that corner and mine is across the way. Glass walls so we can see each other all day."

"Please don't make inappropriate gestures while I'm working."

Simon dramatically gasps. "I would never."

I narrow my eyes. "Yes, you would. It'll be freshman year business management all over again."

"Hey, we both got A's in that class." Simon points to rooms to the side. "I set up two small meeting rooms, so that way if we need to bring clients in we have some private space. Plus, there's a lounge area in the back that will also serve as the space my daughter sleeps in when I have to bring her to the office."

"Smart."

"Why, thank you. I know it's not a big-time firm like you were at in Nashville, but it'll do the trick."

I give his back a pat. "It more than does the trick. It's perfect for us."

I take one more look around and can't help but feel excited. He's right, it might not be big and lavish like my old firm. But the look and design feels as high-end as it comes. Glass walls for the offices and meeting rooms. Expensive desks. Hardwood floors. Modern and sleek lighting fixtures. He spared no expense. "I'm guessing you called in Maeve to decorate?"

"Was my first phone call," he says. "What's the good of having an interior decorator sister if you aren't going to use her for her services?"

Simon chose to use the word "use," but it's not what he meant. Most people would use family members for free services, especially if they are as sought after in their field as Maeve is. But not Simon. If I had to guess, he paid double her normal rate because that's the kind of guy he is. He might talk a big game, but at the end of the day, he's one of the best men I know.

"This is great," I say. "Did you hire anyone for the front desk yet?"

At that moment the front door swings open and I'm frozen. I feel the color leaving my face and my stomach dropping to the floor.

"Stella?"

"Oh! I forgot to tell you!" Simon says as he walks over to where Stella is standing at the doorway, holding a cardboard box. "I'm bringing Stella on to help us get going."

Excuse me…what did he say?

"You're what?"

I try to keep the shock and panic out of my voice, but I don't think I did.

"It actually worked out perfectly," Simon says, not realizing that Stella and I haven't taken our eyes off each other since she walked in the door. "She had to leave her job at the law firm. It was best for everyone involved. So she needed a job. I had a job to give her. What better way to get this place up and running than with a woman who has run the office of one of the best law firms in Nashville?"

Neither of us say anything. Neither of us move. I figured I'd see Stella again at some point. Birthday parties for Lainey. Random get-togethers. Maybe she'd swing through Rolling Hills at some point while I was here.

But never in a million years did I expect to see her so soon.

Or looking so beautiful.

Or in the same room as her brother.

"What's the problem?" Simon asks as the silence becomes deafeningly noticeable.

I let out a cough before speaking. "No problem. Just… surprised."

"Yeah! Surprised!" Stella says a little too enthusiastically.

"Good," Simon says. "I was nervous for a moment. The staring was weird. Almost like you were seeing a ghost. Or even more ridiculous, that you saw each other naked."

Oh Simon…if you only knew.

guide to love rule #97

Check the employee handbook on rules about your boss giving you toe-curling orgasms before you knew he was going to be your boss.

22
stella

Things I didn't realize until yesterday—Emmett and I never exchanged phone numbers in Florida.

I don't know how that happened. I guess we never needed to? We were just always…there. We showed up at times we agreed on. He'd pop over if he wanted to ask me something. I'd knock on his door if I didn't want to be alone. Looking back, it was pretty nice. But yesterday, when I needed a way to tell him that, "Surprise! We're going to be coworkers!", it was very inconvenient.

Normally if I had this problem, I'd pin on my white girl FBI badge and go digging down the rabbit holes of the internet to find some way to get in touch with him. However, that required programs I had access to at the law firm, especially since Emmett is nowhere to be found on social media. My only choice would've been to ask Simon for his phone number, which wasn't an option. I could just hear my question now…

Hey Simon! Can I get Emmett's phone number because I need to let him know that we're going to be working together. Why does he need to know? Funny you should ask. And totally not a big deal or anything. We just had sex one or fifty-six times and I've dreamed about him every night since I've returned from Florida. Now, I don't know if he's been thinking about me like that, which he probably isn't, but I just wanted to give him a heads up so he isn't caught off guard.

Yeah…that wasn't going to happen.

Which brings us back to right now.

Emmett staring at me like he's seeing a ghost.

Me staring at Emmett and remembering how his beard feels against my thighs.

Simon looking back and forth at us, completely clueless.

"How exciting is this!" Simon yells as he claps his hands together. "I already feel like we have a Three Musketeers vibe going."

He starts to go on about what our group nickname should be, but thankfully a phone call takes him away. He excuses himself into his office, shutting the door behind him.

"What the fuck, Stella?" Emmett whisper yells. "What are you doing here?"

"I'm sorry," I say, trying to keep my voice down. Simon might be in his office, but those have glass walls, and I also haven't tested how sound travels in here. "It happened so fast, and I didn't have a way to get a hold of you. Also, why didn't we exchange numbers in Florida?"

"Because we didn't need to." He rubs his hand down his face, taking a second to gather himself. I set my box of personal belongings on my future desk at the front of the office space, not wanting to say anything else until Emmett gets his bearings. I had a day to prep for this. He didn't. "You quit the firm?"

"That's one way of putting it…"

He raises an eyebrow. "How else can you put it?"

I glance over at Simon, who seems to be still in the thick of his call, but I also know I'm strapped for time. "I quit after I told the entire office, while standing on a desk, that Duncan stole from me, liked to be spanked, and had a tiny dick. That, on top of the whispers and glares and rumors that had been going around me, led me to the decision that it was best if I didn't work there. That and I was going to get fired for the whole "pencil dick" comment in front of the senior partners."

Emmett chuckles, and the small smile that pops up immediately eases my nerves. "That's pretty good, Tiger."

Fuck…that nickname…I wasn't expecting that. Is he still going to call me that? How am I supposed to "get over Florida" if I'm constantly reminded? Add that to the list of things I'm going to learn to either forget, or not think about, when it comes to Emmett.

"Yeah, I'm sure it'll go down in Carter, Banks, and Fairchild history as one of the more entertaining days in the office."

"So let me guess," Emmett says as he sits in the chair that will eventually be mine. "Simon swooped in to save the day by offering you a job. And because he's always one for a big reveal, decided to not tell me and make it a surprise?"

"Pretty much. He was also crying about how much work it was when you were gone. Me coming on board felt like the right move." I lean against my desk, which puts me inches away from Emmett. His cologne engulfs me in the best way. God, I've missed his smell.

No, Stella. Don't. Stop. Stop it right now!

Between the nickname and the smells and the beard and the body…I'm in so much trouble. Which is horrible, because Emmett is technically my boss. I'm here to make their lives easier. That's a boss in my book. Granted, I've only had one boss in my life. And they weren't six-foot-four with sexy scruff that you feel hours after it touches you. They didn't have eyes that could see every part of you. And they definitely didn't ruin you for all other men in the sex department.

This is going to be the absolute worst.

I pull myself quickly together to finish catching Emmett up. "I went to my parents, knowing that I was likely going to need a lawyer. Between the suit he filed, the one I plan on counter filing, and maybe now one for my outburst, I figured a good thing to do was go talk to Dad.

Anyway, that talk turned into a family meeting with Simon, Charlie, my parents, and all my sisters involved. They even Face-Time'd Quinn in Arizona. Before I knew it, Ainsley was adding me to the lease on the apartment, my dad was dusting off his laptop to file motions, and Simon was offering me a job with Magnolia Properties. I'm sorry, Emmett. I really wanted to tell you, I—"

He shakes his head and gently touches my leg. I know he's not meaning it in an intimate way, but don't tell that to my body. "I know you did. And I'm sorry for snapping. I was just caught off guard. And I'm sorry you had to quit. I know you loved your job."

"I did, but it's what I had to do. I was delusional, thinking that I could go back there and just take a couple of days of ridicule and stares before everything went back to normal."

"I don't know if you were delusional," he says. "Let's go with wildly optimistic."

That makes me smile. "Sure, let's go with that."

I look up and do a Simon check, and we're still in the clear. His feet are kicked up on his desk, cell phone on his desk on speaker mode. He looks like he could talk for hours.

"So," I begin. "How do you want to navigate this?"

Emmett leans forward, hanging his head and resting his elbows on his knees. I internally yell at myself for missing his touch when he pulls back. "I'm usually not a fan of elaborate lies and secrets—I motherfucked Simon when he pulled what he did with Charlie—but I think that's our best play."

"I agree," I say. At least, my head agrees. My body doesn't, but it'll just have to catch up. "And nothing is going to happen with us again, so there's no sense in telling him about Florida."

"Exactly. We're two adults. We can be in a room together and not tear each other's clothes off."

Speak for yourself, Cap…

"Plus, I'm only in the office a few days a week," he continues. "We can behave and not be weird about what we shared."

"Weird about what?"

Emmett and I both jump at the sound of Simon's voice as he walks back toward us.

"Oh nothing," I say, though I can tell my tone is oozing with suspicion. Adding to the suspicion is Emmett looking everywhere but at Simon. "Just weird that as of a few weeks ago we'd never met and now we're coworkers."

I don't know where that came from but I want to pat myself on the back.

"Crazy how things work," Simon says. "I have a good feeling about this. Like it was all meant to happen."

Simon gives Emmett a pat on the back and me a kiss on the cheek before exiting the building, I'm assuming to go next door and drive Charlie crazy at the diner.

"We can do this," I say. "We've got this completely under control."

"Completely under control."

I move to sit at my desk, only to run into Emmett, who's trying to walk away. I don't know where he was going, but now we're just standing here. Staring. His chocolate brown eyes are burning into me. Our bodies are touching, and I'm pretty sure I'm feeling something else, though I could be imagining it. Or hoping. Not sure which one.

I bite my lip out of habit, needing something to keep me from jumping into his arms and kissing the hell out of him. His breathing is picking up, and I bet if I look down at his fists, they're clenched.

I don't know if makes me feel better or worse that he's struggling with this just as much as I am.

But one thing I do know—this is going to be hard as hell. And I'm not just talking about Emmett's dick, which I'm definitely not imagining.

"I need you to walk away, Stella," he says in his low, growly tone.

If he wants me to leave then he needs to stop using his sex voice. "Why?"

"Because if you don't, then I'm going to toss you on this desk and fuck you for anyone walking by to see. And I'm not going to regret it one fucking bit."

Oh…well then…

Swallowing the rather large lump that suddenly appeared in my throat, I do as Emmett asked and walk toward the back of the office. My feet pick up speed as I end up racing into the bathroom and slam the door shut.

"Dammit, Stella…" I say to myself as I lean against the door, suddenly struggling to catch my breath. "What are you going to do?"

———

"To fucking your cabana boy boss!"

I shush Andi at her fake toast. I don't know anyone here—that I know of—but the way she puts it makes it seem very strange.

"He was never the cabana boy," I say as I play with the stem of my martini glass. "He was…Cap."

I don't know how else to describe him to her, and I know my use of his nickname doesn't help that. I've tried and failed a few times to truly talk about what Emmett did for me in Florida during this emergency girls' night. Maybe a few more martinis will help.

Normally Andi and I meet on Thursdays for drinks. It's our tradition since the first week we worked together at the law firm. But this problem? It couldn't wait another minute.

She's now caught up on Florida. Our vacation fling pact. Our now work relationship.

I did though leave out the threat—or was it a promise—he made today about bending me over the desk. I liked that one more than I care to admit.

"Stella, I'm going to ask you a question, and I want you to know there is no wrong answer."

I lift an eyebrow to Andi. "This sounds like a question where there's actually many wrong answers."

"No. I just need to see where your head's at before I proceed with any advice."

"Go on," I say before taking a healthy sip of my lemon drop martini.

"Do you have feelings for him?"

And I nearly spit out that drink. "What? That's absurd. I don't have feelings for Emmett."

Either my voice got too high or Andi knows me too well, because she's clearly not buying it.

"Is it? He got you through the hardest day of your life. You shared a lot with him, in many ways, while you were in Florida. And the way you just said his name? A nickname, might I add… it just seems like you have feelings for him. Real ones. Not ones you think you have because of orgasms."

I could keep protesting, but it's pointless. "I mean, yes, I have some feelings. He's a friend. A very good friend."

"A very naked friend."

"Then. He was a naked friend then," I correct. "Did we have sex? Yes. Did he eat ice cream off my body? Yes. Did his dick make me speak in tongues? Yes. But do I have romantic feelings for him? No. I do not."

"Okay, when we're done with this conversation, we're going to revisit the ice cream thing," Andi says, turning my barstool so I'm now facing her. "Feelings aren't bad, Stella. You're allowed to have feelings for a person."

"But I don't," I protest. "Not like that. Emmett is my friend. Yes, we shared a lot, and I have affection for him. I think that's normal. But I'm not in any place to be in a relationship, let alone have feelings for a man. Just a few weeks ago I was supposed to get married. I'm not in any place to be having any sort of feelings that are more than friendship. Plus, Emmett is very anti relationship. He made that abundantly clear. So even if I did, which I don't, they wouldn't be returned. So, the answer to your question is, no, I don't have feelings for Emmett. And I won't. I just need to figure out how to forget how he looks naked while I'm at the office."

"Okay then," Andi says, though I can tell from her tone she clearly doesn't believe me. "I just want you to know, it's okay if you do. Finding your person isn't on a timeline. It happens when you're meant to. It's not a check box on a to-do list. Feelings, real feelings, for that person who was meant for you? Sometimes it happens when you aren't expecting it. So if you did feel that way for Emmett, just promise me you won't ignore them or push them to the side. Don't reject them because others are saying it's too soon. When it's right, it's right. Fuck a clock."

She's right. In theory. Except I don't feel like that toward Emmett so it doesn't matter.

"But as for you and Emmett, if you really are just friends, then you're going to need to quickly forget about the ice cream and the penis and remember that you work for him. He's a very close friend to your brother. And if he's not a relationship guy, then it should be no problem pushing any gray-area feelings to the side. Right?"

"Right," I agree, though the word leaves a bitter taste in my mouth.

Which is silly, because I don't have feelings like that for Emmett.

Keep saying it, Stella…the more you say it, the more in denial you can live.

23

emmett

"WHAT ARE YOU DOING HERE?"

Simon looks perplexed as I enter the office from the back door, which leads into the hallway between our two offices.

"Working?"

He makes a show of checking his watch as he meets me in the hallway. "But it's Wednesday."

"Yeah? So?"

"You don't come here on Wednesdays."

Dammit, I hoped he wouldn't realize that…

"Sometimes I come in on Wednesdays."

"No, you don't," he says confidently. "Wednesdays are Nashville days. I know because you never come to Rolling Hills two days in a row. And you were here yesterday. And you've made a point of telling me numerous times that Rolling Hills day is Tuesday."

Since when is Simon so perceptive? Or remembering what day of the week it is?

"Yes, I was," I say, trying to not sound defensive in my response. "But you said it yourself, I need to be in here more now if we're going to really start going full throttle. So here I am."

Don't you just love it when you can hide your motives behind the truth? Because, yes, Simon did say I need to be here more. And I should be here more if we're really going to grow Magnolia Properties beyond our wildest dreams. But I'd be a bold-faced liar if I didn't say a little part of me was coming in here to see Stella.

The woman got under my skin, and I don't know if there's a way to get her out. Especially now that I'm going to be seeing her regularly.

I didn't see her after I told her to walk away yesterday. Once she was out of sight, I made a beeline to my truck and white-knuckled my drive back to Nashville. Was I going ninety miles an hour? Maybe. I'm not sure. I just knew I had to get the hell out of there before I did something stupid.

Like kiss her.

God, I wanted to fucking kiss her. I wanted to prop her up on that desk and run my hands through her hair before pulling her into me. I wanted her legs to wrap around me like they always do. I wanted to feel her smooth skin in my hands.

The second I got home, I took the coldest shower I've ever taken. And I'm not proud that it only took a few strokes, accompanied by thoughts of Stella in her fitted green dress today, to make me come harder than I have since—since I last fucked her.

So was coming in here today stupid? Probably. But, between the cold shower and the restless night, I came up with a plan.

Desensitizing.

The only way to get used to something is to have it around you all the time. It made sense at three in the morning with Winnie snoring at the foot of my bed. And it made pretty good sense as I went over my plan while driving down here this morning. My theory is, the more I see Stella, the more desensitized I'll get. Pretty soon her scent won't make me instantly hard. After a while her smile won't knock me on my ass. And eventually, Stella Banks will be nothing more than the woman I work with.

It will be the perfect plan.

Emphasis on will.

Because I know I'm not there yet. It's why I used the back door instead of coming in the front, where she'd be the first thing I saw. It's why I'm not going out of my way to say hello to her. It's why I want Simon to stop talking so I can lock myself in my office for the rest of the day. In my mind, I'm seeing her, so the desensitizing process is starting, but I'm not jumping in to the deep end quite yet.

"Well, great," he says. "How about you get settled in and then the three of us will meet. I know we chatted a little yesterday, but we should all sit down and go over expectations, what we're going to be doing, and how we can all work together to make this a well-oiled machine."

"Sounds good."

The words are gritty as I shut the door so I can take a few deep breaths. I knew I wasn't going to be able to go all day without interacting with her. She works a hundred feet from me, and the walls are glass. I had just hoped to get through another cup of coffee first.

Yes! Coffee. That's what I need. A cup of Charlie's coffee—that I think has some sort of illegal substance in it—is just what I need. I don't know what it will help with, but is coffee ever the wrong answer?

I drop my laptop bag and head out the back door again without saying a word to Simon. Luckily, Charlie doesn't mind if I use the back door to the diner, which allows me to slip in quickly and snake my way to the front counter.

"Well look who it is," Charlie says. "Two days in a row. I never thought I'd see the day."

Does everyone know I don't come here two days in a row? "There isn't coffee like this in Nashville."

"Sure, that's what it is," she says sarcastically. "Large black coffee?"

"You know it." I pause for a second as I take a look at the

pastry case. It changes every day, and honestly, I've never paid attention. But today a cake pop that's listed as birthday cake flavor is staring me dead in the eyes.

Goddamn it…

"And a cake pop. The birthday cake flavor."

Charlie raises an eyebrow before she gets it for me. "I've never taken you for a cake pop man, Emmett Collins."

"It just looks good," I say quickly as I reach for my wallet. Charlie doesn't let me pay, but I always make sure to leave a hefty tip.

"Would you like a complicated iced latte to go with it? Maybe vanilla flavored?"

I know for a fact that's what Stella ordered one day in Florida. But I can't let Charlie know that I know that—even if she does have a mischievous twinkle in her eyes.

"Does Simon like that?" I say, trying to throw her off the scent.

She laughs. "He does, but he's already had his fix for the morning. But I'm sure your new coworker would love it. It's her go-to."

"Yeah. Sure," I try to say nonchalantly. I can tell that neither of us are buying it. "What are you making her, if you don't mind me asking?"

Charlie starts making the iced concoction with a huge smile on her face. "Iced vanilla latte with caramel drizzle, oat milk, sweet cream cold foam, and cinnamon on top."

That's not hard. I should be able to remember it.

You know, in case I have to make coffee runs in the future.

Wait. No. What the fuck am I doing? It's like my mind and body are being controlled by two different masters. My mind is still listening to me. My body and actions, though? Those clearly belong to Stella Banks.

I don't know what I'm doing. This isn't like me. The me I was before Florida would never just buy a woman a cake pop and coffee because it reminded me of them. Hell, I'd never know their preferences to even attempt such a thing. And my head knows this and is begging me to get back to my old self. It keeps telling my body over and over again that I need to have minimal contact with Stella and any I do have should all be under the context of work.

But every other part of me? Those all split off and are doing things like getting her a coffee and a sweet treat. And saying things like sweet treat. And fantasizing about fucking her in the office for anyone walking by to see.

Who am I? This isn't me. I'm not the guy who does nice things just because. That's dating shit. And I'm not the guy who has uncontrollable sexual urges and fantasies.

I need to get a grip. Right the fuck now.

"Can I ask a question?"

I raise an eyebrow as Charlie comes back over with an armful of drinks. Apparently she threw one in for Simon too. "Sure."

"Does Simon know?"

Fuck…how does she know? Apparently I'm a worse actress than Tiger.

I shake my head. I don't know what she knows, but I need to make sure I shut this down right now. "No. And there's nothing *to* know."

That makes her chuckle. "Whatever you say."

Fuck me.

"Here," Charlie says as she hands me a tray of drinks with three cups in it, and two bags that are way heavier than just a cake pop. "Take these. I made a drink for Simon to make whatever this is less obvious. And he's easily distracted by muffins."

"Thanks," I say softly as I quickly make my way out the door. I'm so focused on getting out of there that I don't even think about exiting the diner then entering the office through the front doors. I swear under my breath, but then quickly notice Stella's not at her desk.

I walk in and look around, finding her and Simon standing in one of the conference rooms. Her smile is shining through her laughter as Simon tells her something that's clearly cracking her up.

How does she keep getting more stunning every time I see her? Her blonde hair is in waves around her shoulders. She's wearing a sleeveless baby blue blouse that's showing off her toned arms. And then there's the pencil skirt and heels that are making me think things that are not at all appropriate for an office.

I know my thought was that I need to get desensitized to Stella. But if this is what she wears to the office, then I don't know if that will ever happen. My aching cock surely doesn't think so.

I take a deep breath, think about baseball stats, and crack my neck before walking into the conference room. I quickly set down the tray of drinks and bags of pastries before taking a seat at the chair furthest from Stella.

"What do we have here?" Simon asks as he starts digging into the bags.

"I needed coffee, so I figured I'd grab a pick-me-up for every-one," I say. Just as I'm about to continue, I see Simon take the cake pop out of the bag. "Actually, that's for Stella."

Her eyes go wide when she hears her name. "For me?"

I shrug as nonchalantly as I can. "Yeah. I thought you'd like it. It's birthday cake flavor."

Her face blushes as the recognition hits her. Fuck, I forgot how much I loved making her blush. Usually it was from things I said or ways I was making her feel. But doing it in this completely nonsexual way? Somehow that feels better than any of the other times.

"Thanks," she mouths as Simon starts yapping about the history of Magnolia Properties. I send her a wink, which only makes her smile bigger.

Winks? Cake pops? Coffee? What the fuck am I doing? Stop it! Right the fuck now!

I hear my brain saying all these things. I know they are all wrong.

So why can't I stop doing them? And why do I want to make sure she smiles like that every day?

And why do I hate myself for thinking that?

————

Today has been a great day.

The sun is shining. The weather is starting to cool slightly, which means that football season—also known as fall—is just around the corner. Not even the phone call I got from my mom asking me when would be a good time to meet husband number eight can ruin my day.

Why is that? Because I don't have to go to Rolling Hills today.

Nope. Today has been an all-Nashville day. Which has meant it's been a Stella-free day.

Well, mostly. I did wake up at five in the morning after a dream where I hiked up that sinful pencil skirt she wore yesterday and fucked her at my desk. Not able to go back to sleep after that, I got up, got in a workout, took a cold shower—because that's apparently all I do these days—and started my day early.

I'm three cups of coffee in, and my stops this morning have been productive and trouble free. I have one more site to check on before I can head home to do some office work. If I keep this pace up, I'll clock out around three today. Maybe go see Maddie and Jack. I could take Winnie over and we could head to the dog park. Or maybe I could head to a bar, grab a burger, and watch a game. Though the last time I did that, I met a woman who has plagued my thoughts ever since.

Nope! Not thinking of Stella. Dog park with the sister and nephew it is.

Just as I'm sending a text to Maddie, seeing if she and Jack are free this afternoon, a text from Simon comes through.

SIMON

Where you at?

EMMETT

Nashville. I told you I wasn't coming in today.

SIMON

I know that. I meant where are you going to be in roughly an hour?

I check the clock and see that it's noon. So in an hour, I'll just be wrapped up with my final stop and be hopefully back home, eating a sandwich, before I spend the rest of the day at my computer.

EMMETT

Should be at my house. Why? What's up?

SIMON

A few contracts and permits came in today that I need your signature on. I know you weren't planning on coming back into Rolling Hills until next week, but I really want to get these processed first thing tomorrow. I'm going to send Stella out to your house and get your signature on them.

Fuck my fucking life…

Today was supposed to be my Stella-free day. And not only is she coming over, but she's going to be in my house?

This is bad. So fucking bad. But I can't tell Simon not to send her, that will raise too many questions. And I know if I volunteer to drive to Rolling Hills, he'll tell me to not worry about it and that this is part of her job, to make our lives easier.

EMMETT

10-4.

An hour later I'm sitting outside on my front porch, Winnie at my feet, as a white small SUV pulls into my driveway. How is she seeing over the steering wheel? I see her straining her neck as she puts the car in park, which makes me chuckle for some reason.

I stand up, not wanting to be rude even if I do plan on being as brief as possible, as Winnie takes off toward her. I call out for her to settle down, but it's no use. My golden retriever is jumping on Stella like she's her new best friend and is here to play.

"Well look at you," I hear Stella coo as I make my way to the driveway. Her laugh is filling the air as Winnie tries to lick her. "You're just the most beautiful girl in the world."

I heard Maddie say one time that seeing a man with a kid was kryptonite, especially to her as a single mom. I thought she was insane. But I get it now. Seeing this woman—who I know biblically and is literally keeping me up at night—playing and loving on my dog? It's enough to do me in.

I won't let it. But it would be enough, especially when my traitorous imagination allows in a picture of me and Stella waking up naked with Winnie pouncing on us in the morning.

The fact that I'm now fantasizing about domestic things is serious cause for concern.

"Winnie, get down, girl," I say as I gently pull her away from Stella. "Sorry about that."

"No problem," she says as she stands up, smoothing down her blouse in the process. Today's blouse is different. A white silk number with short sleeves that she has tucked into a pair of pants that accentuate her legs. She's wearing heels, as always, and if I'm remembering right they are the ones she bought while we were in Florida.

God, I really am done for if I'm remembering fucking shoes…

"Sorry Simon made you drive out here," I say, not making any motion to lead her into the house. I know it's rude, but her in my house is a dangerous, dangerous thing.

Stella reaches into her oversized purse and pulls out a folder. "It's no problem. He's letting me take off early so I don't have to drive back. I should be thanking you."

"Anytime." I take the papers from her and walk to the hood of her car, where I proceed to sign them. I hear Winnie slowly walk back to Stella, who I watch out of the corner of my eye lean down to pet her. I don't attempt to make any sort of conversation and neither does she. Is it awkward? Yes. But is it needed to survive the two of us being alone? Hell, yes.

"Here you go," I say as I shut the folder. "Easy enough."

"Easy enough." She takes the folder from me and starts walking to the car door, before stopping and turning on her heel. "Can I ask you a question that you can say no to?"

No…

"Sure."

"Can I use your restroom? I drank an extra-large Diet Dr Pepper on the way here and—"

I laugh, because of course she did. "Inside. First door on the right down the hall."

Stella does the best she can at walking fast, but not running, inside. I walk behind her, because I'm pretty sure she's going to bite it in those heels.

I also need to be behind her so she doesn't see me physically needing to calm down at the thought of her keeping those heels on…and only those heels.

When I hear the door close to the bathroom, I let out a deep breath and pull at my hair. I need to get a hold of myself. I'm not a fucking teenager who has his first crush. Why can't I keep my brain from going places it shouldn't go? Why can't my dick be under control around her? Why do I want to invite her to stay for dinner? Why? Just…why?

I stop pacing when I hear the door open and Stella's heels hitting the hardwood as she comes back down the hall.

"Thanks," she says shyly. "I'll be going."

"Yeah." The word comes out awkwardly as I open the door.

But just as Stella starts to walk out, Winnie runs in front, stopping her exit.

That's it. No treats or dog park for her tonight.

Stella's close. Too close. I could just lean in and take her lips that I want to kiss so fucking bad. I could hold out my arm and wrap it around her waist, bringing her into me where I could feel her soft curves against me. I could just give Winnie a little kick out of the way and pick her up like I want to, because it's been way too long since I've felt her legs wrapped around me. I'd press her against the door and take her right here.

God-fucking-damn-it, I need this woman out of my house before I go doing things that I swore I'd never do.

Like ask her to stay.

"I'll see you next week," I say with a gruffness to my tone, which I can tell she picks up on.

"Yeah. Sure. See you next week."

She gives me a small smile and a shy wave as she moves around Winnie and heads to her car. Her head is down. She never looks back.

Fuck…I hate that I made her shrink into herself like that. That's the shit Duncan did. I never want to be that man. Ever. Being that man, or that type of man, leads to Stella reverting back to the unsure woman who came to Florida. And that's not the kind of man I want to be.

The only problem is I don't know how to stay away from her without ignoring her. I'm clearly not strong enough to be friendly with her. At least not right now. Maybe over time, but for the immediate future, I think it's best if I keep my distance. Keep my Rolling Hills days to the bare minimum. It's the safest plan to make sure I don't do stupid things like act like an ass again.

Or kiss her.

Or worse, make her mine and never let her go.

guide to love rule #95

Don't settle. Ever.
(Even if he's hot and has made you
pray to gods you don't believe in).

24
stella

I'll never be able to thank Simon enough for giving me a job at Magnolia Properties. And while it's not as busy, or as intense, as my job at the law firm was, it does have much better perks.

One, I'm next door to my favorite diner, owned by my eventual sister-in-law, who makes me the best vanilla lattes I've ever had. Two, the days are usually calm enough that I can listen to an audiobook while doing my work. Who doesn't like to listen to fairy smut while looking at real estate listings? Third, some days my duties include watching my niece and getting baby snuggles.

Those days, like the one today, are the best.

When I showed up to the office this morning, Simon looked frantic. And that's saying something, because my brother's average speed is seventy miles per hour. He was wearing a baby sling with Lainey strapped in as he paced back and forth around his office, yelling to someone over speakerphone. I don't know what it says about my brother, or my niece, that she wasn't fazed by this in the least. She had a toy in her hand, and that's all she needed. She was the definition of unbothered.

Now my brother? He's always bothered about something. Today it was why the city was dragging its feet on permits that he needed to renovate a building he bought a few months back.

When I asked him how I could help, he unstrapped Lainey from his chest and handed her to me. Apparently in his rush to get out of the house today, he left her diaper bag and all her bottles at the house. So I did what any good office administrator and aunt would do—I stole my brother's keys, forwarded the office phone to my cell, and took my niece for a day of Aunt Stella time.

Which includes story time before her nap.

"So then, *she* tried to propose to *him*, and everyone thought he was going to say yes," I say to Lainey as I give her a bottle. "Only it turns out that he broke up with her before the reunion show. Can you believe it! And he was never good enough for her. No he wasn't…not at all…"

I say the last part in my best baby voice as Lainey's eyes start to get heavy. Apparently my retelling of reality television is the trick for her to go to sleep. I quickly burp her before wiping her mouth and laying her down in her crib.

"You're such a good baby," I whisper, kissing my fingertips before gently placing it on her forehead. "Nothing like your daddy."

I stand over it for a few seconds, peacefully watching her sleep before slipping out. Since it was bottle and naptime as soon as we got here, I haven't checked my phone or emails since arriving at Simon and Charlie's. I grab my purse with my phone and laptop, bringing both to life as I take a seat on their over-sized, and quite comfortable, sectional. I haven't missed any calls, but I'm pretty sure there are a handful of emails I should get to sooner rather than later.

A few querying houses we're renting. One from a charity asking Simon to donate.

And one from Emmett.

I know there are more to scan, and probably more in order of importance, but I click on his immediately.

Stella,

Please handle this for me.

Emmett

Wow. So personal. I feel the warmth oozing from every letter he typed.

Then again, that's the most I've heard from him in a week so maybe I should take that as a good sign?

I want to scream at the top of my lungs, but I don't because of Lainey. So instead I toss my laptop to the side and sink into the couch, covering my face with a pillow so I can scream into it.

It's been a week since I left Emmett's house with a folder of signed contracts. Did I know things were weird then? Yes. But I didn't want to press anything. This whole thing has been weird and frankly, I don't know any scenario where I know how the hell to act.

Apparently he's choosing to act with minimal seeing or speaking.

Which is fine. It doesn't bother me at all. I'm sure many office assistants don't talk to their bosses regularly. Or said bosses don't often get them coffees or sweet treats.

This is what we said we needed. A professional, business relationship. No nicknames. No flirting. No talk of him fucking me on my desk.

Though every time I sit at it I remember what he said that first day, and I can't get the image out of my head.

I didn't realize he was giving me the no-contact treatment until he missed his normal Tuesday Rolling Hills visit. He told Simon he needed to handle something urgent in Nashville. Simon seemed to buy it.

I didn't.

Emmett is a man of routine. He likes order, normalcy, and everything in a box. His idea of crazy is actually going to the beach. Him not coming to Rolling Hills was on purpose.

Because he didn't want to see me.

I scream into the pillow one more time for good measure when I feel a dip on the couch next to me.

"Hey, Charlie," I say as I take the pillow off my face. "What's up?"

"I should be asking you that. Was my child so bad you had to yell into a pillow for relief?"

I shake my head and bring the pillow down to my stomach, holding it over me like a shield of some sort. "My niece is an angel. Well done making sure she got as little of Simon's temperament as possible."

"I love that man with all my heart, but I agree. I can barely handle him, let alone him in small child form," Charlie jokes.

Charlie is a true saint for putting up with my brother. And yes, Lainey might have been an unexpected surprise, but she's truly the best parts of both of them, and I can't wait to see how their family grows over the years.

"So, what has you yelling into a pillow on a Wednesday?" Charlie asks.

I start to say something, but quickly close my mouth. What do I tell her? I can't tell her about Emmett. I don't want her having to keep things from Simon. Also, and I don't think she would judge me, but I *did* sleep with a man I'd known for less than a week as a vacation-slash-rebound fling.

"Oh, you know…things," I say. "Duncan. The lawsuit that he's still insisting on filing. The fact that I still have to go to his place and get my things, which hopefully I'll be able to do tomorrow. You know…all that kind of stuff."

Charlie pats me on the leg. "It's not that I don't believe you. I think those things are happening and weighing on your mind. But right now, in this moment, Stella Banks, you are full of shit."

I let out an audible gasp. Did she really see through that? Damn, Emmett was right. I *am* a really shitty actress.

"I don't know what you mean."

Charlie gives me the head tilt along with the raised eyebrow. "We can play this any way you want. We can live in your world of denial that this is only about Duncan. You can tell me what's happening while using hypotheticals and fake names. Or, you can tell me what's going on with you and Emmett that's making you scream into upholstery and making our stoic friend one day buy cake pops then proceed to drop off the face of the earth."

Damn, she's good.

"I don't want to put you in a weird situation," I say. "Simon doesn't know anything and we'd both like to keep it that way."

Charlie nods. "I'm an amazing secret keeper. Plus, this can be payback for him not telling me he owned my restaurant for the first six months."

I still can't believe my brother did that.

"Are you sure?"

"Yes, I'm sure," Charlie says. "If I'm going to have to not react to him buying you lattes, I'd at least like to know what I'm getting into."

I relax into the couch as I tell her everything. Well, not everything. She doesn't need to know about my now deeper love for ice cream.

But I do tell her about meeting him after I ran out of the wedding. And us showing up in Florida. And how when things escalated we made it clear that this was only to be in Florida. That when we got back to Nashville, we'd go our separate ways.

"Except your ways have you now working together."

"Exactly," I say. "We figured we could hold it together if we saw each other a few times a year. But every day? With Simon usually in the room? It hasn't been as easy. It doesn't help matters that Emmett is giving me whiplash. Like you said, one day he's sweet and buying me coffee and the next it's the cold shoulder. I just want to know which way is up."

"As you should," she says. "Can I ask a dumb question?"

"There are no such things as dumb questions," I say. "Just sometimes dumb people. Which you are not."

That makes her laugh. "Why did you two draw the line in the sand? I can understand if you thought it was going to be just a vacation fling. Fine. But clearly you are both attracted to each other. Is it just because of Simon that you're not seeing if there's something really there?"

I shake my head. "Simon is part of it, but not the majority. I'm not in a place to be in a relationship. I mean, I should be writing out thank you notes right now. And for Emmett, he was very clear that he's not a relationship guy. Between those two factors, we thought it made for a perfect, and temporary, situation."

"Nothing's ever perfect."

I let out a quick laugh. "You're telling me."

Though there were moments in Florida when I thought it was perfect. Now I'm wondering if it was just the timing and the excitement or if it truly was.

"I haven't known Emmett for long," Charlie says. "But I've known him long enough that I think I can read him. Until last week, the man was one of schedule and routine. Consistency. Ordered the same thing all the time because he isn't one to rock the boat."

"Oh I know," I say. "Though he does get a little crazy and mix pasta sauces."

"Interesting. I didn't think he had it in him."

I don't even try to hide the smile I know is on my face when thinking back to that first night in Florida. Who would've thought Mr. Don't Rock the Boat would be the one to push me to try something new?

"And I haven't known you for that long," Charlie continues. "But in the time I have, and a majority of that was you being engaged to Duncan, I've never seen you smile like you just did. And it was over marinara sauce. I can't imagine what you'd look like if you told me about the time you spent together in Destin."

I fall back into the sofa, now feeling more defeated. "I don't know what to do, Charlie. I'm never getting back with Duncan, but it feels like it's too soon to be even thinking about being with someone else. But on the other hand, he's all I think about, and I'm going a little crazy. And then there's the major flashing sign that he doesn't want this. He's been adamant about that. With me or anyone. And I do want it. I want it all."

I look down the hallway toward Lainey's nursery. "I want

babies. I want marriage. I want a family. I might have wanted it before because of me feeling like I was missing out on what other's had, but deep down, that's what I want in the long run. And I'm not going to be with a man who doesn't want what I do."

"Good," Charlie says. "You shouldn't settle. You should have everything you want. And if that's a family with a husband, a few kids, and a dog running around, then that's what you should have."

I feel the tears start pooling in my eyes as I think of Winnie jumping on me.

"I wish he could see what I do," I say. "He'd be the best partner."

"I mean, he got you a cake pop just because," Charlie says.

I laugh. "He's all about the little things. Small gestures. And he's quiet, but will say what he needs to when he wants to. And did you know he's a history nerd? And that he built his house with his own hands? You should see it, Charlie. High ceilings. Beautiful hardwood. And his dog, oh my gosh! Winnie is just the most beautiful golden retriever. Oh! And did you know…"

I trail off because at some point during my ramble Charlie's smile is now ear to ear.

"What?"

"You love him."

Well, that's absurd. Feelings? Sure. Love? Ha. She's hilarious.

"No, I don't."

"Yes, you do."

"Charlie, do I like him? Yes. Did he help me in the hardest part of my life? Yes, I couldn't have done it without him. Is it weird transitioning from what we were to apparently what we're being? Yes. But I'm not in…"

I trail off, because fuck. She's right.

I accidentally fell in love with Emmett Collins when I gave myself clear instructions not to.

"Oh no," I say, falling directly into her lap as I start crying. "How did this happen?"

"I'm not sure," she says as she strokes my hair. "But I'm sure orgasms have something to do with it."

I laugh through the tears. "This is so bad, Charlie."

"I know," she says. "But don't change who you are, or what you want, because of him. I know you did that before, and I don't want you falling back in those old ways. You're Stella Banks, and you deserve everything you want. And a person who wants those for you. Nothing less will do."

She's right. I do deserve that. I lost sight of that with Duncan, and like hell I'm ever going back.

Do I wish Emmett would want that too? Sure. More than anything.

But if he doesn't, I'll get over it. I have to. Because I'm not settling. I'm not compromising on things I want more than anything.

Even for the man I love.

25

emmett

"UNCLE MET!"

I kneel down as my nephew comes running into my arms. "Hey, buddy."

Jack plows into my body and wraps his tiny three-year-old arms around my neck, squeezing me as hard as he can. Winnie starts jumping next to me, clearly wanting in on the moment. And I hug him back. I squeeze his little body, and for the first time in what feels like forever, I relax.

This is exactly what I needed. I've been in a funk ever since Stella came to my house last week. I ended up texting Maddie and canceling our plans. Hell, I've barely left my house except for absolutely necessary site visits. I made a horrible excuse to get out of going to Rolling Hills this week. I thought a few days away would make me feel better, but it hasn't. Now I'm behind at work, and I feel like a fucking schmuck.

I need to suck it up. I need to get over these feelings and get back to normal. That's what I've been telling myself for days now. That I'm a grown man and I should be able to turn the switch off. Or at least, stick to a strategy.

Desensitizing is going to take forever to work, if it even does. Being a dick just made me feel like, well, a dick. Avoidance has been my strategy recently, but that's failing on multiple levels. Plus, she doesn't deserve my cold shoulder. I'm the one in the wrong. I got too close when I had no business doing so. And I'm taking it out on her. I don't want to quit my job, but that might be safer for my sanity than seeing her every day.

Because if I see her every day it might drive me mad. I'm starting to think there's no getting over Stella Banks.

"How's my favorite kiddo?" I ask Jack as Winnie continues to run around us.

"Good," he says. "I brought a ball!"

"That's fun," I say as he shows me the foam football he's holding. "Where did you get that?"

"Brock," he says, like I'm supposed to know. Before I can ask any more questions, Jack throws the football, well, as far as he can, and Winnie promptly goes to chase it. The two start playing as Maddie walks up, taking a seat with me on the bench at the dog park.

"Who's Brock?" I ask.

"My neighbor," she says. "Or as Jack likes to say, his new best friend."

"Does this new best friend have a last name?" I ask. Because if there's a man living next to my sister, who is giving my nephew toys, I need to check this guy out.

She lets out a sigh before answering. "Napier."

Did she just say…"Brock Napier? As in pro football player for the Nashville Fury Brock Napier?"

"The one and only," she says. "But before you go all big brother on me, we're just friends. Jack thinks he's cool and likes his cats. That's it."

"That's it?"

"Cross my heart," she says, making the same motion. "Believe me, I doubt a pro football player is just jonesing to get with the single mom next door."

"Why not?" I ask. "He'd be fucking lucky."

Now it's her turn to give me the raised eyebrow look.

"What?"

"It's just funny."

"What's funny?"

"That just the mention of a guy on my radar—who's not even on my radar—and you quickly say how lucky he'd be to have me. Yet, when I say the same thing but about you, that any woman would be lucky to call you theirs, I'm met with a look meant to terrify. Oh! Like that one! That look right there.."

I don't know at what age I stopped being able to rattle Maddie. I think it was when she was two.

"And! Since we're on the subject," she continues. "Do you want to tell me why you canceled on our park date last week?"

"No reason," I say, making sure not to make eye contact with her, instead focusing on Jack and Winnie playing in front of us.

"Interesting. You know. You've been a little weird since you got back from your vacation. You know, the vacation where you had a date that I've still not heard about."

I groan, but that's the only follow up I make to her statements. I know she's going to keep going, and I'm going to let her. But I'm not going to add fuel to her fire.

"You might ask, 'how have I acted weird?' Great question, I'd love to tell you! For starters, your already short and sweet text messages are even shorter than normal. When Jack FaceTimed you the other night, you looked stressed. And, the biggest signal of them all, I heard you agreed to go to dinner with Mom and Gary. You never do that without two weeks of a fight."

"His name's Larry," I correct.

"And you know his name! You're not calling him by a nickname. Something is definitely up."

I hate that she knows all of this. Sure my texts have been short. I felt myself being cold to Jack the other night. As for Mom? That one was just because I'm too tired to fight.

Before she can add on to my list of offenses, I'm saved by my nephew, who comes running over to me and jumps on my lap.

"What's up, buddy?"

"Water please," he says, reaching over to Maddie for his water bottle.

I take Jack's distraction and let myself cuddle him for a second. He still asks to sit on my lap, which I know won't last for too much longer, so I take it in when I can.

I remember when Maddie told me she was pregnant. She was young, scared, and alone after the sperm donor took off after she told him. From that moment, I knew what I needed to do. Step up. Be who she needed me to be. Do whatever I could for her and Jack. Whether that's a babysitter, someone to teach him to eventually throw a baseball, or just to show him what a man should be, I was ready. Being Uncle Met has been the best thing that's happened to me.

"I know you're going to yell at me, but I'm okay with it; you know you'd be a great father."

I huff out a laugh as Jack climbs off me and heads back to playing with Winnie. "Sure. Because I know *so* much about being a father."

Maddie turns toward me on the bench. "Do you think any of us know what it's like to be parents before we have a kid? News-flash: No other parents, books, or Mom hack videos can prepare you for having a child. Do you think I knew what the fuck I was doing when I found out I was pregnant, just because I techni-cally had a mother growing up? I didn't. If I were to write an autobiography of my parenting, it would be called 'You Grew Up with Rhonda: Here's How You Do the Opposite.'"

I laugh, because she's right. Don't get me wrong, we never went without a roof over our heads or food on the table. But how did those things get paid for? That we still don't know, and frankly, I don't ever want to know.

"That's fair," I say. Normally, I'd end this conversation with silence. And I don't know why I don't, but yet again my actions are going rogue from my rational brain. "Do you think I'm like them?"

This catches her off guard. "Like who?"

"Mom. My dad. Am I like them?"

Maddie doesn't answer right away. Which I appreciate. Because she could easily just say "of course not!" and move on.

"I can't speak for your dad, because I never met him," she says. "As for Mom? A little. But in a good way."

That takes me aback. "How's that?"

"You do what needs to be done for the people you love. Mom might not have had the most conventional way of parenting, but she made sure we never wanted for anything. You do that with me. No matter what it takes, or what you have to sacrifice, you make sure Jack and I don't want."

I never thought of it like that. "Thanks, but that's not what I meant."

"Oh. What did you mean then?"

Shit. I've said too much. "Never mind."

"No. Hold up," Maddie says, grabbing my face and turning it toward her. "What were you going to say?"

"Nothing."

"Bullshit," she says firmly. "How about instead of you talking, you listen, and I tell you what I think you've been wanting to say and that I've been thinking for years now."

This ought to be good.

"I think the real reason you've never dated seriously, or considered being a father, is because you're scared you're like them. You're scared that you are either a flake like Mom, who will come and go and never settle down, or that you're like your dad, and that you don't have it in you to be in a committed relationship or take on the responsibilities of a father. So, because you don't like to take risks and would rather have the mundane because it's safe, you've never allowed yourself to try."

Do I tell her that she's spot on? Judging by the smug look on her face, she knows she is.

"I don't want anyone to get hurt," I say in defense of her accurate description. "Why would I hurt someone if I don't have to? Myself included."

Maddie takes a second and looks over to Jack. "When his dad told me he was out, I was hurt. Devastated. But I'd take that pain in triple if that meant I'd still get Jack out of the deal."

I never thought of it like that.

"I think it's too late," I admit. "Can I just turn a switch with someone? For years I've been the anti-relationship guy. And what? Now all of a sudden after one day in the park and light-bulb moment I'm going to be asking her to marry me?"

This gets Maddie's attention as she whips her head back my way. "Emmett Michael Collins, is there someone you want to marry? I was just hoping you thought a girl was pretty!"

I really need to get out of this funk because I have zero control over my reactions or words anymore. "No. Maybe. Fuck…I don't know."

"Is this Florida girl? Please tell me this is Florida girl! I'm not going to stop asking until you tell me so just tell me pleeeeease."

Sometimes Maddie is wise beyond her years. And then at times she's my annoying little sister. "Yes. It's Florida girl."

"Squeeeeeeeeeee." I don't know the sound that just came out of Maddie's mouth, but she's also kicking her feet rapidly.

"You good?"

She lets out one more loud noise before composing herself. "Yes. I'm good. Now where were we?"

"I'm hoping I'm not like my parents because I'm pretty sure the feelings I've thought for weeks were just lust and attraction are something else."

"Oh! Yes. You're in love. Got it," Maddie says. "Just go talk to her. Tell her all this."

"Pass. Second option please."

Love her? I love her? I don't love her.

Why am I even trying to lie to myself anymore? I do. I love her like crazy. I love her smile. I love how she always wants to do a good job with everything she does and puts her whole self into it. I love how she snuggles next to me like she was meant to fit into my side. I love how she feels in my arms. I love how she makes me do things I never thought I'd do, like go to the fucking beach. I love how she's inquisitive and always wants to learn.

Holy fuck, I love her…

Maddie lets out a groan, but doesn't continue because the sound of my cell phone ringing interrupts us. It's Simon—probably calling me to ask when he's going to see my face again.

"Hey man. What's up?"

"What are you doing right now?"

The urgency in his voice takes me aback. "I'm at the park with Maddie and Jack. Why? What's up?"

"I hate to ask you to do this, but I'm in a bind."

"Ask me what? Just tell me and I can help."

"Stella's going to Duncan's right now to pack her things. She's been adamant that she doesn't want anyone's help and she'll be fine but…"

"No. She shouldn't be alone with that asshole."

"Exactly. The problem is, Charlie has to work at the restaurant tonight and Lainey is throwing up everywhere. I was going to just show up so she couldn't protest…"

"I'll go," I say before he can say anymore. "Text me the address."

"Thanks, man. I owe you one."

We hang up the phone and I quickly stand up from the bench. "Can you take Winnie for the night? I need to go to Stella."

Maddie studies me for a second. "Sure. Is everything okay? And who's Stella?"

"It will be."

I don't answer the second question as I start jogging to my truck, but not before I hear Maddie call out to me.

"Emmett!"

"Yeah?"

"It's her, isn't it?"

I nod, not even caring about hiding it anymore. "Yeah. It's her."

"Perfect. Then go get your girl."

My girl.

Mine.

Stella's mine.

Actually, change that. I'm hers. She's had me from the first day we met. She had me the second I saw her in that wedding dress. She's had me from the jump.

Now I just hope I'm not too late.

guide to love rule #35

Find you a man who will haul a moving truck's worth of shoes
for you.
If he threatens your ex? Even better.

26
stella

I'm a strong, independent woman who don't need no man.

Actually…that's a lie.

I'm a strong, independent woman, and I really need a man to carry these heavy boxes.

I fall to the floor of my former bedroom and let out an "umphf" as I stare at the stacks of shoes I've already packed, and the ones I still haven't touched yet. I haven't even started on my clothes or other items that I bought that are scattered around the condo.

Maybe those spontaneous shopping trips with Andi and my sisters have finally caught up with me? Do I have too many shoes?

No. That's just crazy talk.

I drastically underestimated the amount of things I still had here. I also stubbornly refused anybody's offers to help me come pack. Or realized that my tiny car can't fit much in it. In my mind, I could do it myself. You know, because I'm a strong, independent woman.

But now as I sit here in a sea of Louboutins, Minolos, and a wedge sandal in every color, I realize that I'm not strong or independent—I'm an idiot. Because there's no way I'm going to get everything packed and moved to my car before Duncan gets home from work. He agreed to stay out of the condo during the day and I agreed to be done by six o'clock. Which means I'm going to have to make multiple trips here, which is something I'd rather not do. But if that's what needs to be done, then so be it.

I look around to assess just how much I have left, when I notice another row of boots on the top shelf. Lovely. And of course I can't reach them without a step stool. With a groan I get myself off the floor and make my way to the laundry room, hoping this is where Duncan still keeps the stool I bought last year when I needed to put the boots on the top shelf.

Note to self: Take the stool.

But just as I walk into the laundry room and flip on the light, a knocking at the door stops me in my tracks.

Shit…who could it be? My blood goes cold as I run through the list of possibilities. Delivery driver? They don't knock. They just leave the package and go. Is it Duncan? I mean, it could be, but why would he be knocking? If he was going to come in, he would just let himself in. Was Simon not able to stay away? No, Ainsley said that Lainey's sick. A neighbor? I didn't even talk to my neighbors when I lived here.

The knocking continues when I see a broom within my reach. Yes. This will do. I quickly grab it, liking my odds better if I have this as a weapon for when I confront whoever is on the other side of the door.

Broom in hand, I walk down the hallway through the living room. There isn't a peephole for me to look through to see who my attacker is. So I just wield the broom over my head with one hand and open the door with the other, ready to attack whoever is on the other side.

"Danger!" I yell as the door comes open for me to see… "Emmett?"

His confusion is immediately interrupted by a laugh that I hate how much I've missed.

"First a shoe, now a broom? You're moving up with your choice of weapons, Tiger."

I lower the broom and let out a breath. "What are you doing here?"

He takes a step inside, even though I didn't ask him to come in. "Helping you."

"Helping me? I don't need any help. Wait. Did Simon send you?"

Emmett looks around the condo, which used to have a hint of feminine exposure in the decor. Now it just looks like a wanna-be rich boy's frat house, complete with a neon bar light and a flag saying that Saturday is for the boys.

"Yes, he did. But you should've asked me to come. I would've helped."

Is he serious right now? Is he forgetting that he's been MIA for a week? "When was I going to do that, Emmett? After you told me to walk away so you didn't fuck me on my desk? When you were being short with me at your house? Oh, wait. I know. I was supposed to text in the middle of you giving me the silent treatment now that I have your phone number. My apologies. How rude of me."

The sarcasm is oozing from me, and my confidence is soaring. Between taking back my belongings and standing up to Emmett's treatment, I'm feeling like the old Stella. The Stella that's a little crazy and a lot vocal.

I missed her. I'm glad she's back.

"I'm sorry," he says, and in his defense, it does sound sincere. "You're right. I've been an ass. And I want to apologize for that. I need to. But how about right now I start with going to get some of the boxes you have packed and moving them to my truck?"

"I don't need your help."

That's a lie.

"Really?"

"Yes, really. I have everything handled."

I don't have everything handled.

"Stella…how many shoes do you have packed?"

I narrow my eyes. I hate how well he knows me.

"That's what I thought." He gives me a coy smile as he starts walking past me toward the hallway.

"No! Stop!" I yell, needing to put my foot down. I'm standing in a house where I've been pushed around for long enough. I'm not going to let another man tell me what he's going to do and I just have to go along with it. Even if he's trying to help me. A girl's gotta take a stand. "You just can't say I'm sorry and then come in here and run things. I didn't ask for your help. I didn't ask for anyone's. You're the one who stopped talking to me. You were *not* nice to me. Rude, actually. And now you're going to walk in here and just say you're sorry and carry boxes for me? Emmett Collins, it's going to take a lot—"

My words are swallowed by Emmett's mouth suddenly on mine. I clench my fists and bring them between our chests, wanting to protest.

Except I can't. His lips feel too good on mine.

And I feel every strong, independent, woman bone being melted from my body.

How does he do this? How in one kiss, in one touch, does me make me forget everything, including my name and birthday? How with every swipe of his tongue and nibble of my lip do I become putty in his hands?

He slowly pulls away, leaving me panting as his strong hands grip my biceps just hard enough that I can feel them. "I'm sorry, Stella. I'm so fucking sorry. I've been horrible. A jackass. The worst kind of man, and a man I hated. And I'll tell you every single reason why in my fucked-up head I thought it was the best play. I have so much I want to tell you. *Need* to tell you. But can we do it later and not in the place where I know you did things with a man whose neck I want to strangle?"

I nod, not sure what to say. "Okay."

I stand back in shock as Emmett continues walking down the hallway to the bedroom. Between the sincerity in Emmett's eyes, the words he's choosing to use, and the kiss I can still feel, I'm more confused than fall in the South. Is it hot? Is it cold? That's exactly Emmett. Is he hot? Is he cold? I mean, he's always hot. The last week he has been cold. Today he's like that perfect 76-degree day with low humidity that you want to get excited about but you're not sure if it's here to stay.

My mind is all over the place right now. But I can't think about Emmett and analyze each and every word. Right now, the focus needs to be packing up my babies and getting the hell out of this condo.

When I make my way to the bedroom, Emmett already has two full moving boxes in his arms. Holy shit, is he even breaking a sweat? Those boxes aren't light, and he's carrying them with ease.

I remember when I thought my type of man wore a suit and tie and had an overly white smile with a trust fund.

I was wrong. I was so wrong.

It's this man right here. The blue-collar guy who carries my boxes of shoes and kisses me out of nowhere. Whose ass looks damn good in a pair of Wranglers but can also clean up when he needs to. The man who one minute is taking control of the room but I know will let me fight my battles.

Emmett Collins is my type, through and through.

"I'm gonna take these down to the truck," he says. "Keep packing so we can get out of here sooner rather than later."

I snap out of my stare and do as he says. I start going for my clothes that I can throw into the suitcase I brought when I hear a door slam.

"Who the fuck are you, and why the fuck are you in my house?"

Oh shit…

I drop the clothes and race out of the bedroom. As soon as I turn the corner and have an eye on the door, I see Emmett and Duncan staring each other down.

Well, Duncan is staring up, but still…

"You don't remember me?" Emmett begins with a prodding tone. "I'm Simon's friend. Emmett. We met at his baby stag party. You know, the one where you asked me when the strippers were coming. Actually! Now that all tracks. I hear you have a thing for women in that line of work. Though I have a feeling they just see you as the gullible douche and an easy payday."

I watch Duncan's face get red with every antagonizing word that Emmett says. Selfishly, I want him to keep going.

"Duncan, what are you doing here?" I ask as I step next to Emmett. Though I might as well not be in the room right now. They haven't stopped scowling at each other. Duncan is now fully straining his neck to look up at Emmett, and I have to force myself not to laugh.

"I wanted to come see how you were doing," Duncan says, finally breaking his stare-off with Emmett. "Maybe see if you needed a hand?"

"No. That wasn't what we agreed on," I say. "You were supposed to stay away all day. So unless a lawyer's work day now suddenly ends at four-thirty after years of you telling me you didn't finish at the office until at least eight, then you shouldn't be here."

"Fine. You caught me," he says as he holds his hands up in defense. "I wanted to come talk to you. I thought you'd be alone."

With those words, he gives another glare to Emmett. Except Emmett knows he said it to get a reaction out of him—one he isn't giving him.

"We have nothing to say to each other," I say. "And I've been advised to not speak to you without the presence of my attorney."

"See, that's just it," Duncan says, taking a step toward me. I immediately take a step back. "This whole lawsuit thing. We should both drop them. We both filed them in the heat of the moment. We just need to sit down and talk. Figure everything out. Patch things up so we can start fresh."

I wish I had this man's audacity and delusion. This is now the third time he's asked me to get back together. Does he not know the word no? Does he have a rejection kink? Oh, maybe that's it. I should ask Nadia. Oh! I wonder how she's doing. Maybe we should get lunch…

I shake my head and focus back on the task at hand—which is shutting this man down for good.

"Duncan, in what world—either the actual round one or the flat one you think we're on—do you think that's going to happen? The answer is no. It's always going to be no. I don't know how many ways I can tell you that we're not getting back together or patching things up or starting over. If I need to learn another language, I will. But we're done. Over. And as for the lawsuits, I'm not dropping a damn thing until you pay me back the money you stole from me. Do you understand?"

"Stella, baby…let's just talk…"

Duncan reaches for my arm, barely grabbing onto it before Emmett shoves him away, stepping between us.

"Don't you fucking touch her."

"What the fuck?" Duncan says. "Don't you fucking touch me!"

"My apologies. I forgot you only like being touched by women with floggers."

Oh shit! One point for Cap!

"I don't know who you think you are," Duncan says, trying to get back the upper hand. "But you need to leave my house. Or I'll call the police."

"Go for it," Emmett says as he takes a step toward him. Emmett already has a good six inches on Duncan in height. But somehow he gets taller the closer he gets to him. Or maybe it's because Duncan is shrinking into himself, trying, but failing, to not look scared as hell.

I mean, I don't blame him. Emmett's breathing is heavy, and his face is turning red. His fists are clenched at his sides. I have a feeling if Duncan says one more thing out of line, Emmett is going to swing first and ask questions later.

And I've never been more turned on in my entire life.

"Listen here," Emmett continues. "She has made it clear on multiple occasions that she wants nothing to do with you. She is here today to get her things out of your grown man frat house. Beer signs? Really?"

"They're collector's items."

Both Emmett and I can only snort out a tired laugh. "If you say so. Keep your collector's items. I'll keep her. How about that?"

I'm caught off guard and don't realize until a few seconds later what Emmett just said.

Keep me? He wants to keep me?

Oh, we have so much to talk about…

"You? Ha! Hilarious," Duncan says with a sudden flash of confidence. "Who are you, anyway? Simon's lackey? The hired muscle?"

"Who am I?" Emmett asks rhetorically, taking another step closer to Duncan, which makes him physically retreat. Before he knows it, his back is hitting the wall. "I'm the man who's going to listen to her. The man who's not going to tell her what food to eat. I'm the one who's going to make her dreams come true. Oh, and I'm hers. In every sense of the word. And do you know what that means? That means she's mine. And if you ever, and I mean *ever*, touch what's mine again, I'll kill you. And that's not a threat. That's a fucking promise."

I'm his?

He's mine?

What is happening?

And why am I so turned on?

"Stella?" Emmett asks as he looks back to me. "Can you have your things packed in an hour?"

I nod, unable to say anything else.

"Okay, then here's what's gonna happen. You're gonna pack.

I'm gonna call a moving company that owes me a favor. While you pack, I'm going to sit out here with my new buddy Duncan. Maybe clarify any points he didn't understand. Make sure he doesn't bother you. And then we're gonna leave. And the next time you see him, it's going to be in a courtroom when he has to pay you back every fucking cent he stole from you. Sound like a plan?"

Emmett tosses me a playful wink. How is he now playful when five seconds ago he was threatening murder?

I don't know how, but I like it.

I like it a lot.

guide to love rule #64

There's no timeline for finding your person.
You might even meet them
on your wedding day.

27
stella

"Emmett! Yes! Yes! Ah!"

With one more thrust, Emmett lets out a low, loud, groan as he finishes inside me.

And I can now say, for a matter of fact, that I know what it's like to be thoroughly fucked.

It was like he was a man possessed the second we walked into his house. We came back here to talk, and so I could start going through my things, but as soon as the door shut, our mouths were on each other and our clothes were coming off. We didn't even make it into the bedroom.

"God damnit, Tiger," he sighs as he rolls off me. His arm immediately wraps around my stomach, bringing me into him as he lays a kiss on my shoulder. "I swear, that was not my intention."

"Really? You ask a girl back to your house after telling her that she's yours, and you don't think sex is the first thing that's going to happen?"

He laughs and gives me another kiss. I'm really liking this playful and affectionate side of Emmett. "In my defense, I've never done this before, so I really didn't know what was about to happen."

I know he didn't mean to diminish the mood with that statement, but I can't help but feel a pang in my stomach. Because he's right. According to him, he's never done this before. What changed his mind? Why did he come today other than, what I'm assuming, was Simon asking him to? Why did he say those things to Duncan? Was it the heat of the moment? Or is he in this? I don't want to assume anything before I hear the words from his mouth, but it's also really hard not to get my hopes up when he's looking at me right now like I am the only thing that matters in this world.

"Why *did* you come today, Emmett? I figure Simon asked you, but it had to be more than that."

Emmett slightly nods as he grabs a blanket from his couch and drapes it over us.

"You're right. Yes, Simon asked me. Actually, he didn't have to. He told me what you were doing, and I was in my truck before he could finish the sentence."

He stops for a second, and I can tell he's thinking about what he wants to say next. I don't push because I know how important this moment is. Instead I just trace lines up and down his muscled arms. I mean to do it to give him comfort. I'd be lying if I didn't get a little something out of it too. This man could make a career on a spicy site just for his arms.

"When Simon told me where you were, I didn't hesitate. Not because I didn't think you could handle yourself, but because when you realize that the woman you want to be with is fighting a battle, you want to be next to her on the field, fighting with her."

Want to be with? Is this really happening?

"Emmett..."

"For my entire life, I was scared I was like my parents. I didn't want to be my mom, jumping from relationship to relationship, but I was worried I was like my dad and that I'd leave when it got hard. I didn't want to be either of them."

"You were protecting yourself," I say.

"No. I was protecting others," he continues. "Or at least I thought I was. If you don't get attached, no one gets hurt. It was great in theory."

"In theory?"

"Yeah," he says, his quiet smile starting to show. "Because the reason I could stay away was because they didn't mean anything. Not seeing them, or not being with them, didn't drive me crazy. They were forgettable. But you, Stella Banks? You're as unforgettable as they come."

Can you die from swooning? If so, I think I am.

I think Emmett realizes I'm speechless because he leans in for a kiss. I want to touch him and bring him in closer, but my entire body is paralyzed from his words.

"I know what you must be thinking," he says when he pulls away.

"Please tell me, because I short circuited somewhere between fighting battles and being unforgettable."

His laugh fills my heart as he kisses my shoulder. "You're probably thinking, this isn't what either of us said we wanted. We said two weeks in Florida. And that was it."

"Oh yeah. We did say that."

He rolls over and I bask in the feeling of his weight on me. "I know you said you weren't ready. And I don't know what the hell I'm doing. It's probably a recipe for disaster. And I didn't even ask if you want this. I've just assumed. Great job, Emmett. First woman you want to get serious with, and you just tell her she's yours like she's a goddamn piece of cattle at auction. What the fuck am I doing?"

I can't contain my laugher. "Oh my God, Emmett Collins… you're rambling."

And if I couldn't die from swoon anymore, Emmett's face flushes red in embarrassment.

God, I love this man.

I thought I did before. I had more of a feeling earlier. But now? There's no denying it. I'm in love with Emmett Collins.

"I know I said I wasn't ready. And I don't know if I am," I begin. "I'm probably not healed. My ex is suing me. I'm living out of boxes at my sisters. I have a temp job I got from my brother. I'm a hot mess through and through. But what I do know is that I haven't been able to stop thinking about you since the day we met. It's like you picked me off the floor from the bar and haven't let go."

Emmett leans down for a kiss, thinking I'm done. I'm not. I take in a breath to drum up some bravery, because I'm about to be as vulnerable as I think I've ever been.

"This last week, not seeing you, not knowing if I did something wrong to make you avoid me…it hurt, Emmett. It was the worst pain I might've ever felt, and I'm including my botched wedding in that. But that pain would be nothing compared to the thought of not being with you."

I can't say anything else before Emmett's lips are on mine, kissing me harder than maybe he ever has. And that's saying something, considering how we entered his house an hour ago.

This kiss is full of passion and love and a million other emotions wrapped in. But what's striking me the most is that it doesn't feel like it's rushed. We're not against a timer.

No, we can kiss all night. And tomorrow. And the next day, and the next.

We can kiss forever.

"You're going to have to be patient with me," Emmett says as he rolls over, bringing me on top of him. "I have no idea how to be a partner or a boyfriend. Shit…how am I a boyfriend for the first time at thirty-seven years old?"

That makes me giggle. I love strong and silent Emmett, but rambling Emmett is quickly growing on me.

I tilt my head down to press a kiss at the top of his pec. "See, that's where you're wrong, Cap. The man who swept me off my feet? The man who saved me? Just be him, and you'll be the best boyfriend ever. Oh, and make sure you always have ice cream for me. That's a deal breaker."

I melt at his smile before his hands cup my face, connecting our lips once again. Our kiss quickly deepens, and just as I'm about to let my hand start traveling down, he sits up, never letting me go as he stands with ease and starts carrying me down the hallway.

How in the hell did he do that?

"Where are you taking me?"

"My bed," he says as he kicks the door shut behind him. "Do you know how much it has killed me knowing that you slept in this bed? That I could smell you on my pillow days after you left?"

My pussy clenches at his words. Somehow knowing that Emmett was still thinking about me before we met in Florida is making me feel some sort of way.

He sits on the bed, keeping hold of me so I'm now straddling his lap. "I meant what I said earlier; you're mine, Stella Banks. So how I see it, I'm going to have you in this bed. I'm going to make you scream my name in this bed. You're going to come all over it when I eat that pretty pussy. And then I'm going to fuck you so hard that you're never going to want to leave. How does that sound?"

How does that sound? Is he serious? Yeah, Cap…that sounds just absolutely horrible…

He doesn't let me answer as he stands up, still holding on to me, only to turn around and drop me on his mattress. My giggles fill the room as he moves me higher up, allowing him to lay down and spread my legs open so he can fulfill one of his promises.

His hands run down my legs, sending shivers through my body before I feel his mouth on me. Fuck…I nearly forgot what his tongue felt like. I try to lay back and relax, wanting to feel every lick and suck he gives me. Every flick of his tongue and every move of his finger. But I can't. It's like every place he hits is a nerve that sends my body thrashing.

Incoherent words and sounds leave my mouth as I try to grab

onto a pillow. What's the pillow going to do? I don't know. But I'm about to come harder than I think I ever have before, and I need something to hold onto so I don't actually leave my body.

"Emmett! Ah! Yes!"

At least that's what I mean to say when he inserts two fingers in and flicks the switch that makes me combust. Holy shit…I'm physically shaking as the orgasm runs through me. Also, I don't know what time it is, but that might be a world record for an orgasm via tongue.

I can barely catch my breath before Emmett has climbed his way up me, snaking his arms under my back. I wrap my arms around him, holding on for dear life as he enters me.

And I need to. Oh my God, Emmett is a man possessed, but not in a scary way. Or rough. No. His head is buried in my shoulder. He's holding onto me for dear life as our bodies connect at a furious pace. The only thing that slows us down is Emmett clutching me tighter so he can bring me up with him as he sits on his bed, our connection never breaking. I arch slightly, loving the new angle, which gives him access to latch onto one of my tits.

"Mine," he groans before switching to the other.

"Yours."

And I mean that. I'm his. It should scare me, saying that, knowing that I lost myself to the last man I was with. But I'm not. Not at all. If anything, I'm getting stronger because of him. He has reminded me of who I am, and he's loving all the parts of me. Even the crazy ones.

So if being his means I'm more back to the Stella I used to know, then I'm good with that.

No. I'm *great* with that.

"Cap, I'm coming," I whimper as he starts fucking me harder. "Please."

I never need to ask twice. I arch back again, knowing that the slight change of angle will do exactly what we need. He circles my clit with his thumb, and it's the magic switch to orgasms that rock us both.

A scream comes out of me as a roar leaves Emmett. It's at this point I'm glad he lives in the country, because we would have disturbed the neighbors.

"Holy fuck, Tiger," Emmett breathes out as he lowers me back to the bed. His arms wrap around me instantly, bringing me in to put my head on his chest.

God, I've missed this…

"If you were wondering, what we did right there is a good boyfriend thing. We should do that a lot." My joke shakes his chest, and I hug him tighter. "I don't want to leave."

"Then don't," he says, kissing my forehead. "Stay the night."

My body warms all over from the thought. "Yeah?"

"Yeah," his smile is maybe the biggest I've ever seen it. "We'll get dinner. I'm sure there's some show that's come out recently that we can agree on. Have a lazy night in. Do that another three times. Whatta ya say?"

"I say that sounds like a perfect night in with my boyfriend."

We fall into a comfortable silence. His fingers are lazily tracing circles on my back as I listen to his heartbeat come back to its normal pace.

That is until I realize something that neither of us thought to talk about that makes me sit straight up in the bed.

"What?" Emmett asks. "Are you okay?"

"I don't know," I admit. "We forgot something kind of big."

"What? If it's do I have ice cream, the answer is no, but people do get delivery out here."

"Good to know, but that's not it."

"Tiger. Spit it out. It can't be that bad."

That's up for debate…

"We need to figure out how to tell Simon."

28

emmett

"Emmett…earth to Emmett…you here?"

I only catch the last of that after Simon snaps his fingers in front of my face. I slap his hand away, which he thinks is just me being surly. It wasn't. I was daydreaming about Stella's good morning blow job, so now I'm pissed I'm back to reality.

"Sorry. Say that again?"

Simon sighs. Stella snickers.

I give her a side eye from my seat at the conference table we're sitting at. There are a few chairs between each of us, because it would be weird if any of us sat right next to each other.

Even though it's killing me not to be next to her. Hell, it killed me this morning when she left my house to get ready for work. Besides the fact she didn't have any of her work clothes or makeup here—I did get her a toothbrush which looks mighty fine in one of the empty slots of my toothbrush holder—we knew we couldn't show up to work together. That's not how we want to announce this to Simon.

Though we do have a plan to tell him. Which we will. If he ever shuts up.

"What I was asking my faithful number two is if we're ready

to break ground next week on the commercial building in Franklin?"

"Oh. Yeah, we're set," I say. Thank God he asked me a question I didn't have to think too hard about. "Permits finally came through, thanks to Stella, and I talked to the foreman today. All is ready for Monday."

"Excellent," Simon says as he looks down at his notes. I take a glance over to Stella, who apparently had the same idea. When our eyes meet, a rush of warmth shoots through me.

I remember when Stella told me about the honeymoon stage when we were in Florida. I had an idea of what she meant, but had never experienced it.

This. This is it. The feeling that I want to be around her all the time. Knowing that I haven't kissed her in three hours and that's two hours and fifty-nine minutes too long. I want to know what she wants for lunch so I can go get it for her. I'm counting down the hours until we're out of here so I can bring her back to my place and cuddle with her on my couch with my dog as we eat ice cream.

"Stella," Simon says. At least this time I didn't zone out completely on what he has to say. "What do you have for us?"

I look over to her, this time at least in context of work, as she opens her notebook. I don't know why I love that she uses a notebook and not an iPad or her laptop, but I do. "We went over the permits for next week, so I can cross that off. Emmett, all the rent checks have been processed for the month, so that's taken care of. I started on the social media accounts for Magnolia Properties because it's 2024 and you need one. Oh, and Simon, the showing you had for this afternoon? The realtor called as we were walking into this meeting and asked if you could move it up. I told her I'd get back to her."

I look on in admiration as Stella goes on with her updates. She's in her element. We give her a task and she gets it done, none too big or small. Most of the time she's tackling multiple things for us at once, and she never seems to get overwhelmed.

And starting the social media? That's genius that Simon or I would've never thought of. In just a short time, she's already making this office hers. Simon might own it, and I might be his right hand, but it's quickly becoming apparent that Stella is running this show.

"Love it," Simon says. "Whatever you need for the social media, just do it. Whatever you need to buy, just use the card. This is your project, and I completely trust you. As for the showing, can you call her and let her know that I'll come out in an hour? I have a few other errands to run, so I'll just do that and then go relieve Mom since she's watching Lainey for us today."

"No problem," Stella says as she picks up her phone, assumably to relay the message. "Also make sure you take her a slice of pie from the diner."

"Why would I do that?" Simon asks.

"Because you need this realtor to come down seven thousand dollars, so you need to soften her up. Pie has a way of helping that."

"Good call," Simon says. "Okay, other than the pie, is there any new business we didn't discuss?"

Stella and I slyly look at each other, making sure that we're on the same page to tell Simon what we need to. This was the plan. We knew he'd ask this question today, and we thought it was the perfect time to gently tell him.

"Actually yeah," I begin. "There's something I want to talk about with you. Actually, that Stella and I both want to talk to you about…"

Simon starts to respond when his cell phone alerts him to a text. "Oh. Shit."

"Everything okay?" Stella asks.

"I think so. It's Mom. She needs me to pick up Lainey right now. Apparently Ainsley got a flat tire. Dad is golfing so Mom needs to go pick her up."

"You can tell Mom I'll come get her?" Stella offers.

"Then you'd have to drive back up to Nashville," Simon

says. "It's fine. I'll just get Lainey a little earlier than planned. I can take her to the showing. Oh! Maybe that'll help negotiations. How can you resist a man holding a baby who also brought you pie? Oh! Maybe I can get Lainey to say her first word, and it be the realtor's name…"

"She's four months old, Simon," I remind him. "Just get her to not puke."

"Good call," he says. "Oh wait. You had something to tell me?"

I look over to Stella, who's discreetly shaking her head. "No biggie. We can talk later."

"Sounds good." Simon says as he leaves the conference room. "See everyone tomorrow."

Neither of us move as Simon hurries into his office to grab his keys. We stay seated until he's out the back door.

"Tomorrow," I say.

"Yeah, tomorrow," she agrees. "What's one more day?"

An awkward pause occurs between us as Stella stands to exit the conference room. I follow her lead, knowing that as much as I want to sneak her into a hidden corner of the office away from the glass windows so I can kiss the hell out of her, we should probably go back to work.

I don't mean to, and I don't think she does either, but we both walk in front of the door at the same time. "After you," I say as I open the door.

"Well, thank you." Her smile is too much for me to resist. As she starts walking I step behind her, wrap my hand around her waist and pull her back to me. She lets out a small shriek as I pin her against the glass wall and kiss her.

And not just kiss her. Kiss the hell out of her. And just like that, the whole "go back to work" notion flies out the window.

"Cap," Stella whispers, her hands pulling at the waist of my jeans.

"Tell me to stop," I say, though my mouth continues to kiss down her neck. "Because I don't know if I can do it myself."

Stella doesn't say anything, but does move her hands from my jeans to my chest, slightly pushing me back.

"Okay," I say, breathing heavy. "I'm sorry."

"Oh, I'm not stopping you," she says with a wicked look in her eye. "I'm just moving this somewhere a little more private."

I follow her lead as she summons me with her finger to follow her. I'm shocked when she walks toward my office, never taking her eyes off me. It's like I'm following a siren. I know I should ask questions. Maybe even stop this. But I can't. It's like she has me under some sort of spell, and I don't ever want to snap out of it.

"Sit," she says, gesturing to my office chair. Not daring to say no, I do as she asks, watching as she seductively walks toward me.

"So I've always had a fantasy," she says as she leans over, her eyes now even with mine as her hands rest on my thighs.

"What's that?"

"How about I just show you?"

Stella leans in and takes my lips with hers, kissing me hard and deep. She doesn't linger, though, quickly placing two kisses on my cheek and neck before she lowers herself to the ground.

Holy shit is she about to…

"Tiger…"

She doesn't say anything as her hands start working my belt, easily getting it unfastened as she works the button and zipper of my jeans. I help her out, lifting up to push them down as I watch the fire burn in her eyes. She starts slowly stroking my cock, which was hard the second I kissed her in the hallway.

And before I know it, Stella's mouth is wrapped around my dick, and I let out a groan that I'm pretty sure everyone at the diner could hear.

Ask me if I care.

I don't.

Right now all I care about is Stella's mouth on me, sucking me just how she knows I like it.

"Fuck yes, Tiger," I say, gathering her hair off her face with my hands. Her mouth is bobbing up and down, her hand working in tandem. It takes all I have not to start bucking my hips, wanting more than anything to fuck her face right now. Hell, I want to pick her up, bend her over, and fuck her on my desk. But this is her fantasy, so it's her show. And I'm the lucky son of a bitch that's along for the ride.

Stella opens wide, taking me so deep that her mouth is against my pelvis, when I hear a door slam somewhere in the office. Which frankly, I don't know how I notice it considering the only thing I was hearing at that moment were the angels singing as Stella deep throated me.

"Hide!" I whisper-yell, "Simon's back!"

Stella quickly moves under my desk, which thankfully is boarded in the front. Just as I'm about to pull my pants back up, I hear Simon's footsteps coming closer. Knowing I don't have time, I roll under the desk, pants down, dick out, as I try and look as normal as possible in front of my best friend.

"Hey," Simon says frantically. "I forgot the contracts."

"Gotcha." I say, though I internally punch myself. When the fuck do I say "gotcha?"

As I sit there, trying to look casual while also not moving, I nearly jump out of my seat when I feel Stella's hand on my dick. And then her mouth.

Is she giving me a blow job under the desk?

I can't look at her without moving my chair, but somehow I feel her smiling as her mouth works my cock like she never has. Stella's blow jobs are something special to begin with. But this one? It's on another fucking level.

I grip the arms of the chair for dear life, wanting to let out a roar that would wake the town when Stella starts gently playing with my balls as she swirls her tongue around my cock.

"You okay?" Simon asks as he exits his office. "You don't look so good."

"Yup," I spit out as Stella deep throats me again. "Everything's great."

Simon clearly doesn't buy it. "I don't know. You don't look great. Maybe you should head home for the day."

"Yeah, maybe I will."

Simon starts to walk out, before taking a step back. "Where's Stella?"

"Lunch," I blurt out. "Went to get us lunch."

"She really is something," Simon says. "I don't want to pat myself on the back, but it was a really good idea for me to bring her on."

"She's something, all right..." I say as her tongue makes a full twist around the base of my cock.

Simon waves as he heads out. I don't move even after I hear the door close, giving it a few minutes to make sure he's not coming back.

"What the fuck," I say as I gently wheel my chair back as Stella takes her mouth off my dick. "What the hell was that?"

She wipes her mouth as she gives an impish shrug. "Improvising."

I narrow my eyes as I signal for her to come to me. She starts to stand to walk over when I say words I never thought I'd say in my life.

"No. Crawl to me."

I don't know why, but at this moment, that's all I want to see. Stella with her swollen lips, messy hair, and skirt that I'm about to fucking demolish crawling toward me. I wheel my chair back a little farther, wanting the full view as Stella's eyes never leave mine, her hands and legs inching toward me.

"Stand." She does as I say, keeping her eyes on me. "Now come here."

She takes the final steps to me before .

"Don't you remember what I once told you?" I say as I stand up. She shakes her head, though I'm pretty sure her brain isn't working right now as I'm hiking up her skirt and tearing off her lace thong.

"That I always get to undress you. That it's my privilege to do so."

She bites her lip in that way that drives me crazy as I turn her around and bend her over my desk.

"This is going to be short and sweet. Now hold on so I can fuck you right here, just like we both want."

I take a quick look out the windows, making sure we're as hidden as I think we are. My office is tucked away in the back, so you can't see in or out if you're just passing by on the street. Which is good, because if anyone were to see in here for the next few minutes, they'd be getting quite the show.

Or wondering where the screaming is coming from.

"Ah!" Stella yells as I push myself into her. I don't hold back or ease her in. I just fuck her like I want, my body slapping against her with every thrust I give. I give her ass a slap, which makes her purr, so I do it again, loving the sounds I'm bringing out of her.

I watch her grip onto the end of the desk, holding on for dear life as I slam into her. Her face is turned so I can see the redness creeping up, her eyes shut as she just feels every inch I give her.

"Emmett…"

My name on her lips sounds as if she's begging, and that's one thing I'll never make Stella do in her life. I feel my balls tightening, and I lift her up just enough to slide my fingers around to her clit, hitting the spot I know will send her, because frankly, there isn't time for multiples tonight.

"Ah!" Stella yells. "Emmett!"

In that moment, we come together, our bodies jerking into each other as the sensation dies down.

"Holy shit," Stella moans as I do my best to keep my weight off her. But it's hard. Between the blow job and fucking her harder than I might have at any point in my life, my body feels like a blob.

"Holy shit is right," I say, giving her a kiss on the cheek before I stand, bringing her up with me. "I have an idea."

"What's that?"

"We get out of here. Ditch the rest of the work day. Go get lunch—because I don't know about you, but I'm starving. Take said lunch back to my place. Then after we eat, I get my dessert. Which will be you."

She leans in and gives me a small kiss to my cheek. "Sounds perfect."

After we fix our clothing and lock up, Stella and I head back to our separate cars. She sends me a wink, which earns her a last slap on the ass before she gets in her mini SUV.

As soon as I flip the truck on and Stella and I get on the road from Rolling Hills to Nashville, about ten things hit me at once.

Did I just have sex in the office?

Did Stella really just give me a blow job while her brother stood there?

Did I bend her over my desk and leave her ass red and my cum dripping down her leg?

Did I really make her crawl to me?

The answer is yes, yes, definitely yes, and holy shit, yes.

I don't know who I am anymore. Hell, I don't know if I've been the same since Florida. Yes I've always been more dominant in the bedroom, but with Stella it was like I needed to make her mine in a way I've never had. I needed to touch her all the time. Feel her on me whenever she was near.

That's not how I would've ever have described myself before. My sexual encounters were to the point, quick, and done. I wouldn't have described them as rough, but they weren't sweet or passionate. Nothing like I am with Stella.

And I definitely wouldn't have asked any of them to crawl to me. Or told them that their pussy belonged to me. They sure as hell weren't done in a place where anyone could've caught us, and even if they would've, I wouldn't have cared.

That's the Stella Banks effect.

My Tiger…my beautiful, feisty Tiger. Never in a million years would I ever have thought I'd do what we just did. Yet, I now want to make this a regular thing.

Is it crazy? Maybe. Am I going crazy? Possibly. But I'm not mad about it. Because I think a little crazy is exactly what my life needs right now.

And the only crazy I want is Stella Banks.

guide to love rule #86

When you're sneaking around, make sure you have your
stories straight for when you eventually (and literally) get
caught
with your panties down.

29

stella

"HOW MANY OF THOSE SKIRTS DO YOU HAVE?"

I giggle as I feel Emmett's breath on my neck as I stand at the counter in our break room, waiting for my oatmeal to heat up.

I also feel his hardening cock against my ass, which makes me want to christen this room just like we did his office yesterday.

"A few."

That's the truth. I've always loved a good pencil skirt, so I have some options in my work clothes rotation. But after I saw the way Emmett looked at me the few times I wore them? I might have bought some more.

Okay, nine. I bought nine.

"You're trying to drive me crazy, aren't you?"

His growly voice next to my ear sends shivers through my body. It's the same reaction I had this morning when I woke up with him pulling me next to him, his voice rough from sleep as he told me good morning while kissing down my neck.

It was sexy then and it's sexy now. Honestly, it's probably never not going to be sexy, and I'm just fine with that.

"I don't know. Is it working?"

"You know it is." Emmett turns me around, his hands

holding onto the counter so he can pin me against it. "But I'm not complaining."

Emmett leans down for a kiss, which I gladly give him. Yes, we're in the office so we shouldn't be doing this. Then again, I shouldn't have sucked my boyfriend's dick under his desk yesterday, so in retrospect, a kiss is harmless. Especially since Simon isn't coming in until this afternoon.

My boyfriend. I can't get over that word every time I think about it. Emmett Collins, the man who I never thought would have more than a cameo during the roughest part of my life, is now the star player.

I remember Andi telling me that there was no timeline on when you find your person. That it's going to happen when it was meant to, not because you set it on the calendar. And she was right. She was so damn right.

Emmett picks me up and sits me on the counter, our lips never leaving each other as he pushes up my skirt so he can spread my legs apart. I pull him in closer by his button-down shirt, suddenly feeling just as daring as I did yesterday. Which was…I don't know where that came from. I mean, I've always had a fantasy about it, that wasn't a lie. But it had been buried so long because of The Small Dick Who Must Not Be Named that I almost forgot about it.

Until we were in an empty office and Emmett was looking damn good in a pair of khakis and a polo shirt. His hair was styled, and his beard was the perfect length that I like—just enough so I can feel the scratch. So yes, I did have a fantasy come true about having sex on an office desk, but fantasy or no, I would've let Emmett Collins do whatever he wanted to me yesterday, and I would have been a willing, and begging, participant.

Our kiss deepens, and I feel Emmett's hand trace up my leg and inside my skirt. I feel the wetness starting to pool and lean into him, hoping that makes him get there quicker.

"You want me to fuck you again, don't you?" Emmett's low

tone spikes my adrenaline.

"Yes."

"Oh Tiger…" Emmett starts unbuttoning my blouse, which today is a pale pink to go with my black pencil skirt. "You're going to be the death of me."

I let out a low moan as Emmett inserts a few fingers into me, pushing my lace panties to the side so he can find where he wants to go. I close my eyes and throw my head back, loving the feel of him working me like only he can. I hear the microwave beep to signal my oatmeal is done just as Emmett's mouth starts kissing the top part of my breast. I lean back, trying to give him as much access as I can when I hear the microwave beep again. I don't care. Let it go off for hours. A fire could start right now, and it wouldn't make me move from Emmett's mouth cherishing my body as his hand starts to pull my breast free from my lace bra. Actually, I don't think anything could stop me from letting Emmett do whatever he wants right now.

"What the fuck is going on!"

I was wrong. Simon catching us could definitely do that.

"Emmett? Stella? What in the actual fuck!"

Emmett and I both let out a gasp as we pull away and look over to Simon, who's standing in the doorway, eyes wide and mouth agape. Emmett does his best to cover me, which I'm grateful for since I'm a quarter of the way naked, but it also means I can't see Simon's entire reaction.

"Simon," Emmett begins. "It's not…"

"If you're about to say 'it's not what it looks like,' save it. Because it looks like one of my best friends, who happens to be my business partner, is making out with my sister on a counter."

"Okay. Yeah. It's exactly that."

"What the fuck!" Simon marches into the room as Emmett fully steps in front of me as I do my best to fix my clothing situation. I'm pretty sure I get a button wrong, but I don't have time to go back and fix it.

I need to fix this.

"Simon, we can explain."

"Oh, that's the minimum you're going to do," he says. "What the…how the…I'm…"

"I know," I say, popping off the counter and standing next to Emmett, quickly pushing my skirt down. "How about you head into one of the conference rooms. Take a breath. We'll be in there in just a few minutes, and we'll tell you everything."

Simon's eyes narrows as he looks from me, to Emmett, before looking back to me. Eventually he nods, turning and walking out without saying anything.

"Fuck," Emmett says, running a hand through his hair.

"Right? He's not saying anything. That's downright terrifying."

"He didn't punch me. That's a good thing?"

"It's Simon. He doesn't punch. He hires guys to punch. Shit, maybe we shouldn't have left him alone?"

I don't think he's actually hiring people to punch Emmett. Then again, he just walked in on me basically having sex with his best friend, so who knows what's in the realm of possibility.

"Okay," Emmett says, rubbing his hands on both my arms to calm us down. "We're ready for this. We wanted to tell him today. Maybe not like this, but it's here, and we gotta rip off the Band-Aid."

"Exactly. This was the plan." Though as I say that, I get another idea. "Actually, let me go grab something. Stall him until I get back. Give me ten minutes."

I don't give Emmett a chance to answer as I go racing out the back door and around the building into the diner. The only thing that stops me is the counter, which I nearly fall over and slam my hands onto, getting Charlie's attention.

"Stella? Are you okay?"

I furiously shake my head. "Simon just walked in on me and Emmett making out in the office and he's pissed. I need food or pie or something to soften the blow we're about to tell him that we've basically been sleeping together since Florida."

Charlie's face goes from concerned, to shocked, to happy, to damn near giddy in the span of seconds. "Yes! It's out in the open! Finally!"

"Yes. Fine. Tell everyone. But first can you help me with your man so I can tell him about mine?"

"Oh. Right. Yes." Charlie starts furiously making Simon some sort of iced, sugary, who knows how many pumps of things, drink as she calls out to someone in the kitchen to cut her a slice of apple pie.

"Here," she says, handing me a to go bag, as well as coffee for Emmett and a Diet Dr Pepper for me. "I'd come over to help you, but I know I won't be able to keep my poker face in check during all of this. So Godspeed."

"Thank you," I say. "And when he tells you tonight…"

She nods so I don't have to finish that thought. "I'll play dumb. Your secret is safe with me."

God, I've hit the jackpot with my future sister-in-law.

I wave to Charlie as I exit and walk back into the office. I decide to go through the back door again because I'm a chicken shit, and I'm startled when I see Emmett waiting for me.

"I thought you were going to stall Simon?"

He shakes his head, takes the drinks from me and kisses my forehead. "We're a team now, Tiger. We go into battles together. Hand in hand."

As he holds out his hand for mine, I look down at it, almost confused to what he's doing. No, not confused. Just still a little shocked that this kind of man exists. Emmett has done many, many things to make it known he's different from any other man I've been with. Even when he wasn't trying to. Never in the years that I was with Duncan did I feel this kind of support. Or love. Or that I wasn't alone. I never felt a part of a team.

Not until now.

With our fingers locked and a deep breath, we walk down the hallway into the conference room. Simon looks up from his phone and over to us, noticing our hands.

"Here," I say. "I brought you a drink."

Simon rips it from Emmett and takes a big swig.

"And pie," I add. "I got you pie."

"Apple?"

"Of course."

He eyes the bag, but doesn't make a move for it. "Thanks. But you're not going to soften me up with a drink and pie."

Damn. He caught on. Emmett stays back, holding my chair out for me, which I don't know if it's his manners or laying it on thick for Simon, but either way, it was a good move. "We have a lot to tell you. And I'm sure you have a lot of questions."

"Damn right I do." He turns his gaze to Emmett. "How long has this been going on?"

"Which part?" Emmett asks. "There are a few different stages to this."

"Stages! Stages take time. You've…wait. Did this start in Flor- ida? Did I pay for your sex vacation?"

"Technically…yes…" Emmett's words trailing off before I chime in.

"But that's not where we met."

Simon turns to me. "Where did you meet?"

I look to Emmett, fondly remembering the day that changed everything. "When I ran."

For the next twenty minutes, Emmett and I go back and forth as we tell Simon everything that he needs to know. How we met. The day, and night, I ran. Florida. How Florida didn't start like this, but as time went on, we grew closer. How we meant to keep it in Florida. But when I came here to work, it threw everything into shambles. Emmett even admits to being MIA last week because of me.

We don't, however, tell Simon about yesterday. That we're going to take to the graves.

Simon's silent when we finish the recap. I hold my breath as I wait for him to say something. Anything. For some reason, I expect him to grill Emmett, so I'm shocked when he turns to look at me.

"He was the clothes?" It takes me a second to remember that Simon's referring to the day after the wedding. "When you showed up at Mom and Dad's and were wearing a guy's clothes, they were his?"

I nod. "Yeah. They were his. But I swear, at that point, I didn't know you knew him. He was just the guy at the bar who took care of me."

Simon looks over to Emmett. The anger in his eyes has tempered, which lets me breathe for the first time in a while. "I always wanted to thank the guy she was talking about. We didn't know where she was. We knew she needed her space, but we were worried at the same time. So, thank you. Thank you for watching out for her."

"You're welcome," Emmett says. "But you don't need to thank me. I...there was no way I was leaving her that day. Turns out there was really just no leaving her. Ever."

I feel a tear start to form as Emmett gives my hand a squeeze. The way he's looking at me right now, and how I know I'm looking at him, it's like Simon isn't even in the room. But I know he is, which is why I refrain from kissing him.

"Wait," Simon interrupts. "Is this...are you two like actually in love?"

Love? Are we? I don't know if either of us know how to respond to that. I mean, we've never said those words to each other. I've thought it, but also it's so soon. Like way too soon.

Love isn't on a timer...

Except before I can say what I feel, even if it's too soon to say thing, Emmett speaks up.

"I don't want to speak for Stella, but I know I am."

He is? The man who up until days ago was a never relationship guy? I mean, I love him too, but...wow. I wasn't ready.

"I love you too," I say, not able to keep the tears back anymore.

He brings my hand up to his mouth, placing a kiss on it that maybe means more than one on the lips could right now. "Stella Banks, for years I didn't think I could do this. I was scared that I didn't have the relationship gene in me. And I still don't know what I'm doing, I just know I want to try and get it right. For you. For us. Because a life without you? I don't even want to think about that."

I'm about to lean over and kiss the hell out of this man, Simon be damned, but that's until I hear an audible sob coming from the other side of the table.

"Simon? You okay big brother?"

Simon nods, wiping away his tears. "You guys are in love. My baby sister and one of my best friends are in love, and it's all because of me!"

"Excuse me?" Emmett asks. Which I'm glad he does. Because…excuse me? "How is this because of you?"

"I'm your matchmaker!" Simon says enthusiastically. "Think about it. If I wouldn't have hired Emmett last year, he never would've been in Florida. I told him to check on you. I didn't realize he was going to take such a thorough interpretation of that order, but here we are. If it weren't for me, this wouldn't have happened."

Leave it to my brother to somehow make this about him.

"What about me running from the wedding and seeing him at the bar?" I ask. "That was complete random happenstance."

Simon waves me off. "Doesn't matter. Same outcome would've happened. All that matters is you're in love, Emmett's going to one day be my brother-in-law, your firstborn child will be named either Simon or Simone, and it's all because of me! Best matchmaker ever!"

"I—"

Emmett puts his hand on my forearm and shakes his head. "Let him have this. It's the best outcome we could've hoped for."

He's right. I didn't know what Simon would think. The man has become a romantic sap since Charlie came into his life, but

I'm sure it's also weird thinking about your best friend and your sister together. I didn't think punches were going to be thrown, but I expected a good amount of curse words.

At the end of the day, I'll take it.

"This is amazing," Simon says as he pulls me into a vice grip hug. "Wait! Who else in the family knows?"

I take a step back into Emmett's waiting arm. "Actually no one."

"Yes!" He starts actually doing a victory dance in the conference room. "Oh they're going to be so pissed I know before them."

"Don't go bragging," I order. "Let me tell the sisters, please."

"Fine," he groans. "But after you do, I'm rubbing it in their faces that I knew first."

"Deal."

Simon all but skips out of the office, taking the slice of apple pie with him. We watch him walk out of the door and turn to the diner, I'm sure to tell Charlie what's happening. Part of me wants to follow to watch Charlie act like everything he's telling her is brand-new information, but the other part of me wants to stay right here and kiss the man who I love.

The man who loves me back.

The man who saved me.

The man I can't imagine my life without.

guide to love rule #2

Green is a good color for
mint chocolate chip ice cream.
It's a great color for flags.

30
stella

"DO WE HAVE THE PIZZA?" MAEVE ASKS AS SHE GRABS PLATES FROM her cupboard.

"Check!" Ainsley yells.

"Do we have the wine?"

I hold up two bottles of Prosecco. "Check and check."

"Do we have Quinn?"

"Here!" I laugh as we take the iPad that Quinn's face is currently on into the living room of Maeve's house. "I wish I was there, but this will have to do."

Even though I asked Simon specifically to not let anyone know about me and Emmett until after I had the chance to tell everyone, that lasted for approximately twenty minutes before the sibling group chat blew up.

SIMON

I know something you don't know!!!!

MAEVE

Why are you five?

SIMON

I'm not five. But I know a secret about Stella
that you and the other sisters don't, and I need
to brag about it.

QUINN

It's laughable that you think you know
something about Stella and we don't. I mean, I
probably wouldn't. But you think Ainsley
doesn't? Or Maeve? Come on, Simon. You're
better than this.

SIMON

No! It's true! Stella! Tell them.

AINSLEY

Stella?

STELLA

I hate you.

MAEVE

Stella Leigh Banks! You tell us right now.

SIMON

Oooohhhh… you got Mama Maeve mad
at you…

STELLA

No. You did. Because you promised you'd let
me tell them.

AINSLEY

Tell us what?

QUINN

Please tell us, because I don't like Simon
having things he can hang over our heads.

STELLA

Can I tell you all tonight? I'd like to not do it
over a text thread. Especially one that Simon's
on, who, by the way, would fail in the wizarding
world if tasked to be the secret keeper.

SIMON

Rude.

MAEVE

Yes, you can tell us tonight. Come to my place at eight. Jayce is at his dad's, so we can talk as long as we want and I don't have to worry about drop off tomorrow morning. Quinn, we'll FaceTime you?

QUINN

You better or I riot.

SIMON

Can someone FaceTime me so I can see everyone's reactions?

STELLA

No. You lost that privilege when you started this text chain.

SIMON

Fine. Enjoy, sisters! Just remember that I knew before you, and also that everything that has happened is all because of me.

MAEVE

Why are you the way you are?

SIMON

Part of my charm.

So here we are, pizza and wine in hand, sitting around Maeve's expensive coffee table, with all sets of eyes on me.

"Are you going to make us ask?" Quinn says. "Or are you just going to tell us? I need to know how to proceed."

I feel the blush on my face start to creep in. "I've met someone and we're….together."

Silence takes over the room. Which I expected, so I continue on. "And, it's not just a random person off the street. Well, I guess he was when he met."

Another pause. "It's Emmett."

More silence. "Emmett Collins."

Are they seriously not going to say anything? "Emmett as in Simon's friend and business partner."

This time I finally get a reaction.

"Get the fuck out of here!"

Leave it to Quinn to break the silence.

"Holy…" For a second I think Ainsley's going to say a swear word. That's what her face is saying. "Wow."

Shucks. One day we'll get her to crack.

"Wow is right," Maeve says. "I didn't know you knew Emmett?"

"I didn't. Well, not until the day of the wedding."

"The wedding!" If Quinn keeps yelling like this she's going to break the iPad. "I thought you just went and got drunk?"

"I did," I say. "But turns out, I was getting drunk with Emmett."

"How did you not know?" Ainsley asks. "Emmett isn't exactly a super common name."

"Because there were no names that night. I was Tiger. He was Cap. And that's how we knew each other."

I fill them in on the rest of the details of that night they didn't know about, and how when I showed up in Florida he was there. How I tried to defend the house with a shoe. How we started spending time together. How that time started becoming more and more and before we knew it, we were inseparable.

"It was only supposed to be a vacation fling," I say. "Two weeks. He didn't do relationships, and God knows I wasn't in a place for anything serious. And it was a great plan…"

"Until it wasn't."

I tap my nose to Maeve's words.

"Oh! Stella!" Ainsley says, leaping over to hug me. "When you got back and you were on the curb crying, it was because of Emmett?"

I squeeze her back. "Yeah. We had just said goodbye. I didn't expect it to make me as emotional as it did."

"Well, of course it did. You loved him. And I'm not even mad that you've been lying to me about where you've been sleeping!"

She's right. I did love him. I just didn't know it.

"Back up," Quinn says. "You two had a vacation sex pact, which, good for you. And for your sake, I hope the orgasms were plentiful and frequent."

"They were," I say, smiling down at the FaceTime.

"Great to hear. But, I need to know how we went from 'only in Florida' to 'now you're together.' Because I feel like I missed about ten steps along the way."

I go back and pick up from that first day we worked together. The hot and the cold. The few days he ghosted.

"And then he showed up at Duncan's the day I was moving out, " I say. "He said that he thought about us, and him, and his life, and he wanted to try this if I was willing to give it a shot. Then he almost killed Duncan for trying to touch me. The rest is history."

"So fucking hot," Quinn says.

Maeve turns the iPad. "Which part?"

"All of it," Quinn says. "The available men I meet would never come to conclusions like that. Or put their heart out there. Or get all protective and alpha. Maybe I need to move back to Rolling Hills. Does he have a brother, Stel? Maybe a cousin in the twenty-nine to forty-two range?"

I laugh. "No. Just a sister."

"Of course," Quinn grumbles.

Ainsley doesn't say anything, but gives me a side hug. Quinn is rambling on about her lack of man options out in Arizona. Which gives me a second to lock in with Maeve.

"Do you have anything to say?"

I know she does, and I want to hear it. More than my other two sisters. She's Mama Maeve for a reason. She gives the best advice. She has the levelest of heads. She's our logical thinker. And I don't think I'd stop seeing Emmett if she didn't support me, but I'd definitely listen to her point if she did.

"Do you remember what we talked about in Florida?"

I think back to the phone call I know she's referring to. "You told me it was a rebound."

"I did. And now that I know Emmett was your Florida Man, I have to ask again, is this a rebound?"

I take a second to think about my answer. On the surface, it looks like that. I was with a guy for three-and-a-half years who I was supposed to marry. The day that was supposed to happen, I met Emmett. A week after that we were sleeping together. If that isn't a rebound, I don't know what is.

Yet, he's not. And I'm not sure what I know in this life, but I know he's not that.

"It's not," I say confidently. "Emmett…he's steady. Stable. Thoughtful. So many things I thought I had with Duncan that I'm now seeing I had none of. He makes me feel…whole? Does that make sense? I know I've never rebounded before, so I have nothing to compare this to. But there's something about this, Maeve—it feels like he's the one I was supposed to meet. That I was supposed to go through the shit I did to get here."

Maeve's stoic demeanor gradually turns into a smile. "Then you should go for it."

"Really?" Quinn says. "I figured you'd be the Debbie Downer and saying it's too quick and it's just a phase."

"You'd think that," she says. "I've been divorced for five years. When Josh and I split, the last thing on my mind was dating. Hell, it still is. The thought of trying to meet someone and do that all over again sounds absolutely horrible. Especially as I'm a package deal with Jayce."

"I mean, it is horrible," Quinn says. "Not all of us can stumble into a bar and into the arms of a hunky construction man."

"What I was saying," Maeve continues while giving Quinn the eye. "Just because I didn't want to date right away doesn't mean that's the right way. Hell, who am I to say what I know is right? Who are any of us? When it's right it's right. And if he treats her well, she's happy, and he's not getting flogged by a dominatrix, then who are we to object?"

We laugh at Maeve's joke. "Thank you. That means a lot."

"I know you want us to approve, but at the end of the day, Stella, this is your life," Maeve continues. "It's not something you need to have because the rest of us do. Or because you see everyone else having it. If this is right for you, then fucking do it. Be happy. Be in love. And we'll have your back. Like always."

Tears fall down my cheeks as I stand to walk over and hug my sister, Ainsley right behind me, making it a group hug.

"Stop!" Quinn groans from the iPad. "I'm already jealous I'm not there."

"Then come home," Ainsley says as we all wipe our tears of joy away. "Why are you even in Arizona still anyway?"

"Because I have a job," she says. "And friends. And a cat."

"You know the cat can move," I say. "And there are teaching jobs in Tennessee."

She doesn't answer, instead changing the subject like she's so good at doing. "I did just think of another pro in the Emmett column."

"What's that?" I ask.

"He's already Simon approved. At least I assume. Wait! How did he find out first?"

I instantly blush thinking back to this morning. "He might have walked in on us in the break room today."

"Stella Leigh!" Ainsley scolds in the nicest way possible.

"We weren't having sex…yet. Or then."

"Did you have office sex?"

I smile at Quinn. "A lady never tells."

"Bullshit. A lady tells. And brags. Because if she's getting railed on a desk, her sisters need to know."

We all laugh as I fill them in on enough details to assuage their curiosity. They aren't surprised whatsoever that Simon is taking credit for this. But also agree that no one is going to go along with his narrative.

Quinn tells us she has to sign off as she has to grade papers before going to bed, so we start cleaning up. We're just about wrapped up when there's a knock at Maeve's door.

"Who could that be?" I ask.

Maeve tosses down a dish towel before walking to her front door. "I have no idea."

Ainsley and I follow her to see that when she opens the door, there's a teenage boy holding two huge paper bags. "Delivery for Stella and her sisters."

What in the world?

I step in front of Maeve and take the bags as Maeve finds her purse to hand him a tip. Something is cold in here, which makes me even more confused.

"What's in the bags?" Ainsley asks.

"I'm not sure." I put them down on the coffee table and open the first. I start grinning from ear to ear as I see two tubs of ice cream, one birthday cake flavor and one mint chocolate chip, and a note on top.

> *Hope you have a good night with your sisters. Call me and I'll come get you when you're done. That way you make it home safe. And when I mean home, I mean with me.*
>
> *Love, Cap*

"Stop! Did Emmett send us ice cream?" Ainsley squeals.

"He did," I say as I hold the note to my chest.

"Oh girl, you've got it bad," Maeve says.

"In my defense, the man sends me ice cream. Wouldn't you?"

Maeve laughs and gives me a reassuring hug. "If a man sent me ice cream, not only would I actually start dating, I'd marry him on the spot."

31
emmett

There is no reason why I should be as nervous as I am.

Yet here I am, standing in my dining room, staring at a fully set table with Winnie looking up at me like I've lost my mind. All because I've set up a date night for my girlfriend so I can tell her that I love her.

Officially. And not in front of her brother.

Bark!

"I know girl," I say to my golden. "I never thought I'd be doing this either."

My dog is so confused. I don't think she's ever seen my dining table used for anything except a place to put the mail and the occasional blueprints I roll out. Yet, here it is, filled with candles, an array of pastas, sauces, and breadsticks, and a chilled bottle of wine. She also probably is wondering why her father, who she's only ever seen wear blue jeans or sweatpants, is wearing black dress pants, a white button down, and a watch that has special meaning simply because of when I bought it.

Oh, the things we do for love.

A few times today as I was setting this up, I wondered how I made it thirty-seven years of my life and never did something like this for a woman. Well, I know how I didn't, but it's also insane that I never wanted to. That I was so content living a solo life that I never even had the inkling to leave what I knew.

Apparently it does just take the right person to show you what you've been missing. Even if I would've been open to love in the past, I doubt I would've tried this with anyone else. No, I was waiting for Stella to come into my life. I firmly believe that.

Now I can't imagine my life without her.

Since Stella and I got caught last week—though she prefers the phrase 'went public'—there hasn't been a night we've spent apart. Well, until last night. She has quickly started taking over drawers and parts of my closet. Which is fine. They were empty anyway. And I'd be lying if I said it didn't do something to me seeing her clothes next to mine. Though if any more shoes make their way over, I'm going to have to build her a new closet.

Oh…I need to remember that for later…

Now that Simon is in the know, and is still taking full credit, we carpool to the office on days I work in Rolling Hills. The days that I stay in Nashville and she goes down to the office, she'll usually come here straight from work and pick up dinner along the way. Neither of us are much of a cook, so the arrangement has worked well.

Except this morning. This morning has been the first day I haven't woken up with Stella in my arms.

I'm not a fan.

Things popped up in the office last night that kept her in Rolling Hills until well after eight. And because she had to be back in the office early this morning because electricians were coming in to fix a wiring issue, it didn't make sense for her to drive back and forth. Since I had to be in Nashville yesterday and today, that means it's been two full days since I've seen my girl.

And that's two days too long.

I hear a car door shut, which sends Winnie frantically racing to the door to greet Stella. I turn back to the dining table one more time to make sure everything is where it's supposed to be.

Just as I'm moving one pan two inches to the left to evenly space them out, I hear Stella's voice at the entryway.

"Hey, girl." Stella's laugh and Winnie's pants are all I hear as I walk to greet her. "Oh, I missed you too."

I can't help but smile as I lean against the wall and watch Stella love on my dog. I mean, Winnie loves everyone. You show her attention, and you're her new best friend. But there's something about seeing the love of my life play with my first best girl that hits me square in the heart.

"That's enough," I say as I walk over to them, gently moving Winnie out of the way. "Quit hogging my girl."

I take Stella's hand and pull her into me so I can kiss her properly. Her hands finding the back of my neck sends a shot to my cock and I dip her down, kissing her so intensely that I'm about ready to say fuck dinner and go straight to dessert.

Which is an ice cream sundae bar.

"Good to see you too," she says as I slowly bring her back up. "Why are the lights dimmed?"

I keep hold of her hand as I lead her toward the dining room. "This, Tiger, is date night."

She looks back at me, then back to the setup, with shock and awe in her blue eyes. "Date night? For what? Is it an occasion? Crap! Did I miss an anniversary already? I'm usually so good at that!"

"No," I say with a laugh as I take her purse from her and she slips off her heels. "There are a few reasons for date night, and none of them are an anniversary. Unless you want to celebrate a belated one-month anniversary of us meeting and you trying to beat me with a shoe."

"If we don't have to, I'd rather not," she says. "I want our anniversary to be special and hold meaning. Not me running from a wedding wearing a horrible dress."

"Fine by me," I say. "We'll lock down an anniversary that's just for us."

"I like that." Her genuine smile hits me in the fucking heart, and I make it my damn mission to come up with the best damn anniversary there ever was. "So, you said there were a few reasons, care to share?"

I lean down to grab the remote for the sound system on my coffee table, turning it up slightly before pulling Stella in my arms. I found a ballad station earlier, and I doubt it knows what's happening right now, but the lyrics couldn't be more perfect as I pull Stella into my arms. We start swaying to a song talking about waiting a hundred years to find their person, and that they'd wait a million more. I've never understood when people say that they thought a song was written for them, but in this moment, I get it. I fucking get it.

"When we were in Florida, and you were telling me about what you wanted, I was jealous as hell," I begin. "I had convinced myself I couldn't be that for you. And I wondered why it bothered me so much. I had made that choice in my life. I was happy, or so I thought."

I pull her in a little closer as the song changes to a timeless classic. "I don't know if it was that night. Or the night I found you screaming in the rain. Or the night you don't want to remember, when we first met. It might have been all of them and a thousand other little times after, but at some point, I realized that I didn't want to be that guy who lived alone. I didn't want to just coast through life so scared of what-ifs that I never let myself try. I want to be more. I want to be happy. And I want to do it with you."

I see tears welling in her eyes. I didn't mean to make her cry, but I need her to hear all of this. "That night you told me that you wanted date nights and lazy nights in. You wanted random dances in the kitchen and a man who loves you so much it hurts. Well, this might be a date night in, and the dance isn't random, but Stella Banks, I do love you so much it hurts. But it's a hurt I want to feel every day because you're mine. And I'm yours."

I seal my words with a kiss, holding her so tightly I don't know if she can breathe. I slowly pull away, still needing to tell her one more thing. "Tonight was the night I wanted to tell you all of that. To tell you that I love you. And that I'm crazy about you, and I've never been more determined in my life to make anything work."

"Oh Emmett," she says, raising on her toes to kiss me again. "I love that you did that, and all of this, but you didn't have to do all of this."

"That's where you're wrong," I say, twirling her out before twirling her back in. A giggle leaves her body that's sweeter than any ice cream in the world. "I did have to. I wanted to. I wanted to make you smile. I wanted to show you how much I love you. And, contrary to your brother's belief, I did not intend on saying that I loved you for the first time in front of him. In fact, and I know he'd disagree with this, but I didn't want him there at all."

This gets me a laugh. "I mean, what girl doesn't want her brother being there the first time the man she loves tells her that?"

"Exactly." I dip her down low and plant a playful kiss on her neck before bringing her back up. The song changes again, but we don't say anything, again falling into the rhythm of the pop song I think I remember from my freshman year.

"This was my favorite song growing up," Stella says, her head against my chest. "And it wasn't because of the lyrics or anything, it's because it was Maeve's favorite."

I can tell she wants to say more, so I stay quiet to let her gather her words.

"I always felt like I had to be like my sisters. Or have what others did. That I was lacking if I didn't have the same clothes, or a date to the dance, or even if I didn't like the same music. It's how I lived my life. When everyone was getting married, I felt like the odd man out. It's how I almost ended up with…"

She trails off, purposely not saying his name. Which is fine. Fuck that guy.

"But now, as I'm here with you, this amazing and thoughtful night…how you make me feel every day…I don't want what others have anymore. Because there's no way they have what we do. And I wouldn't trade this for anything in the world."

I stop moving, but that's only so I can cup her face and bring our lips together. Fuck…how did I think I didn't need this? That my life was complete without this? For a smart guy, I was a fucking idiot.

"I love you, Stella Banks."

She holds my wrists, her eyes looking up at me with tears and love and forever. "And I love you, Emmett Collins."

Without giving her a warning, I bend down to pick her up, legs in my arms as I start walking her down the hallway to our bedroom.

"Where are we going? What about dinner? I saw breadsticks!"

"Not now, Tiger," I say, kicking open the door. "I think tonight we have dessert first."

guide to love rule #83

Find you a man who fixes you a plate.
Or will bail you out of jail.

32
stella

APPARENTLY THERE'S SOMETHING ABOUT FAMILY GATHERINGS AND me bringing over men in my life that go hand-in-hand.

When I officially brought Duncan to meet the family, it was for my parent's anniversary party. We'd been dating a few months, and even though none of my siblings had dates, it felt right to bring Duncan to meet everyone. Yes, he'd known my dad through the law firm, but it felt big. Monumental even. Granted, that was still early, so he was doing his best to impress everyone. Now looking back, I realize the smiles were fakes. The conversations were forced. His enthusiasm was all an act. It's amazing how blind I was.

Fast forward to today as the whole family, as well as Emmett's sister and nephew, have gathered for my dad's birthday.

The first sign that this was going to be different was that Emmett didn't even ask if he should come or not. It was "what time are we leaving" and "what can I bring." When we got here, his hand holding mine, he didn't hesitate to go say hello to my dad, even though they've met numerous times, and firmly shake his hand. Though I think the winning move came when he handed my mom a bouquet of flowers. A bouquet that matched ones he got me this morning after he went out and got us coffee and donuts and brought them to me in bed.

That earned him a well-deserved blow job in the shower.

Now as I watch him interact with my family, I can't help but realize how natural this all feels. He's talked to my sisters. Simon's excited he has a friend to play with. But the part that melted my heart was when Maeve's son, Jayce, came over and asked him to toss the football around. Emmett didn't falter. He just gave me a quick kiss then told him to go long.

Which is fine, he can have my nephew, because Emmett's has taken it as his duty to be my new best friend.

"More?" Jack asks in the sweetest voice I've ever heard as we stand at the buffet set up in my parent's backyard.

"What would you like more of?" I ask as I take his plate.

"Chips!" He says enthusiastically.

"Okay, we can have some chips." I grab a few, but then load some carrots and green peppers onto my plate. "How about we have some veggies too?"

He shakes his head. "Don't like 'em."

"Oh really?" I say as I scoop on a heaping spoonful of my mother's famous veggie dip. "But have you ever had them with the best dip in the world?"

Jack tilts his head like he's trying to decipher if I'm telling the truth or full of shit. "The best?"

"Yes!" I say as I lead him to an empty picnic table. "Would you try one? For me?"

He thinks about it for a second, his jaw ticking back and forth like it's the biggest decision of his three-year-old life. "Okay."

I smile and break off a piece of green pepper, making sure to thoroughly coat it in the dip before handing it to him. I watch as he reluctantly starts chewing, clearly wondering what his feelings are. Before I know it, he's bringing the plate in front of him, soaking every vegetable in dip before eating.

"What do you got there?" Maddie asks as she sits next to her son.

"I hope I didn't overstep," I say. "He asked for more chips. I threw on a few but made sure to add in a few veggies. Though now I feel like they are the accessory to the dip."

"Not at all. I don't care if he bathes in the dip if he's eating vegetables. I've tried everything to get him to eat anything green. You must be the Jack whisperer."

I laugh at the complement. "Nope. Just a girl who also hated vegetables as a kid."

"Well, thank you," she says. "And not just for performing a miracle with my son's choice of foods."

"Oh," I say, a little confused. "What else did I do, if you don't mind me asking?"

Maddie looks over my shoulder, so I turn to her eye line. Emmett is standing with my dad and Simon, talking like they've done this their whole lives.

"For years I tried to tell him how much of a great partner he'd be to someone. He's the most thoughtful guy I know."

"Is it true you used to call him Prince Charming?"

She laughs with a nod. "Only because it's true. It started with climbing a tree to save my cat then graduated to stepping in as a father-figure role when Jack's sperm donor notified me he had no interest in being a father. He just couldn't see it. But I knew it would just take that special someone to open his eyes, and that person was you. So thank you. I've never seen him smile like this. I was with him on the day he went to help you get your stuff from your exes. You should've seen how fast he moved. He didn't hesitate. I knew he'd love big, but I didn't realize how big until I saw it in person. It just makes me so happy to see because no one deserves it more."

Well, damn, I didn't think I'd cry today and I didn't wear my waterproof mascara.

Maddie and I share a hug, laughing and crying at the same time as we embrace.

"Mommy? Tella?"

We laugh as a clearly confused Jack looks on. "What's up, Bubbs?"

"You okay?"

Maddie nods. "Yeah, we're great."

We share one more smile as I feel familiar lips kissing my cheek. "Hey, Tiger."

Emmett puts a plate of food down for me—God, I love this man—and has barely sat down next to me before Jack's little yell takes us all by surprise.

"Uncle Met! No!"

What the heck?

"Jack, that wasn't very nice," Maddie says.

"No kiss Tella."

It's three seconds of shock, and a whole lot of seconds of trying to stifle our laughter.

"But she's my girl," Emmett says.

"No. *My* girl."

My eyes double in size, and I'm doing my best to not start cracking up. Or to pull Jack on my lap and tell him that he's my favorite and I'm getting him a pony for Christmas.

"All right," Maddie says as she grabs Jack's plate. "How about we go get more veggies and dip?"

Jack stands up, but not before coming around the table to give me a hug. And I don't know if I'm making it up, but I think he mean mugged Emmett before walking away.

"What the fuck?" he asks. "Did my nephew just try and lay claim to you?"

"He did," I say with a smile, leaning back to rest against Emmett's chest as he sits behind me at the table. "But don't worry. I like my men older."

"Damn right you do," he says as he starts kissing my neck.

"That's enough!" Simon bellows. "I might be okay with this, and keeping up my wedding officiant certification so I can one day marry you two, but that doesn't mean I need to see that."

"Oh shush," Charlie says as they join us at the table. "Just think, it could be the other guy."

I flinch a little at her words, which I hate that I still do. Because I don't want Duncan to have any effect on me, good or bad. I just want to be indifferent to his name and know that my life truly began when I walked in on him on his hands and knees.

"Shit. I'm sorry," Charlie says. "I didn't know if he was off-limits topic wise. I shouldn't have said anything."

I shake my head. "You're fine. It's just that sometimes it still stings, thinking of what I could be doing right now. Hell, what I almost did."

"What did you almost do?" Maeve asks as she and Ainsley take a seat around the table with us.

"Almost married a douche," Simon says. "Which, since we're on the subject, have you heard from him?"

Emmett holds me a little tighter, which I appreciate. "Actually, I haven't. Which kind of has me worried."

"Worried?" Ainsley asks. "Isn't that a good thing?"

"On the surface, yes. That means he finally got it through his head that we're not getting back together."

"That doesn't sound like the douche," Simon says. "He filed a lawsuit against you. He was calling you weekly to get you back. He tried to threaten me and dad for information. And suddenly he just stopped? Doesn't track."

"I don't know, Emmett scared him pretty good the day I went and got my things."

I look up to Cap, who has a well-earned prideful smile on his face. "Damn right I did."

He kisses my head, which earns "awws" from Ainsley, Maeve, and Charlie, and a groan from Simon.

"Enough already," Simon says. "Maeve. Please tell us there is something exciting in the world of interior design so we can change the subject."

Maeve shakes her head as she finishes a deviled egg. "Not

really. Men get divorced. Men move to the city and need their new condos decorated. Rinse and repeat."

Leave it to Maeve to completely undersell what she does. Maeve is one of the most sought-after interior designers and decorators in Nashville. And while she doesn't just decorate spaces for men, that's become her specialty. Rich men with no design sense but wanting a luxury condo or mansion to bring their new, often younger, girlfriends home to equals big bucks for my super-talented sister.

"She's lying," Ainsley says. "She has a mystery client coming at the end of the month that she doesn't know anything about."

Maeve shoots Ainsley a look. "I told you not to say anything."

"Well, then you told the wrong sister," she says. "You know I can't keep a secret."

"Spill," I tell Ainsley. "Everything that she told you so I can figure out who he is."

"Good luck," Ainsley says. "I tried. All she knows is that her budget is unlimited. And it's not just a condo in the city. It's a freaking mansion in Franklin. Like, next to the country stars' houses."

"Oh he's rich rich," I say. "And you don't know who?"

Maeve lets out a sigh, clearly hating that she has to talk about it. "I don't know and I don't care. His assistant sent me his color preferences, and I have the specs of the house. I don't even have the exact address, just that it's in Franklin and I'm to meet with him at the end of the month. They'll send me the details the day of the consult."

"Oh that's exciting!" I say. "And I'll find out. I'll dust off my social media stalking skills for you. It's been a minute since I've had someone to investigate."

The six of us start talking over each other, trying to guess who the mystery client is. Well, the four women do. I think Emmett and Simon have branched off into talk about Tennessee football. We're laughing, drinking, Emmett is stealing the occasional kiss, and I don't know if I've ever been happier.

This. This is it. This is what I wanted. A man who blends with my family. Me happy with my love life and getting to be with my sisters and family. Having a job I'm happy with, where I feel like I'm contributing in my own way. I don't know how it gets any more perfect than this.

"Are those police sirens?" Maeve asks as the distinct sound approaches our house. And not just one—it sounds like a convoy.

No one says anything else as we all stand and go walk through the fence and into the front yard. My mom and dad follow as Maddie hangs in the back with Jack and Jayce.

As soon as we step onto the front lawn we see that it's three cars lining the driveway. Two of them are Rolling Hills police cars, and one is an unmarked car.

What the hell is going on?

"Shane? What the fuck?"

That comes from Simon, who approaches Officer Shane Cunningham, one of his closest friends who he grew up with.

"I'm just here for support," he says in a near whisper. "This has nothing to do with me."

"Well then who the fuck does it have to do with?"

"Stella Banks?"

All eyes turn toward the Temu version of the guy from CSI, aviators and all. My blood goes cold as it sets in that he said my name.

I take a step forward, but not before I feel Emmett's hand on my back as he steps with me. "I'm Stella Banks."

"We need you to come with us."

"Just hold on there one second," Dad says as he walks in front of me. "I'm William Banks, her father and attorney. She's not going anywhere with you."

"Sir, you can accompany her if you'd like, but we need her to come with us."

"For what? And who are you?" Dad demands.

"We're from the SEC and the Tennessee attorney general's office. Miss Banks is the focus of an investigation. This will go easier if everyone cooperates."

SEC? The only SEC I know plays football.

"The Securities Exchange Commission? What does the SEC want with my daughter?"

Temu CSI takes off his sunglasses, like some sort of power move he's been waiting to do for years. "Miss Banks is being investigated for insider trading. She needs to come with us. Now."

33

emmett

"Emmett, sit down."

I shoot a death glare to Simon. "I won't sit until I know what the fuck is going on."

It's been eight hours since the police and the federal government showed up to take Stella in for questioning. Insider trading? I love the woman, and she's good for many things, but being savvy enough to buy and sell stocks after illegally obtaining information about what to do with said stocks? I don't think that's in her wheelhouse.

"Well you're making me dizzy, so sit the hell down."

I stop, send him one more menacing look, then reluctantly take a seat next to him. It's the only seat available, and that's because Charlie is upstairs putting Lainey to bed. No one left Mr. and Mrs. Banks' house today after Stella was taken away. Hell, even Maddie refused to leave. Mrs. Banks set the kids up in different rooms upstairs since it's now well past their bedtimes. Even Quinn is taking a redeye from Arizona.

It's good having everyone here, ready to act when the order comes. The only problem is, besides the charge that Stella's being questioned about, that's all we know.

And it's slowly killing me.

"Hey, she's going to be okay." Simon pats my leg as I lean forward, rubbing my temples from the headache I've had since Stella was driven away. "My dad isn't going to let anything happen to her."

"I know," I admit. "I just…I hate that I'm not there with her. I want to fix this for her. Fight it. Whatever it is. I just…I feel so useless."

"We all do," he says. "But I get it. You love her. That's what we do for the women we love."

On cue, Charlie comes back downstairs and I offer her seat back, but instead she sits on Simon's lap. He wraps his arms around her, holding on to her for comfort. It's what they do. They're a team in every way, feeding off each other when the other needs them.

That's what I want to be for Stella. And it fucking killed me that I couldn't go with her. Well, I could've, but William told me to stay. I wasn't allowed in the interrogation room, and who knows how long it was going to last. It was better for me to stay here with the rest of the family and wait.

And wait. And wait some more. No one is speaking or talking, and the silence is eerie. I'm guessing quiet isn't something that happens often in this house. It's so quiet that we all jump when we hear the sound of a door opening and Stella, along with William, walking into the living room.

"Tiger." Her name is a relieved breath on my tongue as I take four huge steps and scoop her into my arms. Her arms are a vise around my neck, and I squeeze her back just as hard. "Are you okay?"

I feel her nodding into my shoulder as she squeezes me even tighter, but she doesn't say a word. I just hold her until she starts to let go, and even then I refuse to take a hand off her.

"Stella, what can we get you?" her mom asks.

"I know I should drink water and it's late, but if you have a Diet Dr Pepper, that would be really great right now."

Demetria smiles and nods. "Of course, sweetheart."

I take a step back as everyone comes in to hug her. Questions are starting to fly, and I see Simon and William whispering something in the corner, so I step away to listen in.

"How bad is it?" Simon asks.

"It's not good," William says.

Before he can elaborate, everyone starts having a seat around the living room. I take Stella's hand, clasping it with both of mine, as I see her gear up to recap the events of the night.

"I know that if anyone was going to be a criminal mastermind in the family, it was probably going to be Simon. But joke's on everyone, it's me!"

"Not funny," Simon says harshly at Stella's attempt to lighten the mood. "That was all Ainsley."

"Hey!" she exclaims.

"Enough," William says, clearly not a fan of his children's jokes. "The charges are serious. According to the SEC and the AG, Stella bought and sold ten million dollars' worth of stocks based on the knowledge of clients at the law firm. They have years of evidence."

"Years?" Maeve repeats. "Stella, and no offense, do you even know what insider trading is?"

"Only what I know from the dumb training videos we have to watch every year," she says. "And even then I'm confused. Stocks? Not my thing. I have to use a tip calculator on my cell phone. You think I understand stocks?"

"That's what I thought," Maeve continues. "So how does the federal government think that you, a woman who would only buy stock in Steve Madden, would be doing millions of dollars of insider trading?"

"And that's exactly what the attorney general wanted to know," William says. "Apparently stocks involving companies that the firm represents have been on the radar for a while. Fishy buying and selling activity, but nothing that popped out. That was until the last year, when heavy buys and sells were happening and the only common denominator was that our law firm represented all of them. Investigators started digging, and when they looked inside, every one of the companies had meetings with us that would've detailed pertinent information about their finances. And that after all of those meetings happened, the files were accessed by Stella."

Audible gasps fill the room.

"We have individual logins for everything at the firm," Stella said. "It's supposed to help with security and tracing things back to people when shit hits the fan."

"But you didn't do it," Ainsley says. "I mean…you didn't, right?"

"Of course not. And that's what I told the investigators," Stella says. "The only problem with that is they don't believe me, since money that was used to buy and sell these stocks has been moving through a bank account with my name on it."

"What?" I wasn't ready for that bombshell. "You had a bank account, and you didn't notice money moving in and out?"

She shakes her head. "No. And that's because I thought that bank account was closed."

"I'm confused," Maeve says. "How do you not know about a bank account?"

"Because I thought my former fiancé closed it."

Fucking Duncan. Of course this has to do with him.

"I'm going to kill him," I growl as I start to stand up. Stella's hand on my thigh quickly stops me.

"Not yet. Because we can't tie it to him if he's dead. Then I go to jail, and I'm sorry, but orange is not in my color wheel."

She's right. I can't kill him.

Yet.

"When the investigators asked me about the checking account I had, I told them about my personal ones and the one that Duncan and I had for the wedding," Stella says. "We did talk a little about the money he took before the wedding, and how he changed my password and alert settings. Then they asked me about a second joint account with Duncan and honestly, I had to think back because I completely forgot about it. We opened it right when we got engaged, but it was hacked within the first week. I told him to close it immediately since it was at his bank. He was hesitant, but eventually agreed. Or so I thought. I signed a paper and everything granting permission to close it."

I watch as Stella's shoulders slump and she hangs her head.

"Hey," I bring her hand up to my lips to give them a reassuring kiss. "You asked the man you were going to marry to do something, and you trusted him to do it. This is not your fault."

"And that's what we told the investigators," William says. "Apparently, the account not only stayed open, but Duncan changed it to Stella as the main, and only, person on the account. That's the document she signed. And with that, he laundered millions through it."

"And let me guess," Simon interjects. "He was using Stella's log-in at the firm to access every client's file because, as the office administrator, she has access to everyone's files, which he wouldn't since he's a lower-level associate."

"That's our theory," William says.

"Oh, Stella," Maeve says. "He knew your passwords?"

Stella shakes her head. "I didn't think he did. But then again, I use the same three passwords. And before you say anything, no, I don't use the strong password suggestion because it's never remembered. And I didn't mean for Duncan to know the password. He figured it out, I guess."

"That's neither here nor there," I say, defending Stella. "We're here now. Does her being with us mean they are dropping the charges and going after Duncan?"

Stella sinks into my embrace as William shakes his head. "They let Stella go because they are still deciding the charges, and she's not under criminal arrest. Yet. They agreed to look into Duncan, but he did a pretty good job on the surface of staying clean on this and pinning it all on Stella."

"Is there more evidence?" Maeve asks. "Like, is there anything that can be dug up that would put a nail in his coffin?"

"Nothing short of a confession from him would be enough," William says. "And I doubt that smug bastard is going to do that."

———

Stella and I didn't get back home until after three in the morning. I don't think we said a word on the drive from Rolling Hills to Nashville. Or before she fell asleep in my arms, completely exhausted from the day.

I don't remember the last time I slept in past nine, but after yesterday's events, it makes sense. I probably could've slept longer if Winnie hadn't started pawing at me to take her outside. Stella barely moved when I rolled out of bed and is still sleeping.

I want to kill Duncan. Murder him with my bare hands. Then I want to bring him back to life so I can do it again.

It was one thing when I knew he was just a shitty human. I've met many men who were and many men will continue to be. But to set her up so she'll go to jail? To blame massive federal crime on her? Anything less than me sending him to an early grave isn't punishment enough.

"Hey," Stella says, her voice still sleepy as she walks into the kitchen. "Please tell me there's coffee?"

I reach into the refrigerator and grab the iced latte I had delivered about an hour ago. "I kept it cold for you until you woke up."

Her smile is small as I lean down and kiss her forehead. When I step back, I can't help but notice how defeated she looks.

"What can I do?" I ask, wanting nothing more than to take this pain away. Or to help get this investigation over. "Please, there has to be something, because I'm dying over here."

She shakes her head and Winnie sits at her feet, sensing her sadness. "I wish there was. Believe me, this isn't like the time I was moving out of his house and thought I could do it all myself. I genuinely don't know what anyone can do."

We walk into the living and sit on the couch, Stella all but on my lap as I hold onto her like the feds are going to storm in right now and take her away.

"I hoped yesterday was a bad dream," she says as I stroke her hair. "It feels like a nightmare."

"I know," I say, kissing the top of her head. "It's going to be a distant nightmare soon. I promise."

"How?" she asks as she sits up to look at me. "You didn't see all the evidence they had against me, Emmett. Thick folders. Like thick with four Cs. If someone on social media made a true crime documentary on me, it would take eight parts just to get through the things I allegedly did."

"I know it doesn't look good. But we'll think of something. We have to. There's no other option."

If either of us know that option, we don't voice it. In fact, we sit in silence for I don't know how long. That's until a few minutes later when the front door is thrown open and a woman I've only ever seen in pictures walks through.

"I've got an idea!"

We're startled as Quinn comes barreling through the front door, Maeve and Ainsley on her heels.

How do they know where I live?

"I'm sorry about her," Maeve says. "The child locks didn't keep her inside the car. Oh, and Simon is on his way. That's how we got the address if you were wondering."

Well, that clears one thing up.

"Fuck your child locks. This can't wait."

I know Quinn has always been described as the blunt one of the Banks family. And she might be. But right now, she's Simon in the female form.

"I had a very long flight with a ton of turbulence and a snorer behind me, so I had plenty of time to think," she says. "And I think I know how we're going to take Duncan down."

Now that gets my attention.

"Wait!" That comes from Simon, who is all but running into my house. "Did you start yet?"

"Nope," Quinn says. "You're right on time."

Stella sits up and looks around with the same confused look that's on my face. "Can someone please tell me what's happening right now?"

Everyone gets settled, but Quinn and Simon look like they're about to bust with excitement.

"Do you know what she's about to say?" I ask Simon.

"Nope. But if I know my sister, who to this day still lives in Rolling Hills High School history for a prank involving a foreign exchange student that never went to the school, it's about to be good."

All eyes are on Quinn as we wait anxiously to hear her thoughts.

"We need Duncan to confess."

"That's what Dad said," Stella says as we all nod in agreement. "The problem is, he'll never just come out and say it. If I confront him, it will be another one of his lies. I don't know how to get him to talk."

"What if we had some outside help?"

We look at each other, not knowing what, or whom, she's talking about.

"Just say the rest, Quinn," Maeve says. "Clearly we're not following."

"And the evil smile on your face is giving villain vibes," Ainsley says.

"Not villain. Let's call me a vigilante," Quinn says. "Because, somewhere over Oklahoma, it came to me. Men say stupid shit. Present company excluded."

"Nope, I do," Simon says. "But carry on because you're not wrong."

"Thank you. Men will say a lot of things during sex. Or to get laid. Or, in the case of one Pencil Dick Duncan Hughes, when he's getting whipped."

I think we all stop breathing.

Quinn is a fucking genius.

"I'm just saying," Quinn continues. "If I liked being spanked and called a good boy, there would be a lot of things I'd confess to my dominatrix."

guide to love rule #23

Men come and go. But female friends you meet in the women's bathroom, or when they're spanking your fiancé, last forever.

34
stella

"Are you sure this is going to work?"

This doesn't feel real. It feels like we're doing a bad reenactment of *Ocean's Eleven*. But instead of robbing a casino with high-tech equipment and a crew of criminals, it's me, Emmett, my brother and sisters, Nadia, and a guy my brother somehow knows who does surveillance that insists on being called Kaos.

And yes, he told me it was with a "K." Which makes sense, with his blue mohawk and gauged ears that you could fit a donut hole through.

"It's working on my end," Kaos says as he tests the camera and audio. "As long as he doesn't see it, we're smooth sailing."

Was Quinn's plan to hire Nadia to get Duncan to spill while we secretly recorded him with cameras strategically set up in the hotel room? Yes.

Is it ridiculous? Yes.

Did Simon then come in saying he knew a guy who could make this happen? Of course he did.

Which is how we're here, at the scene of the flogging crime—the hotel I was supposed to get married at—to catch Duncan in the act.

Hopefully not *that* act. Just the one where he admits that he's a trash human and the SEC can put him in jail instead of me.

He wouldn't last a day, even in white-collar jail.

"This is going to be fun," Nadia says as she comes out of the hotel bathroom, clad in her leather outfit. "I've never done this before."

"You've never got men to confess things?" Maeve asks as she sits at the hotel room desk.

"Oh plenty of times. They're usually accidental. One second I'm asking if they're being good boys, the next they're telling me all the times they weren't. But I've never got to use this power for good. It feels like I'm giving back to the community."

We all laugh. How is this even real life right now?

"I must say, you look stunning," Ainsley says. "The red lipstick really suits you."

"Why thank you." Nadia gives Ainsley a once over. "Now, I know this line of work isn't for everyone. But I'm just saying, you could make a lot of money with that good girl vibe you got going. Throw on a baby doll dress? Honey, you could make bank."

The roar of laughter that comes from the room can probably be heard fourteen floors down in the hotel bar. And Ainsley's blush? Poor girl is redder than Nadia's lipstick.

"Oh, Nadia, that was good," I say, still keeled over in laughter. "I really needed that."

And I did. It's been four days since I was questioned, and since then, it's been nothing but worry and stress and planning. I don't know if I've genuinely smiled since the moments before we heard those sirens. I've been a mess. I can barely eat. Sleeping has been few and far between because my brain won't shut off. And then once this plan was in play, all I could do was come up with the hundred reasons why it wouldn't work.

Honestly, I don't think I'd be standing if it weren't for Emmett and my family. My siblings have been taking care of everything so I didn't have to get my hands dirty. Quinn took the week off from work to help out. Simon found Kaos. Maeve has been the coordinator with Shane and a lawyer she knows to make sure everything is on the up-and-up. Even Ainsley's been all-in. This might be shady and borderline illegal; I think our good girl is finally going a little bad. She was the one who found Nadia. I still don't know how. I'd never Googled "dominatrix near me" before, so I assumed finding her was going to take a minute. Yet Ainsley came through in a pinch, and even went to pick her up this afternoon.

Then there's Emmett, who...I don't know how I would be getting through this without him. And it could be happening. With or without Emmett, Duncan was setting me up. I could be going through this without a rock. A shoulder to cry on. Someone to hold me and tell me that everything is going to be okay. He hasn't left my side, and I don't know how I'll ever thank him.

"Thank you again," I say to Nadia. "I know we met under unusual circumstances, and you could've turned us down."

Nadia shakes her head and takes my hand in hers. "I haven't been able to get the sight of you out of my head since it happened. I know I've been the other woman to many men, but knowing what he did to you? What I was doing to him on the day that was supposed to be yours? Absolutely not. Fuck him and fuck his audacity. Getting him to confess this shit is the least I can do. And I know exactly how I'm going to play him. Sometimes he likes me to be comforting before I start the whipping. I'll play into it nice and thick. He won't know what hit him. And yes, that was a dominatrix pun."

Everyone laughs as Nadia and I embrace. It hits me at what a full circle moment this is.

"He's here. The eagle has landed."

Quinn's voice carries through the hotel suite, announcing that Duncan has walked into the lobby. When we were devising roles and plans for today, Quinn was all too eager to sit in the hotel lobby in disguise, waiting for Duncan to enter. She got very excited when Kaos told her that he had a phone app that could serve as a walkie talkie.

"Places," Simon announces. Which is really just for Nadia and Kaos. Nadia grabs her bag of props and uses the adjoining door to go next door while Kaos takes his spot at his computer monitors.

"I still can't believe he fucking fell for the bait," Emmett says.

I laugh. "Oh I can. I guess four years with him did do me some good."

Once we had Nadia on board with the plan, the next part was the hardest—getting Duncan to show up alone. And, being the narcissist he is, we were able to play him like a fiddle. All it took was one phone call from Nadia, who said how much she missed him, and that she'd give him a free session, and boom, they were making a date for right now.

"Here we go," Kaos says as he adjusts the volume as Duncan enters the hotel suite.

My blood pressure spikes when I watch him walk in on the computer screen. I'm feeling so many emotions as he slithers his way to Nadia like the snake he is.

I'm fucking furious for what he's done to me.

I'm disgusted at myself that I was with him for as long as I was.

But the biggest feeling? Indifference. I couldn't give two shits about him. I want him to confess. I want him to go to jail. And I want him to be a distant memory in the Book of Stella.

Now, Emmett on the other hand? I'm pretty sure he's ready to commit murder.

"Easy there, Cap," I whisper. "Remember, if anyone is going to go sneak attacking him, it's me. I even brought the good shoes to do it with."

My joke doesn't seem to lighten his mood, but I can't concentrate on that. Because Nadia is about to get going.

"There's my good boy," she says, holding out her arms. Duncan walks into them and leans in to start kissing her.

It turns my stomach.

"Oh my God is that how he kissed?" Maeve says with disgust.

"Ew!" Quinn says a little too loudly as she enters the room. "It's like he's trying to eat your face."

"Shhh!" We whisper-yell. The walls can't be that thick, and if we get caught, then I'm fucked. This is our one and only chance to take Duncan down.

"You didn't tell me I was a better kisser?" Emmett says, the teasing back in his voice.

"I figured it was assumed that you're better at everything."

Emmett kisses my forehead as we turn back to the monitor.

"I'm glad you called," Duncan said. "I needed to let things settle down before we met again."

"Of course," she says. "It had just been so long. I didn't want my good boy thinking I was mad at him."

Damn, she's good. She's doing exactly what she said and playing into the comforting role. Her voice is smooth and sultry, and if I were into women I'm pretty sure I'd let her call me a good girl.

"Well, you did seem to side with Stella," he says. I feel Emmett tense next to me when he says my name. And, I'm not going to lie. Watching my man get angry over another man simply saying my name? Fucking hot.

"I need to apologize for that," she says, slowly stroking her whip up and down his chest. "I was just confused. I wasn't expecting your wife to come in and catch us."

"We didn't get married," he says.

"Oh no," Nadia starts gently stroking his face. "Are you okay?"

Holy shit, she's laying it on thick.

"I will be," he says in a sad voice which is completely fake. "I'll be much better once I'm with you, Mommy."

The collective gagging sound of everyone in our room echoes off the walls. Even Kaos can't handle it.

"I want to throw up," Ainsley says. "Stella, he's truly awful."

"I knew he had mommy issues," I say. "But I didn't realize it went this far."

Oh God I was going to wear is mother's wedding dress. What if he wanted me to keep it on that night! And her name is Sheila! And I'm Stella! Is that a coincidence?

I swallow back the bile in my throat and do my best to collect myself. I can go to therapy later for those thoughts, but right now, I need to focus on what's happening. I have a feeling we're about to get to the good stuff.

"That's my good boy," Nadia says, her demeanor hardening as she gets into character. "Now take off those pants for me."

Duncan starts to do so, but looks up at Nadia as he undoes his belt. "Did you mean what you said? This time was free?"

I bite my lip, knowing what we've told Nadia to say next when the conversation turned to this.

"Of course it is," she says. "I called you. I missed you. Of course it's free."

"What a dumbass," Quinn says. "Like any well-respected dominatrix does it for free."

"Well, he's an idiot," Emmett chimes in. "Combine a narcissist with a dumbass, and you get this fucking guy."

The two share a fist bump, which makes me smile. Quinn isn't an easy one to win over, even if she did live here. It's that simple moment that makes me realize I've picked right.

"Why haven't you called me?" Nadia asks. "Is it because of how I acted the last time we were together?"

"Here we go," Simon says, rubbing his hands together.

"Partly," he says. "I had to get some other things in order."

"What kind of things?" Nadia asks, walking a little closer and starts playing with his still limp dick over his boxers. "The wedding?"

He shakes his head. "I had some money troubles."

"Come on..." I say under my breath, starting to rock back and forth. I reach for Emmett's hand, squeezing it because I need something to keep me grounded as we watch and pray that Duncan is the fool we know he is.

Nadia takes her pointy nail and starts tracing it up and down his cheek bone. He leans into her touch. It's like I'm watching him be cast under her spell. "Money problems? But you're so rich. You told me about all the money you had."

"I am," he lies. "Just had a rough patch."

"A rough patch? What happened?"

He shakes his head. "Nothing I want to get into."

"Fuck," Simon grits out. "He's not opening up enough."

"Give her time," Maeve says. "We knew this wasn't going to happen in the first five minutes."

"That's okay," Nadia says as she starts to lead him to the bed. "I know how to make everything better."

"Do we need to be subjected to this?" Quinn asks. "Our eyes didn't do anything wrong. And Ainsley shouldn't have to see this."

Ainsley shudders. "No one should have to see this."

I hold my breath and clutch Emmett's hand while wrapping my other through his arm as we stare at the monitor. Nadia's directing Duncan to undress as she snaps her whip against her hand.

"On the bed," she orders. Her change of tone is immediate and intense. But it seems to light something in Duncan as he immediately listens.

"Good boy."

Crack!

We all flinch at the sound of the whip hitting Duncan's bare ass. I must say, the sound quality Kaos has is top-tier.

"No," Duncan mewls as Nadia cracks him again.

"No?" she asks. "That's not our safe word."

He shakes his head. "No, I haven't been a good boy."

Crack!

"Oh really?" she asks, walking around him and tipping his chin to look her in the eye. "Do you need to tell me about it?"

He nods. "Yes. I've been so bad."

Nadia goes back to her assumed position. "Tell me. What bad things did my good boy do?"

Everyone goes still in our room. No one is breathing.

"This is it," I whisper. "Please God let this be it."

Crack!

"I used information from my company to buy stocks."

Crack!

"Is that all?"

He shakes his head, which earns him another whip.

"I stole money from my fiancé," he says.

Crack!

"Don't hold back. Tell me what a bad boy you've been. Tell Mommy everything."

"I used her for stock information," he says. "I looked at files she had access to and bought and sold stocks. Put the money in an account with her name on it. Then she quit, so I lost her log-in and access. And then I lost the money. I lost *all* the money!"

Crack crack!

"Holy shit," I mutter. "That's why he wanted me back. He thought if we were back together, I'd come back to work at the firm. Once I was gone, he lost access."

"And he probably thought after the wedding you were going to quit," Maeve says. "That's why he filed the lawsuit. He wanted to scare and intimidate you. He knew you usually just let things slide away. No way would you have wanted a lawsuit. He scares you with it, you, in his mind, come to your senses, and after a few chats everything goes back to normal. You go back to work. He has your password. And the trading continues."

"I'm going to snap his damn neck." Emmett growls as he starts to make a move through the adjoining door, but I hold him back. "Just wait. We need to let him bury himself."

"Is that it?" Nadia asks as we all turn our attention back to the main show.

He shakes his head. "The government is investigating. I

made it look like Stella did everything. I think I got away with it. But I lost all the money. It was all for nothing!"

"We got him," Simon says, which is all the permission Emmett needs to go barreling through the door. Before Duncan even knows what's happening, Emmett has him pinned against a wall, holding him up by a flimsy white T-shirt. We all enter the room, and I don't know about everyone else, but I'm doing all I can to not look at Duncan's dick swinging below.

Partially because I think he's about to pee himself.

"You're fucking done," Emmett says. "You think you can set Stella Banks up and there not be repercussions? You're a bigger fucking idiot than we realized."

Emmett slams him against the wall before tossing him on the bed, setting him up for Simon, who comes in with a punch straight across the face.

"I've wanted to do that since the moment I met you." He winds up and throws another one. "Fuck with my family again, and you won't walk out of here alive. Understand?"

Duncan nods, fear in his eyes as his now ghostly white face tries to get a sense of bearings. I grab a blanket as I walk over to him, tossing it over his crotch, because we don't need to see that.

I lean over, making sure that he looks me square in the eye. "I fucking loved you. I wanted to be the best wife, best partner, best friend you ever had. I did everything for you. And what was it all for? Nothing? Con the woman who had access to everything in the law firm just so you could get rich? Was that all this was?"

Duncan shakes his head as he sits back up. "No, Stella. Baby. I loved you. I still do. I can explain everything."

It's been a minute since I slapped someone in the face. Never a man. Then again, is Duncan a real man? Either way, the slap I deliver straight across the face stings my hand in the best way. He falls back on the bed, holding his face that's now received a slap and a punch as I go stand over him.

"I want you to remember this. Remember me. Remember that you could've had everything, and your greed and pride is why you're going to be in jail. Alone. You threw your life away for a few bucks. And as for me? I'm going to say thank you. Thank you for being a greedy asshole. Thank you for being a worthless human. Thank you for being a goddamn idiot and getting caught in every shady thing you did. Because it led me to the happiest I've ever been. With a man who loves me for who I am, crazy and all. I'm going to live happily ever after, and you're going to rot in fucking jail."

I turn on my heel and walk away, head held high and more confident and free than I've felt in years. And why shouldn't I? My name is about to be cleared. Any and all lawsuits are about to be dropped. Duncan is about to be exposed for everything he did. I get my reputation and name back.

Yet, I'd go through this all again if it meant finding Emmett. The running. The shitty relationship. Almost going to jail. If I knew Emmett was waiting for me on the other side, I'd experience it all again.

Because once you know a love like ours? You realize that there's nothing you wouldn't do to have it in your life for as long as possible.

35

emmett

~~ Eight weeks later ~~

I let out a groan as I turn to Stella, who's walking into the bathroom where I'm finishing brushing my teeth. "I hate the sun."

"No you don't," she mewls, coming over to me and placing a kiss on my cheek. "Sun's out, guns out, baby. It's time to go to the beach!"

The last time we were in Florida, I convinced myself I didn't mind the beach. Granted, I was looking for any excuse I could come up with to spend with Stella. But now that we're solidly together and it's November, I figured I could avoid the sandy hell this time around. But no, it's an unseasonably warm day, which means Tiger wants to go to the beach.

Which of course I'm going to do because I love the hell out of that woman. But I'm not going to be happy about it.

"You know I love you, right?"

"Yup!" she says as she jumps up and down in a victory dance. "Now grab your book and your sunscreen. It's beach day!"

She kisses me one more time before skipping out of the bathroom. I finish getting ready, flip the light off, and walk back into the master bedroom of the rental house we're staying in.

And not just any rental house. *The* rental house. The Destin house where so many memories were made and started it all.

It's where I first fell in love with her, though I didn't know it at the time. It's where she tried to beat me with a shoe, and where she rediscovered her love of Alfredo sauce. Where I held her for the first time as I buried myself inside her. Where we spent nights wrapped up around each other and mornings lazily in each other's arms.

I've already talked to Simon about buying the house, which Stella doesn't know about yet. Not that I don't want others to live here—it's just that this is our house in so many ways. I want to come here with her whenever we want. I want to skip away for weekend trips. Bring our kids here one day. Though we won't have our honeymoon here—well, not the official one at least. When that happens, it's going to be the trip of our dreams.

But that's a long way down the line. We've only been together officially for three months, and most of that has been dealing with the Duncan fallout. That's partially why we're here. Stella's birthday is next week, and to say she's been a ball of stress is an understatement. So I told Simon we were skipping out for the week and I whisked her off to Destin. It was the perfect way to make her unplug, relax, and let me celebrate with her privately before her family birthday festivities next week.

The festivities she knows nothing about, that Ainsley and I are planning.

When I walk into the bedroom, I see Stella sitting on the bed in her bikini, and while I'd love nothing more than to peel that thin fabric away, I realize the happiness she had just a few minutes before has faded away.

"What's the matter?" I say, taking a seat next to her. She tilts her phone for me to read, which is an email from her father.

"He pled guilty," she says, the relief evident in her words. "It's over."

Unfortunately, the saga with Duncan, the civil suits, and the fallout with the law firm took much longer than any of us would've liked. Granted, we all wanted for this to be over and done in a day, which we all know was a bold ask. And relatively speaking, it was quick. It just seemed to drag forever.

The video and audio footage we gathered that day was swiftly, and anonymously, sent to the attorney general, the SEC, the partners at Carter, Banks, and Fairchild, as well as Mr. Banks. When William asked Simon about it, he denied up and down that he had anything to do with it. All of the sisters followed suit. But the look of pride in his eye when he realized all of his children were full of shit was undeniable.

Because this was considered an anonymous tip, it was enough for the investigators to start digging. And lo and behold, if people looked past the surface of Stella's passcodes being used and her bank account funneling the money, the next person was Duncan. But the giveaway? The moron used her passcodes during the two weeks she was away in Florida with me.

I was fucking her, and he was fucking himself. I think that's quite poetic.

We knew Duncan was being questioned this week because of William, which was another reason why I wanted to get Stella the hell out of Dodge. I didn't want her worrying about whether or not he'd lie his way out of it again. The investigators seemed to believe that Duncan really did it the last time we talked to them, but who knows what he'd say to change their minds.

"Dad said that he confessed to everything," Stella says as she reads the email. "To using my logins and passwords. To using the bank account. Every stock he bought and sold, some of which they didn't even know about. He admitted to it all for a shorter sentence."

"Damn." It's good to see he did the admirable thing and pled guilty. Oh, who am I kidding? He did it to save his own ass. I have a feeling poor little Duncan wouldn't like being spanked in prison as much as he did by Nadia. "I can't believe he's going to jail."

"Neither can I. Granted, it was jail or pay the money back, according to what Dad told me. This means he doesn't have a penny to his name. So if pleading means a shorter sentence, he's going to sing like a canary."

I bring Stella into my arms, holding her tight as he finishes reading the email from her dad.

"It's over…" she whispers. "It's finally over."

I feel the immediate weight off my shoulders. And if that's the relief I'm experiencing, I can't imagine how she's feeling right now.

"It's over." I repeat, kissing her temple. "You never have to worry about him again."

"It doesn't feel real," she says. "This has been my life for weeks now. And just…all of a sudden…back to normal? What is normal? Is normal before I even met Duncan? I definitely haven't been normal since we've met. Things are going to be boring. Oh no…what if now that I'm a regular person without lawsuits and federal investigations you're bored and break up with me?"

I flip her over onto her back, kissing her because I need her to be quiet. Also this bikini has slowly been killing me since she first showed it off. I am but a weak man who's obsessed with his woman. "Stella Banks, you are the farthest thing from boring."

I quickly untie the top of her bikini and push it to the side so I can start peppering her chest with kisses. Unfortunately, that's not a good enough distraction, as she keeps rambling.

"How do you know that? You've never met me without catastrophic things happening in my life. You're assuming now, Cap, and it's not good to assume."

I sit up on my knees and pull at the strings of her bottoms. Again, she's rambling about something, and I don't even think she realizes that I'm stripping her, between her thoughts of being boring and if she should go on social media and make a multi-part series about "the man I almost married."

I stand up, figuring I might as well take off my clothes while she's distracted. It's not until I grab her legs and pull her so far down the bed that when I sit her up and she's in eyeline with my cock, does she truly realize what's going on.

"Are you going to stop talking nonsense? Or do you need something in your mouth so you'll listen to what I have to say?"

Her eyes heat, and she licks her lips before slowly circling her tongue around my cock.

"That's my girl," I say. "Now, do boring girls like sucking cock?"

She shakes her head no as she takes me in.

"Do they swallow their cum in the office while hiding under desks?"

She shakes her head again, all while doing something wicked with her tongue.

"Do boring girls get fucked over desks? Or on balconies where anyone could walk by and see them?"

Her face blushes thinking back to what we did last night. Which, for the record, was one of the hottest things we've ever done.

"And do boring girls try to get in fights at bars and run away from weddings and befriend strangers?"

With every one of my words, Stella starts working me harder and faster. It's like my praise is fueling her.

"No, they don't. Because Stella Banks, you are the farthest thing from boring. And if you're going to forget that, then maybe I should remind you."

A popping sound comes from her sweet mouth as I pull her off me, but not so hard as she doesn't have her bearings. In one motion I have her back on the bed, her leg on my shoulder, as I line my aching cock up to her and slide in.

"You're the furthest thing from boring," I say as I push into her, her heat wrapping around me as I make sure she's good before letting go.

"You're fucking beautiful."

And she is, really, at all times. Dressed up in her heels and skirts that try to kill me. Wearing my T-shirt with no makeup. Sweaty when we're at the gym. Every time I see her, it takes my breath away.

"You're strong as hell."

I mean, who could run from a wedding, figure out a new life, be threatened to be sued, be questioned by the feds, and come out wearing a smile and never letting her demeanor crack? Stella Banks, that's who.

"You're smart. Funny. The furthest thing from boring."

I lower her leg and slow my thrusts, but just because I want to lean down and take her lips as soon as I'm done saying this last one.

"And Stella Banks? You brought out something in me I didn't know was buried. You make me want to be a better man. I can't wait to show you all the ways you're not boring. Because this life? The one we're about to start? Boring is going to be the furthest word from it."

I capture her lips with mine, burying myself in her deeper than maybe I ever have before. She purrs into my mouth and I hold her closer, wanting not a breath of air between us.

Boring? How could she think for a second that she's boring? Every time I'm with her it's something new. New sounds or touches. New ways she screams my name. Everything with Stella is like the first time, every time.

And I don't think I'll ever get tired of it. I'll sure as hell never think she's boring.

"Emmett…" My name spills out of her mouth as she tilts her head back. "Please."

She'll never have to ask twice.

I place her back down on the bed, this time bringing both legs to my shoulders. I've learned this is Stella's magic switch, and I'm not going to be too far behind her.

Stella's back arches and her legs tense against my chest

seconds before she explodes onto me. It's enough to send me just seconds later.

"Fuck me..." Those are the only words I can think of as I slowly bring her down and fall onto the bed next to her.

"You said it," she says, rolling over so she's now on top of me. "I love you, Emmett Collins."

She places a small kiss on my lips as she starts slowly running her fingers through my hair. The acts are enough to send me into a late morning nap.

"I love you too, Tiger."

That gets me another kiss before she moves slightly higher so her mouth is right next to my ear. "I'll give you ten minutes to recover, but we're still going to the beach."

I groan, but only in jest.

I'll take her to the beach.

I'll take her to the fucking moon.

I'll take her anywhere.

Because that's what you do when you meet the person you were meant to find.

The person who adds a little chaos to your calm.

The person who completes you.

The person you know you're going to spend the rest of your life with.

guide to love rule #71

The best surprise you can have is finding love. The second best is impromptu closet sex.

epilogue

Stella

A YEAR AGO TODAY, I THOUGHT I HAD MY LIFE PLANNED OUT.

I was turning twenty-six. I was engaged to a man I thought was my forever. I had a good job, good friends, a loving family, and nothing seemed to be standing in my way of a happily ever after.

Funny how so much has changed since then, and yet, as I'm celebrating birthday twenty-seven, these same general statements are true.

My friends and family are doing amazing. Andi is still at the law firm, and we still have our regular Thursday night drinks. It's where she gives me the tea from the office, and I tell her about the antics of small-town Rolling Hills.

I always knew I'd move away from Rolling Hills after college, but I must admit, now working there each day, I love being back. Seeing my parents more, as well as friends from grade school, has been a nice change of pace to the hustle and bustle of Nashville.

And speaking of my job, it's not just good, it's great. At first I thought my position with Magnolia Properties was temporary, but turns out, I'm in it for the long haul. And I couldn't be more excited about it.

In the few months since I've come in to run the office and social media, the company is pacing ahead of Simon's goals for year-over-year progress. All of our rentals are filled, and each month we are adding more properties. I want to pat myself on the back for being responsible for that, and while I am a part of it, most of it is because my brother and boyfriend have a knack for going viral on the social media app, *For You*. Who knew having two handsome faces of a company, combined with their unfiltered ways of giving dating advice, could make people flock to a real estate company? We even have merch. Everything from hoodies to tumblers to baby onesies. Because of course, Lainey had to have her own line.

The best part, though, is seeing how energized Emmett is. Because we're ahead of our schedule in terms of growth, it's looking like within the next year, the construction portion of Magnolia Properties is going to begin, with Emmett being the head of the division. I've come home some nights and just stood back to watch as he pours over designs and ideas. He's so determined to make each home truly special. It's inspiring to be a part of.

Then again, what else would I expect from a man who makes it his mission each day to show me how special we are together?

I remember when he thought he was going to be bad at being a boyfriend. Or being in a relationship. That's the furthest thing from the truth. The man could write a book on how to be a supportive and loving partner. Take today, my birthday, for example. After he made me breakfast in bed—and I was *his* breakfast in bed—he handed me gift cards for my favorite stores at my favorite mall. This is even after taking me to Destin last week for a birthday celebration for just the two of us. Apparently, he had more up his sleeve. So he arranged for Maeve to pick me up for a girls' day—which was going to lead into a dinner tonight at my parents' house. When he smacked my butt out the door I was told to use all the gift cards and any credit card I wanted. I wasn't to worry about money or where to put the new shoes and clothes I would inevitably buy.

He's really the best.

And yes, Emmett and I are officially living together. I don't even know when it actually happened. We never had a talk about it. Slowly but surely more and more of my things ended up at his place. I never slept at my old apartment. Then one day I called it "home" and he didn't correct me. Actually, he kissed me so hard my lips bruised.

I know we haven't been together long. And some might say it's too quick to move in with him. Those same people probably thought it was too quick for us to even be together, let alone say we love each other.

And to those people, I'd kindly say, "go fuck yourself."

Emphasis on kindly. I'm a southern lady, after all.

Though that's all hypothetical. My entire family is one-thousand-percent Team Emmett. My dad loves him. Hell, the two of them, along with Simon, have a standing tee time Sunday morning. My mom has told everyone she knows about us. And when her judgy bingo group made snide comments about me just being engaged, she told them to kick rocks.

Literally. She said that phrase. I now know where I get my mouth from.

And as for my sisters? They welcomed Emmett with open arms. And they didn't do it just because they're my blood. Believe me, it took them years to warm up to Duncan, and even then they were never completely sold on him.

That should've been my first sign.

I think about Duncan from time to time, mostly because it's funny that as much as I'd rather erase him from my memory and life, I know I wouldn't be here without him. I hate to thank him for anything, but strangely, I do.

And Nadia. I thank Nadia regularly at our weekly lunches. At our last one, I told her that Duncan is serving a three-year sentence with the possibly of parole in eighteen months. He lost his law license and will be on house arrest for the remainder of his sentence if he does get paroled early.

Fitting that he'll have to move back in with his mother, since the feds seized the condo. And his precious fucking whiskey.

That last one always made me smile.

"What are you cheesing about?" Maeve asks as we pull out of our parking spot in the mall after our day of shopping.

"Nothing particular," I say. "Just how everything has turned out."

"Yeah, it has been quite a year for you," she says. "Hey, can you reach in the back and grab my sunglasses out of my purse?"

I do as she asks, doing my best not to fall as she pulls onto the freeway.

"Here you go." I give her the sunglasses, and that's when it dawns on me we're not going to the right direction to Rolling Hills. "I thought we were going to Mom and Dad's?"

She shakes her head and maneuvers into the middle lane. "I need to run home before we go, so I'm going to take you home. I'll just meet you and Emmett there."

"Oh," I say. "Shit. I think he left already."

"He didn't," Maeve said. "I texted him while you were checking out at the last store."

"Oh," I say, wondering why she didn't tell me. "That's fine. As long as he knows."

We sit in silence for a few minutes as I check my phone, thanking the friends who I never talk to for an entire year except when they post on my Facebook feed to have a happy birthday. I scroll for a minute when I see an article pop up that draws my attention.

"Hey! Did you see the news about Logan Matthews?"

"Who's that again?" Maeve asks.

"Who's that?" I swear my sister lives under a rock. "The video game billionaire? The one who invented the game every kid in the world plays? Your son included?"

"Oh yeah, that guy," she says. "What did he do now?"

"More like *who* did he do," I say, skimming the article. "He was photographed with Sabrina Rome last month. And now last night it's some model."

"Why do we care?" Maeve asks.

"Because this is the fifth woman in three months he's been spotted with."

"Good for him? Sounds like another stereotypical billionaire playboy."

"But see, that's what I think they want us to think."

"Who's they?"

"They! The PR Machine!"

"Is that a new band?"

I roll my eyes. I swear my sister is thirty-six going on seventy.

"You know what I mean. A relationship just to be in the head-lines. Think about it. The man is a video game nerd who hit big. A hot nerd, but still, a gaming geek for all intents and purposes. And the women he's been seen with probably can't spell console. Except Sabrina. She can do no wrong."

"Your point?"

"My point is, all the models he's been with are up-and-comers. Even Sabrina, when they were photographed, she was just getting out of a horrible relationship. All the women have needed him to get their name out there. And maybe he's trying to seem like he's not a video game nerd. Which fine if he is. He's a hottie with his glasses. But at the end of the day, I think this is all for publicity."

"I think you spend too much time on the internet reading about celebrity gossip."

Leave it to Mama Maeve to be a tea party pooper.

"Fine, let's talk about something else," I say. "What about your mystery client? Whatever happened with that?"

Maeve lets out a groan as she exits the highway. "Canceled again. I swear, I don't care how big the commission is, if they cancel one more time…"

"Oh man. How many times is this now?"

"Four," Maeve says as she turns toward my house. *My house.* I don't think that will ever get old.

"I'm sorry," I say. "Can you get out of it?"

"Yes. No contracts have been signed. No deposits paid. But I'm tired of holding times for them just for some rich asshole to keep canceling on me."

"I don't blame you. And you still don't know who it is?"

She shakes her head as she pulls into the driveway. "Not a clue."

Maeve turns off the car, which surprises me. "What are you doing?"

"I need to use the bathroom."

"Oh, okay then." I grab my bags out of her backseat as I start walking toward the garage. Maeve though walks toward our front door.

"Where are you going?" I ask. "Come in this way."

She shakes her head. "Can you let me in over here? Closer to the bathroom."

Damn, I didn't realize her bladder was that small. "Fine."

I walk across the driveway and up the sidewalk to a waiting Maeve on the front porch. I go to put in my key, knowing we usually keep it locked, when the door easily pushes open.

"What the heck?"

I turn to Maeve who has a coy smile on her face. "Happy Birthday, Stella."

I carefully step into my house, which is scarily quiet. Where's Winnie? I'm used to her jumping on me the second I'm home. My heart starts racing as I walk down the hallway and turn toward the living room, where I find every person I love in one place.

"Surprise!"

Noise makers echo off the walls as confetti and balloons start raining around me. I look up and yes, somehow there was a net on the ceiling. How in the world…

"Oh my…" I trail off as I'm completely surprised and overwhelmed. I look around and my heart is bursting. Andi and her boyfriend Max. My parents. Ainsley, who I think might be crying. Maeve, who walks over to a waiting Jayce. Even Quinn is here, waving from the back as she blows into a noisemaker. Simon, Charlie, and Lainey. Mom and Dad. Maddie and Jack.

And of course, Emmett, who is smiling ear to ear right now.

I start walking over to say hello to everyone, when I feel someone run into my leg.

"Happy Birthday, Tella!"

"Thank you, Jack!" I say as I bend down to give him a hug.

"Can I have balloon?"

"Of course," I say. I grab one off the ground for him, and just as I'm about to stand up, I feel a hand on my shoulder.

"You have a habit of stealing my girl," Emmett says.

Jack takes the balloon, looks Emmett dead in the eyes, and presses a kiss to my cheek.

Oh, this boy is something else…

"Did he just—?"

I laugh at Emmett and give him his own kiss. "He did."

My family starts gathering around me, wishing me happy birthdays and asking if I had any idea.

Which I did not.

"Everyone? Can you please grab a drink?" Emmett announces as everyone gathers around. Ainsley hands me a glass of champagne with a wink. "Thank you to everyone for coming. And a special thanks to Ainsley and Maeve who I couldn't have pulled this off without."

"Hey!" Simon interrupts. "I helped too."

"Of course," Emmett says. "You did a great job rigging the balloon net."

"Damn right I did."

Everyone laughs before Emmett continues. "I wanted to gather everyone here to celebrate Stella, because in light of things that have happened over the last few months, I thought her birthday was the perfect day to truly applaud her for everything she's been through."

Oh hell, I'm going to cry…

"I know most by now have heard how we first met, but I've never told anyone my vantage point. I was just sitting at a bar. Having a drink and people watching. Obviously the woman sitting in a wedding dress caught my eye."

"God that thing was ugly," Mom says, which makes everyone in the room crack up laughing.

"It wasn't the best," Emmett says, which makes everyone laugh even more. "But Stella was still the most gorgeous woman I'd ever seen."

A chorus of "awws" go around the room as Emmett turns to look at me. "Some guy came over and started hitting on her. My instincts immediately went onto high alert. I walked around the bar, ready to pummel him, but I stopped and we locked eyes. Somehow, in that moment, I knew she had it handled. That if I needed to step in, and she wanted me to, I'd do it in a heartbeat. But in that moment is when I knew how strong Stella Banks was."

Emmett takes my hand. "Since then, I've been in constant awe of her strength. Of her resilience. Of how she's kept clawing back and facing every obstacle thrown at her. And because of some happenstance, or because of Simon Banks, I get to stand here next to her and celebrate her."

Dad claps Simon on the back as he holds his drink to Emmett. Smart of him just to include Simon in the speech.

"So yes, this party today is to celebrate another year for Stella. But I wanted to also celebrate her and everything she's overcome these past few months. So if everyone could raise their glasses, and let's make a toast to Stella Banks. To strength and beauty."

"To Stella!"

I push away the tears as I take a sip of my champagne. I quickly put it down so I can quickly bring Emmett's lips to mine.

"That was beautiful," I say. "Thank you for all of this. I had no idea."

He smiles and places another kiss on my forehead. "I have another surprise for you. Do you want to see it now or later?"

"Gee, let me think about it. Now!"

Emmett laughs and excuses us as he takes my hand and walks me toward our bedroom. Except instead of turning left toward the master, he turns me to the guest bedroom—with a shut door and a pink bow on the front.

"What's going on? And is this why you had it locked all week?"

Emmett's infectious smile is warming me all over. "When I built this house, I thought it was complete. There was not one more thing I thought I needed. Then you moved in, and I realized there was something very big that was missing."

Before I can ask any more questions, Emmett turns the door handle and ushers me in. I gasp because the room is completely transformed.

The walls that used to be gray are a pale pink. White book cases line the walls, filled with books and trinkets that I'd had in boxes from the day I moved out of Duncan's. Against another wall is the vanity of my dreams. I can see makeup brushes and my hair products all stacked accordingly, along with a jewelry box that I used to have when I was a girl.

"Emmett…" I'm in awe as I look around at everything.

"Check out the closet."

I turn to him first, shocked and nervous about the order. When he gives me a slight head tilt to walk over, I do so timidly. I'm glad I did, because the beauty that I see before me is enough to send me into a coma.

A walk-in closet bigger than I've ever seen.

And it's filled with my shoes.

"You built me a shoe closet?"

I start slowly walking in, Emmett's hand on the small of my back. I'm completely mesmerized by the sight.

"I must say, I really didn't know how many shoes you had until we started this project," Emmett says as he places his hands on my shoulders. "Ainsley said it took her and Maeve two full days to get everything organized."

"How? When?"

"Last week when we were in Destin," he says. "I designed the space. I had a crew I trust come in while we were gone. Ainsley and Maeve put together the room."

I'm in full tears as I turn to a portion that is beautifully displaying my array of Louboutins. "I don't know what to say."

For a man who is all about small gestures, he really knows how to deliver a big one.

Which makes this that much more special.

Emmett turns me to him, and I immediately jump into his arms, wrapping my arms and legs around him. I kiss him with all I have in me. I'll say the words I want to in a second, but right now I need to show him.

This man…how did I get so lucky? How did I stumble into a bar and into the arms of a stranger, who wasn't a stranger, who turned out to be everything I ever wanted?

I know he's not going to, but if he would get down on one knee right now, I'd say yes. I wouldn't hesitate. I want to spend the rest of my life with this man. I want to surprise him just like he surprises me. I want to show him the love that I feel from him every day.

I thought twenty-six was going to be the first year of the rest of my life.

In a way it was, but twenty-seven is going to be so much greater.

"I love you, Cap," I say. "I love you so much."

"There aren't enough ways to show you," he says. "I love you. Happy Birthday, Tiger."

He lowers me to the ground, but our lips meet again before we can step apart. Emmett brings me in closer as my body heats from his kiss.

"We should stop," I say begrudgingly. "What about the party?"

Emmett takes two steps away, but only so he can shut the closet door. "They can wait."

Sounds good to me.

Thank you for reading
Runaway Bride's Guide to Love!

Want more Stella and Emmett? Maybe see how he proposes? If you think the closet was swoon worthy, just see how he pops the question by reading this extended epilogue!

acknowledgments

Starting a new series is hard.

Like so hard.

Are people going to like this new group of characters? Are people going to be sick of Simon's cameos in another four books? On top of that worry, I've never centered a series around the female leads before, which even though doesn't seem like a big shift, really was.

Also please don't get sick of Simon. He'll cry.

This is also the first book I'm releasing as a full time author, so the pressure I put on myself was through the roof. Basically, all this to say I've been NERVOUS for this.

That being said, thank you so much for reading Runaway Bride's Guide to Love. I fell in love with this cast and I hope you did as well. I fell in love with Stella's strength and determination. And Emmett? This man gave me fits (how dare he not talk to me). Then I realized that's who he is, apparently on page and in my head. But what he did tell me I fell in love with. And I hope you did as well.

Thank you for reading Stella and Emmett and I hope you're now invested in the Banks sisters. Maeve is next, and ooh boy, do I have some fun things planned for Mama Maeve. Stay tuned for that!

Now, to the thank yous…

First and foremost, my parents. As always, you're my biggest cheerleaders even if you still have no idea what I'm doing.

You've allowed me to follow my dreams and my path, and for that I am forever grateful.

Amanda, who would have thought when we met nine years ago that one day we'd be here together? Thank you for keeping my life in order. Thank you for reminding me to drink water. And thank you for being my best friend. I promise I won't fire you this week.

Kelly, you've been with me on this book journey since day one. Not only are you an amazing alpha reader, but you are an amazing friend.

Valentine, this is your book. You are Stella. Thank you for everything you, your mom, and the VPR team have done for me. Here's to you finding your Emmett.

Julia, Georgia, Bella, Mae, and Claire: How did I write a book before I met you ladies? All I know is I don't ever want to write one without y'all again.

Kiezha, thank you for correcting my bad grammar habits and being an amazing editor. One day I promise I'll get T-shirt right. Michele, thank you for dotting the Is and crossing the Ts. Jamie, thanks for jumping in with a helpful eye and a good eye for the catnip.

Corinne, I'm here because of you. If you wouldn't have given me a chance I wouldn't have started writing. You forever changed my life.

Last but not least: Readers. I love you all. Whether this was your first book by me, or you've been here since Reformation, I'm truly thankful for all of you. There are so many amazing authors you could be reading. I'm humbled that you chose me.

about the author

Known for her witty sense of humor, Chelle Sloan is a former sports editor who after completing her Master's degree in journalism, decided to become a romance author. You know, because that's the normal path to writing happily ever afters.

An Ohio native, she's fiercely loyal to Cleveland sports, is the owner of way too many — yet not enough — tumblers and will be a New Kids on the Block fan until the day she dies. She does her best writing at Panera, or anywhere that's not her house. When she's not writing, she's trying to learn to bake, fixing up her condo (badly and by watching YouTube videos), or falling in love with a book.

As for her own happily every after? Maybe one day...

Stay up to date with all things Chelle & join the VIP Squad!

also by chelle sloan

THE NASHVILLE FURY, PRO FOOTBALL SERIES

Off the Record: A secret office romance

Off Track: A surprise pregnancy romance

Off Season: A second chance romance

Off Limits: A sibling's best friend romance

LOVE ONLINE SERIES

Thirst Trap: A social media romance

Match Maker: A fake dating romance

Run Run Rudolph: A celebrity, holiday romance

ROLLING HILLS

The One I Want: A single dad / nanny romance

The One I Need: An accidental marriage romance

The One I Love: A friends to lovers romance

The One I Hate: An enemies to lovers romance

GUIDE TO LOVE SERIES

Runaway Bride's Guide to Love: A brother's best friend, age gap romance

Single Mom's Guide to Love: A billionaire, marriage of convenience romance

Roommate's Guide to Love: A small town, single dad, romance

Good Girl's Guide to Love: A fake dating, pro football romance

GUIDE TO LOVE WORLD

Vixen's Guide to Christmas: A rivals to lovers, holiday romance